PRAISE FOR
THE LOUDEST PLACE ON EARTH

"Ken Ziegler's *The Loudest Place on Earth* is a singular reading experience. Why can't more novels be this fresh, inventive, and laugh-out-loud hilarious? Not since *A Confederacy of Dunces* have we gotten to watch such a quirky and against-all-odds-loveable protagonist fumble and gaff his way through the most ridiculous and, in the case of this novel, wildly fantastical of circumstances. I loved it."

—Jacqueline Holland, author of *The God of Endings*

"Such a funny and pleasurable read! It's not often that I come across a story that's completely unpredictable, but that's how I felt reading this one—I had no idea what was around the corner. But rather than feeling random or zany, this is a satisfyingly solid fantasy with the rollicking pace of Ludwig's life aboveground always underpinned by the unfolding and expanding mystery of the fairies down below."

—Julie Tibbott, author of *Members Only: Secret Societies, Sects, and Cults—Exposed!*

"This is a novel for anyone who has ever felt like a 'scavenger for parts' in their own life. It will resonate deeply with disillusioned young professionals who find the 'pivot or die' culture of modern business to be a farce. It's also a perfect fit for fans of contemporary fantasy who prefer their magic to be messy, punitive, and grounded in the dirt of reality rather than high-fantasy tropes. Ultimately, Ziegler has written a 'fresh, inventive, and laugh-out-loud' urban fable that asks us to choose between the easy comfort of apathy and the difficult weight of accountability."

—Manhattan Book Review

"The novel's eloquent, descriptive language verges on poetic. . . . [Ziegler] conjure[s] a New York City that is as magical as the fairy world beneath it. . . . A wild, kaleidoscopic fantasy novel marked by eccentric magic, *The Loudest Place on Earth* is about combating the overwhelming noise of big-city life."

—*Foreword* Clarion Reviews

THE LOUDEST PLACE ON EARTH

THE LOUDEST PLACE ON EARTH

A NOVEL

KEN ZIEGLER

GFB

This is a work of fiction. Names, characters, organizations, places, events, and incidents are either products of the author's imagination or are used fictitiously.

Published by GFB™, Seattle
www.girlfridayproductions.com

Produced by Girl Friday Productions

Cover design: Greg Mortimer
Production editorial: Katherine Richards
Project management: Kristin Duran

Image credits: FilippoBacci/iStock (cover image), paprika/Shutterstock (frame ornaments), nadiya_sergey/Shutterstock (fleuron), Vorobiov Oleksii 8 (rat)

ISBN (paperback): 978-1-967510-41-2
ISBN (ebook): 978-1-967510-42-9
ISBN (audiobook): 978-1-967510-43-6

Library of Congress Control Number: 2025927041

First edition

SOME SORT OF DEED TO A TUNNEL

Winter 2011

1

> The New York City Noise Code claims to balance New York's reputation as a bustling, "world-class city that never sleeps, with the needs of those who live in, work in, and visit the city." It says and offers nothing to protect the myriad, complex sensitivities of the city's oldest and most vulnerable residents by far.
>
> —Granny Num Num, Bronx Fairy Lord

Ludwig hadn't known about the rats before signing the lease.

The sight-unseen, half-aboveground, half-belowground studio offered more surprises than an apartment should, and the fog of pink paws and black eyes scavenging behind at least two of its white, wood-patterned metal walls was just one of many alarming extra features.

Others included an electric hot plate with two burners, only one of which worked; an incontinent faucet that serviced the kitchen and bathroom; a full-size mattress without a box spring or frame that had seen more masters than Sicily; a rusting, oft-painted-over ceiling-spanning pipe that rained yellow-white paint chips down the middle of the apartment when the heat came on, *if* the heat came on; a claustrophobic bathroom with a plumbing system that regurgitated the toilet's demonic payloads up the drain and into the shower, in addition to weeks' or months' worth of tangled hair; a shower enclosure without a ceiling that served as a mezzanine from which passing rats watched a scared, naked twenty-seven-year-old jab at them with the plunger handle; and a desk assembled from two doors, one of which someone had sawed in half to form legs, which supported Ludwig's middling-but-canonical pile of mass-market fantasy paperbacks and swayed at the brink of collapse every time the L train rumbled through North Williamsburg, New York's most obnoxious neighborhood. There was a final surprise, though it numbered more than one: all the rat heads left in all the rat traps.

Where were their bodies?

AN HOUR PAST morning rush hour, when New Yorkers with real jobs were already having dreams crushed by bosses who never once claimed that their employees were like family, the L train was packed with the kind of media and tech professionals who enthusiastically paid six dollars for a single taco.

Except for Ludwig, the passengers wore inflexible wool coats and big wet boots with high, too-hot wool socks pulled over airtight jeans; their heads were topped with itchy, knitted caps, and knotted scarves bound shoulders to faces perched upon by heavy plastic frames all from the same in-vogue, family-owned, century-old Lower East Side optician. If you needed a photographer, copywriter, or graphic designer, there they were, all in one place and usually willing to freelance.

Pressed against Ludwig by the morning crowd, Hassan said, "Don't tell anyone I told you this, especially Charlie, but they're letting you go today." Hassan managed Electric Guacamole's four-person sales team, a position he earned by convincing people to pay for things they shouldn't have wanted, like his building's rat-infested basement apartment. He possessed the seldom-observed, even more seldom-mentioned quality of being traditionally handsome yet deeply evocative of a frog. If someone drove past while he squatted atop some prehistoric lily pad, they might have thought, *That's a big frog,* before they had a chance to think anything else.

"I'd fire me too," Ludwig said.

"Technically, they're 'letting you go.'"

"That's a firing."

"More than half the company is being let go."

"So it's layoffs."

"Yeah. Just layoffs."

"*Just* layoffs."

"Yeah."

"No telling where I'll turn for personal fulfillment without the Under Armour account in my life."

"I thought you liked them."

"Their aesthetic is decent, but they barely have a thesis," Ludwig said, betraying no concern about his imminent execution.

"You're taking this well. Have you ever been fired?"

"Oh yeah."

"How many times?"

Ludwig rolled his head in place like an observatory telescope assigning numbers to stars. "So what happens to you?"

"I've agreed to stay on as an adviser."

"What kind of adviser?"

"They didn't say."

"You said they don't have money."

"Not for you guys."

They transferred to the F train at Fourteenth Street and Sixth Avenue. A wayward shoulder intercepted Ludwig's as they shape-shifted off the train. Its owner growled an unknown expletive. Was it an expletive? It started with an *M*. What curse words started with an *M*? Well, *that* one, but this was a syllable short.

Aboveground, light snow stippled their clothes. Ludwig played hopscotch with the newly formed ice and camouflaged slush until he submerged a sneaker in the latter.

"No boots?" Hassan asked.

"Boots are corsets for feet: difficult to get into, out of, and supremely uncomfortable. I prioritize comfort over aesthetically centered social conventions. I don't own belts, ties, or clothes with numbered sizes, either, just M, L, XL, and so on. I like to look and feel like an urban druid. You ever feel like an urban druid, Hassan?"

"You're taking this better than I would."

"That's because—"

"You, Naveena, and Igor are starting your own shop?"

"Who told you?"

"No one. You just only ever go to lunch with each other."

It was true. Ludwig wanted a business of his own, a workplace where he answered to no authority higher than that of respected partners, but first, he needed resources to cobble it from. So he phoned it in and waited for the implosion that would let him scavenge Electric Guacamole for parts, and in the meantime, he collected the paychecks that he needed to keep living, without giving anything his all.

"Where do you think the money went?" Ludwig asked to refocus the conversation on anything besides the instant discovery of his underhanded plans.

"Where do I *think* the money went? I know where it went. Two Christmas parties in one year, one that employees weren't even invited to; Naveena and Igor's salaries; that time Charlie gave away all the books in the office because we needed to 'think different,' then replaced them with new copies of the same books when he thought we needed to be 'more inspired.'"

"Think they'll bother with a severance?"

"Maybe half your back pay," Hassan said. "They'll treat it like some great sacrifice."

"It's been nice working with you."

"Has it?"

"Not really. I mean, it's been fine."

Electric Guacamole's office wasn't hard to find, but it should have been—no one, including its employees, knew what neighborhood it belonged to. Some said the Lower East Side, the once dangerous, now glamorous collection of walk-ups beneath Houston Street; some said NoLIta, an elegant-sounding portmanteau that denoted a neighborhood north of Little Italy; and some, pointing to the percentage of neighboring businesses who preferred Cantonese to English, claimed their claustrophobic forty-person concrete cuboid for Chinatown. Job applicants and clients from the company's declining rosters of both always doubted whether they had the right building, even when standing in its lobby. It didn't look like the sort of place that an agency profiled by *The Kingdom of New York* would call home.

A renowned pickling operation stuffed cucumbers, peppers, and garlic into jars on floor five. On three, an elderly painter painted photorealistic, scavenged trash two doors from where a celebrated ceramist spun and squeezed clay into vaginal, Hitleresque urns. Two lesser boutique agencies (Antiquity and Sugar Dog) were nestled on floor two, and no floor was without some kind of photography studio. It was hard to love the job, but the building had its charm.

Ludwig and Hassan stepped out of the freight elevator, which was the only elevator, on floor six and arrived next to last—though no one knew it was them and not Charlie, plus an aspiring model half his age, who were dragging wet feet across the welcome mat that said *family* in Hindi.

Postures instantly improved as if someone had cracked a whip. Fingers accelerated across keyboards as though working at full throttle could alter the fates of the bodies connected to them. Mice and touch pads clicked faster and faster until they formed one continuous sound like heavy rain.

Everyone knew about the layoffs; no one knew who would be laid off.

For Ludwig's recently graduated coworkers, this would be their first time receiving a packet featuring a sailboat on its cover, some papers to sign, a few apologies, and as many assurances about their greatness as they wanted.

Ludwig, who had stormed this ridge before, wanted to give them some assurances of his own, namely, that being fired is "liberating," that getting half your waking hours back from people who "only care about you for your labor, anyway, man" was worth more than any paycheck—that you weren't fired, you were free.

Except that this was not the time to start building relationships.

Ludwig wiped his company-issued laptop's hard drive, stepped onto the fire escape, ignited a cigarette, and waited for Charlie, whom he expected to enthusiastically pull the lever.

The midwinter air contrasted with the office's claustrophobic heat from manically banging tenement-era radiators. The fire escape was his favorite place in the office because it wasn't in the office and because out there, no one asked him to do his job, whatever that was. The longer his tenure at Electric Guacamole, the harder his role became to define.

He was on the media team, he told coworkers, and for a while, he was. But as time went on and whatever value he brought to that team inevitably declined in quantity and quality, he told people that he had transferred to the leaderless accounts team, where he mostly damaged client relationships and played *Halo* on the office's projection screen. This was followed with a short stint on the creative team—where his proposed solution to every client problem included either arcane magic, epic quests, or cosmic horror—and then an even shorter stint on the sales team, all of which he made work for months at a time. As a result, he was often mistaken for a polymath free agent, a wild miscalculation that he played into and encouraged. Like gravity, his presence was felt everywhere by dragging everything down.

The last snowflakes waltzed down from depleted clouds. The spaces between them grew and grew until the only snow that fell rode swirling gusts of frozen wind off rooftops in shapes that resembled drifting djinns and frostbitten phantasms as the city sang its song:

> *Woop-woop. Woooooop.* (Sirens, police.)
> *Ee-oooo-ee-oooo-ee-oooo.* (Sirens, ambulance.)
> *Baaaaaaa. Baaaaaaa.* (Sirens, fire trucks.)
> *Gablahblahgyah.* (Guys shouting, other guys shouting back.)

Charlie joined him, but he neglected to prop open the exit door using the two-by-four that prevented smokers and people taking phone calls from exiling themselves to the fire escape in midwinter.

"Fuck," he said. "Someone's going to have to let us in."

"Let's hope they do," Ludwig said, offering his neck to the executioner.

"How's it going, L?" Charlie asked. He wore a silk infinity scarf, designer jeans, and a wool coat with leather shoulder pads that he always found a way to inform listeners was "bespoke." (It was neither a bad nor an uncomfortable look.)

He loved that word and used it to describe everything from furniture to employees with mixed ethnicities. His right eyelid hung half open like a broken blind.

"Y'know," Ludwig said, "fine." He had little else to say; he was ready. Not only did he know his termination was coming, but he knew for sure what came next: freedom from bosses and—finally—opening his own shop.

"Yeah? I'm glad to hear that," Charlie said.

"Smoke?" Ludwig offered.

"Quit."

"OK."

"Yeah, I'll take one."

"All right."

"Give me a couple for later."

Their ashes fell imperceptibly among the storm's churning dregs.

"I don't know if you've heard, but some things have been happening," Charlie said, tapping and then flicking his phone without looking up. "It's never easy to have conversations like this. It's the hardest part of being an entrepreneur. If I could avoid it, I would, but it would be irresponsible to put my interests over the needs of . . ." He became lost in his phone. He swiped up, down, up, down, and for several moments, which seemed to Ludwig like seconds and to Charlie like eons, he forgot about Ludwig altogether. Was the boss who told Ludwig no less than five times that he *loved* firing people nervous about firing him, the person he should never have hired? Was this the genesis of human feeling or the lingering effects of anti-anxiety medication?

"The team," Charlie finally said. "Electric Guacamole is having some problems, most of which were totally unavoidable. We did everything we could to prevent them. No matter how prepared we were, bad things have happened, quite frankly, and they're not good. I've been thinking about how best to break this news to the team and, sadly, concluded that nothing I say will make what I have to say hurt any less. As you've probably guessed, we're making changes that will severely impact our Human Resources landscape. I wish we did not have to make these changes, but like I always say, and now everybody says: Sometimes it's pivot or die."

"Ah, the pivot," Ludwig said, offering no resistance. "Of course."

"Exactly. On Friday, we officially lost the Under Armour account, in addition to several others. Under Armour was, as you know, the source of more than half our annual revenue. I know you loved that account, so I'm coming to you first. I consider you a valuable avocado. I have always appreciated your sense of humor, candor, and commitment to building magical brands. And that makes what I am about to say so difficult. We are letting you go."

"That's fine."

"It is?" A single tear balanced on Charlie's trembling eyelid.

"It's going to be a tough day. You'll make it through. Electric Guacamole will ride again." Ludwig empathetically patted one of Charlie's shoulder pads.

"Thank you, L. Maybe when this ugly business is done, and we finish rebuilding, you can return and lead our media division."

"That sounds great, Charlie," Ludwig said because neither knew what to tell the other except lies.

"No hard feelings?" Charlie extended a curdled milk–colored hand.

"None." Colder than a corpse.

Charlie kicked the fire escape door three times, and together they waited for someone to open it. They silently scrutinized each other's shoes, the weather, and what was happening in the windows of the not-quite office buildings that shared this building's not-quite alleyway. Charlie's executive assistant and acting Human Resources director (checkered blouse, knee-length skirt, flats) appeared, carrying a packet that depicted visor-wearing Caucasians piloting a sailboat over motionless, photoshopped water.

"I'm so sorry," she said. "I know the company is behind on two paychecks, but we can call it even at one if you sign a nondisclosure agreement."

The packet's papers were covered in thought-terminating phrases like "Look to the future" and "The best is yet to come."

Ludwig flattened the packet against the hall's primer gray walls and signed wherever optimistically colored Post-it tabs indicated. The income he lost wasn't worth months of listening to excuses while bartering over email or begging hollow entities like the Better Business Bureau to intervene on his behalf. *Time versus money,* he thought. And the money would come, now that he had secured what would be, by nightfall, the company's most valuable remaining assets: best employee number one and best employee number two.

Ludwig had survived enough cardboard-box send-offs to know that anything superfluous or sentimental didn't belong in an office. From the Spartan desk that he could only work at with his feet up, he gathered his keys, a handful of favorite gel pens that didn't belong to him, a tote bag, and several remembrances pilfered from Charlie's desk (personal lubricant, cocaine mirror, twenty-seven dollars).

As he reached the staircase, he observed Charlie following him with his hand outstretched like a limp homing missile.

"I just want to thank you again for everything you did for us, L."

"Electric Guacamole is going to come back strong. I can feel it," Ludwig said flatly.

"Muumbazza," Charlie said. "Muumbazza."

Ludwig didn't know that word or why Charlie said it. The culprit, he suspected, was the hypothetical, though increasingly theoretical, antianxiety medication moving through Charlie's blood like glue. Ten years prior, this man had almost single-handedly brought hot yoga to the West Village. Perhaps one had something to do with the other.

"What's that, a yoga thing?"

"Is what a yoga thing?"

"What you said."

"What did I say?"

"Muumbazza?"

"What?"

"What?"

"I didn't say *muumbazza*."

"No?"

It must not have been important.

"It's going to be such a long day," Charlie said, forgetting their disagreement. He soaked in the building's chemically enriched fluorescent lights as if they might keep his trembling eyes open.

From the stairwell, Ludwig heard Charlie for the last time.

"Gloria! Do you have a muumbazza?"

With half his waking hours returned to him, Ludwig could do anything he wanted, which wasn't much. So that's what he did.

He wasn't fired; he was free.

EIGHT YEARS AFTER the citywide smoking ban went into effect, International Bar still smelled like a chain-smoker's fingertips. Their beers were cheap, obscure, in cans, and piled into dripping coolers; their regulars were middle-aged or older, inappropriate, and oozing out of their clothes. No matter how drunk or loud a patron became, someone always became drunker or louder. It was New York the way Ludwig thought it should be: a multiethnic enclave full of people who hated each other, the kind of place where a guy could get stabbed without being ironically happy about it.

By age twenty-five, Naveena Chandra's combined social media followings surpassed many of the world's most recognizable three-letter advertising agencies, placing her among the city's best known graphic designers. She wore a black peacoat, black knit cap, lace-up boots, a wool mock neck pullover, and jeans cut from a material you could hear. Comfortableness score: 4/10.

Igor Kavtakpastonovichsky, her eighteen-year-old work husband, was already so sought-after by tech companies who wanted his code that they were willing to deny him a normal transition into adulthood by poaching him right out of Stuyvesant High School, a tuition-free public accelerator school for gifted students. Dressed like every software developer, he looked pretty comfortable. Ludwig arrived last, with the only severance packet between them.

The potbellied bartender's T-shirt read "Bartender [*bahr-ten-der*], Noun," followed by a made-up definition that reinforced the perception of bartenders as something more than people who poured drinks, along the lines of therapists, mediators, and neighborhood encyclopedias. Ludwig ordered three cheap shots plus three cheap beers for twenty-four dollars, plus a three-dollar tip, exactly the amount he had stolen from Charlie. Serendipity.

"This fucking daaay." Naveena used her itchy, scrunched-up knit cap to muffle a performative scream.

"What happened with Gloria?" Ludwig asked.

"They let Gloria go, and you know Gloria: 'Where is all the money? What did you do with all the money?' When they asked her to sign an NDA in exchange for half of what they owed—which absolutely no one did—she said she was keeping her laptop as collateral. Then she got in Charlie's face and chased him around the office, yelling about Schoffenhoofer being vindicated again."

"Schopenhauer. She loves Schopenhauer," Ludwig said.

"Whatever. Hassan walked her out while telling her how great she is. If he didn't have a girlfriend, I'd say he was trying to get with her."

"Oh, buddy," Ludwig said, "having a girlfriend hasn't stopped him before. His bedroom is right above where I sleep."

Naveena retraced the conversation's steps. "Anyway, Charlie locked himself in his office for an hour. People thought they would have to fire themselves."

Igor nodded. He rarely spoke; he didn't need to. His nods were verbose and rich with pointed meanings.

"As far as bosses go," Ludwig said, "I'll take a crier over a screamer any day. Who's left?"

"Everyone you'd expect. Us. You going first surprised nobody. Charlie hates you."

"If only he'd act like it. I don't even feel fired. What did they offer to retain you?"

"Two-thirds of back pay and the same moving forward until they can 'make things right.' Which, y'know, absolutely fucking not," Naveena said. "But it's good to have it behind us, which brings us to what we wanted to meet about."

Uh-oh. It had to be their still mostly hypothetical agency's name—nothing took longer to settle on. To Ludwig, the point was to stand out and create interest, not to capture what the company did. They had spent weeks scavenging for something prickly enough to stick: Suck, Squirm, Spasm, Bandit Camp, Starlight Octopus, Ugly, Wizard Hat, Black Hoodie, Girlfriend, Boyfriend, White Knuckle Nights, Gulag, Quantum Dominatrix, Dinner Party, Filth, Heart-Shaped Balloon, the End of Everything, Bobby, Treehouse, Sisterhood, the Bludgeonator, Blob, Magic & Mythology, Jennifer from Minneapolis, Vermin Milk, Best Supporting Actress, Tyrant,

Bureaucracy, Fairy Lights, Hack the Mainframe. Candidates numbered in the thousands. It was more like naming a band than a company.

Finally, they—but mostly Ludwig—agreed that Vermin Milk was memorable, unusual, and edgy for a company in a field where edginess equaled publicity. It gave them mystique, which gave them free marketing. Their operating agreement divided the valueless Delaware LLC into thirds.

"I'm still into the name. Also, the LLC is formed, and it's a pain plus three hundred dollars to change," Ludwig said.

"No, the name is really good," Naveena said without making eye contact.

"If you're concerned about an office, start-ups start without them all the time. All we need is a client."

"Actually," Naveena said, searching Igor's side of the table for support that never materialized. "We've decided to pursue something different. ColosSys offered us a deal to come in as a team. They're giving us a blank canvas."

"ColosSys is acquiring us?" Ludwig asked. "When? How? We're just names on a piece of paper."

"Well, no. Not us *us*, but *us* us. Last week, they approached Igor and me when we launched that web app for flexible grid systems. Shit exploded!" she said before reeling back the exclamation point. "I'm sorry, man. We just don't want to be in client services anymore, especially after today. Tech pays better, and you get stock options. We asked about bringing you; we just didn't know how to describe your role. *Obviously,* we told them that you're good at names. They asked what else, and, honestly, we didn't know what to say."

"I would have talked to them," Ludwig offered, too late.

"And you probably would have sold them. You sold us on Vermin Milk! You're like the El Greco of bullshitting bullshitters. We love you, but if you did at ColosSys what you did at Electric Guacamole, that would be on us. I'm not judging.

You just don't seem to want a job. Maybe you just have to find your thing. Finding your thing is how great entrepreneurs are made," Naveena said.

"I thought they were made by bullshitting bullshitters."

He congratulated them, and they left. Ludwig knew how to be let go; he didn't know how to be left behind.

SINCE YOUNG LUDWIG couldn't live among the floating lights across the Hudson River, he had created his own New York by pinning posters, magazine pages, and printed JPEGs to the walls of his tourism board–approved bedroom. He had his own World Trade Centers, Empire State Buildings, Chrysler Buildings, Central Parks, Rockefeller Centers, and more than a dozen Times Squares.

His favorite movie was *Ghostbusters*, only somewhat because of its ghost-busting. He watched *Seinfeld, Kramer vs. Kramer, Friends, Felicity, Spin City, The Jeffersons, Manhattan, Will & Grace, When Harry Met Sally, Hey Arnold!, Sex and the City*, and *Mad About You* because of where they took place and not because of who or what they were about. He read New York–centered novels, coffee table slabs of street photography, pocket-sized guides for fast-moving tourists, and Peter Kaplan's *New York Observer*, the thinking New Yorker's steamed salmon–colored tabloid. Ludwig played *Max Payne* and *Parasite Eve*, generally agreeing with critics that the former was too repetitive and the latter too linear.

On real and faked sick days when young Ludwig couldn't or didn't want to go to school, he watched pixelated, dial-up-modem-speed footage from webcams perched above New York's tallest buildings and busiest corners and crosswalks. His favorite days were the rainy ones when the lights from streetlamps and headlights reflected in the dark, wet streets like rippling, enchanted windows into other New Yorks. Except seeing the city wasn't enough—young Ludwig wanted to hear the city too, which no low-resolution, corner-mounted 320x240 webcam made possible in the late '90s.

So in place of sounds in context, he looped Frank Sinatra's "New York, New York," for as long as his strained relationship with his mother and father allowed. It wasn't that they didn't love him or he them, but as life's first authority figures, Ludwig struggled to be their child. Then, when his mother's urinary tract infection became sepsis, and his father's kidney stone became kidney failure, he no longer had to struggle. ("What were the odds?" he and his sister asked doctors, curious about the likelihood of losing both parents to back-to-back urinary maladies. "One in thirty-nine million," they said without hesitating, as if they had wondered the same thing.) With his sister, he simply lost touch. As the older sibling, she, too, bore the mantle of authority.

Young Ludwig ate hot dogs sentimentally and fell for the idea of New York as much as the city itself and as hard or harder than the people born there and far harder than his New Jersey neighbors, five minutes past the western end of the George Washington Bridge. Those people had cars and checking accounts. They paid rent. They could live there, but they lived here, in Secaucus, East Rutherford, Hackensack, Teaneck, and Englewood, places whose only noteworthiness derived from their proximity to the city.

On the night that adult Ludwig lost his job and his partnership, the New York that he saw overlooking the bottom half of his two-story building's trash and recycling bins ceased to resemble the New York of acclaimed fiction and sitcom B-rolls, pastrami on rye and dollar slices, Broadway musicals and casual racism—the New York that put the world within walking distance.

He swallowed his medication, placed a glass of water beside

his pillow, dived onto his mattress, and cycled through the positions that led to sleep, while out of sight all around him, the little brown beasts that had once sacked Europe fought over cockroach parts.

Then, as the meandering blue wilderness between conscious and unconscious enveloped him, someone opened the creaky, waist-high gate separating Ludwig's apartment building from the sidewalk, snuck behind the trash and recycling bins, and pissed all over his windows.

"Muumbazza!" they cried.

2

Shield and storm can't stop what's coming.

—Napkin found at Cozy Soup 'n' Burger,
Broadway and Astor Place, 1991

LUDWIG CAPITULATED TO unemployment by purchasing Shrek-green sweatpants from a grocery store, exhausting an entire travel-sized box of Q-tips in a weekend, and reheating four-day-old pad thai with a space heater because the hot plate that he inherited met its predictable end when a saucepan full of shrimp-flavored instant ramen boiled over the rim and into the device's wiring.

Rather than replace it by spending money that could be allocated toward comfort or leisure, Ludwig explored online classified ads until he discovered a second- or thirdhand PlayStation, a small pile of classic games, and a forty-dollar, hundred-pound cathode-ray television that was more like an asteroid than an entertainment system. Their owner's next of kin let him plunder the departed's medicine cabinet for thirty extra dollars, scoring him five 1 mg Xanax, three 10 mg

Ambien, two 1 mg Clonazepam, and one big blue oval that looked promising.

His expiring MetroCard took him into the city one last time, to the Bowery's Kitchen District, where five cramped blocks of supply stores furnished Manhattan eateries at a fraction of what image-conscious elites paid for comparable hardware found in catalogs designed and photographed almost exclusively by people who shared Ludwig's zip code.

The Bowery was where people went if they owned or managed a Mexican restaurant or nightclub and needed an always-on, LED-studded frozen margarita machine. Ludwig owned little and managed less, but he had arrived with a purpose: to add two years' worth of twenty-five-dollar minimum monthly payments to his credit card, not because he was a drinker, but for the vibes.

If he was going to be unemployed, he might as well be fucking unemployed.

Electric Guacamole faded from his mind in steps, strides, and then altogether, rarely to be seen again, like a stegosaurus-shaped cloud. Yet losing his fledgling company, Vermin Milk, which had immense personal value but no price, was a strain of employment-based indignity to which Ludwig wasn't inoculated. He had never planned to live in a basement for long.

Vermin Milk should have elevated him to some East Village or Lower East Side walk-up surrounded by bodegas and restaurants tessellated with Edison bulbs that had derivative, pretentious names connected with ampersands like *Rosemary & Flint* or *Spatula & Honor.* It never got the chance.

He could relocate to some other city if needed; most of his things weren't even his.

He heard good things about New Orleans, and San Francisco was, well, he'd heard something about San Francisco. There was also, hmm—what else was there for someone in his field? LA, which was like New York without weather or anything within walking distance? Boulder, where guys mountain biked to ad agency jobs, drank disgusting beer, and rolled their eyes whenever someone mentioned religion? What about Atlanta, where people never stopped driving, mainly back and forth from strip clubs? Or Chicago, where locals marched through slush puddles and stabbing, subzero winds, until their arteries froze and they became curmudgeonly ice sculptures? He imagined Boston the same way, but with worse accents and people more annoying to everyone than other Americans found New Yorkers. How much did he need to know about the rest of the country? It belonged to a different country altogether. He considered himself a New Yorker first and an American second.

To stay meant living somewhere besides Williamsburg, which was in the early stages of a prolific gentrification. The warm, timeless redbrick walk-ups built by Italian and Polish immigrants fought for visual dominance with startling, postmodern glass experiments. If it could be renovated and flipped, it would be, first to guys in hoodies, then to guys in cardigans, and then to guys in blazers.

As a testament to the gentrifiers' power and will, the delightfully retro, neon-blue Kellogg's Diner—a favorite meeting place for anyone below a certain income level—began disappearing from sight as a glass-and-slate ziggurat ironically containing over one hundred minimalist hotel rooms rose around it like a dragon guarding treasure.

Overwhelmed with indecision and self-loathing, Ludwig ventured to a place where people only ventured when they were overwhelmed by indecision and self-loathing, a make-or-break spot for anyone thinking of calling it in for the night or in general.

Ludwig went to Union Pool.

PART BAR, PART taqueria, part concert hall, and all meeting place for people who would someday conceive and sire cool babies, friends only suggested Union Pool to friends when they had partied too hard to be admitted anywhere else. You were met with understandable suspicion if you were a man—or a dude, which was usually the case—and ventured there alone on a Friday or Saturday night. Girls went to Union Pool.

They went in threes and fours and danced to "Bad Romance" and *My Beautiful Dark Twisted Fantasy* and *The Blueprint 3* and Tanlines' *Settings* and The-Dream and gloom-pop played by two DJs at once in the early days of the iPhone. More importantly to Ludwig, Union Pool served the ethnically appropriate gut fortification needed to attempt the frozen green gauntlet coalescing one 360-degree rotation at a time back at his apartment.

"ID," the doorman simultaneously asked and demanded. In his cargo pants with stuffed pockets, snow boots, and a too-small ski jacket, his comfort level couldn't be gauged.

"Sure. Remind me how much tacos are here?" Ludwig frisked himself.

"Six dollars. Those sweatpants?"

"They're about to have a moment. I think I left my ID in my other—"

"Sweatpants?"

"Say what you will," Ludwig said, "but I have this thesis that aesthetically centered social conventions are due for a reckoning. The future is all about wearability, which is why I only wear clothes that come in lettered sizes like M, L, and XL instead of numbers. There's a fortune to be made in high-end athletic leisurewear, especially in New York. Think about it. It's too hot when it's hot and too cold when it's cold. Apartments are microscopic, claustrophobic, or glorified closets, and the subways are always crowded. People should be comfortable, and not just once they get home or when they're going to bed but everywhere and all the time. Shouldn't you be the most comfortable that you can be?"

"Did you memorize that?" the doorman asked.

"No. But I believe it with all my heart."

"You still need an ID."

"The same goes for what's in your pockets," Ludwig continued, looking at the man's bulging cargo pockets, lost in possibility. "Soon, we won't even have to carry wallets or keys. Instead, our phones will do everything they do, and we'll have one designated phone pocket."

"ID."

"I'm just getting tacos," Ludwig said, unsure and unconcerned about whether he was telling the truth.

Three young women with purple streamers chasing their hair tumbled into line. The doorman gestured Ludwig aside as if banishing an imp or phantom and examined the girls' IDs one by one. The tallest among them posed with her miniature self, and the doorman made more small talk than he needed to.

"You ladies are all good." He winked. "Muumbazza."

"Muumbazza," they slurred.

"What is that?" Ludwig asked.

"It's a PSP," the doorman said, flashing the device that let users play PlayStation games anywhere.

"No, *muumbazza*? Is that an Internet thing? Like a mee-mee?"

"I don't know what you're talking about."

"You just said it. Those girls just said it."

"I didn't say—what was it?"

"Muumbazza."

"I think I'd remember three white girls saying *muumbazza*. Come back with an ID and some different pants, and I'll think about letting you in. Muumbazza."

"All right, I—*there*!"

"What?"

"You just said it!"

"I know I just said it. I was telling you that I didn't say it. Go home, Costco. It's getting old."

Ludwig unholstered his cracked phone from a sagging pocket. He typed *muumbazza* and hit Return while distractedly listening to a conversation approaching from the direction of his apartment. They were too well dressed to live in a neighborhood still considered up-and-coming, most likely finance guys hunting for women they thought were more interested in meaningful energies than meaningful relationships.

"Since she started, all she has done is fire people and replace them with friends from her last job. Jaclyn is the nicest person at the company, and she's the one who dubbed her Madame Aneurysm. I can't go to Stella again. Should I get out of there? She's killing the muumbazza."

The query loaded:

1. Muumbazza Takes the Lead Against Zurazodan Athletic Debut
2. Mumbassa Songs Download—Free New Songs Online @ LitePoleAB103
3. Enoa Muumbazza Profiles | Facebook
4. Dr. Tiffany Aya Muumbazza—Minneapolis, MN, Family and Pediatric Practice
5. Mombassa Fishing Lodge—Laverno—theisraelifishinglodge.com
6. Muumbazza Chalet is a decadent en suite with shower toilet
7. Khanda Muumbazza Jr.—academians.edu
8. Mumbassa Kalimekwanto—Address, Phone, Contact Info

None of the previews that followed explained why *muumbazza* was flying off the tongues of baffled New Yorkers. Was it a spelling issue? He punched in *muumbazza* and then *mumbaza* and then *moombasa* into the social media app with the short updates and read nothing but noise.

Then he made his own contribution, his first since prematurely announcing the launch of Vermin Milk:

> What does *muumbazza* mean? Why is everyone saying it?

SNOW FELL LIKE sleep across the city; experts called for half a foot. It wasn't enough.

Ludwig wanted snow past his basement windows that he could pair with expired, though probably still potent, euphoria-inducing pills; a humming frozen margarita machine; and nostalgia-centric, out-of-vogue, still-great video games. He yearned to hear other people shoveling snow since nothing made him more comfortable than the sound of the city's upkeep, as long as the manual labor it required was performed by someone else.

A fire truck screamed past, then a police car. Noise followed noise. Even in his practically suburban neighborhood, silence was the exception.

The heat was off again.

Ludwig did the check that all people do when arriving home: this thing here, that thing there, every object and item right where he left them except in the dilapidated hallway that led to the building's dilapidated laundry room where he discovered two new rat heads in two old traps and no blood, fur, peanut butter, or impossible-to-ingest parts (scapula, pelvic girdle) at either scene.

How long had those been there?

He tossed his phone onto the teetering desk, withdrew Terry Brooks's *The Elf Queen of Shannara* from his middling-but-canonical pile of mass-market fantasy paperbacks, kicked off his sneakers, pulled off his jacket, unbuttoned his shirt, peeled off his socks, flipped off his hat, and dived knees first, elbows second, onto his adopted mattress and, unbeknownst to him, a rat the size of a fire hydrant.

IT COULD HAVE been anything: half a set of encyclopedias, two footballs wrapped in a bedsheet croissant, a considerable piece of driftwood, a formidable Thanksgiving turkey, a middle school student's science fair volcano. It didn't resemble a rat as it scrambled from under him and his sheets. It was more like the spoiled dachshund of a childless widow. Ah, that made sense, a dog. Why was someone's dog in his apartment?

Ludwig squealed like a stuck pig, accelerating the Giant's sprint for the bathroom as its gray tail slithered after its scab-covered rump.

It sank its overgrown claws into the shower curtain and climbed as if it knew about the uncovered ceiling and the building's neglected, human-free depths. When it reached the curtain rod, it burrowed its head between the rings from snout to neck as if that could conceal it, binding the beast to curtain and rod.

Ludwig possessed no weapons or special knowledge to deter the invader; if he did, he lacked the courage to apply them. The traps were automated, in a sense, and didn't require him to be present at the execution, let alone at the switch. What he needed was a spear. What he had was a dull, serrated kitchen knife and a wooden broom. How long would it take to whittle the broom's handle into a spear?

The Giant hissed—longer than he had.

Without the time or caution to formulate a better plan, Ludwig retrieved the previous tenant's unopened Max Death Ultimate Roach Killer from beneath the leaky sink. He filled the subdued Giant's eyes and nose with burning aerosol, hoping that the can's contents might work like bear mace, which is effective whether or not one's target is a bear. Instead, the Giant thrashed in place until it unhooked the rod and the curtain from the shower enclosure and tumbled to the floor like a demon in drag. It charged Ludwig, leaving behind a trail of poison and claw marks that recorded the choreography of their duel.

Ludwig retreated, wanting to slow the creature until the unfolding ambush could be assessed, but in attempting to do this, he frightened it more, causing the thing he least wanted to happen to happen. The Giant leaped for his sweatpants and climbed. There was safety at the top of the shower; what would it find at the top of Ludwig?

He whipped the can of poison across the Giant's face to no avail, then madly tore the cables from the dead woman's PlayStation and battered its face with the console until the creature relented and a lucky kick sent it soaring into one of the apartment's white wood-patterned metal walls.

The curtain rings exploded; the Giant was free.

Ludwig sent the PlayStation spinning after the creature. He missed, causing the game inside (disc 1 of *Final Fantasy IX*, 2000) to somersault through the air. Then, with both combatants as distant from one another as the apartment allowed, Ludwig bombarded the Giant with books that had names like *The Assassin and the Enchantress*, *The Prince of Red Dragons*, and *The Bloodbloom Chronicles*.

They also missed.

Nothing that instinct told him would work did, so he did something that he thought wouldn't. He threw himself upon the plastic-and-glass boulder of a television and hoisted it as high as his flabby, unused muscles allowed, then flung it at the Giant like an executioner's wheel. The television bounced off the rodent's neck and onto the floor, shaking the connected satellite dishes and radio antennas, which were fixed to the building's roof three stories above.

Ludwig waited for a receipt of death, such as a sustained lack of movement, a death rattle, or some mortal disfigurement.

The Giant gave no such signal.

As if renewed by black magic, it sped between the apartment's walls like a captured hornet, splashing cascades of black blood across the bed and floor.

Drunk on fight-or-flight adrenaline and still without a notion of what to do next, Ludwig made a decision that wasn't a decision at all but a reflex of last resort like tackling one's kidnapper, and with his bare foot blindly stomped one, two, three times, sending the Giant's skull through its brain.

Ludwig fell into the desk made of doors, collapsing it, himself, and his middling-but-canonical pile of mass-market fantasy paperbacks to the ground.

Then he cried.

Black blood and gray brains painted Ludwig's naked heel. The Giant's proximity to the shower and the possibility that Ludwig's presence could usher its vengeful spirit back into its body made the shower's use unthinkable. He would sooner piss in bottles until his lease expired than risk returning it to life, so he reached for the poison, aimed it at his heel, and sprayed away the blood.

Ludwig's catatonic mind wouldn't let him look away from his vanquished foe, and the Giant's broken body wouldn't let it look away from him; they stared at each other, nothing, and the farthest reaches of the universe together. Time passed, but neither of them knew how much.

There came a knock on the window, a pause, a second

knock, a second pause, and then the unmistakable sound of the window sliding open along its rusted frame, though Ludwig heard none of it. If his faculties could have registered additional surprise, it would have been at the stranger's presence and then at its layered English brogue, which belonged to no one that Ludwig knew. If he could have assimilated the speaker's words, he might have described the accent that flavored them as a sort of "jovial cockney."

It was jovial, but it wasn't cockney.

"Please forgive my intrusion. One wonders why your blinds are all the way open in a neighborhood with such abundant foot traffic," the voice from the window said. "Yet to critique your decisions or idiosyncrasies is not my mission. My name is Lonesome Johnny. Indeed, I should have said so at the onset. Only a villain arrives with a purpose and neglects to introduce themselves, and though I am devilishly handsome, I am no villain!"

Whether any of these statements were true, none but their speaker could say. The voice from the window continued, unbeknownst to the electrical impulses that, in any other circumstance, would have governed cognition inside Ludwig's head.

"I am here at the will of my lady-lord and benefactor, who gave my spirit form both a body and a purpose. An agent in her employ saw your startling and inquisitive post on the blue-bird social-website contraption, and she dispatched me immediately."

The margarita machine veiled their one-sided communication in whirring white noise.

"For us to converse further, I am afraid that I must ask you to join me outside or invite me into your home. The fact that I cannot enter your home—not that I would without an invitation!—might make me appear vampiric, or at least like the kind of 'vampire' that one encounters in slanderous works of supernatural fiction. However, I do not drink blood, I enjoy sunlight more than other spirit vessels, and I can grasp any amount of silver without catching fire. In short, I am no vampire! How could I be, considering how few yet live? From where I am crouching, you have already engaged one unexpected, out-of-the-ordinary guest tonight, and entertaining another might cause you to slip from the brink of sanity on which you appear to teeter to outright pandemonium of the mind. Supposing that you do not trust how well-intentioned I truly am, let me relinquish your doubts about my personage and mission by speaking the following word to you, which, as you have already learned, is gibberish to most and yet carries particular relevance to you. Muumbazza! Muumbazza, muumbazza, muumbazza!"

Had Ludwig heard the speaker's words, he might have wondered whether they would ever stop coming.

"There! I am fully aware of the word I am speaking, and I believe you are aware of it too," the voice said. "If I am correct—and since I speak for my lady-lord and benefactor, I know that I am!—you sometimes hear your kind saying this word without them knowing they have spoken it. My lady-lord and benefactor has not permitted me to explain why that might be, preferring to tell you herself. However! If you join me outside or invite me into your home, I may further describe her operational protocols and schedule a time for the two of you to meet. Oh, you fortuitous goose! Imagine you, coming from such low origins as these, meeting *Her.* If I were you, I would play the lottery tonight because you are on a lucky streak!

"Now, if you consider yourself indisposed or otherwise unable to accommodate my visit, I am perfectly happy to return tomorrow evening or later in the week, whichever suits your arbitrary human schedule. I imagine it brimming with pointless drudgeries, wastes of time, and other regrettable endeavors. Otherwise, please take as much time as you need. I am in no rush. On the contrary, I greatly enjoy being the first and final resting place for falling snow."

Ludwig heard nothing except a ghostly iron bell tolling somewhere that did not exist.

"Right-oh-ho, Joe! I'll come back."

3

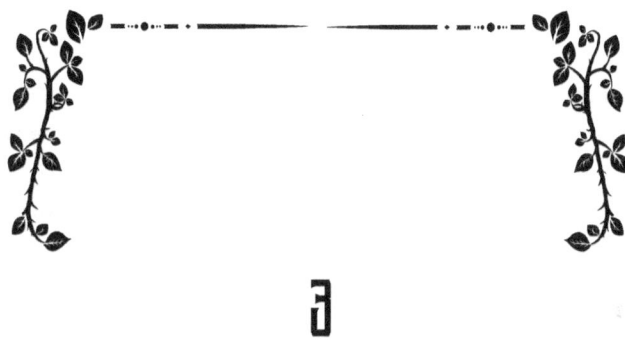

Magic, real? I wish it were. That way, even if I never cast a spell or carried a staff, things wouldn't have to be exactly as science says, so that at least when they bury me, there would be a chance of something other than lying in the dark wearing whatever stupid look the mortician put on my face.

—Lulu Vaillancourt, Auction House Fixer

In the delusional daydreams that every person has, the kind where they dispatch a terrorist with a projectile thrown from across a crowded ballroom or surprise friends by dominating trivia night, Ludwig was himself like a protagonist in one of his fantasy paperbacks—or at least a helpful secondary character such as a flamboyant bard, potion-shop attendant, enchanter-blacksmith, monster-sanctuary caretaker, spell-book collector, or vagabond with a mysterious past. So, although his victory over the Giant was undeniable, the condition it left him in made him question whether any of these fantasies might be conceivable anywhere but his imagination.

Temperatures fell overnight. Predictions about snow became warnings about freezing rain, which had turned intermittent patches of ice into endless skating rinks, camouflaged puddles into salty swimming pools, and last week's plowed hills of gray snow into impassable mountain ranges that Saturday morning crowds cautiously braved one careful footstep at a time.

They were truck drivers and bakers and winter-proof joggers and adulterers and moms with owl, switchblade, cupcake, skull, cat, and rose tattoos who had gotten in early on Williamsburg's restoration as it became the younger set's Upper West and Upper East Sides, places they uniformly rejected until moving to them ten years later. Still traumatized, Ludwig didn't see them, but they saw him winding an extension cord through his basement's unfurnished, unfinished lengths, past the stoop's ice-glazed gate, and out to his building's frigid front steps. The margarita machine followed.

Ludwig cleaned his roach spray–poisoned heel in a shallow mound of hardened snow, then siphoned the margarita machine's bright green slosh into his body not as a procession of slowly savored cocktails but as one continuous swallow, as though enough of it might possess the power to carry him back to some time when he could if not circumvent the night's events, at least prepare for them. His greatest fear was the Giant returning to life, so he waited on his building's stoop for the margarita machine and its contents to fortify him with the courage to clean the previous night's coagulating fever dream from the floor. Unable to pass his bathroom's newly anointed guardian if he reentered the apartment, he adhered to the precedent set by countless other late, late-night inebriates and, with the garbage and recycling bins at his back, pissed all over his window.

Why was it open?

Ludwig remembered every detail about the Giant and the fight; and nothing about the stranger. He only half remembered or even less than that—like trying to recall a minor detail from a days-old dream—that something about the window was worth remembering. The heat was unreliable at its best, and he seldom opened the window in the winter except when the heat was too reliable.

The four-apartment, two-story building's front door, which Ludwig never used since his basement had its own, swung open over the stoop and would have capsized the margarita machine if Ludwig had not lunged to its rescue.

"I thought you were taking unemployment better than this, big guy," Hassan said as he stepped outside. He gave Ludwig the kind of pat on the back that people only give friends or someone they aim to fight. "Or is this how taking it well looks? Have you been out here all night?"

"Only a couple hours. You want some of this?" Ludwig slurred, offering him a drink from his blue plastic Solo cup.

"No, I don't think so. That's all you."

The front door opened again, and a smaller, quieter set of feet appeared.

"Nice to see someone enjoying unemployment. People say you're a big shot with your own agency now. As it happens, I am also looking for a job." Gloria never failed to outdress her competition, even this early, which meant that she looked uncomfortable to the point of being in pain.

Ludwig made a sound that mimicked an upset stomach.

"Gloria?" he said slowly, as though he had forgotten her name in the week since Electric Guacamole collapsed. "What am I doing out *here*? What are you doing in *there*?"

"It's been an emotional week," Gloria said. Ludwig could only stare and pass judgment—another pelt dangling from Hassan's belt. He wondered whether Gloria knew about Emma,

Hassan's girlfriend. Was that his girlfriend's name? Was she even his girlfriend? He had long since stopped keeping score.

"So why *are* you out here with a margarita machine?" Hassan asked.

Ludwig gestured to the open window.

Looking down into Ludwig's apartment from the trash bins, standing in urine she didn't notice, Gloria's eyes scavenged for a narrative. Something happened in there. What was it? Why was the TV broken and on its back? Was that a shower curtain or a blanket? What was all of that paint? "Ludwig! You got a dog!" And then: "Oh no! Ludwig killed his dog!" She directed Hassan's eyes to the life preserver–sized coil of wet fur.

"I guess the partnership didn't work out," Hassan said.

"That is no dog. That is a . . . that is a . . . beast! A fiend! A revenant!" That Ludwig used this last word, which appeared only in scripture and gothic-fantasy fiction, said much about the kinds of media he consumed. "Can't you see that I'm wounded!" Ludwig didn't know how to reveal his lacerated thigh in front of Gloria without revealing everything else, so he didn't. "Why else would I be out here like this? It was hiding under my sheets, and I landed right on it."

This hadn't occurred to Ludwig before. If the Giant had been hiding, what, if not him, had it been hiding from?

"Guess that's what was eating all the other rats," Hassan said.

"You have rats?" Gloria asked.

"I don't. Ludwig does. I've only seen them on my way to the laundry room."

"That eat other rats?"

"Except for the heads," Hassan said.

"And you didn't tell me?"

"If I did, would you be here?"

Hassan and Gloria marveled at the beast, which they could

because, to them, it was just another New York story: the "big" rat in their friend's apartment.

"Hassan," Ludwig said between freezing gulps of bright green slush. "You are technically my super, and while I think of myself as pretty low maintenance, I need help disposing of . . . that. It already came back from the dead once."

"We're getting breakfast," Hassan said. "But sure—can't wait. When I get back, I'll see if I can find where the landlord hid the snow shovel. Where is your shoe?"

They left.

In the backyard, Ludwig sifted through rusted, frozen, decades-old tools. He found hedge clippers and a spade, but his problem was too big for a spade, and the hedge clippers forfeited their usefulness once the battle had ended. He could cut the body into pieces, he supposed, and dispose of them, bloody part by bloody part, or—no, no, he couldn't. Someone could but not him. Through some hybrid, crane-like deployment of the spade and a yard rake, he could lift the Giant into one of the black contractor bags he deployed upright in the corners of his apartment instead of actual trash cans. Or he could wait and hopefully make Hassan do it.

What to do until then?

His bad week had ended with a worse night, but he could still redeem his morning.

Giustina DiPalma, "a saint in a butcher's coat," as she was known to the neighborhood, kept tabs on Metropolitan Avenue, one of Williamsburg's main thoroughfares, through an unblemished window between a laundromat and one of the city's last travel agencies. The neighborhood's Italian origins were alive and well in her. She had made mozzarella from scratch in that storefront and occasionally a sandwich from little more than that since before the United States entered the Second World War. If anything condemned Williamsburg to the long claws of gentrifiers and hipsters, it would not be the institutions coming in but the institutions like hers that were going out.

"Ciao, Giustina!" Ludwig said as he tripped into the shop.

"Ciao," she said, gesturing to the twenty neatly wrapped loaves of warm, minutes-old mozzarella occupying the counter—the perfect food: a colorless ball of flavor that required no utensils or preparation. Fat and warm, comfortably wrapped in a single layer of stretchy packaging, his mind easily did the gymnastics required to see himself in a piece of cheese.

Ludwig never forgot to remind the few friends he let in on this neighborhood secret that Giustina's mozzarella had never been inside a refrigerator because, as he informed them, "refrigerators turn mozzarella into plaster." To the rest, he never said where he got it, especially to Naveena, whose inexhaustible social media following of authenticity-obsessed, camera phone–equipped graphic designers could be dispatched like an ADHD-afflicted tsunami to swallow anything charming, local, or obscure.

Rolls of Italian bread cooled in a shopping cart beneath a shelf containing the few things the store still sold (olive oil, salt, flour, dried pasta). In the back of the faded yellow, one-woman emporium, a slicer sliced prosciutto and, only on Saturdays, roast beef for sandwiches that Ludwig couldn't describe without hyperbole. He bought one of those and a loaf of mozzarella. Because of her advanced age, he knew that any loaf of cheese or dripping, fatty hero might be her last. Nevertheless, he inhaled the sandwich one billiard ball–sized bite at a time.

"Ciao, Giustina," he said.

"Ciao! Muumbazza!" she said.

Ludwig called Hassan. No one answered, so he reapplied his ass to the freezing stoop until his nervous system once again disappeared from his body.

The Giant, though large, had just been a rat, he argued to himself. How could he fear it? In his imagination, he fought wyverns, griffins, warlocks, and trolls—this was just a rat. "Just a rat," he told himself. He saw it depart the living world by his own hand—or foot. He could deal with a dead rat.

The real inconvenience would be replacing the things their battle had degraded past even his accommodating standards. One was only a mattress; apart from its size, it would be easy to replace, unlike the shattered television. Both needed to go to the curb. Just a few things to do, and then back to savoring unemployment, not with the television or the PlayStation or the stack of nostalgia-centered games as he planned but with frozen margaritas and some choice sedatives. All said, this was New York—he should have been exploring, not wasting what remained of his twenties like he wasted his teens. It was just a rat. Yes, just a rat; he could dispose of a rat. The trash was right over there.

The freezing air began to stiffen his mozzarella into the pencil eraser–like consistency that he pedantically warned others about. Newly fortified by something more than alcohol, something that bolstered his fragile nerves with comfort and joy instead of counterfeit courage, he entered his apartment.

To his surprise and relief, someone had already removed the Giant. Hassan, he assumed (who else?), had somehow come through. For such a gesture, Ludwig might gift him his ancillary mozzarella.

Or, no—he wouldn't.

Hassan hadn't come through at all, but something had. The Giant's body was missing.

But its head was still there.

HASSAN WOULDN'T GO this far for a joke if he went anywhere for one. Someone would, but not the kind of digital agency sales director who wore blazers to work on the Lower East Side, tucked in his shirts, and carried business cards in 2011. Nevertheless, it could have been a prank.

Ludwig found nothing he didn't remember depositing in the pad thai–stinking contractor bag that stood in the corner like an abyssal mouth from which nothing ever returned. The same went for the building's trash and recycling bins, which indicated nothing with a tail, blood-matted fur, or claws full of green shower curtains and matching sweatpants.

In the deserted, snow-covered cement slab that tenants generously referred to as *the backyard*, Ludwig found no hidden, dog-sized demons fruitlessly anticipating the return of their higher faculties. The phrase *outright pandemonium of the mind* occurred to him but without reason to think it originated with anyone other than himself. The less he found, the more he searched. The more he searched, the more tangled his mind's switchboard became.

The party or parties responsible could be watching and laughing like on one of those social media prank shows. Didn't Charlie know people in entertainment? Oh, of course! Ludwig got his job at Electric Guacamole writing copy for one of Charlie's friends *in* entertainment!

Ah-ha!

No cramped, ready-to-pounce sound or camera people waited behind his closet door.

He entered the shower on his toes and inspected the building's rotting foundation with a grill lighter, finding only plywood stained by half a century of darkness.

He sleuthed through empty buckets, paint cans, piles of lumber from incomplete renovations, the reverse sides of ceiling panels, the laundry machine (wet clothes, women's), and the dryer (dry clothes, his).

How could there be a more gigantic, hungrier rat than the one he vanquished? And why was he so afraid of this one's dead body, particularly since something had done him the favor of downsizing it?

Dark thoughts appeared.

Doubts about the value of life weren't unusual to Ludwig. Every job made him feel like life might not have been worth it if it looked like nine-to-five employment. No one is immune to morbid thinking. If they claim to be, they have never faced a potential lifetime of carrying two-hundred-pound carpets out of basements or pitching clients named Splash Guard, LLC, while the world remained a wondrous mystery all around, and only your time could unlock that mystery, not for yourself but for people whose only use for you was your labor. Except *these* dark feelings weren't those dark feelings.

In the presence of the Giant's head, Ludwig yearned to stab his own eyes into jelly, run naked through armored police barricades, smash plate glass with his face, gargle razor blades, and other morbid and self-destructive scenarios. Yet he feared the Giant's head too much to approach it long enough to cover the errant appendage with a blanket or towel. It was just a rat, he had told himself.

He had to calm down.

Ludwig opened the bottle containing the dead woman's consolidated pills. The yellow-and-orange labels on the bottle and the easily imagined warnings from her doctors strictly prohibited what he did next. He knew not to take all or even most of the pills at once but ignored the plausible, catastrophic possibility of any or all of them badly clashing with alcohol.

To cease the horror, he would sedate himself.

He took one pill at random, waited three minutes, and took another. Three minutes later, he took another, followed by another, and then another. He felt no braver by the eighteenth minute and the sixth or seventh pill, and it occurred to him that he might have spent thirty dollars on Tylenol and multivitamins. The Giant's head did not indicate whether this would bring Ludwig any closer to concluding the matter of its missing torso.

If the pills were what he thought he had bought, it wouldn't be long.

He flipped his blood-sprayed mattress over and layered it with towels and T-shirts he no longer needed. In the morning, he would leave this house, this neighborhood, and this city.

Was the Giant's head getting more gigantic? Did he hear heavy breathing, or were the pills making his own breathing more noticeable? Was something standing just behind the door?

There it was, the infamous tug toward Earth's gravitational center from the psychoactive sleep aid that made users who defied warning labels passionately nail bananas into trees and overnight jet skis directly from manufacturers to city penthouses and mountaintop South Dakota homes.

The drugs worked.

As the margarita machine turned and turned, a way into the nonsensical night city that we all visit but can only explore alone opened.

For a day, at least, Ludwig left New York.

4

To what species does a higher being belong? Take note of its name. If polysyllabic, pretentious, and more like a prolific title or honorific than a day-to-day alias, you may be in the presence of a demon. For example, Rudy "the Fortress of Stabbing Flames" Giuliani, or Arch Vicar Fran Lebowitz of the Seven Rotting Spirals. Demon ego drenches both.

Spirit names are, quite simply, much simpler. All they require is the name of what the spirit embodies, such as "the spirit of Watawa Falls" or "the Brandenburg Gate spirit." That's it. Their names are as self-evident as they are not.

Fairy aliases, however, are not so simple. As the years pass, they receive an additional name that affixes itself to the preceding one, creating a hyphenated chain of every designation that specific fairy has ever answered to.

Here is a tiny fraction of the name of a "middle-aged" fairy I met on a starlight farming expedition ten or eleven years ago: Diarofitmetzglanfiddish-Bumbledove-Shafopetrium-Blam-Dar Viago-

> Avoverinazdrianel-Lovbishe-Sourfly-Happy Blade-Parohapticaplitz-Metzgovin-Riojada'avitsbladobrian-Giggleglade-Chillyfoot-Brokbee. That is something like 1 percent of 1 percent of it. I forget, or indeed, may never have even absorbed, the rest. For this reason, making a fairy's acquaintance can be time-consuming. However, this is of no consequence to them since their lives are comparable in length to forests and glaciers.
>
> On rare occasions when fairies accommodate the shortcomings of other species, they deploy placeholder names that, like the title of a book, capture the thousands of words that constitute those names while formalizing their order. These placeholders, or "common names," are used when transacting with other species. However, fairies have little concept of what a "common name" should sound like, so even those names have the unintended effect of announcing the presence of a fairy.
>
> —Driftboots the Foggy Juggler

LUDWIG AWOKE TO the furious sensation of an unseen force attempting to excavate his brain. The hour was unknown.

He searched his scalp for the agony's epicenter, then groped blindly for the glass of water that dutifully stood guard against dehydration an arm's length from his pillow.

There it was.

He swallowed a mouthful and then immediately unswallowed it. It tasted like hot dog water, or like he thought hot dog water tasted, which must have been something like diluted hot dogs, which adequately described whatever had snuck into his glass. He also identified unwashed lake fish, cough syrup, vinegar, and pipe resin.

"What the shit?" he said, spitting pink syrup. He added, perhaps more to the point: "What the fuck?"

He wasn't alone. A uniformed stranger squatted like a gargoyle atop the flattened ruins of his desk.

Ludwig recognized its navy-blue ensemble from the eleven-and-a-half-hour American Civil War documentary that he sometimes looped whenever he needed consistent, mellow, friendship-simulating background noise. Living in a basement had made friendships even less likely for him than his idiosyncratic quirks and character defects had before. As he was without even coworkers, the prospect of loneliness grew like a tapeworm. But how to socialize? And whom with?

The uniform belonged to the Union side of that grisly conflict, though, including a pair of snow-white gloves but minus a rucksack, canteen, and rifle that should have completed the picture. A regulation blue-billed cap was also absent. In its place, between the stranger's shoulders and shielding its entire head from scrutiny, sat an inverted metal bucket with two painted brown dots for eyes (a single line representing a monocle circled one) and a tobacco-colored mustache—also painted—that reached almost to the bucket's unseen backside.

"Ah, he stirs! Thank you for inviting me in, Mr. Ludwig! To my order, such a gesture as leaving the window open is an unmistakable sign that you wish to plant the rugged seeds of forever friendship," a voice informed Ludwig from beneath the bucket. "Should I be wrong, know that I intensely aspire to your friendship! Having made my acquaintance only while in a stupor, I doubt that my current assurances are of much value to you. Nonetheless, I assure you that it is in your best interest to finish the dreadful contents of that filthy glass. They will help you process the events taking place currently and those belonging to last night, as well as the news I come bearing now, which I will share once the pain caused by the green, arctic medium within that cyclonic doodad subsides." He pointed a roll of brown paper as wide and long as the trunk of a young birch tree at the frozen margarita machine. "Right-oh-ho, Joe!"

Those words triggered a memory of the stranger, though Ludwig couldn't be sure from when or where he drew the fractured recollection. Nevertheless, he remained tactful.

"Who the fuck—I'll beat your fucking balls off, you motherless fuck!"

Ludwig rolled onto and off his feet and into the apartment's dorm room–era refrigerator, scrambling its depressing contents. He should have been standing on the Giant's head.

Where was it?

"Oh, God," Ludwig said. "Not again!"

Ludwig fired his cell phone at the stranger, which it regarded no more than a person regards a windswept leaf.

"What does it mean, *beat your balls off*?" the stranger asked.

"It means I'll kick your nuts off your shit!" Ludwig barked. "Hassan! Hassan! We have an intruder!"

"My nuts? Oh! Testicles, you mean. I haven't had those in so long, nor would I have use for them if I did. I'm afraid that under this old uniform, you will find mostly straw, a medley of bird feathers, a fistful of witch hazel, a clay jar stuffed with sandalwood shavings where you might anticipate a heart, and under this bucket, an ethereal medium whose name would mean little to you if anything at all."

Ludwig threatened the stranger with his dull serrated bread knife.

"Mr. Ludwig! Put that away! I am excellent at first impressions and know well that you lack the hostility of spirit required to apply that knife during the most perilous of circumstances, let alone against someone who wishes you no harm. And I can see from over here that its blade has less edge than my bucket!" The stranger knocked on its bucket. Was it a bucket, or was it a head?

"I've already killed once today!" Ludwig said.

"Too true!"

"Where is it, you bucketfuck?"

"Where is what?"

"You know what I mean!"

"I do not."

"Right here! They were here! The head! The body! What did you do with them? You like to fuck big rats, you sick rat fucker?" He was trembling. How was this happening? Why was this happening?

"As for the fate of its body, I cannot say, but it is I who have taken its head away!" the stranger rhymed. "I have it stowed in one of these peanut sacks."

The stranger offered a glimpse into a bag that had once presumably stored hundreds of unshelled peanuts. Ludwig approached the bag and looked in, then fell back as though it contained an infinite, screaming pit.

"Yes, best you don't look in there long. Please count the head's relocation as a show of good faith."

With bread knife in hand, Ludwig retreated behind his kitchen counter like someone in a shoot-out.

"It doesn't seem you remember my previous visit, Mr. Ludwig. I saw you from that piss-covered window following your victory over the beast to whom this head belonged. I doubt I am mistaken to believe that its mere presence makes you feel that your faculties are rattling around your skull like coins in a vagrant's tin? Expected! Who among us administers death without touching the abyss, even if only to end a monster from whence it appeared?

"Now, to my purpose. Since you don't remember my

previous visit, you likely don't remember when I recited the rules that govern my ability to visit the homes required by my vocation. Those rules, which are binding, to say the least, only apply to homes with sealed portals, which tonight, yours was not. I took this to mean that, among all this frost and freezing rain, you were inviting me in from the cold—the genesis of our friendship! But, ah! Once again, I fill volumes without introducing myself. I must report this defect. My name is Lonesome Johnny, though you may call me anything you like—my lady-lord and benefactor's client-housemates certainly do! Oh, the epithets they invent! Cruel, yet so clever. Right-oh-ho, Joe!"

The visitor was right; Ludwig did not remember him, though that exclamation, *Right-oh-ho, Joe,* continued to dance along the perimeters of recollection.

"Unfortunately, Mr. Ludwig, I have not had the good fortune to taste 'hot' dogs myself, but my lady-lord and benefactor impressed upon me, to impress upon you, that Dr. Tot's Miraculous Sanity Serum tastes as it does because its ingredients share branches on the alchemical tree with hot dogs and because suffusing it with a more tolerable flavor would compromise its effectiveness as an all-purpose sedative, sanity multiplier, and pain reliever."

"Pain reliever?" Ludwig's fear of the stranger instantly pirouetted, becoming curiosity. "It gets you fucked up?"

"No, Mr. Ludwig. The great Dr. Tot is no brewer of ephemeral euphorias." Ludwig placed the glass on the counter, his interest lost. "But! But! It will relieve pain and confusion, as well as terror and anxiety. Should you find yourself run through with a broadsword—an event that I pray never transpires!—that concoction would numb your nerves to the physical and psychological effects that becoming a human sheath imposes. However, you could still bleed to death, so if cold steel ever does leave your guts dangling like holiday ornaments, remember that Dr. Tot's Miraculous Sanity Serum will not save your life—seek help immediately. In addition, while side effects are possible, they are all unlikely. The most common is the sniffles, while the rarest is immortality."

"That sounds like a pretty good side effect," Ludwig said, gripping the knife.

"Indeed! Though some erroneously believe that immortality is a curse and not the gift it so transparently is."

The glass's contents were bubblegum pink at one angle and banana slug yellow at another. Bits of something swirled around inside like chum. A fish swam past—that couldn't be, could it?

"Ah, fuck me, this is probably a dream, anyway," he said, choking through the serum's deranged flavor as it lathered his shriveled tongue, throat, and throbbing esophagus. He turned ninety degrees, lowered his head to the faucet, and chased the serum's flavor until it couldn't possibly linger. It was no dream—nothing could sleep through that taste.

The throbbing ended, and Ludwig ceased fearing the stranger called Lonesome Johnny, who suddenly felt no more threatening than a short walk on a sunny spring day. As advertised, the tincture offered no narcotic effect, but it relieved Ludwig of all adverse, unwanted feelings, which was itself narcotic-like.

"I'm sorry that I threatened to beat your balls off," he said. "I hope that didn't force you to relive past trauma. I'm also sorry for throwing my phone. And for the knife. It's just a bread knife. It's not even sharp." Ludwig poked his finger with its tip, releasing blood.

"Quite kind!" Lonesome Johnny said. "I hope this brings us closer to that rewarding and lasting friendship."

"You said this stuff is enchanted. What is it really? I've never known a hangover cure to work so fast." Ludwig remained skeptical but grew receptive to the possibility of his world overlapping with another. In a sense, he had trained for this possibility since childhood. Though he may never have warmed to the idea without the serum, which could have been its purpose.

"A powerful elixir, Mr. Ludwig. I do not know its exact ingredients, for I am only an errand boy. That it worked so quickly and without peril is no surprise. My lady-lord and benefactor is a master potion-smith. However, please do not mistake her for some eccentric practitioner of the liquid arts, heating little vials over tiny fires and stuffing corks into oddly colored jars. Pain relief is an ancillary effect, not the serum's purpose, which is to reduce the outright pandemonium of the mind that, in our current circumstance, is caused by—well, my lady-lord and benefactor wishes me to say only so much, preferring instead to say these things herself. All said and done, we now appear on the same—"

Woop-woop. Woooooop.
Baaaaaaaaaaa.

Lonesome Johnny covered his earless bucket until the vehicles retreated into silence.

"Ah, that malicious, malignant racket! It is good that my lady-lord and benefactor sends me in place of herself or her client-housemates, for either would have plunged into madness just now. So fragile are their infinite minds that even the creak of a passing carriage can corrode their souls, leaving them needing days of care. To them, the shrieking sounds of this 'city that never sleeps'—an admission of guilt, I'd say!—are as cruel as any instrument of torture found in any dungeon, including all of the dungeons that my lady-lord and benefactor keeps.

"Once again, I grow distant from my purpose. My task is to investigate the matter of the three syllables that you have been hearing. I refer, of course, to *muum-ba-zza*," Lonesome

Johnny whispered. "The word that you have heard others say, although they have no knowledge of saying it. You are not 'going crazy'—last night and this morning notwithstanding. Indeed, the opposite might be true. Do you ever marvel at the willingness of your species to waste their insignificant lives serving creatures no greater than themselves?"

"Buddy, all the time," Ludwig said. He felt great.

"Terrific! Oh, and we are buddies now, just as I predicted!" Had Ludwig consented to this friendship? For him, *buddy* was just a thing you said. But he supposed any number of friends beat none. "Now, my understanding of your predicament is that you are unemployed. Upon inspection of our surroundings, I suspect that my assumption is credible. Given the dangerous, growing gap in your curriculum vitae, my lady-lord and benefactor is willing to offer you the opportunity to enter her service. I have served her estate in some form or another for two decades. By only the second month, I was so rich and respected that I am to this day the envy of the entire spirit world."

"Do you know that you're wearing a bucket?" Ludwig asked. The words appeared naturally, like speaking to an old and frequent friend, someone in front of whom he had no reason to feel self-conscious or anxious.

"Right-oh-ho, Joe! A slight correction, however. The bucket is my head. There is nothing beneath it but a whistling void leading only to another whistling void."

Ludwig had no reason to doubt him.

"What did you mean by 'unemployed?'" Ludwig asked. "Are you offering me a job? Just to lay it on the table, I was let go from my last job. A lot of people were. So I was definitely not fired. In fact, I was very popular and indispensable to multiple teams. Do you want to see a résumé? They're kind of old. Is this an interview? Because any court would agree that I threw my phone in self-defense."

"So professional, Mr. Ludwig, except there is no need. Hearing *muumbazza* is the only credential required. The arts of enchantment are governed and made usable by certain principles. Chief among them is that things stumbled upon are preferable to things sought. No amount of wand-waving can replace plain serendipity. In my lady-lord and benefactor's opinion, she and you stumbled upon each other. That is serendipity. Immediately, she dispatched me to find you. And imagine my surprise to learn that you live in a basement! My lady-lord and benefactor intensely prefers servants who live in basements."

"Servants?"

"Employees! Same thing."

Ludwig agreed.

"Now, since I am a *servant* to the greatest enchantress of any age, I am very busy. And while I cannot imagine a kinder, nobler, or better-dressed member of your species with whom to ingratiate myself, I must attend to other tasks. So, here, take this."

Lonesome Johnny withdrew a throbbing green organ from a second peanut sack. Pink spots dabbed the body part's surface, and so did the kind of broad, tectonic veins that enmesh the elderly. A cork shaped like a golden bucket sealed the vile, living decanter.

"It is best to overlook the optics of that hollow instrument. It is premium gargoyle's heart and contains more of the serum that protects you even now from your foe's severed head. If you find yourself in need, one sip will tame even your most contentious ghosts."

Ludwig struggled to contain his excitement about introducing a new, comfort-inducing sedative into his life.

"Does it need to go in the fridge?"

"No, Mr. Ludwig. Arcane relics don't belong next to the banana peppers. It is the temperature it needs to be. Likewise, the liquid it encloses must move and rest, making the gargoyle's heart necessary, since it alone is still by day and alive by night. And do not forget what I told you about serendipity. I cannot tell you the way to my lady-lord and benefactor. The place that you must now seek is hidden for the safety of all. When you find her, know that you will require Dr. Tot's serum. Your species is not meant to keep her kind's otherworldly company."

"What kind of pay can I expect?" Ludwig asked. "Are there stock options? I mean, not 'stock' options, obviously, but equity? Is that what you meant by a deed? Some friends with whom I was about to form a company offered me a chance to go full-time at a place that offers stock options, but I decided to entertain other offers. I can go hourly if that works for you. I just need a meaningful, nonrefundable down payment to show you're serious."

"Your rate! Oh, Mr. Ludwig! My lady-lord and benefactor is neither cheap nor a cheat. This work pays in knowledge, adventure, romance, and rubies. You will have more than a career in her employment. You will have a life—the kind you have always sought but failed to find because such a vocation has seldom been within reach of your species."

"Yeah, so, that's good," Ludwig continued. "I still need a number. Do you pay rent? Does she? Williamsburg isn't cheap, and it's only getting worse. I've been thinking about moving. And where I go next could be even more expensive."

"Soon, you will be able to buy any home in this dying neighborhood, if not the neighborhood itself. Don't forget to sign the deed!"

"What deed? What job am I supposed to do? How can I want the job if I don't know anything about it? Who is this lady-lord? Why did you take the rat's head? What happened to its body? At least tell me that."

"Afraid not, buddy! This is how fairy tales work!"

Lonesome Johnny maneuvered out the window into the

frigid night, leaving Ludwig with a gargoyle's hollow, beating heart and an impossibly heavy parchment tube. A purple ribbon and a dollop of moss-green candle wax bearing a little picture of Lonesome Johnny sealed what he now recognized as a scroll.

The window slid shut.

LUDWIG WANTED TO talk about that night and the day before if only to confirm that the report his senses delivered had not been in error. But who would believe such a tale?

He had proof: the hollow heart flask, the magic dumpster runoff that filled it, and an unopened scroll that, given its enormity, must have contained more proof of the supernatural. Then again, talking about the last twenty-four hours might not have been possible, physical or no physical evidence, since the magic he knew of from fantasy paperbacks could seldom be spoken of to the unenchanted. Lonesome Johnny didn't say that exactly. However, he did say a lot, which was a tolerable quality most of the time, but not one befitting a magical matriarch's clandestine, enchanted courier.

Ludwig opened the scroll, causing trumpets to sound. Trumpets weren't uncommon instruments to hear randomly in 2011 Williamsburg, though he couldn't ignore their timing. He closed the scroll and reopened it. Trumpets sounded whether Ludwig opened the scroll a little or a lot.

The scroll's size forced Ludwig to reposition it as he read. His apartment was too small, and it was too big. The letters that formed the words and sentences that formed the content of the deed belonged on banners, not on a legal contract. Were scrolls always so huge? How could the scribes of yore compose secret formulae, plot conspiracies, and write plays on parchment as long and wide as a country road?

The deed read:

The Parliamentary Commonwealth and Republique of the Manhattan Wild Presents: The Enchanted Land Act for the Empowerment and Employment of Non-Magic Entities

Deed Status: *Approved*
Courier of Deed: *Lonesome Johnny, Puppets 1 & 2*
Length of Property Bestowed (Parliamentary Units): *966 human paces; 0.6 crow flights; 19.9 giant snail rides; 7.4 pallbearer processions; 441 standing cartwheels; 1,253 bullfrog hops; 1.0 portals*
Haunted (Yes or No): *No*
Booby-Trapped (Yes or No): *N/A*
Door in Floor Included (Yes or No): *No*

This deed certifies that Ludwig of Williamsburg, Brooklyn (See also: Ludwig of Englewood, New Jersey; Ludwig of Long Island, New York; Ludwig of Astoria, Queens), is the registered proprietor of the land hereby granted, subject to the entries in this register related to the interests set out in Section 1234 of the Enchanted Land Act for the Empowerment and Employment of Non-Magic Entities.

By enacting this accord through the application of his signature, Ludwig of Williamsburg agrees that he will: (a) hold the Deed Issuer's existence, material knowledge, and instructions in the strictest confidence; (b) take all steps necessary to protect the Deed Issuer's existence, material knowledge, and instructions and to implement internal procedures to guard against disclosure; (c) not disclose or make available all or any part of the Deed Issuer's existence, material knowledge, and instructions to any person, firm, corporation, association, or other entity for any reason or purpose whatsoever, directly or indirectly. This deed binds Ludwig of Williamsburg, his employees, agents, representatives, successors, heirs, friends, lovers, mentors, pets, slaves, wards, acquaintances, captives, and blood enemies.

Ludwig of Williamsburg shall only use the Deed Issuer's existence, material knowledge, and instructions as directed by the Deed Issuer and not for his own purposes or the purposes of any other party. The Recipient shall only disclose the Deed Issuer's existence, material knowledge, and instructions received under this Agreement to any person within its organization if such persons have an urgent, essential need to know.

This Agreement, with respect to the Deed Issuer's existence, material knowledge, and instructions, will remain in effect in Perpetuity, or until the Deed Issuer declares otherwise.

Upon request from the Deed Issuer or upon the termination of collaboration between the Parties, Ludwig of Williamsburg will surrender to Deed Issuer all originals and copies of all documents, records, artifacts, incantations, incentives, and other materials containing proof of Deed Issuer's existence, material knowledge, and instructions. Ludwig of Williamsburg shall not be permitted to make, retain, or distribute copies of anything proving Deed Issuer's existence, material knowledge, and instructions, and shall not create any other documents, records, or materials in any form whatsoever that include proof of the Deed Issuer's existence, material knowledge, and instructions. Any notice provided in this Agreement must be in writing and must be either personally delivered by Lonesome Johnny (Puppets 1 & 2) or by Ludwig of Williamsburg.

In the event that any provision of this Agreement is held as unenforceable because it is invalid or in conflict with any natural law or enchantment of any relevant jurisdiction, the validity of the remaining provisions shall not be affected. The rights and obligations of the parties hereto shall be construed and enforced as if the Agreement did not contain the particular provision(s) held to be unenforceable. Ludwig of Williamsburg hereto represents and warrants that he has the full power and authority to enter into and perform this Agreement. Each party knows no law, rule, regulation, order, agreement, force, promise, blood oath, undertaking, or other fact or circumstance that would prevent its full execution. Failure to comply with any of these conditions will, at the behest of the Deed Issuer, reverse Ludwig of Williamsburg's right to the land hereby granted and transferred.

Breach of Agreement and Remedies:

Failure to comply with the terms of this Agreement will result in the maiming or outright eradication of the breached information's Recipient relative to how much confidential information has been disclosed. The timing of said maiming or eradication will be at the discretion of the enchantment that binds Ludwig of Williamsburg to this Agreement. Minor breaches of confidentiality will be met with aggressive warnings, whereas outright and intentional violations of confidentiality will be met with whatever swift suppression the enchantment deems necessary to protect the confidentiality of the Deed Issuer.

On 24 February 2011

Given by my hand and seal of power,
Litzdinera-Fitzerrathort-Dapplecurl-Bralolingiaraian-Hazeltoad-Glittermint-Dorekothia-Roofitnegovia-Sheezelroot-Lorenhapitz-Fogirackamoa-Walahabiniriamoriana-Lopewravaza-Shuutz-Sovitziana-Zalanarianao-Qimifish-Laralandorialazorenwakalopow-Foregia-Walalia-Ifnozapiona-Dagaloiana-Porgroiafinzia-Vergogaria-Lobiaredperetzfugh-Blarndelana-Sandilolo-Ifritzkishganozi-Loperandor-Zutroperianati-Quickthirst-Proraraceptonitzglofidor- (the signature continued like this, eventually covering more square feet than Ludwig's apartment)

Other given names of Deed Issuer:
An Exalted Northwind

Ludwig of Williamsburg's Signature:

____

WHAT DID *LENGTH of Property Bestowed* even mean? Land had to be two-dimensional to qualify as land. And what door? Whose floor? More importantly: Was this another fucking NDA?

Eager to have these and other questions answered, Ludwig produced one of the pens he annexed from Electric Guacamole and applied his little human signature to the deed. French horns sounded this time, though Ludwig's ears failed to discern the difference.

He closed the scroll and then unfurled it just a little. Trumpets played. Where were they coming from? He stepped into his sneakers, shut the window, and tucked the paper cannon under his arm, which reminded him of his time working in the basement of a rug store.

Outside in the near-zero-degree night, Ludwig again unfurled just the corner of his deed. The horn called from somewhere near McCarren Park, Williamsburg's Central Park but without a zoo or open-air productions of Shakespeare and with far more posturing by people who wanted to be seen attempting the first seven pages of *Swann's Way*. Finally, Ludwig regretted not owning boots. At least it was a straight shot. Just eight blocks. He could manage eight blocks in sneakers.

He passed Devoe Street and then the Family Garden, an Americanized Chinese takeout restaurant where Ludwig bought containers of white rice when he couldn't afford the General Tso's Chicken that should have gone with them. It was too late for traffic, so he passed Metropolitan Avenue without waiting for the walk signal and then, to be sure about his direction, peeled back the scroll.

Pah-pa-ra! That way.

These ugly side streets and their names (Conselyea, Skillman, Jackson, Withers, Meeker) blended into one boring conglomeration of vinyl-sided two-story buildings. What had he ever seen in this neighborhood?

He passed homeless encampments huddled beneath the Brooklyn-Queens Expressway (could they hear the trumpets too?), then onto Frost, Richardson, and Bayard, where ongoing gentrification became unmistakable if it wasn't already. He opened the scroll again. *Pah-pa-ra!* The trumpets were louder.

Ludwig searched for the source of the trumpets by circling the park while opening and closing the scroll. The closer he came to where the sound was, the farther away the trumpets' calls moved until they seemed to come from the direction of his apartment.

Is this thing fucking with me? he wondered. The scroll didn't answer.

Ludwig followed the trumpets home, climbed out of his salty, soaking sneakers, and unfurled the scroll. Again, the trumpets played, this time from the direction of the park. He scrutinized the scroll's wording until discovering this line:

Door in Floor Included (Yes or No): *No*

That seemed noteworthy. It couldn't have been included accidentally in such a meticulously considered agreement, especially since Lonesome Johnny mentioned his lady-lord's fondness for servants who lived in basements. Which door did it refer to? Every door that led to his apartment was a door in the floor, so he tried each of them: the door on the first floor that led to the basement, the one in the backyard that led to the basement, the door right outside of his apartment that led to the rest of the basement, and the only door that led into his apartment from the outside. He also tried the closet door, then scanned his apartment for something that fairies might count as doors since fairy magic, which he believed thrived on word traps and double meanings, was seldom explicit about anything.

Ah-ha! The desk.

Ludwig made certain that nothing separated the base of the door that had once been his desktop from the floor, then used his bread knife to pry one from the other. The door opened on invisible hinges, revealing a deep cellar. He'd expected a torch-lined staircase or a long rope made from damsel hair. Instead, he found fifteen flights of ladders joined one floor at a time to scaffolding like the kind that cloaked New York buildings of all sizes. It was like a *Donkey Kong* level without barrels, a princess, or a gorilla.

Ludwig wrapped the slimy hollow heart in a trash bag, stuffed it into his backpack, and dropped the deed to the first and highest level of scaffolding. It quickly rolled from plank to plank.

Thud.

Thud.

Thud.

Thud.

KALEIDOSCOPIC LIGHTS DANCED beneath Ludwig's feet. What colors were those? All of them, it appeared, including a few that he had only ever seen while rubbing sleep from his eyes.

"New colors," he said. "Whatta town."

He hopped from the lowest rung of the lowest ladder and discovered a second, perpendicular tunnel unfurling before him. Although it was too long for him to ascertain its end, if it had one, the same prism of torches radiating unknown colors lined its walls like a runway. Was he standing on purple bricks? What had he expected? Yellow? He supposed so.

Breathing only through his mouth to avoid the taste, Ludwig uncorked the living decanter and took a preventative swig just as an unseen voice growled. Perfect timing.

"Did you close the door?" it asked.

A serumless Ludwig might have scurried back up the scaffolding, dropped the flask, or cloyingly apologized for being there, but the hollow heart's contents erased much of his capacity for fear.

Another bucket-headed stranger sat in a gilded, golden-tufted velvet chair. In place of the friendly and familiar, even cute, face painted on Lonesome Johnny's bucket, this one's resembled that of a cartoonish traffic cop, grave digger, executioner, or member of some other humorless guild. Instead of an American Civil War uniform, its ensemble perfectly matched the one Napoleon wore in Jacques-Louis David's iconic portrait of the megalomaniacal French emperor crossing the Alps. This buckethead hunched over a long, thin sword that resembled a knitting needle.

"I said, 'Did you close the door?'" the stranger asked without Lonesome Johnny's jovial extroversion or enthusiasm for companionship. Instead, its accent belonged somewhere that brought peaty hills and men in kilts to mind. But it was not Scottish.

"Which door?" Ludwig asked.

"The only door."

"Of course I closed the door. That's, like, Magic 101."

"Were you followed?"

"What?"

"Were you followed?"

"Who would follow me? No one comes to my apartment, let alone the secret dungeon beneath it."

"It isn't beneath your apartment. It's beneath your door."

"Same thing."

"No, it isn't. Again, were you followed?"

"No one followed me," Ludwig proclaimed, wondering if it was true.

"Good." Though motionless, Ludwig felt whatever lay beneath the bucket surveying him. "This tunnel is the last of its kind, and it belongs to you now. I will protect this passage until the reclaimed souls that power my corporeal form cease clinging to life. Remember, Upstairs Neighbor, I serve you not. I serve my lady-lord and benefactor. So leave me to the shadows, and pray you do not need me."

"Wow," Ludwig said. "You're nothing like the other guy. What's your name?"

"I am Desolate Phil."

"Perfect."

Ludwig swiped an omni-colored torch from the wall; it burned cold, if a flame that burned cold could be said to burn at all. He couldn't describe it using the adjectives that usually describe fires, such as *hot, cozy, bright, red, warm,* or *blazing.* Once he decided that the torch's flame burned blue, it became pink, which transformed into a simultaneous prism of familiar and foreign shades of green, which turned into some other hue that he didn't know the word for, if such a word even existed, as if the fire were hiding its true color from him.

"Take the torch. I do not mind the darkness," Desolate Phil said. "From it, we arrive, and to it, we all depart."

"That's what I'm always saying!" Ludwig said.

The long, purple brick road that connected Desolate Phil's outpost to the tunnel's farthest end rippled as if it were alive, and at first, Ludwig even thought it might be. The torch only shined where Ludwig wasn't looking, which made light objects dark and dark objects light; yet still, he saw them: worms. The long and wavering path was teeming with them, like some stillborn god of the deep. They covered the purple path and the tunnel's squirming walls and rained from its mud ceiling onto the ground, where they wriggled for the safety and obscurity of dirt to protect them from Ludwig's crushing feet.

"Can I trade this torch for an umbrella?" Ludwig said. "This is the shittiest torch I've ever seen." It was the only torch he had ever seen.

"Let their filth cover you. Your kind once crawled from it," Desolate Phil said.

Ludwig danced around the worms, not out of disgust but a lifelong aversion to cruelty, apologizing each time he missed a vacant brick.

Half a mile later, the tunnel ended where a cement stoop and a high and wide wooden door began. It offered no clue whether it belonged to some great house, fort, or tower. The building beyond—if one existed—could have been a hundred stories tall or a mile wide or not a building at all.

On either side of the great door, four prismatic lamps, totaling eight, circulated more of the same light while radiating like the eyes of some cosmic arachnid. Though they changed color based on perspective, they became black if approached and looked at directly. Not purple-black, either, like the lights that illuminated the basement raves and over-the-counter cough medicine–fueled parties of Ludwig's teen years, but bright, radiating black. The door they surrounded possessed no less than ten—no, eleven—locks.

Hundreds of precisely sharpened, welded spearheads stabbed forth from the door, fortifying whatever lay beyond against not a metal or timber battering ram but the living, soft-tissued version of something like them, as if the door worked part-time as an iron maiden. Except where spearheads jutted forth, carvings depicting hundreds of apocryphal scenes covered the door as if they contained a secret message. If such a secret existed, it remained one—randomness appeared to be their point.

In one scene, a man devoured an hourglass, while a lion slept at a desk in another. Over on that side (no, the other side), three armored geese hung by their necks from sturdy branches, and a flame with four faces watched over a garden where vegetables planted human skulls like seeds. In the illumination below, a tree swinging an ax chopped down a person, and ringed planets filled a coffin while a serpent slithered from a nun's mouth. Above them, a cat climbed a stairway to the moon, while frogs sparred with morning stars alongside a marsh. In the red-and-black transom that united these and other carvings, three fates quilted a wooden river that knocked blacksmiths and apothecaries into other arenas.

The building's directory, which accompanied a set of buzzers, read:

5G
5F Uncle Basement
5E Muck Interpreter
5D Sweet Tooth the Trapdoor Spider
5C Coral-Horned Hallucination
5B Admiral Toenails
5A
4G Granny Num Num
4F Duke Runeberg
4E Spell Book Lexicographer
4D Calamity Broker
4C
4B Peckish Impropriator
4A Trampoline Shark
3L An Exalted Northwind's Archives (cont'd)
3G
3F Arachnid Meringue Pie
3E The Moss-Covered Witch of Castle Cold Rock
3D The Itty-Bitty Mushroom Man
3C Cave Girl
3B The Emperor of Technicalities
3A Ye Olde Cattle Thrower
2L An Exalted Northwind's Archives (cont'd)
2G
2F Slime Maiden

2E Déjà Vu Collector
2D Tuttle the Twelve-Headed Turtle
2C Bottomless Unbeliever
2B The Collision Brothers
2A Beelzeblob
1L An Exalted Northwind's Archives
1G A Vision While Drowning
1F
1E Tambourine MacGriddle
1D Frozen Pond Apparition
1C Graverobber Ballerina
1B
1A Otter Committee
B1 Lonesome Johnny

5

We saw a very good piece of ground: and hard by it there was a Cliffe, that looked of the colour of a white greene, as though it were either Copper or Silver Myne: and I thinke it to be one of them, by the Trees that grow upon it. For they be all burned, and the other places are greene as grasse; it is on that side of the River that is called Manna-hata. There we saw no people to trouble us: and rode quietly all night, but had much wind and raine. A sailor called Muyskens beheld a building five windows high by thirteen windows across. He told the captain, and the captain laughed well.

—Robert Juet's Journal of Henry Hudson's 1609 Voyage: The Unauthorized and Unabridged Edition

Neither the deed nor Lonesome Johnny told Ludwig whom to buzz, so Ludwig buzzed Lonesome Johnny. The button lit when pressed. No sound issued, and no one answered.

He easily imagined that upbeat, bucket-headed sentinel's apartment full of hanging swords, disintegrating books, and antiquated art mounted in bulging gold-painted frames. His vision stopped at what kind of books Lonesome Johnny might read and what kind of art he might hang. Oil-painted pastoral landscapes of an England that no one living knew, except because of other oil-painted pastorals? Depictions of Romantic-era figures staring out over yet-to-be-conquered lands with hands resting on sheathed blades and holstered pistols, their backs forever facing the viewer? As the basement apartment, it might not have been an apartment at all but a glorified storage unit populated by other sentient, self-aware Civil War ensembles.

Ludwig fruitlessly pressed the buzzers of random, strangely named tenants until another way to make his presence known occurred. He peeled open the scroll. But this time trumpets didn't sound.

Since he might have been too far beneath the city, he beat out a melody on that colossal carved door as though he were drumming on a redwood tree *(dun-de-de-dun-dun, dun-dun)*, then again *(dun-dun-dun, de-de-de, dun-de-dun-de-dun-de)*, and then again *(dun-dun-dun-de, dun-dun-de, dun-de, dun-dun-dun)*, announcing his anonymous presence to the pseudonymous somethings populating whatever lay beyond the passageway's inane, nonsensical edifice.

He half expected someone to emerge and chastise him, and someone half did. The heavy, baroque door cautiously slid ajar on well-oiled hinges, and a white glove attached to a blue uniform attached to a bucket with a painted-on, mustached face appeared.

"Oh, Mr. Ludwig! Of course it's you. Your timing is fortunate; I've only just arrived myself. I hope all these eyeless, limbless little freaks haven't impeded you," he murmured, motioning to the tunnel.

The worms seemed to writhe at the insult.

"These buttons create no sound, only prisms of soothing light. Please note that from now forward, impressed as I am by your mastery of the percussive arts, we request that you make no sound louder than, say, the crackling of a campfire, bird song, ocean waves heard from a distant bluff, or soft raindrops rolling from leaves onto the roof of an old cabin. In other words: Keep your voice down, buddy," Lonesome Johnny whispered. "Now, for your benefit, I must ask whether you remembered Dr. Tot's Miraculous Sanity Serum."

Ludwig plucked one of the taut straps connecting his backpack to his Neanderthal frame.

"Wonderful," Lonesome Johnny whispered. "And I imagine you have met Desolate Phil, my most austere colleague. I believe you are the first human to cross his path in a century. I would call to him, but as mentioned, rackets of all volumes are ill-advised within range, or even range of range, of this building."

"How come you don't get a sword?" Ludwig whispered. "Desolate Phil got a sword."

"My lady-lord and benefactor thought it wise to disarm me after the Madame Tussaud's incident," Lonesome Johnny whispered, referring to the museum of lifelike wax celebrity sculptures sandwiched between Seventh and Eighth Avenues.

"What made it an *incident*?" Ludwig asked.

"The helicopters, I believe."

"Are you two the only two, uh, bucket people?" He considered calling them bucketheads, which felt right, as he had done before, though it sounded like a slur. "Or bucket persons?"

"I'm afraid not. A third *bucketbearer*—one word!—exists. However, we do not engage with or speak of him unless we must. He is an unfortunate necessity."

"What's his name? You guys are two for two on those."

"I must leave the matter there, Mr. Ludwig." It was the first time that Lonesome Johnny had been anything but congenial. In deference to his chaperone, "there" is where Ludwig left the inquiry.

"So where are we?" Ludwig asked while inspecting the muddy ceiling, as if a location could be divined through it and the worms. "I mean, in a tunnel, but in a tunnel under what? The East River?"

Lonesome Johnny returned to form.

"You stand before the Parliamentary Republique of Manhattan Fae, also known as Broken Throat, which serves as a temporary home to my lady-lord and benefactor and the forever home of her fairy clients. Supposing this information may not yet be useful to you, we are deep beneath what you know as Times Square."

"Can't be," Ludwig said. "I didn't walk far enough. Times Square should be forty or fifty blocks from here."

"Your impressive knowledge of New York geography notwithstanding, need I point out that you just passed through a wormhole?" Laughter erupted from Lonesome Johnny's bucket until it seemed like it might blast off of his shoulders. "Pardon me, I know better than to hoot and holler so near to my lady-lord and benefactor and her client-housemates. As to our location, starting from your door in the floor, the length of your tunnel is always the same, regardless of where you open it. Before we enter, might you suffer some more serum?"

"I've already suffered quite a lot."

"Ever the right candidate you are! To your sanity!" Lonesome Johnny retrieved a dainty blue glass vase from his pocket and toasted Ludwig. Then he placed the glass on the cement stoop and covered it with a handkerchief.

"One more thing, Mr. Ludwig. Please step on and break that glass. If for some reason you are being watched via a crystal ball or even some tarot cards, breaking blue fairy glass will disrupt the observer's view."

Ludwig stepped on the glass, and Lonesome Johnny beckoned him into a foyer packed with hundreds of neatly piled leather shoes too large even for his cryptid feet. None showed even a day's worth of wear; it was as if they had been created not for any reason that people usually cobble shoes, such as to protect and support feet in motion, but to pass the time.

A rolling cabinet bearing two silver trays impeded their journey into the receiving room.

Sliced bread (white, wheat, whole grain, potato) layered one tray, while the second supported unblemished silver bowls full of peanut butter (crunchy, creamy); five ceramic jars containing strawberry preserves, raspberry preserves, raspberry jam, grape jam, and apricot jam; a ceramic basin brimming with marshmallow creme; a perspiring silver pitcher filled with unpasteurized milk; and presiding over the entire hospitable offering, a stout barrel labeled Hot Koko.

"Please, help yourself. Platters such as these are scattered about the building. These two are specifically for guests, what few we can have. I would happily dine with you, except I have no guts, tongue, or teeth and cannot experience the phenomenon you call flavor. Luckily, the tenants of this house more than compensate me for my defects by eating a dozen displays like this one each day. Besides the roasted birds once enjoyed at their fairy banquets, no nourishment brings them greater joy," Lonesome Johnny whispered.

Ludwig haphazardly composed a sandwich, creamy peanut butter and strawberry preserves on white bread, which he hoped would soak up the potentially toxic serum. Was it toxic? He remembered something about side effects. (The sniffles were one, weren't they? While the other was . . . what was the other one? Impotence? That conversation had been, and still was, a blur.)

A dormant fireplace was centered in the warm and comfortably furnished receiving room that met them past the peanut butter and jelly station. Above it, a placard hung, which appeared to be written in and perhaps by the same enormous hand that had inscribed his deed, detailing what appeared to be rules:

1. *No Talking above a Whisper.*
2. *No Whispering above a Whisper.*
3. *No Enchanting in Common Areas Without Approval.*
4. *No Gathering in Common Areas Without Approval.*
5. *No Gathering in Apartments Without Approval.*
6. *No Use of Fireplaces Without Approval.*
7. *No Gathering on the Stairs.*
8. *No Archival Access Without Approval.*
9. *No Name-Calling.*
10. *No Nickname Giving.*
11. *No Stomping.*
12. *No Knocking.*
13. *No Slamming.*
14. *No Dropping.*
15. *No Thumping.*
16. *No Clicking.*
17. *No Clacking.*
18. *No Barking.*
19. *No Whistling.*
20. *No Scoffing.*
21. *No Scraping.*
22. *No Spilling.*
23. *No Stone Carving in Common Areas Without Approval.*
24. *No Chiseling Without Approval.*
25. *No Woodworking in Common Areas Without Approval.*

26. *No Sawing Without Approval.*
27. *No Sanding Without Approval.*
28. *No Cobbling in Common Areas Without Approval.*
29. *No Shipbuilding in Common Areas Without Approval.*
30. *No Unoiled Hinges.*
31. *No Excess Foot Traffic.*
32. *No Sleeping in Common Areas.*
33. *No Drawing or Painting on Walls.*
34. *No Climbing on Walls.*
35. *No Open Windows.*
36. *No Eating in Common Areas.*
37. *No Use of the Kitchen Between 19:00 and 66:66 Hours.*
38. *No Falling in Love Without Approval.*
39. *No Lovemaking Without Approval.*
40. *No Music, Including Flutes and Fiddles, Allowed.*
41. *No Guests Allowed.*
42. *No Upstairs Neighbors Permitted, Even to Torture.*
43. *Report Symptoms of Blueness Immediately.*

Individuals in Violation of These Rules Face Banishment to the Construction Site.

"I hate it," Ludwig whispered. "But I think I also admire it?"

"Yes, there is much to admire. My lady-lord and benefactor cares deeply for order, especially since her fairy client-housemates do not."

Lonesome Johnny led Ludwig around the floor's surplus turns and sudden dead ends. Every stair, railing, table, couch, chair, ottoman, and shelf appeared at least a foot higher than they should have if someone human-sized had designed them.

Doorknobs appeared at the shoulders, not at the hip or ribs. Ludwig seldom felt small, but he had every reason to in that building. It went against much of what people believed about fairies, which were typically depicted as sprite-like humanoids with translucent, blue-green wings that left sparkling pixie dust in their wake. If fairies lived there, they scaled up to match the city above them, or vice versa. Even roped-off staircases, which appeared out of nowhere like memories, hung so high that he could pass beneath them without crouching. However, while he still had a chaperone, curiosity and the impulse to explore took a back seat to courtesy.

In what the placard called the building's common areas—all empty—stalactites with painted faces drooped so far from the ceilings that they rendered some rooms unusable. Sometimes they intermingled with floating lanterns and candles whose familiar, omni-colored flames created haunting, natural chandeliers. Rather than liberate entire rooms by chiseling them down, it appeared that someone simply conjured new rooms and furniture into place at the ends of equally new hallways. It was just one floor, but it never ended. There was always another turn leading to another never-before-seen room lined with more windows than a house that only overlooked dirt should have had. And each room among them was empty, or so they appeared, until Ludwig saw a bare green leg bolt around a corner. Only the serum prevented him from following it.

"Someone is up past curfew! I must report this," Lonesome Johnny whispered.

Atop tables, desks, and other flat surfaces, jigsaw puzzles portrayed castle ramparts packed with tight-lipped green men and women, some with animal faces, cheering the burning pyres full of medieval Europeans. Others depicted carriage-sized spiders dragging terrified families apart limb by limb, and great snakes swallowing fleeing children as long green people in trees pointed, gobbled roasted birds, and laughed—quietly, Ludwig imagined.

Equally grim paintings by presumed amateurs whose work suggested little passion for the art form leaned against walls, ten canvases deep, and stacks of scattered, open, frequently earmarked books wilted over shelves, ottomans, and couches.

Ludwig and Lonesome Johnny passed abandoned card games and apathetic forays into balsa-wood architecture (gallows, guillotines, more pyres) and ships in bottles, either already finished or halfway through development, that dotted shelves and end tables. A coat of green dust and boredom layered everything.

In what Lonesome Johnny called the large big great room, which was more medieval dining hall than any other kind of room, great or not—the kind that every fantasy novel had at least one of, usually with a throne at one end—a sequence of lifelike paintings illustrated thirty-five cheerful green people in cloaks. When an additional, much taller fairy began to appear intermittently and then persistently, the number of guests at the long table dwindled in correlation from frame to frame, as did the cheerfulness of those who remained. In each successive picture featuring the long-fingered, precisely dressed, and menacingly calm matriarch, the number of guests dropped by at least one, until seven seats were empty. Even the number of roasted birds unhappily fell.

"Now to my lady-lord and benefactor's grand archives," Lonesome Johnny said, "where she fearlessly stares down dense books and glowing cauldrons. Of course, you cannot know how excited you should be, so I forgive your perceived lack of excitement as originating in ignorance, not indifference."

"It's mostly the serum," Ludwig said. "I'm just chilling."

Like those that announced the end of his tunnel and the start of Broken Throat, the door blocking their way had been carved from a single massive slab, despite lacking the spear tips and mercurial carvings that confused and disoriented visitors, if such visitors existed.

Lonesome Johnny pressed the doorbell.

Light emanated from beneath the door, changed colors several times, then returned to its original tint and hue. One moment of silence followed another as the well-oiled knob soundlessly turned and the open door revealed a dress twice as tall as Ludwig wearing boots, both of which few had ever seen. A delicate green hand like a verdant branch descended from on high and beckoned them inside. If the hand and arm were the branch, here was the trunk. She had to be fourteen feet tall if not more. The words *Jolly Green Giant* crossed the threshold of Ludwig's mind, but out of fear or something like it, he banished them.

Tight, midnight-purple robes and glittering embroidery unfurled from her neck to her boots. She wore a corset (two corsets?), many bracelets, decorative belts around her biceps and forearms, and twice as many around her waist. Around her neck, Ludwig spotted three collars: one made from smooth velvet, one made from coarse leather, and another made from stiff lace. At some angles, branches full of dying leaves grew from her scalp, while at others, hair as profoundly green and prickly as pine needles spilled down until it claimed the small of her back. Her skin was green and so were her fingernails and teeth. Even the whites of her eyes were green and thus not *whites* at all.

Were those limes in her hair?

Ludwig cringed through a long swig from the hollow heart. Cryptic energy poured from her as though she were lit by a secret sun. It wasn't her size that infected him with unease, but something that he could not place, as if his senses needed recalibrating to comprehend her, as if one of them did not belong on whatever plane of reality they occupied in what the building's directory and Lonesome Johnny called a grand archive. Her age wasn't apparent or perhaps even knowable.

"You're *Lood-vig*," she whispered, making her the first in years to pronounce his name as his parents intended, though perhaps this was because he had always presented himself as more of a *Luhd-wig*.

"And you are taller than I expected," he whispered back.

"Yes, almost one-tenth of a giant snail ride. I see you are taking Dr. Tot's serum. Without it, you would be seizing on the rug or trying to stick me with something unequal to the task. You will not lack for that serum in my employ, at least until you no longer need it. I can refill it without physical access since the gargoyle who provided it had a twin, and I possess that twin's heart, which connects to the one in your possession. Speaking of connections, how did you like your tunnel?"

"I can imagine worse tunnels," he said. "Probably wormier than it needed to be. But I'm not one to judge. You should see my apartment. Last night, I killed a rat that was more mountain lion than rodent."

"So I've heard, though I wouldn't call our vermin a problem. Think of them as intruder detection. When stepped upon, they cry out, but only our ears are sensitive enough to notice their tiny screams." She rolled foam cylinders between her spider-leg fingers and stuffed them into her ears.

"Sorry," Ludwig whispered. "Was I being too loud?"

"Not at all. I'm just taking precautions. Your volume is exactly appropriate, just like your name, which I love. It's as at home in a fairy tale as in an entomologist's display case. My name is An Exalted Northwind. My fae name has grown unwieldy even for our long-winded formalities, so I do my business using this epithet."

Instruments for calculating, calibrating, measuring, leveling, mapping, and other uses that he could and could not easily imagine covered eyeball-high tables that he could only scrutinize while on his toes. A compass and an abacus were easily recognized. Other instruments, like a jar filled with children's teeth attached to a hand crank, were not. Then he noticed the books.

Rows of encircling bookshelves rose and rose until they reached the ceiling, which was three An Exalted Northwinds or six and three-quarter Ludwigs above. They sagged under the weight of tomes that were more like slabs of sidewalk than books, bending the shelves at angles that shaped them into rounded points, like dull arrowheads, indicating the bubbling cauldrons full of colored drafts below, any one of which could have accommodated three of him.

"You're a witch?" he whispered.

"Pardon?"

"I thought you were a fairy."

"Please clarify."

"The cauldrons. Aren't those for witches?"

"Do you know many witches?"

"No. Well, not the real kind. Though I've worked around women who would probably disagree."

"Well, you know one now, according to your kind's understanding of what designates a witch," she whispered. "For millennia, humans have invented explanations that rationalized our existence without understanding what they uncovered when they happened upon us. They even co-opted the color of our skin into their stories. Notice, green?" she said, pinching her ageless skin. "In those cauldrons sleeps the liquid form of my enchantment. As it boils, the actual enchantment rises through this place into the city above. Where it goes from there is a mystery to me. Under a bridge? Shopping? Does it run for office? What is it up to? I don't know. But you might."

Her familiar, humongous handwriting packed the pages of every open book in sight. How many of these had she written? How many had she packed with notes instead of prose or verse? They must have been what made it an archive and not a library, though it seemed more laboratory than either of those.

"There's no way you've read all these," Ludwig said, indicating the shelves. "I mean, maybe you have. But I know how it is with people's home libraries. Nobody reads shit anymore."

"You're half right," she quietly countered. "Some are just resources for when things escape me. As for the rest, I rarely read them because they're still fresh in my mind. I wrote them since moving into this building two human decades ago. They are filled with equations, formulae, incantations, and observations, all to help me create an apex enchantment that will, when complete, be no more than a page long and capable of splitting our overlapping fae and human realities into distinct worlds. This will let my client-housemates occupy Manhattan again without subjecting them to your kind's urban cacophony or you to their existential hysteria. Are you a reader, Ludwig?"

She extracted a stool from beneath a table for herself and motioned for Ludwig to take another, but they were too tall to accommodate him without a potentially embarrassing climb, so he stood.

"Mostly fantasy. Some history, mainly of New York."

"Oh? My niece is writing a book about New York—*The Decline and Fall of the Fae Kingdom of Manhattan* or some such pretentious thing. I'm sure it will be adequate if she's half the writer that she is a reader. Either way, it keeps her busy, which is necessary during these difficult times. I owe you an apology. I sent my puppet to your home rather hastily. I have one in my part-time employ who can access your computer webs when necessary. He notified me once you announced that you heard *muumbazza*, a simple test of my enchantment that I'm afraid got away from me. I also see that you brought your deed. You no longer require it. However, I will hold on to it for you since theft from my archives is impossible."

God, she was big.

"Thank you. Carrying this thing is like carrying a rug

around." He dropped it onto the table like a felled tree, causing An Exalted Northwind to cover her ears. "I used to work at a rug store. You ever work at a rug store? Sorry, dumb question."

"Manual labor is why I have my puppets, though it is positive to hear that hard work is not foreign to you." So far, the conversation was pleasant. It seemed clear that she was not the one who was assembling the gallery of antihuman art in the common rooms.

"If I'm known for anything, it's hard work," Ludwig said flatly. "No doubt about it."

Ludwig traced the path of a rolling ladder from the first to the second floor, where he detected an eavesdropper. Even under the serum's influence, she startled him. She was beautiful and nearer to his height than the living tree called An Exalted Northwind, though still vast, as she was likely two feet his superior. Her moss-colored hair was decorated with black flowers, dark gemstones, and leafy branches full of bright orange leaves. Her green robes fit loosely and followed her every motion. She looked comfortable, which was more than he could say for some other, taller parties in the room.

"You brought an Upstairs Neighbor into our home, Auntie Northwind?" the eavesdropper asked. "This one looks fresh from the construction site. Don't let the others find out about him. We don't want another mutiny."

She was a thrown stone away, yet Ludwig heard her whisper as though her lips somehow touched both of his ears. "If he doesn't prove useful, perhaps we can saw off his limbs and graft them back where they shouldn't be, then hide food around the building that we can watch him clumsily scrounge for if he wants to live? Or perhaps we can pluck out his eyes and implant them backward so he's forced to stare at the grotesque source of his feeble, limited consciousness? Oh, I've got it! Let's use his bones to build a tiny fort, then use what's left of him to furnish it. Ah, childhood!"

"Ludwig, this is Galilea Dazzledark," An Exalted Northwind said. "She is the niece whose manuscript I mentioned. Her abbreviated alias is like my own. Unlike my own, she gave it to herself. Galilea, this Upstairs Neighbor is a part of my work now. Please refrain from reconfiguring him. Galilea is the one who convinced this city's fae to get serious about their human problem by summoning me."

"I like your name, Ludwig," Galilea said, echoing her aunt. "Perhaps you would let me read your tarot cards? If only I had some."

"Not now, Galilea. Take what you came for and go back to your apartment."

"I'm skedaddlin'. I'm skedaddlin'. Just borrowing some of your notes for my book," Galilea said. "I pray for your death, Upstairs Neighbor. I hope the flames that kill you take an eternity to do so."

"What did I do to her?" Ludwig asked halfway through another swig from the hollow heart.

"It's just how they are. Mischief and cruelty are far more common in our natures than I would like. My client-housemates would not be in such a bad way if they focused on practical solutions to their problems instead of on the hundreds that make them feel good, though I cannot entirely blame them for being this way, especially now. Because of your kind, we are trapped down here. Though we can leave at any time, doing so risks a fate worse than death—one not unlike burning for eternity. In a way, my client-housemates brought this on themselves. By departing Fairie to settle here, they ensured the prosperity of your colonial ancestors. Have you never wondered how your city outpaced so many others? There's more to its success than rivers and musicals. Surely you can see how founding a city on a fountainhead of enchantment could benefit its growth?"

"Uh-huh, kind of, yeah, sure," he said.

"Naturally, my client-housemates tried and failed to stifle the growth they caused," An Exalted Northwind said. "So many failures: the stock market crashes of 1929 and 1987; crime in the 1970s and 1980s; the blizzards of 1888, 1947, and 1996; the election of the corpse-licker demon Rudolph Giuliani. They successfully crossbred rats with cockroaches, but no one noticed. They even helped found Tin Pan Alley, thinking it might do to human ears what your city did to theirs. But their plan badly backfired, leading to your 'roaring twenties.' Then the invention of jackhammers, sirens, and car horns brought the fae of this building even closer to defeat. Their options were to flee, which is not so simple since fae cannot leave their wilds except to return to Fairie, a prospect that is for you like moving back in with your parents; forfeit their sanity by braving the noise, which would turn them into something more dangerous to you and themselves than they already are; or take shelter.

"Back when this city still slept," she whispered, "they deployed an old enchantment that granted this building badger legs, which let it dart from neighborhood to neighborhood. When the fae chose a place on this land to shelter, one that was distractingly busy enough for no one to notice a five-story building digging into the earth, it dug fifteen stories beneath surface level. This solution worked for a while, except now they suffer from isolation instead of noise."

"I thought fairies liked it underground? In your, uh, burrows?" Ludwig asked. He only ever encountered this word when fairies appeared in one of his middling-but-canonical mass-market fantasy paperbacks. Most would call them holes in the ground. Fairies and those who feared them called them burrows.

"Not for one hundred years, Ludwig. Yes, you have your boroughs and we have our burrows, but you must occasionally desire to leave your five boroughs?"

"Not really," Ludwig answered honestly, then shrugged to signal that he wouldn't apologize for being a New York supremacist.

"Regardless, I believe it is possible to create an enchantment that lets my client-housemates occupy the city as you do, without hurting humans or vice versa. To accomplish something so ambitious would secure my legacy as the greatest enchantress of any age. Of course, the fae of this house won't see it that way; they would prefer that I drown you all in an inferno of gargantuan, flaming mosquitoes. Can you guess why I accepted this challenge?"

"Because you care about human life?"

An Exalted Northwind leaned back and soundlessly laughed; a phantom gust of late-autumn wind moved through the room. Was that how they laughed? Leaves fell from her hair and the ceiling too, as if they were under a forest instead of Times Square. A lime bounced off the floor.

"Because you love to win?" he asked.

"Yes, Ludwig. Because I am an entrepreneur." Ludwig unstuffed the cork from the hollow heart and drank. He could endure all the allusions to human-crushing cruelty, but no more of entrepreneur and CEO culture.

"My lady-lord and benefactor, you are already the greatest enchantress of any age!" Lonesome Johnny whispered.

"Not quite, puppet. Not while that Gilda Fiorella keeps blinking in and out of existence. They say she lives in Italy and has a crystal ball now. The last of its kind, I suspect. If we had one, I wouldn't need you, Ludwig."

"Gilda who?" Ludwig asked.

"Gilda Fiorella. Some might call her my rival, but never to my face. Knocking her off her high unicorn would bring me satisfaction equal to saving ten times this building's fae."

Perhaps because she was trying to make a positive impression, she had not yet betrayed the kind of malice that was so readily on display throughout the rest of Broken Throat. But at the mention of Gilda Fiorella's name (was it Italian?), Ludwig felt his blood turn cold and itch beneath his skin.

"Maybe, instead of a crystal ball, try giving Galilea Razzledazzle some tarot cards? Isn't that what they do? She sounds like she knows her way around them," Ludwig said.

"Dazzledark," An Exalted Northwind said, correcting him. "Unfortunately, the last real deck, which belonged to my niece, disappeared centuries ago. Gilda Fiorella may have that too. But tarot cards are fickle and cannot offer me the clarity of a crystal ball, which shows you what you want to see. In contrast, tarot cards show you what the sun, an errand boy with a questionable number of swords, and a chariot mean, for your second cousin's second marriage. Please don't mistake me; I would pay a high price for either. But to develop my enchantment without them . . . well, the stars would sing my name until long after they died. More importantly, they would stop singing hers. Gilda this, Gilda that! Gilda, Gilda, Gilda!" she exclaimed at a volume not suited to her own presence, so Ludwig shushed her, and she returned to whispers. "I am sure that Gilda has servants and allies up there attempting to sabotage me as we speak."

"I'm not sure how involved I want to get with fairy politics," Ludwig whispered. "My English and Irish folklore are weirdly up to snuff. So I know what happens to humans who meddle in fairy affairs."

"Those are just stories," she declared, though the paintings and puzzles he had seen earlier suggested otherwise. "And, like it or not, you're already involved. The distortions in reality that afflict you were an uncharacteristic miscalculation on my part, one that won't go away until I complete my enchantment, so it's in your interest to help me. Enchantments are not, as you might believe, spells. They are living things that trick reality into doing what you want. They court trouble while young, and they mature with age. They have mischievous personalities, so our species must nurture their potential and help them grow. The process," she said, gesturing to her bookshelves, "requires reductive guesswork that can last centuries. Our long lives uniquely qualify us for this role. If you want riddles, turn to spirits. If you want weapons, turn to demons. And if you want enchantments, you have only us. Forgive me. I am talking more than my puppet. I suppose that I am just excited. I have been at the foot of a mountain pass with a sprained ankle for two decades, and just now, a donkey appears."

"In this scenario, am I the donkey, or is Lonesome Johnny?" Ludwig asked.

"My puppet?" Lonesome Johnny perked up, then saluted her. "He is an errand boy—a spirit and some souls that I gave second wind to by attaching them to a hamper full of laundry. I can't involve him in matters of complex enchanting. It would be like using plutonium to detect radiation. I expect to work without rest until completion, which could be a century from now. With your help, it might only take a tenth that long. I require a similar commitment from you."

"I haven't agreed to anything yet," Ludwig cautioned. "Ten years? I'll be thirty-seven. The last years of my youth will be over. So if I do this, whatever *this* is, it will require pay enough to compensate me for that." Ludwig paused. "Millions—up front. And once the project is over, millions more. And they can't disappear as soon as the project is over. No trickery."

"Millions of what?"

"Dollars."

"Ah, your currency. Will this make you so rich that you don't have to work?"

"Not in New York," he lied.

"Since I have never transacted in dollars, I cannot offer you compensation denominated in them without creating a separate enchantment. And as I said, they are time consuming, and we do not have time. But I can give you a kind of universal-value faucet."

Ludwig tried to imagine what form a universal-value faucet might take. A tree that grew gold? A cloud that rained diamonds? A bag of holding filled with bearer bonds?

"Tell me more about the job," Ludwig said.

"I need you to locate things that neither of us knows exist," An Exalted Northwind said. "They are the unintended side effects of the enchantment I am calibrating into existence. In the same way that the computer code that controls your human machines can have 'bugs,' so can my enchantment. Think of these bugs as distortions in reality if that's easier for you. You have already found one such distortion in the form of *muumbazza*. Your assignment will be to help me find more. While I can't see my enchantment's deployed state from the ground, I might through steady reports from you, my crystal ball. Report what you find to me through my puppet. Summon him anytime by leaving a fish in a gin-filled mug on your windowsill. Together, we can save these fae. Together, we can show that frizzy-haired, squat, mushroom-shaped bitch, Gilda, who is Fairie's supreme enchantress."

Ludwig's blood again turned itchy and cold.

"Will I know what I am looking for?" he asked.

"No, but that doesn't matter. As my puppet told you, the enchanted arts are governed and usable by certain principles. Chief among them is that things stumbled upon are preferable to things found by seeking. This is serendipity. However, since you won't know what you seek, every bug or distortion in reality that you find will be one you stumbled upon. And the more you search, the more you will find. Expect to spend many hours a day on your feet. You love this city, don't you? Then explore it. Work will multiply luck. Every day will be an adventure."

A job. A boss. Hours on his feet. Exercise. So far, adventure wasn't what he'd call it.

"This sounds like manual labor." Ludwig reached for the hollow heart but stopped himself because he didn't want to reveal his misgivings before she gave him the value faucet.

"It is manual labor. But it's just walking. It's not like you will be—where did you say you worked? At a rug store? You won't be carrying anything that heavy." He was, he knew, usually at least that heavy.

"Will I know how many of these reality-distorting bugs I am supposed to find?" Ludwig asked.

"I don't know. If I did, I would say."

"So my job is to walk around until I find an unknowable number of unusual . . . somethings?"

"Yes."

"In New York?"

"Yes."

"And if I don't succeed, all the fairies in this building will, what, die?"

"No. Something much worse than that."

"In that case, we need to do better than a dollar figure," he said.

Ludwig stepped back from the table, raised a fist to his chin, and scanned the room. What sort of valuable things did fairies have that he wanted? Swords? Potions? Ancient relics? Enchanted clothes? From what he thought he knew, fairies could produce anything, so long as it was magic. They could even grant wishes. Then again, those same books weren't aware that fairies and witches were the same thing, making them dubious sources of insight.

"Besides monetary compensation," An Exalted Northwind said, "I am willing to include immaterial compensation. How does being king of New York sound?"

"I appreciate you starting high," he said. "But too many people want to be kings or queens of New York or one of its boroughs. I have no interest in being anyone's king, and, for that matter, I don't want anyone to be mine. I want to be something the city's never seen, like an urban druid."

"A *druid*?" she spat. "We *hate* druids. They are pet-sitters who barely rise to the level of gardeners. We hold pyromancers in higher esteem, and they are our natural enemies."

"I have a better idea," Ludwig said, smiling hopefully. "One that I'm surprised didn't hit me sooner. What if you taught me magic in lieu of money? Nothing fancy. Maybe one spell that shoots magic arrows, another that lets me walk through walls, and, I dunno, something that lets me stop time if I clap my hands? These are rough ideas. I think we can workshop them if you're willing. I'd trade the 'value faucet' for, say, five spells? No, let's make it six. But I choose the spells!"

An Exalted Northwind impatiently closed her eyes and exhaled.

"Let's not use the *M* word. I am not pulling rabbits out of hats. Even though teaching one of you the craft of enchanting is the kind of challenge I usually cherish, your lives and attention spans are too short even to crack the art's surface. I'll think about the urban druid concept, even if it is a contradiction in terms."

"Let's stick with the value-faucet idea until we get there," Ludwig suggested. "One more time: I want what I want, not some nefarious fairy interpretation of what I asked for—and maybe some health insurance too."

"I understand your request," An Exalted Northwind said. "I am not my niece, who once pretended to be a djinn in order to grant a young woman's wish to make every day of the year her birthday. Two months later, the young woman died of old age. I am interested in the task at hand, nothing more. I am on your side in this endeavor, and you are on mine—the first human-fae alliance in nearly a century."

"How did it go for the human in that alliance?"

"She was melted down and used to put up this building's

wallpaper. Puppet," An Exalted Northwind put her fingers to her lips and whistled, though Ludwig heard nothing, as if it were a dog whistle. "Puppet, we are near an accord. Bring Ludwig a universal-value faucet. One should momentarily appear in 2G's bathtub."

Lonesome Johnny quietly jogged from the room.

Could he trust her? She was a boss, and to him, like in a video game, bosses were something to be defeated.

Lonesome Johnny reappeared carrying a long-haired, feral-faced golden piglet. An unexpected patch of amethyst fur surrounded its right eye.

"Is that the faucet?" Ludwig asked, flummoxed. "I think maybe you don't understand what millions of dollars look like, and you know what? That's my fault."

"Oh no," An Exalted Northwind said. "It is you who draws the wrong conclusion. Puppet, if you don't mind, I would rather not be the source of so much crassness."

"It's a fairy piglet, Mr. Ludwig!" Lonesome Johnny said, almost dancing. "Give him a good shake on a full moon night, and he'll defecate flawless rubies. You'll never fret about the weight of your purse again!"

"What will he defecate the rest of the year?" Ludwig asked.

"Turds!" Lonesome Johnny said.

"What does one feed a fairy piglet?"

"Copper coins!"

"Do they have to be shiny, or can they be whatever?"

"He's a pig!"

"So much has happened that I almost forgot: What happened to the rat?" Ludwig asked. "The one that I bravely faced like a valiant knight and killed against all odds?"

Lonesome Johnny sought permission to speak. An Exalted Northwind held up a candlestick finger.

"There is more hiding beneath this city than those in this building, Ludwig. If I were you, I would consider moving. You now have the means. Alert my puppet once you have made a discovery. Keep that serum near." She tossed her fingers as if to shoo a fly away, and Ludwig found himself in his apartment clutching the hollow heart of a gargoyle, an enchanted piglet, and a backpack filled with peanut butter and jelly sandwiches.

"Whatta town," Ludwig said.

> *Woop-woooooop.* (Sirens, police.)
> *Baaaaaaaaaaaa. Baaaaaaaaaaaa.* (Sirens, fire truck.)

The city agreed.

LONESOME JOHNNY MADE his rounds, inspecting self-replenishing pitchers of milk, trays of soft bread, bowls of jam, and basins of peanut butter. The thing that had gone unsaid bothered him. His lady-lord and benefactor knew it, of course, but he needed to be certain for her safety and Mr. Ludwig's, so he softly journeyed to her archives and depressed the doorbell without a bell.

"Come in, puppet," she projected with a whisper.

He found her deep within the stacks, folded over a free-standing magnifying glass with a rose lens that she used to locate and scrape the incandescence from a pile of moth wings.

"My lady-lord and benefactor, I wish to bring something to your attention. I am sorry for not doing so sooner. I thought it unwise to raise such a potentially controversial matter in front of Mr. Ludwig."

"Speak, puppet."

"Mr. Ludwig's home possesses an aura. It is what made him so easy to locate; this could explain why he alone appears to be the exception to your enchantment."

"Nevertheless, puppet, things stumbled upon are preferable to things acquired by seeking. Serendipity and coincidence rule the arts of enchantment from their twin thrones atop the glowing moon. Is Ludwig the perfect candidate? No, certainly not. But I don't think we will find someone more able to help us troubleshoot my enchantment. Perhaps a superior alternative could present itself in some other epoch, but look at my client-housemates! They called upon me to save them, and except for the one who shares my blood, they have followed my rules, so save them I will."

"Forgive me. I doubt that I am communicating my full meaning."

"Tell me your full meaning."

"I felt what I thought was one of Broken Throat's previous tenants in Mr. Ludwig's basement, faintly on my first visit, then unmistakably on my second. After all, this is why I and the others exist, to protect you and your client-housemates from them. Its presence, it follows, is why Mr. Ludwig required Dr. Tot's Miraculous Sanity Serum a full day before he crossed the threshold of Broken Throat. This confirms my suspicion." Lonesome Johnny placed a nearly empty peanut sack on the shoulder-high table. From it, he withdrew the wet, severed head of the Giant. "I am sorry. I know that you despise these."

"I believe you are right, puppet." She uncorked the twin to Ludwig's hollow heart and choked through the taste; even someone of her power and prestige trembled before the Giant's severed head. She inspected it through the rose-colored glass; its wet neck shone violet. "Even their saliva sparks the frenzied flame of madness now. Unfortunately, the longer Ludwig works for me, the more drawn the creatures will be to him."

"Is that why you withheld the truth? To keep him focused? I fear this may put Mr. Ludwig in tremendous danger."

"It may. And, yes, Ludwig seems easily distracted. But he

has the hollow heart, which he has not been afraid to use so far. It should protect him until I have no choice but to tell him."

"So . . ." Lonesome Johnny said.

"Yes, puppet?"

"You know that Mr. Ludwig has a blue guy?"

"Yes."

THE MOST COMFORTABLE MAN ALIVE

SPRING 2012

6

> There are two New Yorks: the one you experience when you have to fret about money, and the other one.
>
> —Wanda "Millions" Mosley

LULU VAILLANCOURT HAD more reasons to hate the auction houses than the number of bracelets she had on (for warding and manifesting) or rings (for binding and healing), and all nineteen or more of those reasons were clients: rising, new-money New York families scavenging the functionless heirlooms and decadent bric-a-brac of declining, old-money New York families. The dregs of the once-estimable house she represented on that misty, silver spring day belonged to the latter category.

If thirty-three-year-old Lulu was honest with herself, her dream job was no longer a dream. But she did it with a smile and countless compensatory hand gestures because Lulu Vaillancourt treated every job like it mattered, even when that job was frothing lattes at an interstate rest stop or convincing shoppers that the turtlenecks in their closet weren't as fall essential as the meticulously folded turtlenecks piled beside her. A lazy eye was the laziest thing about her.

Following the 2008 housing market collapse, Lulu, who worked all sides of New York's auction houses as a proxy buyer, seller, connector, and sometimes appraiser, encouraged clients to prioritize the sale of hard assets like precious gems since, like gold, they were seen as safe havens during economic turmoil and would be in demand. When the economic recovery threatened this strategy, she reminded her clients that the banks had grown even bigger and a second calamity was "like a pet alligator flushed down the toilet"—closer and more dangerous than they thought.

After three years of pushing clients to part with stones more valuable than some museum wings, they capitulated; or, put another way, they saw how much money their Upper West and Upper East Side rivals were making by listening to Lulu the Magician's rivals, but not before chastising her for their mistakes.

"Why didn't we list sooner?" they quizzed Lulu, whose profession required her to stay calm under fire from some of New York's most entitled and undeserving matriarchs.

"Well, I did recommend selling last year, but as always, markets are fickle, and I respected your wisdom and caution," Lulu would say, furling and unfurling eyebrows so broad and impenetrably dense that they formed a natural sweatband. On nights when she couldn't sleep, or could but instead chose to stay up casting make-believe spells on her clients, she imagined turning them into toads, eels, rats, pigs, chickens, and on one noteworthy occasion, a ghastly amalgamation of all five.

These experiences desensitized her to the preposterously high prices of items that moved through Hazlitt & Hazlitt Auction House, unlike her rural Massachusetts parents, who claimed not to believe (they did anyway) that someone paid $33,000 for a rusting end table with something called a "rare blue-and-brown patina," or $183,000 for six unframed drawings of fish. She sat through these sales not because she wanted or needed to, but because when her aging clients tuned in to live streams of the event—something that she was still adjusting to them doing—and didn't see her sitting among the watchers and bidders, proxy or otherwise, they told her so.

"Why weren't you there, Lulu?" they demanded. "I was watching, and I didn't see you. What if I wanted to bid on those wonderful pandas? Did you see Teddy Roosevelt's hat? How couldn't that go up in value? You know, I fancied that rug from Abu Dhabi, the one with the three medallions."

Lulu's specialties were gems, jewelry, and timepieces, things she could easily carry to and from underground vaults until her clients remembered purchasing them. Once upon a time, these and other auction house staples had seemed like enchanted objects to her. What An Exalted Northwind had called the *M* word was all she wanted from life, but this business had long since forced her to stop believing it might exist.

When the jewelry (or "jewellery," according to the parlance of auction house catalogs) event began, Lulu, jingling like a wind chime from her woo-woo accoutrements, vacated the bidding pit for a fuller view of who was in it. Having done the job for years, she could roughly gauge buyers' appetites. With engagement season a couple of months away and talks of post-recession inflation circulating, she anticipated cutthroat bidding for her clients' lots, whose listing prices Lulu kept artificially low to fuel competition between bidders. This strategy carried risk, but risk could be limited if you knew what Lulu did.

A well-kept secret of high-end auctions is that winning bids are often secured before bidding begins. This behind-the-scenes chicanery saved Lulu, her clients, and the auction houses from embarrassment in the unlikely scenario that a $5,000,000 blue diamond generated no interest. Auction houses were not, as they seemed, free markets. They were carefully rigged ones that utilized absentee bidders played by people as high up in auction house organizational charts as vice presidents and C-suite executives when they didn't have their own Lulus pulling strings. On the auction block, reputation mattered, and failing to sell important lots for double-A clients could deter business from any triple-A client.

Lulu's client wasn't herself a collector of gems, though her departed father was. In his will, he had left his beachcombing, permanently vacationing loaf of a daughter several pieces prominently featuring African and Southeast Asian rubies. When a Ponzi scheme ravaged the daughter's finances, she held a twelve-course dinner to announce that she was parting ways with the famous gems, which the heiress's father had bought not for her beloved mother but for his beloved mistress, whom he called "my flame." She expected millions. Whether she got it depended on Lulu.

Beatrice Drake, Hazlitt & Hazlitt's only female auctioneer, conducted that day's bidding. Whether man or woman, auctioneers must be English, as some unwritten law decreed, so she was, despite making her reputation by defying other tropes like the one depicting auctioneers as monosyllabic, fast-talking automatons. Instead, she orchestrated slower, friendlier auctions with a higher joke-to-sale ratio than the ones administered by her rubber-stamping, gavel-swinging peers.

The event began, and diamond rings, emerald brooches, and sapphire pendants flew off the block to the beat of the auctioneer's gavel, a reassuring sign that meant Lulu's advice to clients about rare gemstones was, as usual, well-founded. Because Lulu received her pay on commission, she could finally make that down payment on a one-bedroom Upper West Side apartment with a washer, a dryer, and possibly even a dishwasher.

Her client's first lot was a pair of 1928 Cartier earrings featuring 28.68 carats of round Burmese rubies, 2.64 carats of brilliant-cut diamonds, and 18-carat white gold frames with English assay marks. The earrings' designer, Germain Lafaille, had signed the inside of the pair's custom-constructed mahogany box—20 percent of their value derived from that signature. Bidding started at $830,000. Lulu estimated their true value to be no less than $980,000. If the words she had said while sitting surrounded by chalk lines and candles on the floor of her apartment last night worked, they could go as high as $1,150,000.

"Ladies and gentlemen, but primarily ladies for now, this fabulous lot is a steal at $830,000. I might even steal them myself! Imagined into existence by Germain Lafaille, brother to acclaimed Dior designer Beatrice Lafaille, these masterfully crafted earrings are the fiery sister to a pair of emerald Germain Lafaille earrings sold at twice the listing price only last month. They feature 28.68 carats' worth of Burmese rubies and 2.64 carats of brilliant-cut diamonds set in heavenly 18-carat white gold. I am looking for bids starting at $830,000. Do I have $830,000 in the room? Do I have $830,000 on the phone? I am happy to repeat myself. One of France's all-time masters of colored stones, Germain Lafaille, designed this magnificent pair whose emerald-focused siblings sold at two times appraisal just last month."

The auctioneer searched the room for paddles as if looking for moles to whack, repeating highlights as she looked, "Germain Lafaille. $830,000. 28.68 carats of beautiful, rare Burmese rubies. Am I at a funeral home or an auction house? Once again, I am looking for $830,000 in the room. $830,000? $830,000, anyone? Closed."

She dropped the gavel.

"Well, as Jigga Man once said: On to the next one," the auctioneer said.

In seven years of working the auction houses, Lulu had never sold an item at less than 10 percent above appraisal, let alone not at all. Failing to sell went on the permanent records of lots like this, especially if they were offered below appraisal. Not selling embarrassed everyone, from the auction house to the item's owner to the Lulus of the world. So what did the bidders in the pit and on the phones know that she didn't?

Her client's second lot was a true wild card, a necklace with an unusual, unforgettable statement piece, a severe yet playful, whimsical yet elegant, salamander-shaped pendant set with 27 carats' worth of rare-cut rubies and 2.88 carats' worth of yellow, internally flawless diamonds. It was a Frankenstein piece, but Frankenstein pieces developed followings, and on the block, followings mattered. The pendant, which had initially belonged to a Cartier piece, was repurposed to look like it emerged from a volcano. For contrast, it came in a wintry jade box signed by all three of the piece's designers.

"Next, we have a truly unique lot: a rarest-of-the-rare collaboration between renowned French, Swiss, and English designers. This cross-generational arrangement possesses a whopping 27 carats' worth of flawless rubies, which combined weigh almost as much as the Hope Ruby. Except the Hope Ruby is a dark stone that lacks the brilliance of the ones uniting this Buckingham-caliber masterwork. Bidding starts at an awfully specific and fittingly unusual $2,329,600. This is the second listing in a row that our jewelry department has informed me is probably too low. It seems like someone out there is trying to stoke a bidding war! Once again, the listing price is $2,329,600. Do I have $2,329,600? I'm looking for paddles. You, sir, did I see your paddle? No? There must be a draft. Do any of you gentlemen have a wife with a heart full of fire? How about a mistress? My, where are the bids? Remember that our appraiser values this lot at 10 percent above listing. That is money on the table. On three, do we have takers? On two, do we have any bidders on the phones or in cyberspace? Going once and for the last time—closed! It seems the rich no longer wish to be richer."

Was this how failure felt? Where were Lulu's arranged bidders? Where were any bidders? Anxiety corkscrewed up her spine like clouds attempting to climb the Himalayas only to return as a drizzly chill once it failed to pass her impenetrable eyebrows.

Lulu expected her client's third lot, a 1947 Michael Ramsey ring featuring a 20.01-carat Burmese mixed-cut ruby, 9.65 carats of pear-shaped, brilliant-cut diamonds, and a size 7.5 high-platinum-and-white-gold band, to generate international attention. The ring rested in a tiny spruce box without a trace of opulence, which was the point. It didn't need any. The ruby was rare and enormous.

When Lulu's client had encouraged her to "Try it on, girl!" in a vault stacked with safety deposit boxes that likely contained at least a few comparable, if not competing, stones, it felt like sliding on an apple. It was the kind of stone that people named, such as the Luck Sapphire or Sunrise Ruby.

The appraiser valued the almost unprecedented stone at no less than $4,900,000. Lulu expected bidding to reach at least $5,500,000. There weren't many who could afford such a stone, and even Hazlitt & Hazlitt didn't know their identities: kleptocratic dictators, royal families from gradually destabilizing autocracies, diversifying hedge fund managers, people with a global network of safety deposit boxes and shell companies, and other fantastically rich, privacy-conscious scoundrels hidden behind walls of proxy buyers.

Auction houses referred to the stone at the piece's center as an anchor item, and auction houses built entire events and catalogs around them. Indeed, that day's event catalog featured the ring on its cover.

"Ladies and gentlemen, if I may finally have your attention.

Is everyone ready? About time someone plugged that carbon monoxide leak." It was an audacious preamble, Lulu thought, but audacity sold exclusivity.

"Bidding starts at an inconceivable $4,900,000. This once-in-a-generation lot features a platinum-and-white-gold band; 9.65 carats of pear-shaped, brilliant-cut diamonds; and today's showstopper: a 20.01-carat ruby that is one of the few known gemstones, let alone rubies, comparable to the Sunrise Ruby, which recently sold privately at the highest price ever paid for a colored gem. It is a crime to offer so much ruby for so little."

The auctioneer raised her arm in anticipation of imminent bids. Once again, all she could do was talk. There were no in-house bids, telephone bids, online bids, or absentee bids; there were no bids for Lulu's lots.

Then her phone rumbled to life.

What had just happened, and how hadn't she, someone who visited a tarot reader more often than her local coffee shop, known that it would happen?

FOUR MONTHS BEFORE the auction, the rightfully incredulous private gemstone broker told Ludwig, "For a ruby of that size and clarity, you need to know someone at a major designer or retailer; have a deep, deep black market connection; or be willing to deal with an auction house. That is at least a $250,000 ruby."

"And what about all these other rubies?" Ludwig asked.

Ludwig sold rubies wholesale and at steep discounts because inflated prices only mattered to sellers without an infinite supply.

Everyone in the jewelry business wanted to work with Ludwig for the low, instantly profitable returns on his rubies and his casual, back-of-a-pizza-shop way of doing business.

Privacy was his only condition, and he could have stipulated any additional conditions without resistance for flawless, half-priced stones. The lucky few jewelers who discovered him early asked few questions and paid promptly. The ruby market caved in on itself a day before the auction at Hazlitt & Hazlitt, and Ludwig never rode the subway again.

Ludwig had named his enchanted pig Mr. Blueberry, which he declared more creatively defensible than something as on the nose as Mr. Ruby. When asked, "Why Mr. Blueberry?" which people often did, he said, "I don't know, man. He's got a blue thing over his eye. What are you supposed to call a pig?"

When New Yorkers with dogs scooped up after their pets, they did so by turning plastic fruit and vegetable bags into gloves that they used to pick up shit and carry it until reaching a trash can. If you had an enchanted pig, it worked the same way except on full-moon nights, when Ludwig gave Mr. Blueberry a good shake and then triple or quadruple bagged his hundred-thousand-dollar bowel movements and carried them incognito past the front desk at one of the hotels where he had rooms. When he got the package to his suite, he broke the turds apart in the toilet, then washed their lustrous fruits in the sink. It was unclear whether Mr. Blueberry knew why.

Instead of settling on a new apartment, because of its proximity to Giustina's mozzarella shop, Ludwig gave 5 percent of his and Mr. Blueberry's time to his Williamsburg basement, which he rented month to month and protected with twin cattle prods that hung by the door and the uncovered shower—the only ways in or out for rats.

He gave the remaining 95 percent of his time to sprawling hotel suites and penthouses in downtown neighborhoods where he might someday live once he had reconnoitered their vibes. He wanted to live where musicals were set, not performed, and nowhere worth going was more than fifteen minutes from his lobby, driving or walking. So he narrowed his search to the borough where he knew he belonged, the leg-of-lamb-shaped island whose perimeter he had beat around for twenty-eight years without accumulating the resources needed to call it home.

His renting days were over. Ludwig wanted to own.

It wasn't the search for a perfect apartment that stopped him from committing to an address but the amount of work he associated with packing the almost nothing that he owned, moving it into a truck or cabs, transferring utilities, learning the neighborhood, setting a time to meet the Realtor, paying Realtor fees that in practice he could easily afford but in principle regarded as serfdom, inventing a lie to tell friends who asked how he could afford a $5,000,000 penthouse, and finding a co-op board that would tolerate the comings and goings of at least one flamboyant, eternally optimistic pile of laundry, plus a pig who might someday weigh hundreds or thousands of pounds. How big did fairy piglets get? He might have to buy an entire floor.

Everything was becoming a lot, which is what being rich without limits became.

Until he could decide on an apartment or the building that contained it, Ludwig contemplated relegating Mr. Blueberry to some upstate farm that he could visit to sift through bowel movements in search of flawless stones. Except that after barely a year with that congenial swine riding shotgun, Ludwig had collected more fond memories than he had ever accumulated in offices or shared living arrangements. So when he checked into hotels, he asked whether he could bring his service dog, which was not a dog at all, but an oinking pet carrier covered by a tiny velvet curtain because, he told whoever was at the desk, "Mr. Blueberry, my dog, is *epilectic*."

Until they discovered a spacious, livestock-friendly building where they could hang up their fly-by-night lifestyles, this was their tradition. Whenever a hotel's housekeeping discovered the pig (plus all the pennies and, on one occasion, a palm's worth of fine rubies), Ludwig switched to a different Manhattan penthouse or presidential suite.

Through it all, An Exalted Northwind's assignment remained uninitiated. In winter, he reasoned that it was too cold to walk all day. In summer, he reasoned that it was too hot. In spring and fall, when temperatures oscillated twenty-five to thirty degrees in hours, he blamed his inertia on not knowing how many layers to wear. Was all that walking really worth the money? Magic was a fair reward for any kind of labor, but she had not offered magic.

A year went by without so much as checking in with An Exalted Northwind or Lonesome Johnny. Yet she made Ludwig rich in far less time than that, so by the metric of any person who had ever worked a real job like carrying two-hundred-pound rugs up narrow staircases, An Exalted Northwind was not just better than all the bosses he had known, but all the people. Ludwig didn't know where to find her enchantment's bugs, or "distortions in reality," so besides peeking down a few alleyways and watching the city through binoculars, he didn't look.

And so far, she didn't care.

Despite not needing it, he continued bringing the gargoyle's hollow heart to hotels and on mozzarella runs, knowing all too well that every manager's favorite time to call was when you least wanted them to.

For Lonesome Johnny's eternally optimistic companionship, on occasion, Ludwig thought to summon the bucket-bearer via a fish and the mug of gin that An Exalted Northwind prescribed. Lonesome Johnny was, like Mr. Blueberry, a great hang, and besides what the pig provided, Ludwig still wanted company. Yet Ludwig never created the lure for fear of destabilizing his unemployment equilibrium. To call on Johnny was to call on An Exalted Northwind, who might want to know about his assignment or to inform him of an upcoming or lapsed milestone. Perhaps she had found another solution to the fairies' problems and forgotten him. If she had, that left Ludwig with a problem. He still heard *muumbazza*.

People said the word only a little more frequently, but since he was helpless to stop whatever the reason was for hearing it, its appearances felt very frequent indeed.

Muumbazza made conversations challenging, particularly since walking Mr. Blueberry forced Ludwig into so many as they strolled past bars with outdoor seating, slithering lines of sneakerheads and tourists, cigarette-smoking nightclub congregations made of gorgeous people who worked in real estate and finance and used *insane* and *crazy* in place of all other adjectives and hyperbole, and launch parties for recklessly funded fashion start-ups that would only exist beyond the deepest depths of closets and thrift stores for another year or two.

The things that these start-ups sold were difficult to rationalize: hoodies tighter than straitjackets that made no one feel like a druid, whether they zipped up or pulled over; hundred-dollar T-shirts that hid nothing, not even flaccid nipples; and formfitting jeans that EMTs had to cut people out of during emergencies. Ludwig could appreciate a nice waist-to-ankle taper, but not at the expense of a comfortable sit. Why did people care so much about looking good, and was there a correlation between tightness and attractiveness? Could some compromise be made? He contemplated his comfortable maroon sweatpants. Surely, they could be the new thing with the right vision and some funding.

Especially with a nice taper.

THE GRACE BANK on Spring and Broadway belonged to two worlds.

Outside, it looked the way that commercial banking did to

bankers: Its Colonial-inspired redbrick exterior embodied tradition and security, while its soaring two-story bay windows promised transparency. Just below a portcullis that centered the building's facade like the face of a grandfather clock, two Doric columns supported a concrete lintel that SoHo shoppers took shelter beneath during sudden rain, exemplifying the bank's benevolence and good-neighbor status.

Inside, the bank looked the way it did to customers: like the secret source of all the world's misery. Interrogation room–colored fluorescent lamps unflatteringly shone on yellowing walls full of brochures featuring smiling, cynically selected multiethnic couples enthusiastically embarking on exciting next steps facilitated by the bank (painting a house, opening a bakery, giving child actors piggyback rides, symbolically driving over a bridge). It was unclear whether the bulletproof glass shielding tellers was meant to protect customers' deposits from bank robbers or customers. Bowls filled with complimentary lollipops bloomed everywhere, demeaning employees and customers alike.

As with most retail banks, employees wore their names and condescending titles on tags instead of on desktop placards because no desk belonged to any employee, a trick that customers weren't supposed to notice since it placed them under the illusion that employees were critical financial experts who merited real estate at the city's most abundant bank chain instead of part-time, glorified retail workers.

"I'd like to open an account for my LLC," Ludwig said to the fortysomething with drooping willow hair whose persistent, expansive smile seemed to Ludwig like it had been pinned in place by some stiff, rule book–wielding branch manager.

The "Relationship Partner," according to her name tag, motioned Ludwig over to a shabby fiberboard desk that seemed unlikely to become a magic door if, for some reason, he fell through it.

"Thank you for trusting Grace," she said; it was as much a formality as an admission. "I'm Ayonia. I'll be your Business Banking relationship partner today. Is your business a Delaware LLC, a New York LLC, or something else? I just need your muumbazza papers, your ID, and a first deposit. What is your company called? Muumbazza."

"My business is called, uh, Vermin Milk." Gradually, even he became uncertain about the name, though not enough to do all the paperwork required to go back on it. "It's a Delaware LLC." Ludwig handed her his driver's license and company formation papers, which he had folded more times than origami. "It's a fashion start-up," he said, then added "I'm in fashion," in case she didn't believe him.

Ludwig knew how much An Exalted Northwind's deed would let him say about his business and its funding without an incident, like the one three months earlier when he started to tell Hassan about the fairies beneath Times Square. He stopped when he noticed an ornately armored, saber-wielding scorpion the size of a moving van squeezed into Hassan's kitchen. The scorpion disappeared in a bristling gold mist when Ludwig changed subjects by asking about Gloria, whom, he was surprised to learn, Hassan had not yet traded in for a new model.

"What an unusual name for a fashion brand! I actually went to school for fashion," Ayonia replied. "I was so happy, even though I never made much muumbazza. I used to lose myself in sketchbooks for months and months. Now I work at a bank, but you know how it goes—gotta work!" Ludwig begged to differ but didn't because he saw her soul seeping through her tear ducts. "And how much would you like to deposit at this time? Muumbazza."

"Not everything," he joked. Ayonia produced an artificial laugh from her bank-approved repertoire of humanizing sounds. "Are there incentives for depositing more?"

She had no reason to expect that the unshaven, unkempt, six-foot, two-inch totem of blended cotton, drawstrings, and elastic would even meet the minimum deposit requirement, let alone greatly exceed it.

"That is a muumbazza question, Mr. Ludwig! If you deposit $2,000 or more, you qualify for Grace Total Business Banking, which comes with free checking, a Grace Total Business Banking debit card, and a monthly service fee of just $15. That can be waived if you maintain a minimum daily balance of $4,000. If you deposit $3,500 or more, you unlock Grace Total Business Plus Banking, which comes with free checking for up to three accounts, two Grace Total Business Banking Plus debit cards, and a monthly service fee of $50. That can be waived if you maintain a minimum daily balance of $7,000. However, if you deposit $5,000 or more, you unlock Grace Total Business Platinum Plus Elite Signature Banking, which comes with free checking for up to four accounts, three Grace Total Business Platinum Plus Elite Signature Banking debit cards, and a monthly service fee of only $75. Once again, that's waived if you maintain a minimum daily balance of $10,000. Muumbazza."

A young woman in line to speak with a teller resembled someone who Ludwig, despite all of the daring adventures he had survived in his imagination, could never summon the courage to engage in a conversation longer than it took him to mumble *yo* as he passed her in the hallway that Electric Guacamole shared with her employer. She had big eyes, big teeth, and unnaturally colored hair (mercury and lilac). Although this alternative version of her caught Ludwig's attention, she did not hold it.

Behind her, just outside the bank, three chanting, upright alligators in wizard robes walked in circles. Through the glass, he couldn't determine what they were chanting. No one seemed to notice them except Ludwig and the iridescent butterflies as big as open books that danced in their reptilian wake like cyclones of swirling leaves. By the time Ludwig had turned to ascertain whether Ayonia could see them, which she gave no indication of, and then turned back, they were gone.

Should he write that down? Is this what An Exalted Northwind meant by a distortion in reality? Were those the "bugs" she had spoken of, whose forms she, and therefore he, could not anticipate? She had said he would know the bugs when he saw them, that they would appear as distortions in reality, but right then, he didn't know shit. Their appearance was unusual, even for that neighborhood, or so he thought. But reporting it could disturb his enviable levels of ruby-fueled unemployment, so he didn't.

"I'm sorry. I thought I saw someone. Could you repeat all of that?"

Ayonia did.

"What do I get if I deposit $1,000,000 and maintain a minimum daily balance of about the same?" Ludwig asked. "When I upgraded my personal checking account a few months ago, they told me I was a Private Tungsten customer. Or Personal Cobalt patron?"

"Oh!" she exclaimed. "Sir, I am so sorry—I am *so* sorry. I did not realize that you were a Private Titanium client." She made a nervous, confused face at something on her screen.

"What are you sorry for?" he said. "What did you do?"

"I did not realize that you were a Private Titanium client."

"That's fine. Neither did I."

Ayonia searched the room for searing, punitive stares. Had her managers seen or overheard her offer a Grace Total Business Platinum Plus Elite Signature Banking account to a customer whose titanium debit card could stop a small-caliber bullet? Had they heard her mention minimum balances or—far, far worse—*complain* about working at a bank to someone whose business was worth far more to her employer than her employment? Private Titanium clients switched banks over less. Private Titanium clients asked to speak to managers over less. Oh no, had she really implied that retail banking was just a job and not her passion? Ludwig read every unspoken anxiety.

Ludwig the Telepath.

"Lady, look, I am wearing the same clothes I wore yesterday. I have a toothpaste stain going straight down my shirt. I haven't gotten a haircut in months. I have a honey-mustard packet in my pocket, even though I can't remember the last time I ate anything with honey mustard." Ludwig dropped the packet on her time-share desk as if that would settle her anxiety.

"We get in trouble for nothing here," she whispered, assured by his assurances, though still visibly distressed. "I'm a model employee and I've already got two strikes." She returned to speaking at the employee handbook–approved level. "So, considering your considerable personal wealth, I recommend the Grace Diamond Monarch Business account, our most exclusive business account. Can I interest you in something like that? Muumbazza."

"You can."

"And is there anything else I can help you with today?"

"Do you know if there's an art supply store around here? Sketchbooks and shit?"

An apartment downtown used to be something that Ludwig wanted—suddenly he required it. To conquer fashion, he needed to live where fashion happened.

He tallied the pros and cons of neighborhoods where a fashion empire might be founded: SoHo (noisy, expensive, populated by tourists and established fashion brands, unclear where to get lunch); the Lower East Side (noisy, gentrifying, still a little dangerous, lots of foot traffic, Goldilocks supply of lunch options); NoLIta (noisy, difficult to picture, skewed older than the Lower East Side, somewhere you walked on your way to other places); TriBeCa (noisy, out of the way, celebrity and media-executive retirement community, too many private drivers waiting in front of buildings with hazard lights on); Alphabet City (noisy, the East Village's remora, not dirty in a fun or fashionable way, too far to one side of Manhattan); NoHo (noisy, more parking garages than expected); the East Village (noisy, everything going for it except a reputation for fashion); the West Village (noisy, older, whiter, and less edgy than the East Village); the Garment District (noisy, less fashionable than it sounded); the Meatpacking District (noisy, more fashionable than it sounded but just as lifeless, which is how Ludwig saw the industry he aimed to conquer); and other neighborhoods that had been considered "bad" and were all "good" once immigrants had been priced out.

Rather than spend another year living out of hotels and developing internal SWOT charts of neighborhoods, Ludwig caved and contacted a broker, a group of professionals whose number had been ceaselessly growing within his circle of relationships.

"I'M LOOKING FOR a not-too-fancy penthouse, maybe on the Lower East Side. And by *not too fancy*, I mean nothing too modern. And by *nothing too modern*, I mean no apartments where everything is at a right angle from everything else, and all the fixtures are black, white, or gray. I appreciate minimalism and even advocate for it, especially in leisurewear, but not in architecture. It's not very comfortable, you know? So I'm looking for something with the vibes of an old theater, dusty library, cellar speakeasy, or Florentine astronomer's tower. Do you know what I mean?"

The broker's assistant said nothing. She was average-looking, yet not in an unkind way, but in a way that makes a person impossible to describe or remember ever having seen. She was more like fog than a receptionist.

Ludwig took a seat, noticed all the home-decorating magazines fanned across the table, and stuffed them into his backpack beside the gargoyle's hollow, stone heart. A few minutes later, the receptionist's opposite, the kind of person someone would never forget meeting, hovered over him.

"Hello! Welcome to Branagh & Bloom." Boy, what a smile. It was more like a bleached seawall than a collection of teeth. It outshone even his fox-colored mustache and anvil cloud of similarly colored hair. "I'm Kenneth Branagh. No relation."

"No relation to who?" Ludwig asked.

"Kenneth Branagh."

"Who's that?"

"Never mind. If you'd like, you can also call me Kenneth 'New York Pinnacle of Prestige Boutique Realtor of the Year' Branagh."

"I think Kenneth Branagh is fine," Ludwig said.

"It hasn't failed me yet. Anyway, welcome to our little full-service agency. Perhaps you'd like to join me in our conference room?"

He moved so quickly and with so much energy that Ludwig expected to find a power cord plugged in between his shoulders. Few who worked in real estate did so out of passion, Ludwig believed, assuming instead that it was a field for people with few options who hadn't found their passion. But there he was, the prancing, happy exception to that rule. "I hear you're searching for a Lower East Side penthouse, Mr. Ludwig?"

How did he know that? Not only had he not given anyone

his name, but the receptionist had moved less than the plastic orchid that was sitting beside her.

"At this moment, there are only two for sale. One is $5,200,000, and the other is $11,600,000." By immediately throwing out the price tags of premium listings, Realtors usually sought to filter out those without the means to buy them but with the time to waste the broker's. To an inexperienced agent, someone dressed like Ludwig should never have made it past reception, but experienced brokers knew that people with extravagant means cared little about showing up to an auction house, opera, or Michelin-starred restaurant in a stained hoodie and avuncular sweatpants. They knew how much they were worth, and their money showed by not caring whether you did too.

"The $5,200,000 listing is toward the northern border of the Lower East Side, just a block and a half from Houston Street. The $11,600,000 listing is on the intersection of NoLIta, Chinatown, and the Lower East Side. What do you do, Mr. Ludwig? Oh, and, um, muumbazza." He said the word almost as if he knew Ludwig expected him to, like he'd been counting down the seconds until it was required.

"I'm in fashion. Also, auctions and shit," Ludwig said.

"I used to work in fashion, as well as *auctions and shit,*" Kenneth Branagh said. His smile grew until his cheeks touched his eyes. "Let's start with what I would call the jewel-box listing: It's smaller in size, but every inch of it shines. It has four bedrooms, three and a half baths, central heat and AC, a 270-degree view of the city, and a rooftop hot tub for those cold winter days and wild summer nights. And, of course, it's all renovated with exposed brick walls, cherrywood beams, and reclaimed java-wood floors. It sits on Ludlow Street between Rivington and Stanton. You'll forever be halfway to everywhere worth going, *Ludwig of Ludlow.* That has a ring to it, doesn't it? You can call yourself LOL, L-O-L."

It *did* have a ring to it.

"Would anything stop me from putting a little grassy pasture and a big, climate-controlled doghouse up there?" Ludwig asked.

"I can't imagine what would."

No matter how many pennies he fed Mr. Blueberry or how hard he shook him, it would be many full moons before they could afford the $11,600,000 apartment. Furthermore, already grappling with loneliness, he couldn't justify the far more expensive apartment's easily imaginable plethora of additional bedrooms.

"How many floors up is the Lower East Side apartment?" Ludwig asked.

"Technically, the penthouse covers two floors. It commands the building's entire fifth floor and continues to your roof, where there is a gazebo, a foyer, a micro kitchen, the fourth bedroom, and so many memories yet to be made. Think of your penthouse as one and a half stories. It's also a true walk-up, made years before elevators. You know, I used to install elevators for a—"

"But not an actual walk-up?"

"No. You have a private elevator."

"I'll take it."

"Just like that?"

"Sure."

"Don't you want to see it?" Kenneth Branagh asked, then added "muumbazza muumbazza muumbazza," as though he were catching up for all the times he had forgotten to say it.

"I strongly feel that the listing speaks for itself."

"Indeed, it does."

"I need to move some money around. Can I make a down payment to hold the apartment for, say, four or five weeks?"

"You don't want a mortgage?"

"I'd rather not involve a bank."

"I understand. I used to work for a bank. Do you have that kind of cash on hand?"

"That depends."

"On what?"

"On whether you know when the next full moon is."

7

There are four types of guys: smart smart guys, dumb dumb guys, dumb smart guys, and smart dumb guys.

Smart smart guys are the rarest of guys, unlike dumb dumb guys, who outnumber the stars. Everyone thinks they are a smart smart guy, and yet, almost everyone is a dumb dumb guy.

That brings us to the worst guys: the dumb smart guys. These are your starchy know-it-alls, politicians, Beltway journalists, Ivy League graduates, social media philosophers, op-ed writers, investment bankers, art critics, CEOs, self-proclaimed entrepreneurs, guys named Hugh, and people who regularly say stuff in Latin. No one likes dumb smart guys, yet they're always finding their way into positions of influence, usually with the unequivocal support of the dumb dumb guys they exploit. Dumb smart guys are the guys most likely to be seen as smart smart guys, despite being the most like dumb dumb guys.

Finally, there is the smart dumb guy. The

> smart dumb guy is knowledgeable but not so knowledgeable that it makes them condescending or superior. They are intensely aware of the limits of their intelligence, which the dumb smart guy never is. Above all else, even when they aren't knowledgeable, the smart dumb guy is consistently wise, which any smart smart guy will tell you is what makes a guy smart.
>
> —Mickey Napkins

One month and several piles of Byzantine paperwork later, Ludwig paid a cab driver $2,000 to wait outside while he packed the few things that he couldn't just as well relocate to the curb: favorite clothes, gallon ziplock half full of pennies, classic video games, restaurant-grade frozen margarita machine, rat-induced trauma, middling-but-canonical pile of mass-market fantasy paperbacks stuffed into bursting Key Food bags. He left the cattle prods and the door in the floor to separate work from life.

The thought of contacting the dozen or more retailers featured in each of the magazines stolen from Branagh & Bloom felt more like work than anything he had contemplated since his rug-store days, so he furnished his new apartment with similar-looking items from the only furniture company whose name came to mind, thanks to a mid-'90s television jingle. The aesthetic he achieved fell somewhere between a Tuscan villa, a Georgian town house, and a gamer cave.

No rats, bodiless or otherwise, were discovered.

The frozen margarita machine hummed as Ludwig clipped Mr. Blueberry's harness to a leash and called the elevator. On the street, and even from six stories above it, the neighborhood was noisy, which, like everything lately, worked to his benefit. Things were again looking up until he looked down and saw that day's *Post*.

On that May evening, it wasn't the *Post*'s 72-point headline ("What the Truck? Intoxicated Driver Plows Through Zabar's Window") or 36-point headline ("Fight My Wife, Please: Moody Mistress Upsets Billionaire's Nuptials") that seized Ludwig's notice, but the 18-point headline crammed beneath both:

Plague of Rat Heads Plagues Union Square Station

The Union Square station was where the L train rumbled along subway tracks one block from Ludwig's basement apartment. Could their proximity be a coincidence? Was whatever had happened there endemic with Manhattan's greater rodent community?

He unfolded the energy drink–stained, radioactive yellow newspaper.

> If they're dead, is it still an infestation?
>
> That's the question NYC Transit and NYC animal control authorities are asking in response to a sudden and shocking wave of rodent cannibalism. Dozens of rat heads—from the snout to just above the shoulder—have been piling up on and off the L train platform at the 14th Street–Union Square station.
>
> "Never seen anything like it. I've worked for the city more than twenty years," L train conductor Leon Suzuki said. "They're everywhere. This morning I found one in

the conductor's cabin. No blood or nothing. Just a head. I've got friends who operate the N, the A, the 6—they haven't seen a mouse. Must be something in the air down here, you know?"

Police and transit authorities ask commuters who see anything unusual to notify NYC animal control.

As reported last week by the *Post* in an as yet unrelated story, a growing number of violent, push-and-shove incidents between commuters have also been reported on the L train, more than on all other lines connected to Union Square's station last year.

No explanation for either phenomenon has been discovered.

An Exalted Northwind never did explain the rats, and Ludwig knew that was intentional.

Having made so many excuses to bosses, Ludwig knew that her rationalization was more excuse than explanation and more outright dodge than either of those. Were there more giant rats, ones that ate big rats, that ate intermediate rats, that ate bite-sized rats, like cannibal nesting dolls? Had these rats been hiding like the rat that had ambushed him in his basement? And if so, what were they hiding from? Had the events in the subway happened because of something he did or didn't do? All he knew for sure was that it 1) had something to do with him and 2) might lead to further encounters with not only more giant rats but whatever was eating them. He could wait and face the cause or act immediately and face An Exalted Northwind—a classic devil-you-know-versus-the-devil-you-don't scenario.

Shit.

Questions multiplied. To answer them, he purchased Pennsylvania gin (she never said what kind to buy) and a tin of boneless sardines in olive oil.

THE CHRISTENING BY magic of Ludwig's sixth-floor micro kitchen began. He combined the ingredients to summon Lonesome Johnny, left the mixture on his windowsill, then tested his penthouse's acoustics by loudly looping "New York, New York" within the confines of his walls and floors that were bomb-shelter thick. How long would it take Lonesome Johnny to find him, and could he reach the penthouse once he had? Did Lonesome Johnny, a headless fixer working for a fairy matriarch, ring doorbells and ride elevators? Did An Exalted Northwind teleport him like she once had Ludwig?

Around the forty-second loop of "New York, New York," the city's anthem began sounding even to Ludwig like some existential torment or urban banshee's wounded wailing.

A gloved hand knocked upon the sliding glass door separating the roof from his penthouse.

"Permission to enter!" Ludwig called.

"Right-oh-ho, Joe! I am ever so glad to see you, Mr. Ludwig!" Lonesome Johnny entered and slid the door behind him from latch to jamb. "I suppose you couldn't hear me knocking over that old songbird's raucous crooning! Nevertheless, how can I, a humble wardrobe spiced with the souls of the lost, be of service today?"

Lonesome Johnny's usually crisp and proudly kept uniform was soaked with something wet and brown that clung to him in globs like French onion soup and stank like old eggs. Tears and rips revealed bits of frayed straw and black feathers. Even the bucket that concealed his missing head bore fresh dents. Were those climbing spikes?

"You look like shit, no offense," Ludwig said.

"Offense from you? Impossible! Can I inquire, however, about the provenance of the fish and gin you placed in yonder mug? I'm afraid that when the ingredients used to summon me are low fidelity, the signal they send becomes difficult to notice and follow. I have had quite a start to the evening! And yet, to see you again, my good buddy and colleague, I would do it all over in a heartbeat, despite lacking one."

"I used tinned sardines. I don't know about the gin. I think it's from Pennsylvania."

"That explains it, then. The Anabaptists have never had a reputation for distilling the devil's medicine. May I suggest you use a nice rainbow trout, some fresh mackerel, or lovely sea bass next time? And some hearty English or Scottish gin, of course!" Mr. Blueberry happily oinked as he nuzzled Lonesome Johnny's boneless shins. "Oh, piglet! You've grown! How've you been?"

"I named him Mr. Blueberry."

"Yet another addition to your expansive portfolio of talents. Mr. Ludwig and Mr. Blueberry, what a pair. And this flat! Ludwig of Ludlow Street is so serendipitous! Now, why have I the good fortune to be called upon this evening?"

"I want a one on one with An Exalted Northwind."

"That's perfect, Mr. Ludwig! She wants one with you too!"

LUDWIG NO LONGER wanted the one on one.

When employees wanted one on ones, it was to make demands, seek answers to questions that bosses didn't want to be asked, cement a career path, and other things that benefited workers.

When bosses wanted one on ones, it was to patronize, test out platitudes, suggest work-intensive remedies to problems they caused, and tell employees things they only ever disclosed to other bosses, such as the truth. And although Ludwig had accomplished much lately, none of it benefited An Exalted Northwind. He thought of the girl who had been reduced to glue, the morbid puzzles that the fairies assembled piece by hellish piece, and the medley of tortures that Galilea Dazzledark sought permission to inflict on him. Perhaps he should have been doing his job.

He extracted the hollow heart from his backpack and swallowed a revolting mouthful.

"Why do you require Dr. Tot's Miraculous Sanity Serum, Mr. Ludwig?" Lonesome Johnny asked. "The one on one's purpose is to review your performance, which, despite the self-evident fact that I have not heard from you in over a year, has no doubt exceeded even my skyscraping expectations! This is a cause for celebration! I would not be surprised if you were given some sort of trophy or commemorative battle-ax."

A performance review already? This could jeopardize his unlimited income, apartment, and even the future of fashion.

He took another swig.

If An Exalted Northwind's exhortation about the fairies' sensitivity to noise was credible, which all circumstantial evidence suggested it was, she could not easily break through New York's cacophonous force field to make Ludwig attend the review. However, she also knew magic and was very tall, which led him to imagine an engorged version of her reaching up through the Lower East Side and dragging him out of his penthouse. But if she couldn't do that, she could only demand meetings and be furious with him. So what? That was every boss, he told himself with the serum's support.

"I guess I can swing by sometime soon," Ludwig suggested without actually committing to a visit.

"Excellent, Mr. Ludwig! I will give my lady-lord and benefactor the wonderful news and prepare a peanut butter and jelly spread just for you. How does two days from now sound? Upon passing through your ramshackle, possessed basement, please give Desolate Phil my regards!"

Ludwig handed Lonesome Johnny $2,000.

"Oh, Mr. Ludwig! That is very kind, except I have no use for it. Our currencies are mostly hen's teeth, fish feathers, monkey horns—fairy-tale stuff. Now, would you mind if I used your elevator?"

Two days later, Ludwig skipped the meeting.

LUDWIG DREW SWEATPANTS like generals draw battle plans—with great intent but little style. The process of turning ideas he saw in his head into something that shoppers saw in stores was haute calculus.

The fashion world was unusually merit based; he couldn't undercut his way to success like he had selling gemstones.

He could draw clothes, just not well enough for his designs to avoid the ugly fate of brands that automatically ended up on discounted department store shelves. That route may have been more profitable, but profitability didn't interest him. The goal was to make a statement, not another zero.

The truth was that he lacked experience, and to close the gap between what he did and didn't know, he needed other people's experience. It would cost him, but at least he'd have company, which was, besides pay, the only benefit of having a job.

But people weren't something he could buy—at least not outright. So first, they had to be convinced that changing how New Yorkers dressed was more deserving of their time and expertise than doing whatever else, wherever else. Money could do that. So could a mission. He could provide both.

At Vermin Milk, these hypothetical people would be part

of reimagining everyday fashion as something presentable but comfortable, work appropriate while gym appropriate, inexpensive, though never cheap, and bougie yet grassroots revolutionary. They would make a more comfortable New York.

His movement needed a name, and unlike the weeks it took him, Naveena, and Igor to agree on Vermin Milk, a thing that he still believed had happened, he didn't have to search for it.

He called it athleisure.

KIPPER'S SEVEN-PAGE MENU was compounded with items that drew their namesakes from the brand, such as the Kip Burger, the Classic Kipper, the Kipper Special, the Double Quarter Kipper, the Fried Country Chicken Kipper, and the Kippers and Cream Shake. Everything came with a signature sauce, and no side was served without a dunk in the deep fryer, including the coleslaw.

Like many Midtown eateries, Ludwig felt it belonged somewhere off a midwestern interstate, not nestled between *Times*-profiled restaurants. It called home a congested, gaudily lit corner one block away from ColosSys, the company that had stolen Naveena and Igor from Vermin Milk. Naveena wouldn't ordinarily eat like this—it conflicted with her brand—but she went where Igor went and vice versa.

"Sweatpants?" Naveena laughed.

"Not just sweatpants," Ludwig countered. "V1 is sweatpants and hoodies. I see us expanding. Say what you will about sweatpants as an instrument for revolution, but I have this thesis that aesthetically centered social conventions are due for a reckoning. There's a fortune to be made in high-end athletic leisurewear, especially in New York. Think about it. In New York, it's too hot when it's hot and too cold when it's cold. Apartments are microscopic, claustrophobic, or glorified closets, and the subways are always crowded. People should be comfortable, and not just once they get home or when they're going to bed but everywhere and all the time. The same goes for what's in your pockets. Soon, we won't have to carry wallets, cash, or keys. Instead, our phones will do everything those things do, and we'll have just one designated phone pocket and no others."

Igor nodded approvingly. It got better every time Ludwig said it.

"This won't work for girls. Muumbazza," Naveena said.

"It will work in the world I'm envisioning," Ludwig said.

"So you're envisioning now?"

"Laugh all you want. Women's clothes need even more reimagining than men's. Girls wear either the most comfortable shit you've ever seen or the most uncomfortable shit you can possibly imagine. There's no middle ground. What is the first thing that girls do when they get home?"

"Change," Naveena said.

"Into what?"

"Into something more muumbazza."

"*Exactly.* Sweats or pajamas. Vermin Milk asks, What if your going-out and staying-home clothes were one and the same?"

"You're really sticking with that name? Muumbazza. I might do this to see how you fuck it up. Where did you even find funding?"

"Let me ask you a question," Ludwig said, stepping around hers. "Are you happy at ColosSys?"

"No one is. They sold us on being able to work on anything we muumbazza, then canned our project after a month. Now they've got us muumbazza a content tracker for refrigerators. Apparently, seeing inside your refrigerator from your phone is the future."

The door blasted open, and a bald, bearded, middle-aged man with pale pink cheeks like pork chops barreled into the room. His pin-striped suit and oval frame gave him the appearance of a zeppelin.

"I can't believe I had to come all the way down here. I want to speak to the manager!"

"I'm the muumbazza, sir," a twenty-something ginger bravely confessed.

"Then you'd better listen up! Muumbazza is no reason why I should have to wait an hour for delivery. Explain to me how it takes an hour to get my cheat-day treats from Thirtieth Street to Thirty-Second Street."

"Yes, sir. When we are busy, we don't always have enough delivery people to—"

"Him! Him! He's the one who took so long. Muumbazza! This one! This one right here!" The middle-aged balloon put his finger in the face of a forty-something-year-old, bicycle-riding delivery person from somewhere else. "You! Do you know how much money I muumbazza given to this restaurant? Enough not to have to reheat chicken in the microwave! I'm the reason you have a job!"

"You are right, sir," the ginger insincerely admitted, seizing the opportunity to make her fault the fault of someone further down the ladder. "There's no reason why a muumbazza as important as yourself should have to wait an hour for delivery. This will never happen again, will it?" the manager inquired of the orange-vested courier, who shook his head from side to side, visibly disappointed with something but not himself.

"I hope you learned your lesson."

He floated away.

"You know, I accept that we all have bad days," Ludwig said. "I'll be right back. I'm going to have a quick word with that guy."

"A word?" Naveena asked.

"Yeah. A word."

"What kind of word?"

"A confession."

Ludwig followed the inflated man until they were far enough from Kipper's sidewalk-illuminating sign that he wouldn't be incriminated for what happened next.

"Excuse me, sir," Ludwig said.

"I don't have any money. Get away from me, you filth. I said get away."

"No, no," Ludwig said, "I'm not asking for your money; I'm asking if you want to know how I made mine. You see, I have this enchanted pig . . ."

LUDWIG HIRED NAVEENA and Igor, then stood outside until the abused employee returned from delivering a pyramid of takeout orders that he somehow balanced for miles on a rusty mountain bike.

Ludwig put $2,000 in the courier's hand and asked if he wanted a different job. He said his name was Uchu, and he had been a photographer for a major newspaper in Belize. Serendipity.

An Exalted Northwind would be proud if Ludwig ever saw her again.

LUDWIG HELD HIS nose and returned to the bank.

"Hi, Ayonia. Any chance you remember me?"

"Of course, sir, you're Ludwig. I never muumbazza a Private Titanium client," she said, hoping that one of her always-increasing number of managers (Paul, Paul, Balaji, Kate) was within earshot.

"You mentioned that you went to school for fashion design."

"That's correct, though not just to school. I worked at a minor fashion house before my twins were muumbazza. That was before I fell in love with banking."

"So you're happy in banking?"

"Of course!" she chirped, scanning the room.

"What if you received an offer to make more money working in fashion? What if that offer was on the table right now? Would you take it?"

BRANAGH & BLOOM'S waiting room hadn't changed since Ludwig last visited, except for new magazines that Ludwig immediately pilfered. The receptionist was out (had there been a receptionist?), and Kenneth Branagh's office door was open.

"Back again, Mr. Ludwig?" He asked five steps before Ludwig entered his office.

"Do you remember when I asked about commercial real estate?"

"*Do you remember* when I told *you* Branagh & Bloom is a *full-service* agency?"

FINALLY, WITH A frozen margarita in hand, Ludwig called Hassan.

"Why are you calling? Just come upstairs."

"I haven't lived there in like a year."

"Then why are you still paying rent?"

"It's my storage room."

"Your storage room?"

"Yeah. My storage room."

"Your storage room for what?"

"Uh, some shit? I dunno."

"Where are you living now?"

"Somewhere I can sleep without hearing you thrusting."

WHAT VERMIN MILK still needed was someone who could tie it all together, who could go to meetings and manage operations, who knew people in the arts, who had experience launching successful businesses, who could challenge him whenever they detected a slide toward mediocrity, and whom he could challenge if he detected a slide toward corporatism.

He needed someone people listened to, even if he never would, so that he could apply his time to imagining instead of managing. Ludwig didn't want to be anyone's boss, but he wouldn't need to if such a proxy could be found.

Hassan was a leader, it was true, and it was inadvertently thanks to him insisting that his building's basement studio was "pretty fucking great, man" that Ludwig had an amount of money he might never be able to explain. Still, he didn't want to place that much responsibility on a friend (was that what they were, friends?), knowing how those arrangements usually ended.

That night, Ludwig shook Mr. Blueberry until he dropped nearly $400,000 in front of a boutique burrito chain half a block from their apartment, and Ludwig scanned sidewalks and outdoor seating for abandoned copies of the day's *Post*. There was always one around, and he quickly found it.

It didn't mention rats, though it mentioned something else of interest:

BLOWHARD IN THE WIND

Columnist and Movie Critic Hospitalized

After "Tornado of Burning Hair" Carries Him from Kippers to Madison Square Park

"We haven't seen a hairnado since the '70s," a police captain remarked.

"Excuse me, are you Ludwig?"

Even though she was clacking along on towering pumps and loudly slurped an after-work Frappuccino, Ludwig didn't hear her coming or see her until she was close enough to dump it on him.

"What?" Ludwig asked, stepping behind Mr. Blueberry.

"Are you Ludwig?"

"Who are you?"

"My name is Lulu Vaillancourt. I'm looking for a Ludwig. I was told that a Ludwig lives in this building and owns a pig, which I presume makes you him."

She was alone, which made her unlikely to slap cuffs on him, something he still didn't know if he should be concerned about since he hadn't committed any crimes except for failing to declare his gemstones. But at what border could he declare them? And to what world?

"Are you with Homeland Security?" he asked.

"Why would you think I'm with Homeland Security? Are you worried about Homeland Security?"

"I don't know who you are. You could be anybody."

"No, I'm somebody. I used to work in auctions, primarily gemstones." Ludwig made a stupid face—uh-oh. "Yeah, that's right. And I'm sure that your concern about Homeland Security has nothing to do with the fact that you're a smuggler. Muumbazza. I bet Homeland Security would like to know about your blood-gem operation. Where are you getting them from? Southeast Asia? Africa? Do you even know how muumbazza people died in mines for them?"

"Way to care about that now, lady," Ludwig said. "So it's fine if an auction house sells blood gems as heirlooms or historical pieces. But if a guy in a reversible Champs hoodie opens shop in the back of a pizza place—actually, I'm done. I have nothing to say to you. Go away," he said, tapping his key fob against his building's front door to make a quick escape.

"*Go away?* Fuck you."

"Fuck me? How about you go fuck yourself, she-devil." Ludwig made a cross with his fingers and held it at arm's length, an act that might have made her recoil if the magic she pretended to have had was real.

"Go fuck myself? Where do you get off telling me to go fuck myself, you muumbazza? You look like the superintendent of an apartment building by the airport." Admittedly, he didn't look like how she imagined a multimillionaire smuggler capable of destroying an entire asset class would look. Her private investigator had described him as big but harmless looking, like a manatee or winded Saint Bernard. This was no hardened criminal. She felt pretty sure about her ability to twist him into submission behind a Key Food.

As she scrutinized him for further proof of his crimes, Ludwig scrutinized her for something to lash out at, something about which she could be insecure or vulnerable. Yet nothing about the scowling, bejeweled, dark-haired vulgarian with the prospector-mustache eyebrows indicated insecurity or vulnerability.

"Yeah? Well, you look like Martin Scorsese in a onesie," Ludwig said.

She pitched what remained of her Frappuccino at him. It bounced off his Supima-cotton hoodie and split open over a terrified Mr. Blueberry.

"I—I am so sorry!" she pleaded.

"He's barely a year old! You attack people's animals? Is that who *you* are?"

Lulu dropped to her knees and dried Mr. Blueberry with an unending supply of café napkins that she pulled from her purse like a magician. There was nothing she could do about the sticky residue the Frappuccino left behind, which only mattered to her until she noticed Ludwig's undulating backpack.

"What the fuck is in there? What, you smuggle animals too? Is he smuggled?" She pointed at Mr. Blueberry, who changed places with Ludwig by sheltering between his legs.

"Oh, now you join PETA!" Ludwig said.

"Answer me this one question: Are you smuggling or counterfeiting rubies? Did you figure out how to inject chromium into some kind of manufactured stones? Muumbazza? Are you some start-up douchebag who doesn't want people to know what he discovered? That's it, isn't it?"

"That's, like, six questions."

"Answer them!" The interrogation wasn't going as she planned.

"I signed an NDA!" Ludwig said.

"We all sign NDAs! My business is broken because of you. My reputation. I worked my way up from serving coffee at an interstate rest stop in Maryland to working at the world's most prestigious auction houses."

"Look, you should just go. You don't want to get involved in this," he cautioned.

"In 'this'? What is '*this*'? Are you warning me? No, threatening me? Oh, I'm so fucking right. You're counterfeiting. That's why you're afraid of the government."

She pushed him off his feet and into his building's front door.

"OK, fuck it. I warned you." A careful application of the deed's privacy-protecting enchantment had defeated one opponent without mortal injury. Why not a second? "The rubies come from an enchantment placed on this pig"—the dome of the world turned intestinal pink—"that makes him shit flawless rubies on the full moon"—a bolt of polka-dotted lightning (parakeet green, candy-apple red) cleaved the engine block from a two-door sedan across the street, while a second polka-dotted bolt (terra-cotta orange, sunflower yellow) popped the lid off a fire hydrant beside them, knocking Lulu out of her pumps and onto the sidewalk. Mr. Blueberry paid no attention; perhaps magic was only miraculous to the nonmagical.

"Whoa, whoa! That's enough! That's enough!" Ludwig said, pleading with the sky. "I'm sorry! It's never sent lightning before," he said, causing a third bolt (blueberry blue, neon violet) to incinerate her painful-looking footwear. Like the carvings that covered Broken Throat's front door, punitive decisions made by the enchantment that governed his deed appeared random by design.

Lulu scurried to her feet and ran.

"At least a cloud of bearded hornets dressed like movie pirates didn't carry you back to Maryland!" Ludwig apologetically shouted.

She'll do, he thought. If she would, after that.

8

It is easier to hate New Yorkers than New York.

—Renowned Carp Flautist

IT WAS A windy, cloudless day in May, and Ludlow Street smelled like whatever was piled into the black trash bags that lined it like headstones. That stink was a reminder. Summer in New York was a calendar page away, and though it would be beautiful, the smell of death would drift like lost souls across the boroughs.

Kenneth Branagh had offered to show Ludwig available office spaces, and he met Ludwig in front of his building in a white, top-down, restored Ford Bronco.

"You ever roll in one of these honky-tonk cherry poppers, Mr. Ludwig?"

"A car?"

"If this is just a car, then your penthouse is just an apartment. Zoom-zoom!"

"Where are we going?"

"You'll see soon enough! I hope you like Toni Braxton!"

Ludlow Street carried them south until they hooked right onto Rivington and charged through a stop sign, honking pedestrians from their path as they passed a bodega, a liquor store, a nail salon, a pizza place, another liquor store, a dry cleaners, and another bodega before blowing through a questionable yellow and swinging right onto Allen Street.

"Can we try to keep it under Thirty-Fourth Street? I'm willing to keep an open mind, but, you know?" Ludwig pleaded. It was farther north than he usually went, except for doctor's appointments. Still, he wanted to give neighborhoods that were foreign to him an unbiased look because he needed to nurture his growing, imagined reputation as a New York oracle.

"Mr. Ludwig, I know my clients! I'm taking you to 345 Park Avenue in Midtown South. It's not the most fashion-forward neighborhood, but it has terrific spaces available at better-than-average prices because of a push by developers to fill buildings that the dregs of my profession failed to fill. Where does your business stand as far as start-up, boutique, mid-sized, and so on?" Ludwig suspected that Kenneth Branagh knew the answer, but he entertained the question, nonetheless.

"This is all just an idea right now. So I have to start small and own the start-up designation. Though some form of enterprise is always the goal, isn't it?"

"For most. Muumbazza muumbazza muumbazza. However, I've found that the boutique-agency lifestyle allows me the freedom and flexibility to focus on doing the kind of business I was born so long ago to do." He couldn't have been born that long ago; he didn't look a day past his forties. "I know you said you're in fashion, Mr. Ludwig. To what end?"

"Well"—Ludwig wound up—"I'm not trying to take over the runways or dominate fashion week. If I'm successful, those might not exist much longer. My thesis is that aesthetically centered social conventions are due for a reckoning. Comfort is my aim, and not just once you get home or go to bed, but everywhere and all the time. I want to end the tyranny of suits and ties, jeans and wingtips, heels and belts. There's a fortune to be made in high-end athletic leisurewear. Think about it. In New York, it's too hot when it's hot and too cold when it's cold. Apartments are microscopic, claustrophobic, or glorified closets, and the subways are always crowded. I'm talking elastic. I'm talking drawstrings. I'm talking cotton, Supima cotton, Tencel, jersey knit, French terry, and maybe even fleece. Spandex? It's possible! I can see poncho-style cloaks in my company's future and many hoods in all sizes, especially the big ones. I want to leave New York a more comfortable place than I found it."

"My God, Mr. Ludwig. You have a believer in me." Kenneth Branagh undid his tie, yanked it from around his throat, and threw it out of the car as if it were a poisonous snake. Then he fished inside his worn leather jacket until he produced a napkin filled with candy-colored pills.

"Do you like Molly?"

Ludwig didn't know. "The drug?"

"I prefer to think of them as epiphanies in pill form—or powder form if that's how you party." Kenneth Branagh jostled the pills.

"Is that Molly?"

"I keep telling you Branagh & Bloom is a full-service agency! We cater to *all* our clients' needs. That's why we were named the New York Pinnacle of Prestige Boutique Realtor of the Year by the New York State Association of Realtors three years running! I've got the keys to this town." He jingle-jangled a crowded keychain.

Ludwig knew that with Dr. Tot's serum in his possession, he was immune to the uniquely joyless hangover that Molly allegedly produced, a good thing that was also bad since consequence-free drug and alcohol use might be more curse than gift to someone constantly searching for new ways to relax. But it seemed rude to turn down Kenneth Branagh, who had cleared all sorts of important people from his calendar to take Ludwig office hunting.

Ludwig swallowed one of the sea foam–colored tablets that had been stamped with—what else?—a fairy.

"These are specially made to be highly water soluble, so they hit fast. No thirty-minute, bullshit waiting periods for my clients," Kenneth Branagh said.

"Speaking of water, do you have any I can wash this down with?"

"There's a six-pack of brewskis in nondescript cans in a cooler behind your seat. I get them from a guy. They're the finest Belgian lager, but look like Diet Coke, so you don't have to look over your shoulder just for enjoying a road soda. Cops in this town don't mess with me, though. My name rings out."

They obeyed the red at Stanton and Allen. A deli to their right was called Gourmet Deli, as were many others. The light turned green, and they burned rubber past Sixty LES, the hotel with a colossal Andy Warhol portrait looking up people's swim trunks from the bottom of its pool.

"I used to work at that hotel," Kenneth Branagh said. Where hadn't he worked? How could one man have held so many positions at so many places? Perhaps he *was* older than he looked.

Allen Street transformed into First Avenue as it crossed Houston Street. They passed an old bar (One and One) and some new bars and a very old locksmith (Speedy Lock & Door), and someplace Ludwig knew and liked but couldn't remember anything about because a bus blocked it from sight, so at that moment it both did and didn't exist, like Schrödinger's Hookah Bar or Organic Grocery, eventually placing them beside nondescript twenty-story apartment buildings that spiritually and aesthetically clashed with everything.

"What did you name your penthouse?" Kenneth Branagh asked. "A home that magnificent needs a name."

"Zeal." The name had only just occurred to Ludwig.

"Is that biblical?"

"No."

"Science fiction?"

"Kind of."

"Fantasy?"

"Both. It's from a video game. It's a floating city in the clouds that aristocratic magic users escaped to during their planet's ice age to study magic and rule over non–magic users trapped in the frozen world below."

"Talk about real estate! Do you believe in magic, Mr. Ludwig?"

"No," he lied. "Still, I'd give up all my success to learn some."

"If only I weren't but a humble real estate agent! Even for my little full-service agency, helping clients learn the mystic arts might be out of scope. Who knows? Perhaps I'm wrong. Consider my ear to the ground."

Did he mean it? Since Kenneth Branagh's relentless smile was painted over every intent and emotion, Ludwig couldn't tell. Perhaps he was reading too far into it. If there's one thing real estate agents weren't, it was magical.

Then it was goodbye to Sixth and Seventh Streets and hello to St. Marks Place, the three-block, Asian food and punk rock thoroughfare with a very high yakitori-to-septum-piercing ratio.

Whoosh! Tenth, Eleventh, and Twelfth Streets, where the avenue rapidly lost its identity, and empty retail spaces that could become a Starbucks at any moment grew in number.

They turned left past Stuyvesant Town, an 11,250-apartment residential development that spanned Fourteenth Street to Twenty-Third Street and First Avenue to Avenue C. Its layout made it look from above like puzzle pieces that a hallucinating person had started assembling until they realized that in the metaphysical sense, there was no correct way to assemble a puzzle and that every configuration was equally valid.

"People frequently make the mistake of assuming that Union Square is in Gramercy. Do you like Union Square, Mr. Ludwig?" He did. It was an artery bursting with culture and commerce.

"I love it. What's not to love? I love Union Square. Love bookstores, love farmers' markets, love scammers, love chess, love chess scammers." The drugs were speaking. Kenneth Branagh's claim that they were extra water soluble sounded like one of those things that drug people said, and yet they really were. "Did you used to work there too?"

"Of course! I spent many years as a traveling merchant. It's among my favorite crossroads."

They passed Union Square and entered claustrophobic Midtown South, where every corner could be any other corner, and every deli was a neutered grocery store, where food without provenance sat under heat lamps. Where did all those trays of room-temperature lo mein, mass-produced California rolls, grill-marked chicken cutlets, leaky shepherd's pies, lifeless mozzarella caprese, unsalted macaroni and cheese, and odorous hard-boiled eggs come from, and who ate them?

"Mr. Ludwig, meet 345 Park Avenue South, one of the hottest spots for start-ups. It's—"

"Pass!"

"Pass?"

"Yeah."

"Are you sure?"

"I couldn't ask people to work here. I haven't seen a worthwhile lunch spot since Fourteenth Street," Ludwig said.

On Molly, he liked this neighborhood. But once he sobered up, he doubted whether he could abide it without more. It was difficult to tell whether people lived or worked in these buildings, from each of which you could read the sign on the

MetLife Building. It belonged in the background of a movie, not at the outset of a fashion revolution.

Heading west, they caught a green across Madison, which had once been a barracks for ad agencies but was known, mainly to cab drivers, as an expedient, traffic-free thoroughfare.

Ludwig crossed his fingers as they approached Fifth Avenue, where he hoped they wouldn't stop, and they didn't. Kenneth Branagh did know his clients.

Then came Broadway, the misunderstood diagonal avenue that was less about Broadway shows than thirteen miles of the city's most photogenic intersections, all of which Sixth Avenue—the deserted-looking Avenue of the Americas—made look like Mardi Gras.

Where they were headed soon became obvious—to low-energy Chelsea, where authentic, noncosmopolitan bodegas began to reemerge and buildings whose residential-versus-commercial identities were instantly apparent.

Seventh Avenue loomed, and with it, some flooring and discount this-and-that stores and more buildings whose purposes were dubious except for one called the Fashion Institute of Technology, a place that Ludwig the Euphoric imagined himself being made an honorary graduate or guest lecturer at.

The area was noisy, but not the good kind of noisy, which got you dive bars and acclaimed restaurants and foot traffic, but cheap noise, primarily cars, all heading somewhere else as if they shared Ludwig's assessment of this place.

"Mr. Ludwig, allow me to introduce you to—"

"Pass! I'm sorry, KB. If I'm on Molly and not instantly feeling a place, maybe that place isn't for me."

"Nothing to be sorry about! You are a man who makes decisions! If only more of my clients did. Now hand KB a cold one!"

Ludwig handed KB a cold one, and they drove south on Seventh Avenue. For a moment, Ludwig saw a Macy's Thanksgiving Day Parade float–sized apparition identical to Thomas Nast's caricatures of William "Boss" Tweed, the Tammany Hall bureaucrat so crooked that he was known nationwide even to Americans who had never heard of the Lower East Side. Surely *this* must have been one of An Exalted Northwind's bugs, a theory whose veracity intensified alongside a suspicion that only he could see it.

"Does Molly make you see things?" Ludwig asked.

"No. Acid will. Have you ever done acid, Mr. Ludwig?"

"I don't think so."

"There's a splotchy piece of brown paper in the glove compartment if you want to give it a whirl. Just tear off a nickel-sized piece and suck it like a lozenge."

"What else do you have in here? A gun?"

Kenneth Branagh reached into his jacket and produced a compact revolver. "Let me know if you ever need one. They aren't easy to get in New York, but, well, you know—full-service agency!" That smile!

Ludwig felt himself crashing. He wondered whether his high was fading because of the pill's fast-in, fast-out water solubility or because the serum's lingering magic qualified the high as an "adverse, unwanted feeling" and suppressed it. His head throbbed, so without removing the hollow heart from his backpack, he closed the cork in his fist, lifted his backpack to his mouth, and swigged, neutralizing the crash. Loose change rained all over the car.

"Antichrist almighty!" Kenneth Branagh said. "What have you got in there?"

"Long story." He expected some sign that the deed's enchantment was watching and would threaten Kenneth Branagh's life. No sign appeared except the numbered ones they passed.

Twenty-fifth, twenty-fourth, twenty-third, twenty-second.

South on Seventh Avenue, graffiti reappeared on windows and metal shutters, which meant that young people, even if they didn't live there, at least went there. Liquor stores multiplied. So did nail salons with tattered awnings and poorly chosen, fading typography.

Twenty-first, twentieth, nineteenth.

They drove through Eighth Avenue and onto Ninth, which put even experienced drivers one wrong-lane switch from New Jersey. Then came the Chelsea Market, a conglomerated tunnel of boutique food stalls, micro restaurants, and stores that served the deep pockets of people who suddenly cared about fracking and wanted to know if you'd seen the latest Banksy.

Seventeenth, sixteenth.

Ludwig didn't hate the West Village, far from it, but he perceived it as lacking diversity, whether it did or not, and diversity was why he loved New York, and a lack of diversity is why quaint cafés proliferated there like head lice. It was where Carrie Bradshaw lived, which meant that a nonzero percentage of Caucasians bought homes there in order to emulate her frankly unenviable lifestyle.

Fifteenth.

Oh no—the Meatpacking District! The neighborhood where tourists and bridge-and-tunnelers congregated for discounts on six-hundred-dollar blouses from brands like Diana Von Fartenberg and Stella McFartney. The Meatpacking District was more parking lot than neighborhood, and fittingly, it offered an amount of parking found nowhere else on the island. It was Lower Manhattan's only real strip mall.

"Mr. Ludwig, allow me to—"

"Pass! This isn't even New York. It might as well be the downtown of a small to midsize Southern city trying to reimagine itself." Kenneth Branagh failed to turn Ludwig on to new neighborhoods, but he had cemented Ludwig's belief in the ones he already loved.

"You are a man who knows what he wants! Perhaps you can share some of that with me."

"New York is my country," Ludwig opined. "I've felt that way since long before I lived here. So I'm looking for a space that couldn't exist anywhere else, somewhere that sits not only geographically at the intersection of multiple cultures but spiritually. Ideally, it should be downtown, though not too downtown. It should be somewhere that journalists can point to when they talk about how far my brand has come—something that testifies to our creative roots without upending them. It should be more than an office. It should be a symbol. Do you know what I mean?"

"Mr. Ludwig, I have an idea! It's a little unusual, though it might be right for a challenger fashion house. It's not very bougie, but from the sounds of it, that's not what you're into—muumbazza, muumbazza, muumbazza." The last was added all at once, as if he were trying to cover up all the times he had forgotten to say it. "On the other hand, it's an easy walk from Zeal, and there's plenty of room to expand. The tenants are hodgy-podgy, and it is, like your apartment, within walking distance of everything cultural. It has edge, and more than that, guts."

"Show it to me," Ludwig said.

They traveled back below Fourteenth Street to the neighborhoods that Ludwig could navigate blindfolded and then to Houston Street and beyond, where they stopped in front of a nine-story cement building without a neighborhood to call its own.

The drugs came back.

"What floor?"

"Six."

"Right or left side of the elevator?"

"Right."

"All the way in the back?"

"All the way in the back."

"Did it hit the market recently?"

"Within a year."

"Why didn't I think of this?"

"You know this place?"

"This is where I planted the seeds of athleisure."

9

The city of New York carried out three Great Magicides against the fae kingdom of Manhattan. Dutch settlers unknowingly carried out the first, while the second naturally resulted from the city's expansion into a noisy, calamitous global trading center.

Robert Moses, New York's only real monarch past or present, implemented the third Great Magicide as part of a highway infrastructure plan. The Manhattan fae believe that Moses's ulterior motive was to suppress any challenge to his power by keeping them underground, as he had suppressed so many others by building interstates on top of them or consigning their dwellings to the infinite shadows of skyscrapers. Following Moses's death in 1981, as part of an amendment to the rescue deal struck by the Manhattan fae with An Exalted Northwind, her associates followed Moses to Hell, where they oversee his torture to this day.

—Excerpt from *The Decline and Fall of the Fae Kingdom of Manhattan* by Galilea Dazzledark

LUDWIG HAD HEARD nothing since blowing off his meeting with An Exalted Northwind. But that didn't stop him from looking over his shoulder and opening doors slowly to inspect what might wait beyond them.

At his request and as a parting gesture, Kenneth Branagh put Ludwig in touch with Katrina "Tag 'Em and Bag 'Em" Camaro, a private investigator that Branagh & Bloom kept on retainer for reasons that weren't clear. She quickly discovered Lulu Vaillancourt's haunts and hangouts.

Ludwig harbored ethical reservations about locating Lulu this way. However, he reasoned that she had not only "started it" but traumatized Mr. Blueberry in the process, so . . .

Even without a PI, Ludwig could have narrowed the location of a careerist, high-society minion to the Upper West or Upper East Side. Anything deeper than that superficial but astute conclusion required too much sitting in parked cars with binoculars and bags of fast food.

The only neighborhood with four right-angled corners besides the minuscule Theater and Garment Districts, the Upper West Side started at 59th Street or 110th Street—depending on your location—and spanned sixty-one streets north to south by four avenues east to west. The area's simple geometry gave New Yorkers who couldn't help arguing about where neighborhoods started and ended little to argue about. On a map, it looked like a stick of gum. What was there to argue about?

Someone always found something.

When New Yorkers became bored with New York and had the resources, they moved to the Upper West Side and spent their twilight years preparing to depart their earthly forms by listening to heirs joust over inheritances.

Depending on where you started, the Upper West Side's residents and visitors could walk half a mile along avenues like Amsterdam without encountering *real* New York culture, unless they were old enough to consider *real* New York culture to be cosmetic lasering, macaron shops, family lawyers, funeral homes, omnipresent dry cleaners, fruit stands where geriatric millionaires haggled with immigrants over the price of kiwis, and businesses that struck gold downtown then opened satellite locations in the neighborhood, giving residents the impression that they lived in the city's most revered cultural center instead of its most populous retirement community. Lulu likely lived there because it was where her auction house clients lived.

Her favorite café wasn't unlike the others, except for their stable Wi-Fi, free-refills policy (if you bought a drink and a pastry), and Wiccan-chic, quasi-witchcraft aesthetic (eucalyptus wreaths, pentagram tapestries, crystal necklaces for sale, visiting palm reader). Ludwig caught himself gawking at Lulu's eyebrows before noticing that he had found the person attached to them.

He pulled out the seat across from her. She looked up from her yellowing laptop, anticipating a far too forward and unwelcome romantic suitor, but this was not that kind of suitor.

"Please go away. I'm not interes—oh, fuck! Get the fuck away from me, dude!" she said.

"I'm sorry! I'm sorry! The lightning thing wasn't my doing!"

"Lightning *thing*? I almost died! Get away, or I will scream." Lulu was bluffing, she would never scream. She'd throw a big mug of hot coffee at his face but never scream.

"You've got me all wrong. I am not smuggling or counterfeiting rubies, for starters. And what happened with the lightning was not me. I signed this agreement that unfortunately scrutinizes everything I say so that I don't give away any of my employer's—" The sky rumbled, and aggressive, throwing star–shaped hailstones bombarded the neighborhood. What would the *Post* say? *The Far East Upper West Side? Ninja Better Run for Cover? Holy Shurikens?* "If I say too much, that happens. That's why I can't say more about you-know-what, at least not without a mutant crocodile dressed like one of the Golden Girls exploding out of the bathroom and devouring you." Ludwig watched the bathroom for precisely that—nothing yet. "Besides, I'm not here because of *that.* I'm here because I want to hire you."

"You want to hire me? You don't even know me. I won't launder gems for you. You've done enough damage to my career." As much as he hated the idea of people spending their lives at work, he never wanted to cost anyone their job.

"I'm not here about gems. I want you to manage my fashion start-up."

"Your fucking *what*?"

It was as if a bison had proposed opening a trapeze school.

"Listen, to your point, I don't know a lot about you or you about me," Ludwig said. "But I'm good at seeing people's potential. My problem is that I don't know much about *managing* people, but you do because you manage the worst people in the city. I have this thesis that hiring talented people who've had opportunity stolen from them by the lack of balance in our economy is both a new and advantageous way to hire."

"The economy didn't steal opportunity from me. Muumbazza. You did! Go stand out in your fucking, whatever—ninja stars!" She had yet to process the significance of this strange weather phenomenon. "How did you even find me? What are you, a stalker too?"

"Stalker? Is that how *you* found *me* the other night?" he demanded.

Touché, she had to admit.

"And I didn't find you. An associate of Kenneth Branagh's found you."

"Kenneth Branagh?" she asked.

"Yeah."

"You know Kenneth Branagh?"

"We did Molly last week. He's my real estate agent."

"Who's your real estate agent?"

"Kenneth Branagh."

"The actor? The Shakespeare guy?"

"Actor? He's a real estate agent."

"Your real estate agent is named Kenneth Branagh?"

"Yeah."

"Oh. What is Molly?" That she didn't know even basic drug slang testified to how old her old soul was.

"It's the stuff they put in ecstasy that creates the high. People take it pure now. Less risk or something, I don't know. I'm not a drug person," Ludwig said, even though he was.

"But you did ecstasy with your real estate agent."

"We're getting off track. I will pay you a $250,000 starting salary with equity in the brand."

"So that you can threaten me with lightning? Muumbazza, dude. I don't want to work for you. I want you to leave here and forget we ever muumbazza."

"I can't leave," he said truthfully. "It's raining ninja stars."

"And I bet you're a bad fucking boss too."

Ludwig's life had taken him to many unexpected places lately, and each made him question what he knew about himself, especially since becoming the first human in a century to contact the Parliamentary Republique of Manhattan Fae. But there was one fact, one axiom, one irrefutable truth that he knew about himself, regardless of whether anyone else did too: By loathing every boss he ever worked under, he knew enough about what made a terrible leader to avoid becoming one.

"First of all, *Lulu,* how could someone who has spent most of his life in direct conflict with bad leadership be a bad leader? I understand better than anyone what makes a manager suck and therefore know the most about not becoming one. I would hardly be a boss at all, but a co-visionary, leading the charge against uncomfortable outfits from the front. Is Santa Claus the boss of the elves? No! If anything, he works for them."

"Have you ever considered that you might be the reason why your relationships with bosses are so bad?"

"No. They're eel people. Toothy, slippery horrors looking for life to suck." Ludwig pantomimed an eel by holding out his arm and curling his fingers to simulate teeth.

"Maybe you're unmotivated," Lulu said.

"What is there to be motivated by?"

"Self-fulfillment? An income that lets you pursue your passions? Making your family proud? Having something to do? Health insurance?"

Ludwig blew a raspberry. He kept blowing it until she gestured for him to stop.

"Let's do some math. You ready?" Ludwig asked.

She wasn't.

"There are fifty-two weeks in a year."

"Strong start," she said while checking the window. The spaces under doorways and awnings overflowed with people seeking shelter from the impossibly shaped hail. People ran for the subways and vacant cabs. The jackets and sweaters they pulled over their heads provided little shelter from the storm's piercing projectiles.

"If you're one of the lucky ones who only work eight hours, five days a week, and get two weeks off per year, then you work two hundred fifty days a year"—Ludwig continued—"that's 2,000 hours a year. You also commute to work, so add an hour each day. You probably work from what, age eighteen to sixty-five? That's 105,750 hours of your life lost to employment. So out of 657,750 hours in a seventy-five-year life, you spend 16 percent on work. Not so bad, right? It's also inaccurate."

Lulu stared into her bowl of coffee as if a portal to some other café might appear.

"My math"—his math!—"assumes that your job only eats forty-five hours a week for forty-seven years. These numbers are unrealistic for people who work two or three jobs, are forced into overtime, have longer commutes, or aren't able to retire at an age that spares them any dignity. Plenty of jobs also follow you home in the form of texts and emails or phone calls or worry. And if you lose your job? Maybe you accept an even worse job, working even more hours.

"And what about the long-term health effects of a physically and mentally punishing job? That chips away at your time. Your job sucks, and because of that, your life sucks, so you drink or maybe see a therapist—more time. At work, you eat what's available, unless you are willing to spend time chasing healthy food. So now your job is punishing your body. Well, you might exercise it out, which costs even more time. Then there's the other, often unspoken, institution, working with employers to claw away at a life that belongs uniquely to you."

"I can't wait," she said as if she could. "What is it?"

"School!"

"Of course!"

"You do not go to school to receive an education. That's a myth, a fable, a rumor," Ludwig said. "Schools train you to work. Oh, *that's ridiculous,* I hear you thinking."

"Wow, you can hear what I'm thinking?"

Icy throwing stars continued inflicting millions in damage to the paint jobs of parked cars.

"Ask a kid who's bad at math what kind of math their school won't let them graduate without knowing. It's the kind that lets them manage a register, stock shelves, use a tape measure, and budget processed groceries that will eventually kill them. When tech companies sponsor initiatives to 'teach kids to code,' do they do it to help kids? No, they're flooding the market with the only labor force still scarce and essential enough to demand things. Everything ties back to work. In conclusion—"

"Nooo," Lulu pleaded. "Keep going."

"You give 16 percent of the only life you'll ever get making bosses rich," Ludwig said. "Except if you run the math, it's closer to 50–60 percent—all that for enough money to live in a condo. Then you get cancer, the lights go out, and some other pawn takes your place at the toilet of life. How's that for motivation?"

To Lulu, the whole thing sounded rehearsed, which, of course, it was—in front of mirrors, pacing around his apartment, lying sleepless in bed, quietly on aimless walks around his neighborhood, and sometimes audibly on walks when no one was present. Lulu could multiply 47 by 2,250 in her head, but him?

"You want to hire me, and that's your pitch? That you're Santa Claus, I'm an elf, and a life spent working is cold, wasteful, pointless, and muumbazza?" She had a point. Perhaps his pitch didn't sound as good to other people as it did to him, a person viscerally biased against every facet of employment.

"Bottom line, I'll pay you more than an auction house, and you will keep more of your time," Ludwig said as he leaned back and nearly tipped his chair over.

"The auction house didn't pay me! Clients paid me. Clients that the scheme you're running cost me. I want to know where your rubies come from. Tell me that, and I'll consider your fucking, whatever, 'fashion start-up.'"

"Do you remember what I told you the other night?"

"Some shit about your pig is magic or whatever?" She wouldn't admit it, but she wanted to believe him. Like Ludwig, harnessing magic was all she wanted.

"Well, that is the—" He stopped himself and analyzed the English language for a way to complete the sentence without giving the enchantment a reason to send down Lulu-seeking rattlesnakes with kangaroo legs or a spinning circle of dancing, psychokinetic swords. "What I said the other night is the t-r-u . . . Do you see where I'm going with this without actually going there? What I told you the other night is the opposite of a five-letter word that starts with *f* and ends with *e*." The ninja stars fell harder. He braced for polka-dotted lightning, but none appeared. So either the enchantment couldn't spell, or it was occupied, perhaps by the hailstorm or by sending a track-and-field-proficient demon lord after some friend or co-worker of some other magically indentured human in service to An Exalted Northwind.

"If you can't tell me," she said, "then show me."

Ludwig produced a near-empty tube of nicotine lozenges from the pocket of his hoodie. From it, he extracted a folded paper towel that, when unfolded, revealed two immaculate Asscher-cut rubies nearly the size of M&M's.

Showing the rubies had never triggered the enchantment since they were just rubies, and on their own and out of context, they revealed nothing of their fairy provenance.

Lulu produced an optical magnifier from her purse and inspected the stones. Then, with one in each hand, she held the bloodshot rocks up to the light and, entranced, seemed to disappear from the table, the café, Amsterdam Avenue, and the Upper West Side.

"These are, well—they don't rule out smuggling, but they certainly rule out counterfeiting. I don't understand," she said. "It took months to prepare one stone of this quality for auction. All the hours I spent negotiating with auction houses to get it on the cover of their catalogs. All the potential buyers I put it in front of. All the certifications. My god, I had a security detail for two weeks! And you're carrying around rival stones like they're cough drops."

Could it all be true?

"I want a $300,000 salary, a considerable equity stake, and a $30,000, nonrefundable advance. And no more fucking lightning."

"Deal. At least not on purpose."

"What?"

Rather than furnish the office that had once belonged to Electric Guacamole with hard surfaces and stiff chairs composed entirely of right angles like Charlie, its cheap yet somehow spendthrift former master, Ludwig called once again on the only furniture company whose name he knew.

He stuffed the office with recliners, Tuscan leather sofas, and lounge chairs. They devoured space, but with less than a fifth of Electric Guacamole's head count, space was abundant.

By design, Vermin Milk's office looked like Ludwig's apartment, except for the void in the corner where he placed three adjustable desks (Uchu, Naveena, Igor), a drafting table (Ayonia), and four $1,500-a-pop ergonomic office chairs.

For their first meeting, Ludwig dragged sofas and lounge chairs into the center of the office and spun them in place until they faced each other. When his coworkers (he refused to call them employees) started to file in, Ludwig had already fallen asleep in one.

"You better be kidding me," Naveena said.

"About the furniture?" Ludwig asked as he groaned from stasis.

"This isn't an office; this is a living room. Muumbazza."

Igor fell into a La-Z-Boy and fumbled for the footrest lever.

"It's a power recliner," Ludwig said. "A remote in the arm lets you control the footrest. I think there's even a massage feature; I just haven't found it."

Igor instantly found it.

Uchu hopped over the arm of one sofa and sank into place, fiddling with the sixty-megapixel, studio-quality camera Ludwig had left on his desk. The rest of the team, the ones who already knew Ludwig, exchanged looks. Was this a trap?

"Who gets Charlie's office?" Naveena asked.

"You do if you want it," he said.

"Where's your office?"

Ludwig pointed to the fire escape, where he had once spent weeks avoiding work. With work on his terms and aimed at his goals, its luster admittedly diminished. This was a job, no question. But surrounded by peers and people he considered friends, regardless of whether they felt the same way, at least he no longer felt alone.

"No *Halo*?" Hassan asked. "*You* didn't install a projection screen for *Halo*?"

"Yeah, about that. Many companies, especially start-ups, offer beer on tap, yoga, and video games to make you happy with less pay. Vermin Milk won't offer any of those perks, not because I'm cheap but because this is still a job. You are all here to make money, so all that will go to your paychecks."

"Maybe some of your salary could pay for the perks?" Naveena asked. "I bet it's pretty nice. You're talking about doing things differently. Start by being transparent."

"Jesus, Veena. One, I don't take a salary and don't plan to. Two, I have equity, just like all of you. Right now, it's worthless. So you guys get my salary distributed between you, which is one reason we can overpay. I just want my vision realized. As long as I feel like a cool urban druid, I'm not in this for the money. Speaking of doing things differently, no matter how successful we get, I'll never force you to clap for company milestones, do one on ones unless you want them, refer to our company as a 'family,' or make you expense things out of pocket. Finally, we are not here to 'change the world.' We are here to, at best, make comfortable clothes that look cool and let us retire early. Any questions?"

"So, I'm sorry," Hassan said. "How can you overpay? How can you pay at all? You lived in my basement not even a year ago. I saw you reheat pad thai with a space heater."

"Great question. I got it from this enchanted—" The lights went out, all the laptops switched to battery power, and a minor earthquake rattled the building. "An earthquake in New York City!" Ludwig exclaimed. Was it an earthquake? An iron golem in the lobby could have wielded a fabled, peasant-crushing hammer.

Lulu's eyes rolled. Whatever she knew, thought she knew, or was still deducing about Ludwig's wealth, it was more than what the rest of the team knew. They had only read about the Upper West Side Ninja Star Hailstorm of 2012. She had lived it—and she wanted to know more. This dipshit idiot knew magic or was connected to it somehow, and she wanted to be too.

"Now, some of you know each other, and some don't," Ludwig said. "So I'd like to introduce Ayonia Green, who is coming out of fashion retirement to be our creative director for product; Uchu Escalante, who comes to us from Belize's second-largest newspaper and is now our director of photography; and Lulu Vaillancourt, who doesn't like me very much, but has nonetheless agreed to leave behind her career as an auction house drone to become our COO. Lulu, take it away."

Lulu rose to her feet before New York's most comfortable employees in tiny, paralyzing heels and a knee-length body-con dress, both wildly off-brand for the team she had come to lead. She unsheathed the smile that charmed hundreds of auction house clients and, while she spoke, swung her arms as if a phantom whiteboard floated beside her.

"Hi, everyone. My name is Lulu Vaillancourt. Me llamo Lulu Vaillancourt," she said, tipping her head to Uchu.

"You speak Spanish?" Ludwig asked.

"Sí. As Ludwig pointed out, I previously worked in auctions at Hazlitt & Hazlitt, Christie's, and Sotheby's. Vermin Milk is my first foray into fashion, and I understand that, except for Ayonia, that is also true for all of you. But this opportunity is new for me in more ways than that. VM—"

"Vermin Milk." Ludwig interrupted. "We don't abbreviate it. Takes away all the punch."

"OK . . . Vermin Milk is my first chance to upend an industry, something that auction houses never gave me a chance to do."

"Hi, Lulu. I have a question," Hassan blurted through a sip of coffee. "Where does the money for this come from? Muumbazza. He's not telling us. You're COO. You must know."

"That's a great question, Hassan. Thank you for muumbazza. As unusual as it sounds, the truth is that Ludwig hasn't disclosed the source of our funding to me." That wasn't the truth. "That said, I have seen our bank statements, and we are very in the black. So as long as paychecks arrive on time, I don't intend to make Ludwig's business my business."

"I'm sorry to keep interrupting, but did you two just meet? He just learned that you speak another language." Whether or not he knew it, Hassan spoke for the room. "You're a serious person. He's . . . I mean, look at him. Look at that. You're dressed like you work at a law firm, and he's the Most Comfortable Man Alive. He's probably got sweatpants under his sweatpants."

"Nonetheless, I have faith in his vision."

For half the room, that was all that they needed. Lulu inspired confidence. For the other half, whatever faith they couldn't have in Ludwig, they could at least try to have in her.

"What should we do about a photography studio?" Uchu asked. "I'm happy to work outside and scout locations for future shoots. Just know that for catalog-quality product photography, you need a lot of control over light."

"I leased an empty studio a couple of doors down if you want to set it up and start thinking about light," Ludwig said. "Hassan, help me move Naveena and Igor into Charlie's office."

"If Gloria asks you for a job here," Hassan whispered from the opposite end of a colossal desk that they attempted to maneuver through a doorway, "please don't give her one. I don't want to work with the person I live with. I think she's trying to keep tabs on me."

"Done," Ludwig said. "But if you philander in this office, I'll make her a VP."

"Funny. So where does the money come from?"

Ludwig knew that people's questions about his wealth might never go away, and employees invented their own answers to questions they never asked him directly: *I heard he won a lawsuit. I heard it was something called bitcoin. I heard that he stakes card counters.*

"Mean aunt. Millionaire. Left everything to my sister and me," Ludwig huffed.

"What was her name?"

"Whose name?"

"Your aunt's."

"Gilda?"

"What's her last name?"

"Fiorella?"

"Bullshit."

"I'm not bullshitting!"

"Your fingers are literally crossed." Ludwig's tells were countless and unmistakable. He was a gifted bullshitter but not much of a liar. "Just be careful, man. Whatever you're doing, it's working. Don't get someone hurt."

LUDWIG ROSE WITH a sun the color of an old bloodstain and dived into a rattling black cab to Williamsburg. Because Giustina's mozzarella shop opened early and sold out almost as early, he was glad that his job gave him an excuse to be there and be gone before commuters migrated into the city from Brooklyn.

More this time than the last time, which was the case every time, Ludwig saw the effects that people with Naveena's level of influence had on this once culturally rich, now rich rich neighborhood.

The hotel that towered over Kellogg's Diner approached completion, and only time and rapidly deteriorating city-landmark laws prevented Giustina's shop from sharing its fate.

"Ciao! Muumbazza!" she said. Whether she remembered Ludwig, he couldn't say. Her more than ninety years on earth made him doubtful. Her English had always been limited, despite having lived in Brooklyn since the 1940s, so their conversations never contained more than a few words and, since she was Italian, several times that many hand gestures.

He bought bread and mozzarella and brought both to the stoop of his former building, where he had once taken refuge from the creature's corpse that still made guest appearances in his nightmares.

Ludwig ate blissfully and fast, hoping to avoid an out-of-context encounter with Hassan or, god forbid, Gloria, who might wonder why he had hired Hassan and not her. But just as his mind turned to them, the lights of Hassan's apartment, just over Ludwig's shoulder, illuminated, and voices from within reached out. Ludwig grabbed his breakfast and stealthily went down the stoop, around the gate, by the trash bins, and into his old apartment.

What a contrast! Few New Yorkers had ever gone from rented basement to owning a downtown penthouse in just over a year, and even fewer, possibly none (he wouldn't rule it out completely), had made their fortune courtesy of an enchanted butthole.

Far more from curiosity than necessity, he checked the contents of his refrigerator. What could be in there after all this time? Only the shadows of shadows of things. It was nearly empty except for cheap margarita mix, cheaper tequila, and something leaking through wax paper that he couldn't identify.

Ludwig unhooked the cattle prod he had installed by the door and flicked it on and off, forgetting what movies never told you, which was how loudly they crackled. Ten or so flicks later, he heard the door to the basement open.

"Ludwig? Is that you?" Gloria's voice called down the stairs.

Shit!

Footsteps descended the creaking stairway. Though all the doors into the basement's shared spaces were locked, the door from Ludwig's apartment into the rest of the basement was not. It had been, once, but not since Ludwig kicked it in after throwing his keys onto a neighbor's roof during an Ambien stupor. Would Gloria enter his apartment unbidden? He recalled how she had handled being terminated from Electric Guacamole, full of threats and intimidation, and even confiscation of company property. If that was how she lost work, how might she pursue it?

"Ludwig? Are you in there? I haven't seen you in so long!"

He opened his door in the floor. If nothing else, since only he could open it, it provided an unparalleled hiding spot.

"Ludwig?"

With the door into the deep still open, Ludwig prepared to descend. But Gloria gave up and went back up the stairs.

Didn't Lonesome Johnny say that this apartment, where they met, was haunted or possessed? No, he definitely said possessed, though what was the difference? He considered the question and Lonesome Johnny's meaning until the lockless door into his apartment edged open.

10

There is a worst way to die. Contrary to Tolstoy, it's happiness that is subjective, while suffering is mostly objective, universal, and agreed-upon. We have all read an obituary that made us glad something happened to someone else, an explicit confirmation that there are better ways to have your ticket punched, such as expiring in bed, than weightlessly somersaulting through space while your oxygen tank depletes—or worse, while it doesn't.

Do you remember how it ended for that person, the one in the article, that made you glad it wasn't you? Some rare bacterium? Radiation burns? Flaying? Crucifying? A limb-at-a-time deep frying? Starving at sea while the sun cooked their shrinking skin? Maybe they were devoured by insects, a fate always worse than, say, a shark or lion attack, since suffering in this scenario is multiplied by the number of mouths at the table. It doesn't matter. They can have the bronze; they can have the silver.

> To my knowledge, there is no final experience more deserving of the gold than the one known only to those unlucky few who encounter a fairy without its sanity.
>
> —Bluebane the Onionscourge

THE THING WAS cute, whatever it was—big and powder blue with an onion-shaped torso and two dinner-plate eyes centered with tiny, featureless black pupils. A thin black shadow spanned its surface where an enormous mouth might yet be concealed, and a crowning tuft of unkempt green hair sprouted from where grasslike scapes usually crowned onions. Even its noodly arms and legs resembled those of a sports mascot, cartoon character, or plush toy.

For a few seconds (or was it a few minutes?), Ludwig and the adorable blue burglar contemplated what the other might do next, or in Ludwig's case, what the other was. Then the creature's mouth opened, revealing an ironing board–sized tongue.

Ludwig's eyes turned bloodshot, and the unpleasant intensity he remembered experiencing after discovering the wet, severed head of the Giant returned with infinitely greater potency. That event had made him feel afraid and paranoid, self-destructive, and more than a touch suicidal. Now, those feelings were desirable, like things worth doing again, such as a long summer's-day drive through the country or having dinner with an old and admired friend.

Ludwig's limbs turned tired and ancient, and his hair, teeth, and fingernails fell out. Whatever essence had flowed through him since he could recognize his own name, such as his wants and beliefs, likes and dislikes, passions and memories, the very things that made him Ludwig, poured out of his mouth and onto the floor just before he did.

The puddle of his rejected insides constituted punctured, pregnant spiders evacuating their younglings; blood-bloated, marble-sized ticks; spitting botfly maggots that bounced across the floor like fleas; and hissing, furling-and-unfurling armored centipedes that fought one another for the right to Ludwig's teeth and fingernails. He could barely see the liver spots that formed up and down his arms through the concord of putrid insects clamoring for real estate across his skin.

He heard his long-dead mother cry for help, and then his sister, wherever she was, and then his friends, what few he had, which made their appeals all the more urgent and desperate. Their cries reached out from the blue onion's eyes, as did arresting visions. Ludwig saw his loved ones' faces pressed into the cold, hard ground by huge, muddy boots connected to unseen faces and gloved hands with serrated jackknives that, one by one, cut the throats of every familiar face, leaving their bodies to decay impossibly fast in some cruel wilderness he had never seen and couldn't look away from, leaving him to explore it alone.

The next scene placed Ludwig beneath the sterile lights of an operating room where he, the patient, lay with his belly surgically opened and pinned back. Around him, all of the women that he had ever loved or secretly loved, even Giustina, all of them geriatric and feeble like her, their battles with time lost, danced to accordion music played by the headless Giant as they unspooled Ludwig's infinite guts into hand-operated meat grinders, the products of which were stuffed into cans with his face on them. Their yellow-and-green corporate logo read "100% Ludwig, No Artificial Colors or Flavors Added." No one recognized him. No one administered an anesthetic, either, which couldn't have been a mistake, so he felt every rip, tear, and mangling of his insides. Ludwig wanted to die. He could open his mouth but couldn't create the sounds needed to beg for a scalpel to the brain. They knew what he wanted and ignored his desperate, mute ad-libbing. Even in that packed room, he was again alone.

Both scenes were terrible in different ways, samplings of all the horror the blue onion could project. So in the nightmare's next act, Ludwig occupied an uncomfortable seat at a Maryland customer-service call center—or was it an insurance company? It could have been a call center at an insurance company. He wore a suit and tie, and the Most Comfortable Man Alive was no longer comfortable at all.

As the first-person menagerie unfolded, a manager beckoned Ludwig into a badly carpeted conference room and hurled profanities at him, insisting he deserved abuse because of his universally poor performance reviews. This boss, whose face shape-shifted to become the faces of his most tyrannical managers, told Ludwig that because he made spreadsheets so incompetently (he had made a single mistake within a two-hundred-page document), he didn't deserve his own time; he'd just use it to mess up something else.

The Ludwig whose body the real Ludwig occupied in the vision wore no calcified, anticastigation armor or enthusiasm for being fired and therefore freed. As the changeling tormented him, an impossibly beautiful, shape-shifting world revealed itself on the other side of that corporate penitentiary's unbreakable, magically reinforced windows.

When the many-faced manager stormed away to shout at coworkers who all looked like Ludwig, making the only person he could speak to himself, real Ludwig's computer displayed happy scenes that would never be: love that he had no time for because he had to make his impossibly escalating rent; the birth of children that in life he never knew if he wanted but in the vision did; and a fifth- and sixth-floor Lower East Side penthouse that he lived in with a plump pig, given to him by fairies that made him finally the protagonist of something other than his ordinary nine-to-five life, reducing all of them to fleeting daydreams that would never be.

Then Ludwig saw his funeral, which was empty except for his corpse and screaming, boss-faced flowers, and corporate condolences from his nameless call center employer that reflected how much they valued the time that Ludwig sacrificed, such as a used condom, an overflowing toilet, a bowl filled with spit, and papers revealing a pancreatic cancer diagnosis. Life was over, and he had made nothing of it. All of these events had felt real. Were they?

The blue onion's transmogrifying gaze could not be avoided, except when it let him inspect the platoon of vermin storming his skin. Whenever it allowed this, it did so only for seconds, then like whirlpools, the blue onion's eyes drew him back into the looping vision, adding a new setting each time: Mr. Blueberry stuffed squealing into an oven; Lonesome Johnny torn asunder by fishing hooks, crying for mercy and for Mr. Ludwig to rescue him; New York emptied of all immigrant culture until it looked like Finland or Cupertino. How many times had he watched these scenes? They played for minutes, hours, days, weeks, months—when could he die? He wanted to die; it was all he wanted. He'd happily do it himself.

Ludwig's dull, serrated bread knife, which he had threatened Lonesome Johnny with on the night they met, was just over there. The telepathic onion trapped his mind, but did it trap his geriatric arms and legs? If Ludwig had the knife, even if he couldn't reach the beast, he could stab out his eyes to break its hold over him. How could he even get the knife, which was somewhere in a drawer, a place so high up that it might as well have been in the clouds?

The creature betrayed no malice or antipathy for Ludwig; it simply continued to block the door and exist without any spark of aggression. Did it know what it was doing to him? The monsters of films, games, and books were blood-starved horrors with crescent claws and vast rows of crooked teeth hungry for soft human parts. They did not resemble the cuddly, eight-foot, nightmare-broadcasting vegetable before him. Ludwig tried closing his eyes. He couldn't even blink—the creature demanded his attention.

He struggled to form words, tripping over vowels and consonants, to tell the beast how he made his money, to tell it everything he knew about fairies, to tell it every secret that the deed forbade him to speak of, hoping that it might smite his mysterious and unexpected opponent. Forming words without teeth repulsed him; his dried, shriveled tongue stuck to everything. When he managed "tunnel, fairies, pig, rubies," nothing happened. No tornadoes of burning hair, no polka-dotted lightning, no ornately armored saber-wielding, moving van–sized scorpions came to his rescue, as if the creature already knew about the tunnel that led to the fairies beneath Times Square.

The tunnel.

Could he just . . . fall backward? Could his brittle, useless body survive the fall as it slammed the enchanted door behind him if it could reach the door? Would the creature follow? Was he too old now to outmaneuver the buoyant cerulean vegetable?

Ludwig the Ancient.

Since he couldn't lift the cattle prod to electrocute the invader, he commanded his muscles to cease holding him upright, letting gravity sprawl him across the floor, unfurling his cattle-prod hand toward the intruder.

Zap.

The electrifying current should have crippled the invader long enough for him to climb into the tunnel. Instead, it only tickled the creature's naked blue leg, causing uncontrollable, cartoonish giggles. The attack hadn't even registered as such.

"Bubbles of Earth! Bubbles of Earth!" it cheered in a voice even more cartoonish than it looked. Its round, ocean-blue body and forest-green hair, in addition to its cloud-white eyes, gave it the appearance of a bubble of earth, whatever one was.

A rat dashed past the blue onion's feet as if it knew what it was and wanted to avoid becoming its next victim, which disrupted the vegetable's concentration. Though the visions dissipated, Ludwig still couldn't move. For a moment, the blue onion forgot about him and chased the circling rodent like Jupiter chasing its largest moon, knocking over or throwing planks of wood and brooms and empty buckets out of the way.

Anything is better than this, Ludwig told himself at the eroding edge of his remaining sanity. An idea occurred, if it could be called an idea, just as stomping barefoot on the head of Ludwig's once-greatest, now-distant and quaint-seeming second-greatest opponent had been an idea. He had seconds.

Unable even to crawl, Ludwig turned the cattle prod on himself, causing uncontrollable spasms that dispersed the abyss of insects like a bright and sudden light.

When Ludwig's soul reentered his body seconds later, his muscles and bones were still tight but no longer locked. His fingernails, hair, and teeth were back, and so was control of his vision. His eyes were his other enemy in that fight, so he closed them and blindly scoured the floor for his backpack. Ludwig reached over there, but it wasn't there. He searched the opposite direction and found only a hollow space where the tunnel door lay propped open on invisible hinges.

Where was it? *Where was it?*

Idiot!

Ludwig unlooped his backpack from his body. The hollow heart felt heavier, as if it had been filled with liquid grief, so without removing the vessel's stone form from its holster, he closed his lips and teeth around the golden topper and pulled until they separated. Then he rolled onto his back and tipped the hollow heart's brimming contents into his face, unconcerned with how much he spilled, thankful for every drop of demonic flavor that made it past his reacquainted teeth.

His body and mind were his again, though noticeably reduced. Ludwig opened his eyes only enough to scan for the tunnel, whose position he had lost while on his back. Then, just as he made that mistake, the onion caught the rat, lifted it by its thrashing, snapping head, and with one clean, bloodless chomp, bit off its body.

"Oh, God."

Ludwig closed his eyes. He knew he couldn't fight the creature even if it could be harmed, so he lunged for the tunnel as the vast, blue onion dived after him.

The door sealed.

With his backpack and several left-behind fantasy paperbacks unintentionally in tow, Ludwig rolled down four flights of scaffolding.

Thud.

Thud.

Thud.

Thud.

Desolate Phil drew his sword and ascended to the sound like a plumber searching for a leak. He found only an unconscious doorbearer with a shattered leg.

"Pitiful Upstairs Neighbor. That blue guy has waited in your basement to ambush you since your first visit to Broken Throat. They can wait centuries if necessary."

He retrieved Ludwig's hollow heart and backpack from where they came to a stop two scaffolds above. He weighed the stone heart in his gloved hands—nearly empty but also chipped. When the sun once again set, the hollow heart's missing piece would become a tear. “Remain here,” he instructed Ludwig, “though I doubt you are capable of much else. This needs mending.”

Like an olden-days prophet, Desolate Phil parted the river of worms between him and Broken Throat. An hour later, he returned with Lonesome Johnny, a silver tray of peanut butter and jelly sandwiches, a thermos of hot “koko,” a considerable length of rope, and An Exalted Northwind’s twin to Ludwig’s gargoyle heart. Lonesome Johnny and Desolate Phil devised a stretcher and pulley from the rope and a wooden plank and lowered Ludwig into the dirt eleven stories down.

“I saw you die,” he whispered. Lonesome Johnny’s gloved hands dripped serum into Ludwig’s parched throat. The stained and soaking uniform he had worn to Zeal appeared fully laundered, even new, if clothes from the Civil War could be called new. “I saw everyone die. I saw myself working at a call center in Maryland. I saw, I saw—Oh, *God*.” What exactly had he seen in that operating room?

“You saw far greater, stranger, and realer versions of your sweatiest nightmares,” Lonesome Johnny said. “The blue guy’s gaze woke your dormant insanity much like how noise wakes the dormant insanity of fairies. Forcing someone to confront their nightmares is far from cutting edge as far as phantasmal powers go, but it’s like my lady-lord and benefactor always says: ‘Execution is everything.’”

“Brother Johnny, you reveal too much,” Desolate Phil grumbled.

“Our lady-lord and benefactor has permitted me to speak, correctly believing that my dear buddy Ludwig might prefer to hear these painful truths from a friend. Oh, how I hate them, Brother Phil! How I despise the blue guys! First, they defy our lady-lord and benefactor, and now they attack the most talented and benevolent Upstairs Neighbor to ever emerge from that raucous metropolis! Though they are still fairies, and are related to our lady-lord and benefactor's client-housemates. May I ask, Mr. Ludwig," Lonesome Johnny's tone softened, "how you escaped its imaginary onslaught?"

"I didn't do anything. A rat distracted it. I drank Dr. Tot's Whatever It's Called, then I rolled down here."

"Rescued by a rat? Once again, serendipity aids our purpose," Desolate Phil said.

"What are they? Why wasn't I warned?" Ludwig no longer noticed the serum's taste as it dribbled past his trembling lips. It could have been a frozen margarita.

"They are the fairies that my lady-lord and benefactor banished years ago," Lonesome Johnny said. "She believed—correctly, since she isn't capable of error—that you might reject or avoid her assignment if you knew of their lamentable existences."

"Terrific leadership," he scoffed. It seemed bosses couldn't help but be bosses, even at the edges of enchanted, overlapping realities. "Was anything I saw real?"

"It was not, though I have little doubt that it felt more real than a dagger to the ribs. Oh, Mr. Ludwig! I wished to warn you. I did! But I am only a servant and can only act as I am order-bound to act."

"It giggled through thirteen thousand volts."

"To kill or injure a blue guy, you must pierce them, hence this." Desolate Phil waved his needle-shaped blade before Ludwig's apprehensively open eyes. "Bluebane the Onion-scourge's Sword-Spear of Puncturing. But even with the right weapons, killing them is not so easy. Only immortals and those who bear the bucket can withstand their gaze since neither is alive as you know life. When they were still green, our lady-lord and benefactor sentenced the fairies who would become the blue guys to exile amid the construction site's noise. Fairies intentionally take many forms, yet madness forces them to take another unintentionally. You surely noticed that the blue guys look like liquid-filled balloons, which is what they are and why they fear sharp weapons. Should you consider retaliation, know that the blue guys are not to be killed since the point of their banishment is punishment, not death. My sword and allegiance are a last resort should one or more of them pile past a door in the floor, of which only yours remains."

Days passed, Ludwig missed work, and Lonesome Johnny fed him tiny peanut butter and jelly sandwiches, hot cocoa, and more serum. Quirk by quirk, defect by defect, cloying idiosyncrasy by cloying idiosyncrasy, Ludwig's mind returned.

"Couldn't you guys drag me to the house, maybe?" Ludwig complained. "I know there are at least a few empty rooms that—I'm just guessing—must be pretty comfortable."

"Mr. Ludwig," Lonesome Johnny said. "You are still healing, and until your mind is fully mended, we thought it unwise to add to your psychic injuries the mind-rattling task of fathoming creatures from an overlapping reality."

Ludwig gradually relearned how to make a fist, wiggle his toes, sit up, stretch, and walk. He raised and lowered his legs, shaking the dust from them until he could rotate each like a helicopter blade. He flexed and tightened his flabby core until he could stand long enough to piss.

"Oh, look at him go! What a powerful stream!" Lonesome Johnny said, applauding Ludwig. "Those heinous freaks can't stop our golden boy!"

"Indeed," Desolate Phil muttered. "Normally, such comprehensive rehabilitation takes weeks. Very well. Our lady-lord and benefactor waits for you, Upstairs Neighbor. You know the way."

Unfortunately, he did. Whether he liked it or not, he was

in for an employee performance review with the mightiest of all conceivable bosses—the most significant test yet of his commitment to never committing.

He took three long swigs from An Exalted Northwind's twin to his hollow heart and, with Lonesome Johnny in tow, limped the length of the cryptically colored tunnel without sidestepping its intruder-detecting worms.

He wanted her to know he was coming.

NEW, MORE BELIEVABLE and genuine-sounding fairy names filled the building's directory.

5G
5F Peachflame Spiderbite
5E Candlelocks Ironcloud
5D Fluttertoad Jellywhite
5C Stardash Moonbreeze
5B Cinnamontail Neverloop
5A
4G Suncorn Bubblerose
4F Bloombird Pollenvale
4E Pinewhite Tangleglade
4D Stormriver Summercool
4C
4B Timehorn Spiralpuff
4A Bubbleveil Nightbloom
3L An Exalted Northwind's Archives (cont'd)
3G
3F Amberbell Birdgrass
3E Moonplume Applecloud
3D Glittersnow Whisperlace
3C Seabraid Doomdance

3B Gempool Briarwind
3A Hollowsail Rotmoon
2L An Exalted Northwind's Archives (cont'd)
2G
2F Silverberry Sugarwort
2E Bluebluff Nightseed
2D Celestialstorm Poppyfield
2C Rainspite Peppercloud
2B Turtlefield Lotuschain
2A Featherweb Graydance
1L An Exalted Northwind's Archives
1G Slithersun Brittleblade
1F
1E Peachsplash Coppertoes
1D Moonmask Howlstone
1C Wormsong Jestergrove
1B
1A Swampheel Bitterbottom
B1 Lonesome Johnny

"Are these the same fairies?" Ludwig whispered. He wanted to shout, yell, and assault the door, but not if it meant getting Lonesome Johnny in trouble.

"Indeed. Since fairy names steadily proliferate like tree rings, my lady-lord and benefactor's client-housemates regularly update this directory, though these are not even real names. They could just as well be drawings of cats. It is impossible to say what is in their infinite minds."

Lonesome Johnny removed his bucket, revealing nothing. He held the bucket at arm's length while another white-gloved hand reached forth from the bitter darkness within, placing a thick, blue, single-flower vase and a little branch ending in eleven key bits into his hand. He reattached his head and inserted the multifaceted key into all eleven locks. Before opening the door, he placed the tiny blue vase on the stoop and covered it with a handkerchief.

"Apologies. A daintier glass could not be found on short notice. Please give it a stomp."

Ludwig's wounded leg and bruised body could only crack the heavy glass. To save face, he pocketed what remained and dragged his feet to simulate sweeping away shards. If someone with a crystal ball was watching, they would see him just fine, which he wanted.

"Aren't you worried about Phil?" Ludwig whispered. "What will happen if more blue guys attack?"

"Worry not for Brother Phil. As he noted during your rehabilitation, we bucketbearers are not susceptible to the blue guys' phantom aggression. Worry not for Brother Phil."

Inside, the pile of unworn shoes had grown so that it approached Ludwig's shoulders.

They exited the foyer without impediment from the previous year's peanut butter and jelly cart. Ludwig scanned the room for the spread and found it pulled up to a couch beside a familiar fairy with dark gemstones and bright autumn leaves freckling her seaweed-green hair.

"Oh, it's buckethead and blunder face. No, buckethead and buttface? Lonesome Johnny and the Lonesome Imbecile? Give me a moment."

"I remember you," Ludwig whispered. The fairy instantly warmed to what she perceived as a compliment.

"How could you not? I am nature's unlimited grace, worshipped by the sun, moon, and rain. Birds sing my ancient name. Stones hold my footsteps in their fondest memories. Light races light to announce my presence, even in the shadows." Beyond the room, in a hallway that Ludwig had once explored with Lonesome Johnny, he saw the broad green face and eyes of a fairy he had not yet met. It was the most he'd seen of any fairy who wasn't An Exalted Northwind or Galilea. Ludwig waved, and just as suddenly, all sign of it vanished. Had it been afraid, and if so, why? Was it An Exalted Northwind's omnipresent list of rules that kept the creature from further interaction with Ludwig? Had the fairy suddenly remembered something that had happened to one of its own for doing what it was?

"Mr. Ludwig, I am honored to reintroduce Galilea Dazzledark, whose cruelty to me is only ever of the highest caliber and utmost originality," Johnny said congenially. "Playing the popinjay to my lady-lord and benefactor's client-housemates is just one of my many functions."

"How's the book going?" Ludwig asked.

"How books go," Galilea said.

"What does that mean?"

"Many things."

"Is this your first book?"

Galilea considered the question as if she didn't know, or perhaps couldn't know, how many books she had written. Was this book just a book, or was it multiple books? It was possible that, like her great-great-great-great-great-great-great-aunt, she had filled hundreds of tomes with beanstalk letters, though something gave Ludwig the impression that she was more a painstaking stylist than a prolific stenographer.

"I don't know," Galilea said. She slathered blobs of creamy peanut butter and marshmallow creme onto a folded slice of bread that disappeared in two bites.

"What is it with fairies and peanut butter?" Ludwig asked.

"Soods da mind an buddredges ow-er zanidy, bowd of widge are weeded wahn woo wiv in da gown," she pronounced as she chewed.

"Lady Dazzledark, a pleasure." Lonesome Johnny nudged Ludwig out of the room toward An Exalted Northwind's archives.

"Wet me whoa if woo fine some Ta-whoa cards. I pway for your det."

Broken Throat hadn't changed since Ludwig's visit a year earlier, except that, this time, An Exalted Northwind's tablet of rules included a fat red line beneath its final clause: No Turning Blue. Stay Busy Whenever You Are Not Sleeping. Report Symptoms of Blueness Immediately, and a sign-up board for something called Trivia Night with Lonesome Johnny. No takers.

The archives' color-conducting bell illuminated, and the door quietly opened, but An Exalted Northwind was nowhere to greet or chastise him.

Ah, Ludwig thought, *classic power move.*

While Lonesome Johnny searched for his lady-lord and benefactor, Ludwig swigged settled solids from the twin to his gargoyle's hollow heart as he assayed the room. She'd been busy, which boded ill for him. Twenty or more tomes lay open across shoulder-high tables, and the unnamable instruments that accompanied them looked either recently used or in use.

Lonesome Johnny returned in the fairy matriarch's long, rippling shadow.

"Oh, Ludwig. It is good to see you again," she whispered. Was it? "You have my apologies; my work is more urgent than ever, so from these stacks, I rarely ever escape except to eat, which evades my mind more and more. Fortunately, my puppet is a committed caretaker. It feels like you and I saw each other only yesterday."

"It does?" he whispered back, in tune with her.

"A year feels different to us. To you, at your age, a year is, what, 4 percent of your life? To us, well—math, you know. Anyway, don't worry about the meeting you missed. I assumed you had been busy with your task."

From fairies, he couldn't know what to expect. But if he had expected anything, it wasn't that.

He didn't buy it.

Before Ludwig learned to enjoy termination, he had

walked into every performance review—even the few good ones—heavy with anxiety. Without money or demand for whatever services he provided to fall back on, managers held his livelihood in their hands. This time, though, it wasn't only his manager who had legitimate grievances, and thanks to Mr. Blueberry's wealth-generating powers, she needed him more than he needed her, which removed much of her bargaining power. The real question remained: Who would strike first?

If it was her, he expected soothing body language and feigned empathy, like the kind she had already deployed, the kind that bosses opened bad performance reviews with to play the benevolent supervisor who just wanted to help a direct report live up to their potential.

"How do you feel?" she asked. "Have your visions ceased? Is the serum helping? I'm afraid that the blue guys, who, as fae, once only acted like monsters by openly flouting seven or more of my rules, which led to their banishment, are now actual monsters. The fae here objected to me turning their friends and family members into blue guys; hell, they still object, but without me to rescue them, the same fate would have awaited them, creating a fae wild consisting of only blue guys. Broken Throat's fae may not have supported my actions, but Fairie's did."

"I'm feeling"—no, best not to open on her terms. He imagined dodging her questions as though they were sword strikes. "I don't know how it works with fairies, but in human working arrangements, employees have rights!" It was only sort of true, depending on where you worked and what you did for a living, but how would she know that?

"Please lower your voice, Ludwig," she commanded.

He didn't.

"Chief among those rights is the right to workplace safety!" he said. "By not informing me about the *blue guys*, which on top of everything is an awful name for such dangerous creatures!—you put my coworkers and me at incredible risk, like leasing me an office that you neglected to mention had an active volcano under it!" Whether or not Ludwig's prior bosses meant to, they taught him the playbook for all future bosses.

With a finger, An Exalted Northwind scribbled something in the air, and a rope flew from a drawer that tied itself around his neck and tightened whenever he raised his voice.

"Your *coworkers*? I have not authorized coworkers," she hissed.

"Yes, *coworkers*. I launched a, uh, fashion brand," Ludwig whispered. Shit. It was a confession he wanted to avoid making since it undermined points he still hadn't gotten to. And yet, there it was, which meant there was just one thing left to do. "My thesis is that aesthetically centered social conventions are due for a reckoning. I want to end the tyranny of suits and ties, jeans and wingtips, heels and belts—"

"Puppet, wait outside." Lonesome Johnny left the room as if yanked offstage by a long, invisible cane. "Ludwig, I don't need to hear your business pitch. Here I thought that something had gone wrong aboveground, either with you or the world itself, and that was why I hadn't received any notes. I assumed you had been working through whatever it was. But it seems you have been shirking us. Listen to me carefully. You alone are capable of performing this task. You alone out of eight million. Lives greater than yours depend on you. You must focus on the task I have given you and not on those you have given yourself. If all you've done until now is make trousers, we have a problem."

Ludwig resented the categorization of flexible, tapered, breathable cotton joggers as trousers and halfway raised a finger to object. At least she wasn't a screamer. Could she even be?

"Oh, we have a problem," Ludwig deflected. He felt the rope tightening but pushed on. "It's you! Why didn't you tell me about the rats? Because it would force you to reveal that the blue guys were searching the city for my door? Because maybe I wouldn't want to work for you if I knew what they could do? And for what? To further your own goals at my expense, the very thing you're criticizing me for doing? I *thought* we were on a team. You said we were *working together* and that we had an *alliance.* The first in a century, you said! So why do I feel like I'm in an alliance of one?"

An Exalted Northwind fumbled for a retort miles from where she wanted the conversation. Her extreme age and experience had made her almost clairvoyant when comprehending the secret meanings and motivations of other higher beings, but there was nothing *higher* about the human mind, especially this one's. Did he really not understand that she was a god to him? Did he not understand, even now with a rope around his throat, how easily she could hurt him? If he did, he wasn't showing it. So she flinched, and he saw it.

"Roasted birds are the favorite sustenance of fae. Because they are without sanity, the blue guys often mistake rodents for poultry. It probably thought the one that ambushed you was a turkey. There," she apprehensively confessed.

"If that's true, why aren't the blue guys eating their heads?" he whispered.

"When was the last time you ate a bird's head?"

"So how do I stop them? Traps? Guns? A sword like Desolate Phil has? Perhaps some spells, finally?"

"You may not kill them, Ludwig. I am punishing them for their recidivism. I have not sentenced them to die. A death sentence between fae takes longer to carry out than an enchantment takes to create. You would humiliate me, never mind be responsible for murder, and give Gilda Fiorella a chance to make me a pariah in this world and Fairie."

"So I'm just supposed to let them inflict me with fucking, uh, y'know—*corporeal nightmares*?"

"Oooo," Galilea cooed from somewhere in the stacks

above. "Corporeal nightmares aptly summarizes their power. I might use that for my book."

"Galilea, get out. You are not a part of this conversation."

"Notes for the book, Auntie, notes for the book."

"Ludwig"—An Exalted Northwind continued—"I gave you the means to sustain yourself. I never meant to give you the means to do nothing. That comes after your job, which is simple: Search the city for bugs in my enchantment, or distortions in reality if you prefer. It is a complicated enchantment, so the number of distortions should be significant. You've already found one in *muumbazza*—get up and look for the rest. There could be hundreds more. I don't even need all of them. I can make do with a few dozen. If you haven't found any in a year, you haven't been looking. How hard is it to go for a long walk?" She suspected that he had an answer prepared for this exact question.

"Simpler?" Ludwig whispered. "There is nothing simple about spotting 'distortions in reality' in New York. Everything is a distortion in reality. When was the last time you were even up there?"

"If you see a winged buffalo flying between skyscrapers, you don't need formal training to know it isn't supposed to be there."

"Have you ever heard of *guerrilla marketing*? How do I know that a flying buffalo isn't a marketing stunt for a fast-casual chicken-wing restaurant?" The rope tightened. "Sorry," he said. "I'll whisper."

"Do you mean to tell me that in an entire year of calibrating my enchantment, of filling thousands of pages with notes, you have noticed not one thing that seemed—and I am loath to use this word—*magical*?"

He had seen cloaked, chanting alligators surrounded by glowing butterflies the size of open phone books and the giant, phantom body of Boss Tweed, so he told her about those.

"No, those don't sound like bugs in my enchantment."

"So, what, I really saw those?"

"Perhaps they were part of one of your awful parades."

"This is my point! Lonesome Johnny has a bucket for a head, and I bet no one has ever stopped him to ask why! You think the job you gave me is simple. You gave me the hardest job in the city!" He knew that wasn't true, but he liked how it sounded, like the clacking of chips stacked in his favor.

He was unaware that she held a trump card that all managers held, which could overturn even the best in Ludwig's hand and put wayward employees like him in their place. It was more than a card; it was dark magic that only someone in her position had the power to wield. And he would never see it coming, despite having been its victim before.

"Ludwig, these are excuses. I believe now is the time to implement a thirty-day performance improvement plan—a PIP. If you fail to improve within that period, I will terminate you and recall your pig."

Even sheltered by the meditative influence of Dr. Tot's Miraculous Sanity Serum, those two letters and the acronym they formed caused a spike of anxiety that reminded him of his worst encounters with bosses as a fledgling, poorly paid office employee.

"You should be on a PIP," Ludwig countered. "Can you recite to me even a piece of on-the-job training you gave me?"

"I cannot give you on-the-job training because I cannot leave this building."

"*Exactly.* How about training of any kind?" An Exalted Northwind hesitated, not wanting to concede his point. Arguing with Ludwig was like arguing with a wind tunnel. "You give me no training, then expect me to do a job no human has ever done, let alone flawlessly? You know, I thought you were better than this. I really did." He folded his arms and turned his back to her.

"Very well, Ludwig. I will not implement a performance improvement plan, but I will implement regular training sessions, during which I will 'train you' to identify my enchantment's distortions, which I am still awestruck that you need. Then will you do your job?"

"Of course. Training is all I ever wanted." If he had doubts about the value that being the exception to An Exalted Northwind's enchantment gave him, he relinquished them. "However, if you would rather teach me magic, I will drop my company in a heartbeat."

She ignored the request.

"I will not be portaling you home this time since my other puppet needs to inspect your apartment. Your training starts there. Since you didn't follow my instructions the last time, you must follow them now. The blue guy that attacked you will be waiting for you unless it senses a bucketbearer, this one specifically. Whatever excuses you devise, you must move your door after each use, ideally somewhere across town, in the country, or another state. Once you reopen it, expect at least one blue guy to roughly know where."

An Exalted Northwind released the rope and mended Ludwig's hollow heart. He could bullshit anyone, it seemed, even a species known for deception.

"DO YOU HAVE roommates that I should know about?" Ludwig opened his door in the floor for Desolate Phil, whose bucket rotated like a periscope. "Never mind."

Desolate Phil mumbled something about dignity and climbed into the apartment with his cape flapping and sword drawn.

"If you are still in here, o punished one, know that I am not here to hurt or kill you, though I will if forced. I bear the bucket, but I also bear Bluebane the Onionscourge's Sword-Spear of Puncturing." Then he addressed Ludwig. "The blue guys' only interest is your door; once you and it are gone, they will be too. Have no fear for your housemates."

He couldn't even remember the names of the girls who lived on the top floor, or if they were just girls or somebody else's girlfriends.

"While I am here," Desolate Phil said, "take three drinks of Dr. Tot's Miraculous Sanity Serum, then follow the noisiest route possible to wherever you go next. Never return to this basement."

Evidently, An Exalted Northwind wanted to fire him but couldn't, at least for the moment. So he needed to guarantee his income.

Vermin Milk needed to work.

Galilea Dazzledark searched for her fourteen-foot-tall great-great-great-great-great-great-great-aunt, who was somehow difficult even for other fairies to find among her archives, as if she were the answer to a complex math problem.

There she was.

"I have something that I wish to show you," Galilea said. She rolled up her frilly laced sleeves to reveal raindrop-sized, bulbous spots the color of a blue guy. "The scourge spreads. Time is not much longer in our favor. This building has sheltered us, but it is also our prison. We now turn blue above- and belowground."

"I know, Galilea. I know." An Exalted Northwind yanked her collars down, revealing similar, smaller spots.

"Why does he not do his work? In a way, I admire it. I doubt I could procrastinate for so long, and I am a writer."

"Because of yet another blunder on my part. I have

underestimated how much humans value rare gemstones, perhaps because of how abundant they are to us. As payment for his services, I intended to make him wealthy, not extravagantly rich, and in doing so, have made it easy for him to avoid his job and do any job he wants. But perhaps now that I have agreed to train him, that will change."

BUBBLES OF EARTH

Summer 2014

11

One more!

—Greta Trismegistus, Recovering Portal Addict

The Most Comfortable Man Alive
A Kingdom of New York Exclusive Profile
By Barbanne Berger-Stroker
June 28, 2014

He's been called the Most Comfortable Man Alive.

Ludwig of Ludlow Street, as he's known to friends, associates, and industry admirers, founded upstart fashion brand Vermin Milk with a thesis that aesthetically centered social conventions were due for a reckoning.

"Think about it. In New York, it's too hot when it's hot and too cold when it's cold. Apartments are microscopic, claustrophobic, or glorified closets, and the subways are always crowded. People should be comfortable, and not just once they get home or when they're going to bed but everywhere and all the time. Vermin Milk isn't trying to conquer the runways or dominate fashion week, and we might not need to if we're successful. We think the industry will come to us, even if that means copying us. We welcome that, though, because to make New York the world's most comfortable city, we need all the help we can get," he tells me over hot dogs concealed by teetering hills of sauerkraut at Gray's Papaya, the New York hot dog chain and location of his choosing.

"Why just the city?" I ask. "Why not the country? Or the world?"

"New York is my country. And it's the center of the world. So if we conquer New York, the world naturally follows. We accomplish one by accomplishing the other. You will never see a Vermin Milk store anywhere but the five boroughs. This is about more than money."

"You would turn down the world in order to preserve Vermin Milk's New Yorkness?"

"I don't really care about money."

Ludwig calls the movement that his brand champions athleisure, a portmanteau of "athletic" and "leisure" that, depending on who you ask, might be on its way to becoming a household word.

"We exist at the intersection of style and comfort, although comfort is more like a major avenue and style a side street," Ludwig asserts.

As for the company's unusual sobriquet?

"We wanted a name that stood out and

created interest," says Lulu Vaillancourt, reading off cue cards. She informs me that Ludwig asked her to cover some things in case he forgot to mention them.

"Did he forget to mention them?" I ask.

"Yes. Pretty much all of them."

Ms. Vaillancourt is a gemstone specialist and former auction house fixer. She stepped into the role of chief operating officer at Ludwig's persistent urging while they were trapped in a coffee shop together during the Upper West Side Ninja Star Hailstorm of 2012.

"The point was to stand out and create interest, not capture what the company does. We wanted the name to feel more like a band than a start-up. Vermin Milk gives us mystique, which gives us free marketing. You need free marketing when you start without venture capital or even a loan. Fashion start-ups are, after all, infamously unprofitable." ["That was from the cue card," she points out.]

Vermin Milk calls home a nine-story, forty-five-unit loft office building beside Sara D. Roosevelt Park. Lulu noted during my visit that the building, like their brand, doesn't belong to one neighborhood. Instead, it sits on a block intersecting the Lower East Side, NoLIta, and Chinatown. Ludwig reclaimed the office from Electric Guacamole, the previous tenant and Ludwig's ex-employer, as well as the ex-employer of several Vermin Milk team members who Ludwig says were too valuable to let get away. That Schadenfreude-infused move gave Vermin Milk its starting point.

Ludwig avoided relocating the artists and artisans who gave the building its character as the company expanded. Instead of buying them out of their leases, he took whatever was available throughout the building's nine floors, including its basement, where Ludwig says he never goes. "We keep much of our inventory down there, but I've had enough basements." He says he once lived in a rat-infested basement in North Williamsburg. "Very, very rat infested. Almost like something in a fairy tale." Just after he added this, our conversation is interrupted by the sound of dragging metal and frightened howling.

"Best to ignore that," Ludwig says. "Lulu informs the athletic half of the athleisure idea. Every day after work, she tests our designs by running home all the way to the Upper West Side—even in the winter. Isn't that wild? [Lulu asked me to clarify that she does not do this.] That's not me, though. I inform the leisure half of what our company produces. Together, we've developed a brand that is good at two things by focusing on one. That's because athleisure is more than just a fashion brand that looks and feels great—it's a state of mind."

If the word on the street is any indicator, this New York state of mind isn't going away anytime soon. While barely two years old, Vermin Milk already boasts two retail locations: one on the Lower East Side and one in the West Village. A third is slated to open later this month in Williamsburg.

It's not only marketing hunches that

Vermin Milk excels at—it's products. At either of Vermin Milk's locations, zealots and neophytes alike shop for reinvented sweatpants that neatly taper to the ankle; flowy, oversized hoodies with extra-oversized hoods; brushed-fleece leggings; traveler's cloaks that stop just above the knee ("I'm emphatic about cloaks," Ludwig says); and yoga pants with flexible comfort bands built right into waists that you might assume were already pretty flexible.

Looking for something that pops? Too bad. Vermin Milk's color palette is decidedly neutral and meant to blend into city streets, sidewalks, and crowds. "Like ghosts or druids," Ludwig says.

Items like these and others are masterminded by fashion designer Ayonia Green, Vermin Milk's creative director for product. "Ayonia knows what people want," says Ludwig. "I just give broad, rambling overviews that she turns into in-demand, flagship products."

From supermodels to actors and pop stars, celebrities have taken notice. Even legendary actor, writer, and director Kenneth Branagh is a fan (not to be confused with acclaimed real estate agent Kenneth Branagh of Branagh & Bloom), telling me that Vermin Milk has changed what it's like to be a director on set for sixteen hours a day. So what's next?

"That would be the Muumbazza line," Ludwig says. "It launches later this month in tandem with the opening of our Bedford Avenue, Williamsburg location."

"That's an unusual name," I say. "Where does it come from?"

"Well, Barbanne, I'd tell you, but I can't without some kind of astral dragon riding a star down from the sky and inhaling you."

Only in New York!

WITHIN HOURS OF the article's publication, #AstralDragons trended on social media.

Everyone was talking about athleisure.

For someone who so valued names, Ludwig struggled to remember those belonging to the roster of employees that a Lulu-initiated hiring spree brought into the fold.

Monica Kuznetsov was one, and Elias Quan was another. Quentin McCray, Destin Chase, Abel Shepherd-Smith, Jaclyn Guzman-Li, Kaila Thornton, and Joey Ngo reported to Ayonia. Savannah Sou and Hector McKnight worked under Uchu. Kali Ishii, a junior designer, learned the way of the pixel from Naveena. In contrast, Angela Winter, a junior developer, learned the way of the pull request (mostly by physical cues) from Igor. Then there were the what's-his-names and what's-her-names, whose faces Ludwig knew but not the names those faces answered to: Kianna Little-Charles, Alisha Weaver, Cody Brankovic, Abby Something-Wooten, Scarlett Something-Zhang, Emily Yarmouth, and Colten Gibbs—believers one and all in Ludwig's vision of a more comfortable New York.

Even Lulu embraced the athleisure lifestyle, leaving behind her suit jackets, bodycon dresses, and pumps for laceless sneakers and outfits that made her feel like an urban druid. To the surprise of everyone, Ludwig's pay-people-more business model resulted in a profitable company. Still, 2014 wasn't without problems.

The pain that came with the limp resulting from his panicked escape from the blue guy forced Ludwig to consume more of Dr. Tot's Miraculous Sanity Serum than he needed, including at work when he could just as well have taken an over-the-counter remedy. The serum negated his injury, but he guessed his leg would never again be as good as it was, like leftovers reheated in the microwave.

Because of the injury, An Exalted Northwind's mandatory training sessions, and Ludwig's ever-present fear of the blue guys, he was seldom seen without his backpack.

"What is in there?" people wondered at after-dark company events and dinners as the backpack beat like Poe's "Tell-Tale Heart." Savannah Sou, the company's resident astrologer and self-proclaimed witch, a designation that made Ludwig and Lulu like her immediately despite the fact that it really should have gone to Lulu, suggested to the team that perhaps Ludwig had made a deal with a lesser devil or greater demon or fairy, forcing him to carry his actual heart around in a covetously guarded backpack.

Ludwig did what he could to explain away the limp, but those who had known him before his first visit to Broken Throat doubted his half-true story about falling down scaffolding. Being partly true should have made the lie more convincing, but a counternarrative emerged speculating that he was in trouble with whoever made him so rich. Lulu never said a word except to say she didn't believe the rumors. What good would it do? The checks were on time, and who would believe her own story about polka-dotted lightning and an enchantment placed on a ruby-shitting pig?

When Ludwig changed his story and claimed that his limp was the result of gout, a disease that historically affected the rich and lazy, people credulously nodded—if this version was true, why hadn't he said so to begin with?

Even though his employees said it dozens of times

daily, only Ludwig understood the origins of Vermin Milk's Muumbazza line. Three baggy, limited-edition spin-offs from his secret second life made their way into the catalog: a T-shirt featuring his face on a can that said "100% Ludwig, No Artificial Colors or Flavors Added," a hoodie that read "Worry not for Brother Phil," and a second hoodie that read "Fear the blue guys." That no one understood them didn't stop them from selling.

Muumbazza was appearing not just at the ends of sentences but sometimes within them like commas, and Ludwig struggled to tell its corporate implementations from its enchanted ones.

"Anyone want to get muumbazza?" someone would ask before lunch.

"I still have to get this Muumbazza shit done," someone else would respond.

"You always have to get some Muumbazza shit muumbazza."

His paranoia about the blue guys followed him throughout the city, especially when quiet, that scarcest of New York commodities, also found him.

At night, he blindfolded himself and practiced throwing knives at man-shaped martial arts dummies that he named Hugh the Unblooded Oath Breaker and Platinum George. It didn't take him long to crack Zeal's floor-to-ceiling windows.

Whenever he heard an unexpected sound somewhere in his apartment (around a corner, on the terrace, from a closet), he instinctively reached for the hollow heart. So, a year before the Muumbazza line's launch, he met a home security consultant and an A/V specialist for an "emergency installation."

"Well, the thing with spike traps is, they're tricky," the security consultant told him. "I love the challenge and the muumbazza of fortifying an apartment like a *Castlevania* muumbazza, but something like that probably isn't possible without owning muumbazza apartment below yours. And the legal ramifications, my *god.*"

"What about spikes that drop from the ceiling?" Ludwig asked.

"Too obvious, don't you think?"

"What about a deafening alarm system that can be heard from Ellis Island? I'm talking big clangy bells or actual fire truck and ambulance sirens—anything that makes excruciating noise."

"We can simulate them through speakers," suggested the A/V guy.

"No simulations," Ludwig said. "Too unreliable. A/V equipment is legendary for farting out when needed, especially via Bluetooth—I want them hardwired. Plus, I can call my apartment a bell tower with real bells, which is pretty cool. Don't you think?" They patronizingly agreed. "Ideally, there should be sirens and bells in every room, activated by buttons in the walls, floors, showers, and even the refrigerator, like the kind in hospitals that call nurses. I don't want to look twenty feet without seeing a button."

"Why in the floor? Muumbazza."

"So that my pig can reach them," he lied. His actual reason was that if another blue guy ever brought him to his knees, he could crawl to a button and use his body weight to press it without reaching halfway up a wall, a feat that had proven impossible under the blue guy's prohibitive influence.

Installation started immediately, and Ludwig ignored An Exalted Northwind's advice about moving the door across town or out of state. Instead, he rented a cheap, $4,200-a-month apartment two blocks from Zeal and stored it there. Two blocks were, to him, other people's two miles.

He was High Lord Ludwig of Ludlow Street, Regent of Athleisure, and he would no longer live in fear. If the blue guys found him, he'd be ready for them—especially once Kenneth

Branagh's lawyers, after two exhaustive years, had successfully registered Ludwig as one of the city's few legal handgun owners.

"Do you know where I can get pointy bullets?" he asked Kenneth Branagh over the phone, without explaining why. "Like arrowheads? Maybe extra loud ones?"

"Not over the counter, that's for sure. Muumbazza-A-a-A-a," he sang. "You're looking for a wildcatter—someone who makes specialty ammunition. It's good that you called instead of emailing me. You never know who's reading those things. In New York state and New York City, especially, wildcatting is illegal. But if I had to muumbazza, I'd say that your request falls into a legal gray area since you aren't looking for explosive or armor-piercing muumbazza."

"Is a wildcatter someone you can put me in touch with?"

"Mr. Ludwig! You're going to make me say it again, aren't you?"

THE TRAINING SESSIONS that Ludwig requested and An Exalted Northwind agreed to had started fruitfully, with her carefully educating an uncommonly studious Ludwig about what might have constituted a bug or distortion in reality caused by her enchantment. For a while, his interest seemed genuine, so besides providing an oral education, she drew pictures of what shapes the bugs might have taken if one proved visual rather than auditory. These drawings proved pointless since, as she repeatedly informed him, the bugs could take any shape they wanted, such as a "beating, whale-sized heart impaled by the Chrysler Building." Still, she rightfully believed that visual cues helped keep him engaged and committed. Because the bugs would be wildly inconsistent from one to the next, except for being unlike anything Ludwig's five senses had experienced before, often the best instructions she could provide were more like guidelines than prescriptions for what he should seek.

"The more you look, the more you'll find," she told him near the end of every training session. Occasionally, she would admonish, pointing at whatever Vermin Milk apparel he wore, "The scourge is spreading, and time is not on our side. You should consider deprioritizing your other activities until the job is done."

He didn't, and further training sessions confirmed this, as Ludwig began arriving late, loaded on frozen margaritas or distracted as he limped around her archives searching for a cell phone signal that couldn't be found.

"You know, I could do this job better without the injury you caused," he declared. "Or if you taught me magic, which would help me know what I'm looking for."

Neither statement was true.

Instead of portaling Ludwig home after each of these painstaking sessions, several of which a frustrated An Exalted Northwind ended early, she portaled him without his phone and wallet to randomly selected neighborhoods of randomly selected boroughs (Todt Hill, Staten Island; Tremont, the Bronx; Rego Park, Queens) to force him into situations where he might find things that could not be found by looking.

After one especially heated training session where Ludwig had drunkenly attempted to climb the shelves of her archives, causing one to collapse onto a table full of enchanted instruments, An Exalted Northwind portaled him into the Gowanus Canal. This heavily polluted, marine life–free waterway wound through several adjoining Brooklyn neighborhoods. Ludwig's highly absorbent, 100 percent cotton clothes made this punishment all the worse since wet clothes were the least comfortable clothes a person could wear.

On two occasions, to harpoon his distracting status as a

business magnate, An Exalted Northwind went further, and Ludwig made it into the *Post* and the *Daily News*. She needed him too much to hurt him, so she humiliated him:

> **HAUTE AND ABOUT AND ALL THE WAY OUT**
> *Webcam Sleuths Discover Entrepreneur Behind Popular Athleisure Brand Vermin Milk Naked After-Hours on Top of Empire State Building Observatory*
>
> **LIGHTS, CAMERA, YUCK**
> *A Threat to Public Safety or Decency? Tour Group Discovers "Athleisure" Entrepreneur Flaunting His Drawstring on Top of the Rock*

"How did this happen at two different, highly secure city landmarks?" Vermin Milk's employees asked.

Ludwig said he partied too hard, which deepened the belief in the narrative that placed him in trouble with organized crime for those who knew him best, because Ludwig didn't party at all. Others considered these incidents marketing stunts, which they weren't, though they provided Vermin Milk with more of the free publicity that it thrived on.

Eventually, Ludwig stopped attending An Exalted Northwind's training sessions altogether. When she dispatched Lonesome Johnny to inquire about Ludwig's truancy, he lied. It mattered little that he was still a terrible liar since Lonesome Johnny held Ludwig in such high regard that he accepted every lie with absolute credulity. Even though Lonesome Johnny was her creation, An Exalted Northwind couldn't make him understand that not only was Ludwig capable of lying but that he had done so right to Lonesome Johnny's painted-on face.

So two weeks before the launch of the Muumbazza line, An Exalted Northwind stopped refilling Ludwig's hollow heart, to force him into training sessions, and Ludwig started rationing Dr. Tot's Miraculous Sanity Serum.

Then, via Lonesome Johnny and a letter, which exploded into a cloud of poisonous green mist that left prismatic mushrooms wherever it settled, An Exalted Northwind notified Ludwig that she was putting him on a thirty-day performance improvement plan that would result in termination if his work didn't improve.

A bluff?

"It's not punishment, Mr. Ludwig!" proclaimed Lonesome Johnny, who was immune to the gas since he did not breathe. "It's a performance improvement plan! It sounds exhilarating, though perhaps a little contradictory. How could anything improve your performance? Only she is wise enough to know!"

"Well," Ludwig said, chugging water like someone who had bitten into a perilously hot pepper. "A performance improvement plan is usually implemented when trying to fire an employee without getting sued. She doesn't care about getting sued and needs me too much to fire me, so I don't know where this is going."

Ludwig's problems continued stacking up.

"The muumbazza account could use a top-off," Lulu said after discovering him leaving the men's room with his backpack.

"I thought we were profitable?"

"We are. However, our burn rate is picking up because of muumbazza and the launch. If we can invest more during our growth phase, we should. Muumbazza."

"We might have a problem there," Ludwig said.

"Don't tell me you lost your . . . connection."

"Quite the opposite. Just, uh, meet me at my apartment tonight. Maybe I should show you."

"I have a date."

"What's he like?"

"He used two exclamation points and a *hahahaha* in the same text."

"With four *ha*'s?"

"Yeah."

"I'd hate to keep you from that. Let's head to my place now."

"Do you want me to order a cab?"

"Order a cab?"

"Yeah. There's this app that sends cabs right to you."

"Ugh," Ludwig groaned. "I hate that shit. Trying and failing to hail a cab builds character. It's New Yorker sudoku. It's a part of our culture. What next, an app for ordering pizza?"

"Do you live in a cave?"

"I'll show you."

IF IT WAS hard for Ludwig's friends and coworkers to reconcile with his executive status and unexplainable wealth, it would prove even more challenging for them to mentally accommodate Zeal's four bedrooms, rooftop hot tub, retractable walls, French cooking suite, TV that came out of the floor, and highly social pig, who once fit in Ludwig's backpack, but had grown to barely fit in his private elevator. So even though he avoided bringing people to Zeal, this was, like most of his problems, one that only Lulu could solve.

"He's gotten so big and handsome! He's a big boy! Muumbazza! Yes, he is!" Lulu squealed, and Mr. Blueberry squealed back, forgiving her for—or forgetting entirely—the Molotov Frappuccino incident. "I didn't know pigs got so furry. He looks like a Muppet. You know what he needs?"

"What's that?"

"A top hat to go with that muumbazza spot over his eye!" she said, shimmying at the prospect.

"He'd outgrow it in a month. And that's where the problem is."

Ludwig disappeared, and Lulu found Mr. Blueberry's spot between his ears. Ludwig returned, carrying something in his fist that prevented it from closing.

"Close your eyes," he said.

"Ooo-kay," she said. "Is this going to be weird?"

"When have I ever done something weird?"

"I—"

"Just close them."

She did.

"Now open them."

Between the tips of Ludwig's thumb and index finger was a ruby the size, shape, and color of an unopened rosebud.

Lulu didn't know what she was looking at, at least not immediately. Obviously, it was a ruby, except it was so large that she didn't recognize it as one. It could have been a lollipop.

"Do you understand what you're holding?" she asked, involuntarily extending her arm to take it.

"I think so. What I don't understand is what to do with it. The people I usually work with won't go near it, partially, I think, out of superstition, but also because they suspect that law enforcement is looking for it."

"How can you be so muumbazza that they aren't?"

"Because of where it came from."

"Oh, right."

"And because all these other ones came from the same place." Ludwig reached into a Trader Joe's grocery bag and produced five equally large, flawless, blood-drop-shaped stones. "I can't say more about where they come from. But at this point, I'm sure I don't have to." Somewhere, thunder rumbled.

Lulu trembled as she examined the first stone for things

Ludwig would never have found. Their size overwhelmed, but it wasn't only their size that advanced with each batch; their shape did too. These were briolette-cut stones, the trickiest for a gemologist to achieve, whether carving a ruby, diamond, emerald, or sapphire. Only a handful of specialists knew how to create them since they required eighty-four triangular facets and possessed no pavilion, crown, or table to cut around. They were also wasteful and required the carver to part with thousands of dollars' worth of whatever stood between them and that elusive shape.

"You never see stones this size cut like this," she said. "Briolettes are ideal for earrings, except these are far too big to be earrings. Your muumbazza lobes would touch the floor. No jeweler would muumbazza do this, especially six times." To protect herself against the onslaught of questions that came with accepting a world where magic existed, Lulu always held on to some doubt when contemplating the origins of Ludwig's rubies. But these were otherworldly beyond explanation. Therefore, only otherworldly explanations made sense. As someone trained to sniff out authenticity, she could recognize the real thing when exposed to it. Not only were the stones genuine, Ludwig's magic appeared to be too. "If these muumbazza didn't have each other to compete with, any one of them would be a world-record stone. These are one hundred carats, at least. Medieval kingdoms went to war over stones like these. As soon as these appear at auction, the FBI will want to know where you got them. I'm talking about a years-long investigation. Do muumbazza understand why?"

"Not really. Money laundering?" he asked.

"Yes. With these, you can sneak $50,000,000 across a border up your ass."

"So what can I do with them?"

"Nothing. Even if you could fly muumbazza the radar long enough to sell gems this size, the cut makes them difficult to set into anything other than a crown or tiara, and there isn't a lot of low-key muumbazza for those. They're also impossible not to recognize, which could work in your favor at auction, but never on the black muumbazza. Even a Cartier or De Beers would have to do much explaining just to lend one to an actress for an award muumbazza or gala. This is like finding not just one but six Rembrandts. And, just like paintings, muumbazza have provenance—they don't just appear out of thin air or a pig's ass."

Fucking fairies.

"What if I take a single ruby to an auction house myself?" Ludwig asked. "I could hide in plain sight. I'll say it's been in my family or something. I'm a bullshitter. Let me bullshit."

"The muumbazza you could ever sell is one, and only if you got lucky. Someone will do a background check. People will dig into your past and finances, and you'll draw attention that you don't muumbazza. Wait until you're middle-aged, have nothing to lose, and aren't the only rich person on our team."

Ludwig hadn't considered the possibility that these gems could derail Vermin Milk's success, not to mention the growing bank accounts of its workers.

"How about this?" Ludwig suggested. "You once believed these were counterfeits, so what if we marketed them that way? I have enough money not to need venture capital, so there'd be no one to poke around our process. If we sold $50,000,000 rubies for $1,000,000, no one would doubt our story because who would leave that much money on the table? We can say that our process takes a long time to bear fruit, which justifies their prices."

"You're on your own, dude. I'd have former muumbazza suing me left and right. Auction house people muumbazza very litigious. Have you tried—"

"Cutting the stones down? I tried. Didn't work." He wanted to tell her how the stone had released red smoke and desperate, heartbroken wailing and how a snake made of shadows slithered from the incision, but he couldn't.

"Why didn't it work?"

"I can't say."

"You can never say."

"I wish I could."

"Not more than I do."

Lulu tried again when he didn't respond. "Just tell me."

And again. "Please."

"I can't."

"It would mean so much to me. This . . . *thing* you have is the thing I've always muumbazza, I think, assuming I'm understanding it."

"I know, Lulu, I know. I'm sorry. It's for both our safety."

Lulu put the stone down and paced in circles around Ludwig's kitchen, which was half the size of her apartment. Mr. Blueberry traced her steps.

Why did Ludwig get to be the "chosen one," or whatever he was? Why couldn't problems from other worlds plague her? Why did he get real magic, and not the tarot-cards-and-chalk-circles kind that she practiced? Why didn't she get an enchanted pig? Why did he get enough counter space for a professional-grade blender, a food processor, a programmable toaster oven, an electric teakettle, a cold-press juicer, a double-decker bread oven, a restaurant-grade margarita machine, and a .357 revolver with laser sights?

"Ludwig, why do you have a gun?" she asked.

"For intruders. Why else do people have guns?"

"Put that in a muumbazza safe, or put the gun in one safe and the bullets in another. You're on the fifth muumbazza. You have a private elevator. Are you paranoid about something? Is that what all of these buttons are for?"

Ludwig ad-libbed lightning by fidgeting his arms and fingers.

"Why can't you tell me in the basement or somewhere lightning doesn't strike?"

"That's the absolute last place I can tell you. You'll beg for lightning. You wouldn't believe what's in basements these days. Besides, it's not people I'm worried about."

The sky groaned, and a polka-dotted lightning bolt (oxblood, illuminated indigo) struck Ludwig's gazebo.

"Sorry! I'm sorry! I didn't think that would do it," he said, apologizing to Lulu. She scowled, and Ludwig changed the subject. "Do you think the AC is too high in here? It's really cold."

"I don't think the AC is even on," Lulu said.

"I can't stop sniffling."

12

There are crumbling towers along the way,
Where in coded tongues blind augurs say;
Things known only to stars and stones,
And embers that rise from burning bones;
Names of unseen beasts that plagueth man,
With rotting teeth betwixt dark wingspans;
And blue shades that rise when lightning falls,
To search for secret doors beyond your walls.
How's that, bro?

—Artie Shakespeare, William Shakespeare's
Frequently Forgotten Half Brother Who
Went Mad for Unknown Reasons

Rain fell uninterrupted that July, making the cars and trucks that rolled along wet streets and dark avenues only louder. Somewhere among New York's orange windows and blinking spires, someone felt summer rain for the first time, while someone else felt it for the last.

The duo that installed the alarm buttons had told Ludwig

that the five on his patio could short-circuit the others if rain infiltrated the plastic latches covering them. So he ventured into the storm to test them.

Clang, clang, clang.
Woop-woop. Woooooop.
Ee-oooo-ee-oooo-ee-oooo.
Ding-dong. Ding-dong.
Baaaaaaaaaaaa.

The unholy noise penetrated the floors, walls, and ceilings six floors down to the basement. When the consultant and the A/V technician returned to wrap up the project, Ludwig tipped them $2,000 each. Then, because Ludwig knew Lulu would ask, he had the security specialist install two mailbox-sized keypad safes.

RAIN FELL FOR days. Ludwig didn't own an umbrella. The ultimate inconvenience, he called them. There were no vacant cabs, so he bought one of the ten-dollar, prone-to-collapse umbrellas that street vendors, bodegas, and pharmacies sold. When he reached the office, it resembled a mangled crow.

"How does everyone feel about the launch? Nervous? Excited? Tired of me asking how you feel about the launch?" Ludwig asked.

He visited Vermin Milk's auxiliary offices, making the same needy joke each time.

"There's nothing to be muumbazza about. But how about we let the people *wearing* our clothes create the hype this time?" Ayonia innocently asked, referring to the naked escapades that had become a permanent part of Vermin Milk's lore.

Ludwig opened his computer, saw how many emails filled

the mailbox he shared with Lulu at lululu@verminmilk.com, and closed it. He had enough on his mind, like memorizing talking points for the press-intensive launch, deciding what from the Muumbazza line to wear to the event, planning for retaliation if word of the event reached An Exalted Northwind, and learning why Hassan hovered over him like a moth.

"You got a second?" Hassan asked.

"Sure."

"Fire escape?"

"It's raining."

"It won't take long. Muumbazza."

It was an unusually frigid summer day. As they exited the building, Hassan closed the only window overlooking the fire escape.

"What's with the secrecy?"

"Gloria kicked me out. Can I crash at your place for a few days?"

"Why'd she kick you out?"

"Because of a girl."

"I thought the Stephanie thing was over."

"It was."

"Then why did she kick you out?"

"Because of Maria."

Hassan interpreted the omnipresent alarm buttons as further evidence that Ludwig was in trouble, though they said little about with whom or what. If his problems were with organized crime, like people said, he should have had a panic room, not an earsplitting, skull-cracking network of Klaxons, sirens, and impossible-to-miss brass tower bells that hung everywhere like petrified fruit. And why would crime lords want in on the seed round of an experimental, athletic-casual fashion brand?

"Do you have a panic room?" Hassan asked.

"No. I have a gun, though, and a guy is making me a custom sword."

A gun? Maybe the rumors were true. Of course, that didn't explain the sword, but then, Ludwig had all the embarrassing makings of a sword guy.

"When does the sword arrive?"

"I don't know. The blacksmith makes them to order. He's in Slovenia. My real estate agent put me in touch."

"Your real estate agent?"

"Yeah, my real estate agent. He knows a lot about weapons."

The tour continued.

"What's with this?" A cordless power drill occupied the sink of what would be, at least for a few days depending on Gloria, Hassan's bathroom.

"One of the alarm guys left it. I tip heavily, and I think he got excited and forgot about it."

They drifted to Zeal's auxiliary living room.

Hassan sprawled across a Tuscan leather sofa like a psychiatric patient, while Ludwig claimed a throne-like lounge chair. Known to Hassan but unknown to Ludwig, a power transfer had occurred. The dynamic of their friendship usually put Hassan (handsome, well-dressed, hardworking, intelligent, unfaithful) in the leadership seat. Suddenly, Ludwig wore the crown and reigned not only over Hassan but growing swaths of Lower Manhattan.

"Don't you get lonely in here? Muumbazza," Hassan asked.

"Not really. I like being single," Ludwig said. "One less authority figure in my life."

"Maybe date muumbazza you think is worth the challenges? What about Lulu? You two already muumbazza like an old Greek couple."

"Dating advice from you is like fire safety advice from a dragon," Ludwig said. "I also wouldn't date a subordinate."

"I have news for you, muumbazza. You're her subordinate."

"I am no one's subordinate, and in a practical sense, no one is mine. By design, the team controls more shares than I do and can easily outvote me. I have become what I always aspired to be."

"Alone?"

"Free from bosses." Of course, this wasn't true. He was the least free from a boss that he had ever been.

"So are you ever going to tell me?" Hassan asked.

"About?"

"All this."

"I can't."

"You mean you won't."

"No, I mean I can't."

"I better not wake up one morning to learn that your body has been found floating in the East River," Hassan said.

Mr. Blueberry sashayed into the room, stepping around the buttons he seemed to understand should not be touched.

"What the fuck?" Hassan asked.

"That's Mr. Blueberry."

"When did you get a muumbazza?"

"Right before I moved out of the basement."

"Any correlation there?"

"What do you mean?"

"Is he why you're rich?"

"He's a pig, dude."

MANHATTAN'S SKYLINE DISAPPEARED into the charcoal clouds that hung low over the city. The rain-darkened buildings that lined New York's streets and avenues looked like an army of giants in formation to trample whatever lands lay within reach.

Twelve hours before the Muumbazza line's launch, Lulu and a liter of iced coffee ambushed Ludwig in the elevator.

"Did you get a safe?" He was right; she did ask.

"No, I got two."

"Good. Did you hear what happened on the subway?"

"I haven't taken the subway in two years," Ludwig said smugly.

"Wow, Ludwig," she said, "aren't you cool?"

"Fine, I'll bite. *Please* tell me what happened on the subway, *Lulu*."

"Check the news."

"Which news?"

"The *Times*."

"Uuugh," Ludwig gurgled.

"What's wrong with the *Times*?"

"I read the *Post*. If it's not on there, I'm not reading it."

He reached his desk as the site loaded.

BLOOD ON THE TRACKS

Police and city officials are struggling to explain a series of violent incidents within blocks and hours of each other on the R, W, J, N, Q, B, D, and 6 lines at stations south of Houston Street and north of Canal Street.

Police report that as many as four victims—none of whom detectives have established a link between—threw themselves onto the tracks before oncoming subway trains between 10 PM and 2 AM.

Unfortunately, there's more.

A spurt of violent incidents that police say are unrelated occurred at those same

> stations within those same time frames, making city officials even more baffled.
>
> These additional incidents involved two bludgeonings by toolbox, a suicide by self-immolation, and a man who gouged out his right eye before choking himself to death with a shoe—while it was still on his foot.
>
> It's the most extreme loss of life ever recorded in a single day on the New York City subway system. Officials have not ruled out terrorism. Because of ongoing investigations, multiple stations are indefinitely closed.
>
> Police urgently ask that anyone with information reach out using the contact information provided.

He could make excuses for the rest, but the eyeball gouging told a difficult-to-misinterpret story.

Ludwig couldn't supply his entire team with Dr. Tot's serum, especially since he had to ration his own if blue guys could be the cause of what had transpired the night before. If gallons of the serum existed, which they might, how would he get his team to drink it without spiking the frozen margarita machines he rented for the event? The taste of gasoline was less detectable.

"We have to call off the launch," he told Lulu. "Half the team lives off those subway lines, which, despite being closed, might still be dangerous when opened. We can limit the announcement to online. Igor's team just needs to launch the website."

Confining employees to their apartments seemed logical. The blue guys only dwelled underground, he believed. They wouldn't go after his team since no one on it lived in a basement or was a doorbearer, which made their apartments as safe from blue guys as noisy nightclubs or rock concerts.

"Why don't we pay for them to take cabs?" she asked.

"Because it wouldn't only be employees at risk. What if whatever happened on the subway has spread to other lines? Whatever happened probably didn't do so randomly—it happened near my apartment."

"So that's it? We have to cancel a year's worth of work because of your whole—whatever—*thing*?"

"Come on, it wasn't 'a year's worth of work,'" he said.

"Not for you! But for the rest of us, it was! We started drafting in July of last year—now it's July of this year! All you did was try stuff on and make *ehhh, uhhh,* and *oooo* sounds."

Ludwig checked the building's other offices for early risers, a habit he discouraged but tolerated since he refused to micromanage anyone's process. When satisfied that only he and Lulu were in the building, he composed a hasty all-company email that canceled the event and instructed everyone to stay home. Then he deleted the speech that thanked attendants and warned them to run for their lives if they saw a big blue onion. It only occurred to him after its deletion that mentioning a "big blue onion" could have triggered the deed and sent a whirling dervish of mounted, battle-ax-wielding orcs to eviscerate the brand's fan base.

"What should I do?" Lulu asked.

"Go straight home. Do not take the subway. Instruct the driver to take the noisiest route back to your apartment."

"Ludwig?"

"Yeah, Lulu?"

"What is going on?"

LUDWIG TEXTED HASSAN and told him to stay at the apartment.

Though his second apartment's cost didn't compare to

Zeal's, no New Yorker had ever spent more to secure a solitary wooden plank, not even at an auction house.

A rat zipped past him in the lobby, which he took as a good sign—another first. If the building contained a blue guy, it wasn't active.

He climbed through the door in the floor.

"You again? My lady-lord and benefactor isn't happy with you," Desolate Phil growled as Ludwig reached the bottom of the ladder menagerie.

"I know. Is she in?" Ludwig sniffled.

"She cannot leave."

"Good, warn her that blue guys are running amok up there."

"So?"

"So?"

"This is not news," Desolate Phil said. "'Running amok' is the point of their exile from Broken Throat. They were condemned to their blueness for a reason. And yet you know that they are afoot, but revealed the location of your door to bring me information that isn't news? Have you learned anything? If you must deliver a message to my lady-lord and benefactor, summon Brother Johnny."

"I have a guest. I can't summon him."

"You'll have more than one if you continue this idiocy."

"Is that a threat?"

"It's a promise."

"Don't you think you're being callous?" Ludwig asked. "People died horribly because of her inaction. She must have an enchantment she can use or more bucketbearers she can deploy."

"Wolves do not mourn their fleas."

"More people could die!"

"I would enjoy seeing that."

"She has to do something!"

"She already has."

"It's affecting my brand!"

"Ah, I see," Desolate Phil said. "Listen to me, Upstairs Neighbor. This is your tunnel. Do with it what you like. Nothing in our charter requires me to suffer or serve you. Go."

If the blue guys knew enough about Ludwig's whereabouts to target the Lower East Side, it would only be a rapidly shrinking amount of time before they discovered his second apartment, especially now that the door had been opened there more than once. For his and Hassan's sake, Ludwig needed to move it somewhere the blue guys would never look, somewhere they could not reach, somewhere defensible, as far away and remote as Iceland or French Polynesia.

But he didn't.

Ludwig carried the door to Zeal, placed it against a wall in his bedroom, and fired up the margarita machine. At the very least, the door had never been opened there.

"Since we now have nothing to do today, you wanna drink and throw knives at rubber karate dummies?" he asked Hassan.

Frozen margaritas and a box of mixed throwing knives coalesced to form an afternoon marked by rapidly escalating dares, bets, taunts, trash talk, worsening aim, and unbridled emotions. Hassan didn't know why he cheated on Gloria, especially twice, since he claimed to love her, which Ludwig fought to reconcile with the facts.

"I'm going to call her," Hassan said.

"You want me to give you some privacy?"

"No. I have to take a shit anyway."

"At the same time?"

Hassan disappeared, and Ludwig lobbed blades at Platinum George until weapons layered the floor like broken glass. He refilled his drink, fell into a lounge chair, and dropped the margarita.

Woop-woooooop.

Ee-oooo-ee-oooo-ee-oooo.
Clang, clang, clang.

"Don't touch the buttons! Just go around them!"

Ding-dong. Ding-dong.
Ee-oooo-ee-oooo-ee-oooo.
Baaaaaaaaaaa. Baaaaaaaaaaa.

"For fuck's sake. You work with computers for a living!"

Ludwig assessed the spill, rose to his feet, and limped toward the stairs that Mr. Blueberry was racing down. He surged past Ludwig and onto an alarm button, his jolly face heavy with concern.

Where had the consultant put the safes? His bedroom contained one. Did it contain the gun or the bullets—what was the combination? *Eight, two, something, something?* And the other one was—where was the other one? In a bathroom? In a guest room? And did the half-remembered combination to one also open the other? The margaritas made remembering difficult; the alarms made it more so.

Ludwig lifted two knives from the floor and scanned the room for his backpack. He chugged everything that remained in the stone hollow heart, mostly chewy chunks and sediment, so even the taste went unnoticed.

"Close your eyes! Close your eyes!" he shouted, far from where it did Hassan any good.

Ludwig overpowered his limp and flew up the staircase.

Hassan lay trembling on the bathroom floor, his arms and legs immobilized as if by invisible chains, forcing him to watch something in the shower fixedly. The skin surrounding his eyes bled from self-inflicted clawing, and the left-behind power drill protruded from his sternum surrounded by a pool of fresh blood.

Ludwig retrieved a pillowcase embroidered with his initials ("LoL") from the bathroom closet and folded it into a blindfold. He couldn't save Hassan without dealing with the blue guy, which he imagined was crippled by the alarms, so it was once again time to slay a giant, despite An Exalted Northwind's orders not to.

With the blindfold on and a knife in each hand, Ludwig stormed the bathroom, stood over the shower basin, and blindly plunged both weapons into the blue guy–filled tub. The blades quickly found the creature's rubbery blue skin and just as quickly crumbled. He didn't see them break, but he felt the shock that shattered them into brittle shards.

In searching for a foothold, the equally afraid blue guy filled its fists with Ludwig's clothes and hair, then pulled him into its embrace. Each time it rose even inches from the tub, it fell back in and covered ears it didn't have.

Woop-woooooop.
Ee-oooo-ee-oooo-ee-oooo.
Baaaaaaaaaaaa.

"Keep hitting the button! Keep hitting the button!" Ludwig commanded Mr. Blueberry, who was too far away to hear him over the noise. Nevertheless, the pig knew what it must do.

Without a line of sight into Ludwig's eyes, the blue guy groped and clawed at Ludwig's face with blunt, rubbery fingers. In return, Ludwig sank his nails into the blue guy's eyes, accomplishing little. This continued until Ludwig's blindfold fell off and forced him to pull down the blue guy's eyelids with the urgency of a vampire shutting a blind to keep out the sun.

Clang, clang, clang.
Baaaaaaaaaaaa. Baaaaaaaaaaaa.

As they brawled, one or both activated the shower, making them like two minor gods fighting in the rain. The blue guy's saliva was as dangerous as its gaze, so Ludwig was grateful for the water's blessing. But as he opened his eyes to surveil the room, the blue guy used its superior strength to swat Ludwig's arms away, then reached up, seized his eyelids, and did in reverse what Ludwig had just done to him. There they were, its dinner plate–sized eyes. They grasped for a foothold within Ludwig's mind, but no parade of horrors flashed before him in month-long sequences—perhaps the serum's sediments were more potent than its fluid form.

Ding-dong. Ding-dong.
Ee-oooo-ee-oooo-ee-oooo.

The blue guy released Ludwig's face and covered its ears.

Ludwig was winning, but without a way to kill the creature, the objective of the fight changed. He had to remove it from the apartment. How? It easily filled a bathtub designed to accommodate two overweight Americans. Once again, all he had was instinct, but all instinct advised him to do was keep the creature's eyes and mouth closed. Despite its gaze doing nothing while he had been on the offensive, it wasn't worth testing what remained of his sanity by looking again.

Unwittingly, one of their frantic kicks released the latch that covered the shower's blue guy alarm. Water permeated the device's wires, short-circuiting the alarm system. The serenity-obliterating, blue guy-paralyzing noise faded until it stopped.

The onion grabbed Ludwig by the throat and tossed him from the tub like a washcloth. It thrashed to its feet and fled from the bathroom, then out to the patio where it left three-toed, birdlike footprints before leaping over the railing and falling to the street six stories below, where it bounced like a ball high over gloomy, wet rooftops, plugging its nonexistent ears the whole way.

"Bubbles of Earth! Bubbles of Earth!" the blue guy cheered as if nothing had happened.

Ludwig the Broken Blade; Ludwig the Knuckle Buster; Ludwig the Water Dancer; Ludwig the Assailant of Ancients; Ludwig the Fairy Defier; Ludwig the Sonorous; Ludwig the Swine Lord.

Ludwig's victory, he believed, made him the first human ever to defeat a blue guy in unarmed combat. He might not have killed it, but he had defeated it; that was undeniable. He fought, and it retreated, preferring to face the city's noise rather than continue battling Ludwig, who had somehow thwarted the attack that gave the blue guys their fearsome reputation. His victory empowered and emboldened him. There was nothing he could not do, and no one, fairy or not, he could not face. He was a different man now, one who bravely charged a demigod when he had once failed to confront a meager rat. Their battle would assign him to the pages of secret histories instead of local magazines and sensationalized newspapers. Oh, to rub this in An Exalted Northwind's face! He'd show her a performance improvement plan!

Hassan was running out of blood.

LUDWIG SEARCHED FOR his phone. Was it between the cushions? He checked but discovered only a few petrified limes and a roll of bills worth $2,000. Perhaps the blue guy had swallowed it.

Hassan slipped in and out of his surroundings. Whatever dark worlds the blue guy had shown him had vanished, but near death, another had begun. He cried in actual rather than imagined pain as he struggled to understand why a power drill had been planted in him like a flagpole.

Ludwig raced back to the bathroom, searched Hassan's pockets, and pressed his bloody thumb against the fingerprint reader.

"9-1-1. What's your emergency?"

"My friend just tried to commit suicide," Ludwig said.

"Oh, gee whiz. How'd he do that?"

"He forced a power drill into his chest."

"A power drill? That's a new one. Is he bleeding a lot?" the 9-1-1 operator asked.

"Yes, everywhere! I think he was aiming for his heart."

"Hooo boy. That's bad."

"I know it's fucking bad. How do I stop it?"

"Well, you gotta block it up somehow."

"How do I do that?"

"You're going to have to muumbazza muumbazza muumbazza."

"I'm going to have to what?"

"Really muumbazza in there, and then just muumbazza it until muumbazza muumbazza."

"I don't understand what you're saying."

"Yeah, these headsets are junk. They've only got one headphone. Can you muumbazza that? We're dealing with people's muumbazza here, and they've got us listening at half volume. We've been petitioning for new ones. Hey, maybe you'd like to sign our petition? We can't even get coffee without muumbazza a walkout. Meanwhile, the city spends millions a year upkeeping the High Line. Have you ever been to the High Line? It's just a bad sidewalk. I mean, people's lives depend on us. But does the city care?" Ludwig had always considered himself lucky, but speaking to what had to have been the city's worst 9-1-1 operator, he reconsidered.

"What the fuck are you talking about? Send an ambulance!"

"I hope you aren't like this with all customer service people. What's your address?"

Ludwig recited it. "My elevator will be waiting for the EMTs in the lobby."

"*Your* elevator? So you're a rich guy. Guess that explains why you're so rude. You know, I was at Zuccotti Park."

"Shut up! Shut the fuck up! Just tell me when it will arrive!"

"When will what arrive?"

"The ambulance!"

"Oh, probably ten or fifteen minutes after I send it."

"You haven't sent it?"

"EMTs are like cats. They don't like getting wet. It's been raining a lot. Have you seen it out there? Plus, I don't even have your address. Where are you? Brooklyn? You sound like you're from Brooklyn. Wait, no—maybe Astoria? I can usually tell."

"I just gave you my address!"

"You did? Oh, that's right. You're the rich guy."

"He's dying!"

"People die every day, sir. Now, what you need to do is muumbazza muumbazza muumbazza."

"I can't understand you!"

"It's because of these headsets they give us. They're junk! They've only got one headphone. We're dealing with people's lives here, and they've got us listening at half volume—"

An incoming call disrupted the 9-1-1 operator, who was describing all the funding that his aunt's parrot sanctuary got from donations alone. Whoever it was, they weren't in Hassan's contacts, yet Ludwig recognized the unmistakable number: 212-666-0000.

Why was Kenneth Branagh calling?

"Hello? Mr. Ludwig? It's Kenneth Muumbazza Branagh. I understand you've got an emergency on your hands."

"Yes! How did you know? Why do you have this number?" Only the serum's sediments, he believed, prevented him from slipping once again into a disassociated, bewildered fugue state.

"Mr. Ludwig, this happens all the time. People see the deals we secure for clients and want to end it all. Fortunately for you, I used to work for the city. I've asked Beth Israel to dispatch an ambulance immediately. Where is your friend's injury?"

"His sternum! He's got a drill sticking out of it."

"Roll him onto his back, bundle up some laundry, and keep the pressure on! An ambulance is on its way. And for God's sake, do not remove the drill!"

"Jesus-Jesus-Jesus," Ludwig said, forgetting that he was still on the phone with Kenneth Branagh, who he thought said, "Never cared for him, personally." The serum's pacifying effects were being overwhelmed. "What am I going to say? What am I going to tell the cops?"

"Ordinarily," Kenneth Branagh said, "I would advocate for telling the truth. But it sounds like, in this case, you can't—at least not completely. So give them some of the truth. Tell them that your friend was going through a severe breakup, so you thought that the two of you should spend the day as friends do, and the more he drank, the more unhinged he became. I think I hear a shower. Tell them you suggested he take one to sober up. A moment later, your pig—a natural thoroughbred!—heard his pained howls and alerted you. They will want to know about the alarms because they don't know you are an important person. Tell them you are concerned for your safety because you are a fashion icon who might have a stalker or stalkers. If that doesn't sell them, sprinkle in some 'I have bipolar disorder, so I go through bouts of paranoia.' That should do the trick. Oh, I almost forgot—muumbazza!"

The ambulance arrived.

Ee-oooo-ee-oooo-ee-oooo.

And so did the police.

Woop-woop. Woooooop.

13

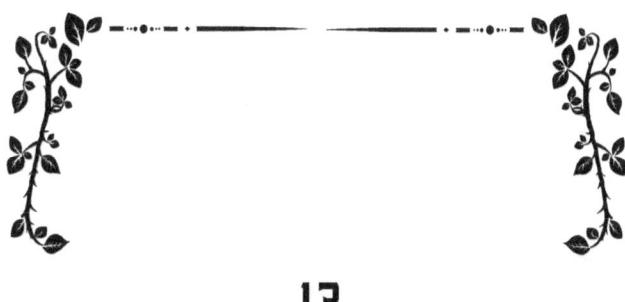

> Life is a slide. You start by climbing a ladder until you can't climb anymore. Then, from the peak of health and happiness, from the summit of all that could be, you assume a resting position and follow the path of who knows how many before you, accelerating to an end only feet from where you started.
>
> —Esmeralda Esperanza

THE SOCIAL MEDIA–LED destigmatization of mental health eventually turned every progressive New York office into a competition where anyone seeing a psychiatrist vied for the title of Most Afflicted Person in the Workplace. No position, not even president or CEO, was more sought after than that of the afflicted, especially the most afflicted.

"I have seasonal affective disorder. It's *so* crippling—"

"Me too! But I also get anxiety, and that's *way worse* than SAD—"

"My doctor told me that I might need to go on *Zoloft*—"

"I suffer from *acute* ADHD. Please don't joke about attention spans—"

It wasn't enough to suffer; other people needed to know that they suffered, unless they had mental health problems that prevented them from keeping a job or finding a partner, like manic depression or schizophrenia, which they couldn't reveal without being stigmatized by their politically correct peers. If someone was willing to admit it, having been to Bellevue was an affliction trump card.

Besides being the country's oldest public hospital, Bellevue distinguished itself by serving as a temporary storage facility for those whose psychological afflictions were deemed incurable, "lost causes" who debated the wind and could decipher secret constellations in the cracks of city streets. The hospital's patients didn't wear straitjackets because its walls were one—they were even white yellow with pandemonium-induced, sweat stain–colored accents, as if the building had been committed to itself.

On winter nights, homeless New Yorkers drifted to Bellevue, not for treatment but protection from the elements, making it a hospital and shelter for those who had stared into the abyss. Many patients didn't remember their names, and when asked to sign admission papers, they often signed as an Abrahamic prophet or *Sesame Street* character.

Some patients claimed to have made contact with higher beings or were themselves higher beings, except for Hassan, the sanest among them on any other night, who didn't know what he had made contact with.

So when the nurse at Beth Israel's intensive care unit told Ludwig that they transferred Hassan to Bellevue, he knew he was in the clear—whew! Accountability had been evaded. Kenneth Branagh's advice had worked.

He wasn't proud of himself for dodging responsibility, but what else could he have done except tell a mixed truth: Hassan and his girlfriend were breaking up (mostly true); because of this, Hassan tried to take his own life (not true); Ludwig installed the alarms because he was paranoid about stalkers (somewhat true).

The magazines in the waiting room beyond the ward were at least half a decade old. The room itself was barren to the point of sterility. No family members or well-wishing friends waited on their delusional, admitted loved ones because the inner ward did not allow visitors. All anyone in the lobby could do was wait, which Ludwig did until a nurse buzzed open the used Band-Aid-colored doors and said, as though he were a game show contestant, "Come on down, Mr. Ludwig!"

A disheveled woman who didn't want a bed because she had "bad butterflies" paced the haunted hallways; the nurses said she had akathisia, a perpetual motion disorder usually caused by erroneously prescribed antipsychotic medication, which forced her to walk without end until she had enough Xanax to sit, if only for a few minutes. She said she had a tornado inside of her. Though not as nightmarish as the blue guys' powers, he still found the concept of akathisia truly cruel since it forced the afflicted to move perpetually, making a long night in a La-Z-Boy with your pig and some margaritas impossible.

Ludwig also wanted Xanax and scored a handful, which he imagined would go against one policy or another. They forked it over anyway. How had that been so easy? It was a giant step down from the serum, which Ludwig believed could have cured the permanent residents of New York's sidewalks and parks if only he had enough, but better a step than a nosedive.

Hassan's health insurance netted him a room of his own, something few patients received because they didn't work for a brand trying to revolutionize athletic wear, which made him more entitled to health insurance in the eyes of society than people with lasting, incurable conditions. So a private room seemed positive until Ludwig noticed Seclusion painted on its door.

"You look like shit," he told Hassan. The nurses had bound him to the hospital bed's rails with cloth restraints; the skin circling his eyes was still puffy and red like geraniums.

Hassan didn't respond. He just stared, but at what? The blue guy had departed hours earlier.

"It's me. It's Ludwig."

Nothing. What had he seen, and was he still seeing it? Was this what became of humans who faced a blue guy without Dr. Tot's Miraculous Sanity Serum?

"Can you hear me? It's still Ludwig. You know, Ludwig from the basement."

Nothing.

"I need to call your family. I need to tell them what happened," he lied. He didn't need to add Hassan's family being consumed by a deed-issued kraken dressed like Martha Washington to his list of psychic injuries.

Because of the haphazard way Vermin Milk was formed, Ludwig had never collected the emergency contact information of his employees. He only knew Gloria's number.

"Good," she said seconds into the call. "Fuck him. Fuck him to death."

"Can I ask you to call his family?" Ludwig asked.

"You're on his side?"

"I'm not on a side, Gloria. He almost died. You see? This is why I didn't hire you." This also wasn't true. "You're like a human hand grenade."

"You're goddamn right I am. Fine, I'll call. You know, you should read Knausgård."

Gloria called and told them everything she knew, especially as it concerned the cheating. Given all that had happened, it wasn't much.

"I will do something about this," Ludwig told Hassan.

Hassan turned his head to Ludwig, startling him. He reached out his hand as if from a grave and took Ludwig's wrist.

"You're going to get people killed."

Ludwig sniffled.

He already had.

Lulu picked up on the first ring.

"Hassan won't be in for a while. I might not either."

"What happened?"

"I can't say. I will leave it there."

"Is he OK? Ludwig, is this because of you-know-what?"

"He's going to be OK. He's with family."

"That doesn't answer my question. We need to talk; this is a problem."

"No shit," he said.

Ludwig placed an immaculate rainbow trout with Scottish gin into a coffee mug and switched on the frozen margarita machine. He played "New York, New York," which no longer sounded like the anthem for everything New York offered but everything it could take away.

Magic was less and less something he liked, and so was being the boss, though he still yearned to control the former since he believed its problems were its practitioners, not its practice. The latter he wasn't sure about. He wanted to avenge Hassan, though how he would without being killed or tortured, he didn't know. Was Hassan worth those possibilities? Then again, he had his own scores to settle with An Exalted Northwind.

Ludwig saw the shape of Lonesome Johnny's bucket before the servant attached to it could knock.

"Come in," Ludwig called.

"Oh, Mr. Ludwig, this awful song again?"

"My bad." He switched it off. "I thought it might help. It's been a rough few days."

"Hopefully, I can stand in for it since seeing you always fills me with joy!" Lonesome Johnny said. "If only our business required more such meetings. What can I do for you on this fine summer evening when hot flowers bloom, and young lovers know they will never die? Look at those storm clouds yonder. I have often said that no piece of art can ever surpass a dramatic change in weather."

"I need a meeting with her, but I am out of serum."

"Unfortunately, that is quite intentional. My lady-lord and benefactor believes you have neglected your obligations to her and her client-housemates. I, of course, insisted that this was impossible and that some misunderstanding existed. Perhaps overwork has pushed her to make the kind of mistakes that one expects from one of you—but not *you*-you, of course!"

"There was another blue-guy incident," Ludwig said, "only I don't understand how this one found me. I managed to save someone from it, but it wasn't easy."

"Oh, Mr. Ludwig! Even without metal plates, you have all the makings of a knight in shining armor. Still, I am sorry for this dark turn of events. The blue guys are insubordinate, loathsome creatures whom I infinitely despise. But they are still the family and friends of Broken Throat's fae. I cautioned my lady-lord and benefactor that the blue guys might again arise to impede your work, but she has been so distracted—even steel bends under a great-enough burden. I hope this event does not deepen the rift between you. My lady-lord and benefactor would never wish harm on anyone, especially you. She values your employment, despite the erroneous PIP, which careful due diligence leads me to believe was meant for someone else. So I agree that you should meet and overcome your differences. As a diplomat, I can testify to the power of words. May I ask, how did you defeat the creature?"

Ludwig explained everything. The scroll's privacy-shielding enchantment posed no more threat to the bucket-bearers than fairies or blue guys.

"Mr. Ludwig, allow me to take this news to my lady-lord and benefactor. I believe that I can arrange a sit-down between the two of you. Give me twenty-four hours. May I use your elevator? Unfortunately, scaling your building has proved challenging since I misplaced my climbing spikes."

"Why not use the buzzer?"

"What buzzer?"

LUDWIG MEDITATED ON a means of retaliation.

Retaliating against bosses was something that he preached more than practiced. Just contemplating revenge was often enough to satiate his desire for it, so Ludwig lost himself in imagined, metaphorical backstabbings. But conceivable means of revenge against someone who was almost immortal were limited.

He could smuggle air horns into Broken Throat and fire them from his hips like a gunslinger until An Exalted Northwind turned into a blue guy, but that depended on her not teleporting him into an active volcano. He could set fire to Broken Throat, he supposed, if she didn't transform the flames into snow or moth-eaten sweaters—even if he succeeded, he would be responsible for the deaths of others caught beneath her enormous boots. Perhaps he could bullshit his way back into her good graces and continue to do nothing, which would frustrate her more than a wrist flick could alleviate.

He could imagine no revenge that did not end in An Exalted Northwind easily deflecting his plans back at him tenfold, except for one that she might struggle to overcome, though it was risky: attacking her reputation. Whatever he decided to do, it wasn't enough to hurt her; he wanted a green-tufted blue scalp to go with it.

Exactly twenty-four hours later, the buzzer rang. Ludwig cautiously checked the surveillance camera, and though he could see his downstairs neighbors queued behind Lonesome Johnny, he let him in.

"What wonderful neighbors you have! I've never met so many creative directors."

"You can talk to people? Isn't that against the rules?"

"Not at all. I am an irresistible, consummate gadfly. Muffling me would be like denying a great poet her quill."

"Come to think of it, I've never met my neighbors."

"How very New York of you, Mr. Ludwig! You are a true scion of this raucous metropolis. After some discussion, I can report that everything is in order! My lady-lord and benefactor agrees to meet, though she impressed upon me to impress upon you that your PIP expires in three days if nothing changes, meeting or not."

"Great. I care *sooo* much."

"Oh, Mr. Ludwig! I knew you would. A few doses of Dr. Tot's Miraculous Sanity Serum should enter your hollow heart within the hour. Unfortunately, I must attend to other matters. I trust you know the way home by now."

The way "home" could be anywhere: in a dumpster, on a beach, in an airplane. Wherever he placed the door, the length of his tunnel would be precisely the same.

Lonesome Johnny left almost as soon as he arrived, and Ludwig rented a cabin upstate for the weekend. He couldn't imagine the blue guys driving cars or taking the bus, never mind that they could not leave their "wilds," so he drove his door to it and drank the serum that An Exalted Northwind supplied.

Desolate Phil said nothing to Ludwig. Neither had any patience left for the other.

He was met at the front door by a dainty piece of blue glass but declined to step on it. Why give An Exalted Northwind more of what she wanted by following her rules?

Galilea once again commanded the lobby. This time, instead of smearing marshmallow creme onto peanut butter sandwiches, she dipped her long mantis fingers into the sweet goo; her saliva left swirling green streaks among the sugary emulsification.

"Don't tell anyone," she purred as she licked her fingers. "You know, Ludwig, you're quite brave to defy my aunt. So few would. You're either very stupid or very, very courageous. I'm into both," she crooned.

Was she trying to seduce him? Nothing about that seemed appropriate. Her beauty was undeniable, but he didn't like the idea of becoming romantically entangled with someone so keen on hurting people, especially someone with the physicality and knowledge to do the hurting. Plus, she was, what, hundreds or thousands of years his senior?

"I won't tell anyone," he said.

"Good boy. Now, have you reconsidered letting me read your tarot cards? Bucketface stole me a novelty sorcerer cat–themed deck. The pictures are very cute, but augur nothing. Still, they're something to do. It's good to brush up on the old razzle-dazzle."

"Maybe some other time."

"Well, thanks to your incompetence, you know where to find me."

Ludwig boldly ventured to An Exalted Northwind's archives.

"You fended off a blue guy with your fists?" She couldn't conceal her admiration or curiosity as she poured herself a black drink from an omni-colored decanter. "That's like putting out a forest fire with your spit."

She lowered her voice to a whisper, and Ludwig followed suit.

"I didn't have a choice. My knives broke—"

An Exalted Northwind's fingers curled, and her veins rose like mountain ranges, but she held back her frustration for the sake of discovery.

"Who do you think you are, Bluebane the Onionscourge? They are gods to you, and you felt that—"

"You're a god to me. And I'm pretty sure that I could whip you with a flügelhorn."

Without taking a step, An Exalted Northwind wrapped herself around Ludwig like a centipede trapping its prey. She unfurled one long tree-branch finger and pressed it against his lips. "Be careful."

Whenever she had touched or come close to him before, serum or no serum, his mind had started to "rattle like coins in a vagrant's tin," as Lonesome Johnny said. But this time, with her finger across his lips, he felt nothing, as if he spoke to Lulu or Ayonia. But he did sniffle.

"Where did you even get the knives?"

"Amazon."

"*The* Amazon?"

"It's a store."

"In the southern hemisphere?"

"What? No. It's online."

"On the webby nets?"

"Jesus, yes."

His frustration moved her little, whereas her frustration could have moved him anywhere geographically.

"The blue guy who attacked me in my apartment might not

have hurt me, but it injured someone else. I'd like to give him some of Dr. Tot's serum, but I only have what last you gave me left," Ludwig whispered.

"You are in no position to be making requests. Your PIP expires in three days. You should be asking how you can help me, not asking for more help than I have already given you. And if you revealed the hollow heart's existence to a friend or even your worst enemy, they would be stomped into gravy by, oh, I don't know, perhaps a constipated, bodybuilding cyclops or something. That enchantment is honestly so inconsistent," An Exalted Northwind whispered.

"I don't understand how the blue guy found me. I moved the door to my apartment the night of the attack, but never opened it. Other than that, it's never been there. Did you tell them? Is this part of your PIP, an attempt to make me take my assignment more seriously by hurting my employees?"

"Tell the blue guys, the fae who revolted against my governance? What, walk up to them and tell them my plans? They are illiterate and nonverbal, except for babbling about 'Bubbles of Earth.' I am not conspiring with the blue guys. I'd rather conspire with Gilda Fiorella. Only my puppets can approach them. And do you think the one you call Lonesome Johnny would betray you? He is almost more loyal to you than he is to me. He is defective beyond repair, but his dedication is beyond question, making his defects mostly moot. Where was the door the last time you opened it? You're so lazy that you surely kept it nearby."

"Two blocks away! So what did it do, search all the apartments in between for my door?" Ludwig asked.

"Possibly. More likely is that you let slip your location via some misstep, and the enchantment did the rest. Perhaps you said too much, and it revealed your location by sending down an incinerating, divine light—"

"No."

"A torrent of brimstones—"

"No."

"Raining, phantom daggers—"

"No."

"A cosmic wyvern—"

"No."

"Exploding hornets—"

"No."

"An ent or two—"

"No."

"Or unusual lightning bolts that helped them triangulate your position."

"Shit," he said.

"Ah, I see. The blue guys started looking for more than your door once they realized you could not stay silent. Illiterates have outsmarted you. It brings me no joy to say this, but you are an embarrassment to yourself, your family, your friends, and your profession," she whispered.

"My profession? We've sold thousands of—"

"Not that profession—*this* profession, the one that makes the other possible. The one I paid you beyond fairly to do. I could have made you king of New York! If you had just done your job as you were supposed to, your friend's injuries would not exist."

Her eyes became the color of bile, so he reached down and finished the second-to-last dose of serum.

"Your PIP expires in three days. After that, we are finished."

"OK. Can you just warp me out this time? I'm not in the mood to fuck with a mile of ladders right now." She wrist-flicked him back to his apartment, but the door was still upstate, leading to a two-hour cab ride back to the house, the door, and his rental car.

Could she terminate him, or was it a bluff?

Did he care?

THE SWORD FROM Kenneth Branagh's "favorite blacksmith" arrived. It was bright, balanced, and tapered down to an invisible edge; no detail from its point to its pommel went unconsidered. Ludwig hacked off Platinum George's head, then stuffed the blade into the closet beside the Swiffer, but not before cutting down several imaginary enemies.

The hollow heart's lingering magic led him to have recklessly brave thoughts. Did he owe it to human and fairy society to do something about her? What was the saying? "The only thing necessary for bad guys to triumph is for good guys to not stop doing good shit."

Something like that.

An Exalted Northwind had insisted that since Ludwig failed to do his job, he was responsible for Hassan's fate. However, deflecting responsibility was something that bosses always did when they failed to do *their* jobs. He accepted that this new life he led was like a rolling boulder that crushed Hassan; he did not accept responsibility for setting it in motion. He had a plan to strike back, but he needed more courage than even the serum delivered. Roaming or resting somewhere below the streets of New York, perhaps in the basement of his building, the blue guy who had defiled Hassan's sanity waited for Ludwig to reopen the door.

Ludwig filled glass after glass with frozen margaritas and guzzled as much as intermittent brain freezes allowed. He took the gun from his bedroom safe and the razor-tipped bullets from the other safe, locked Mr. Blueberry in his room, dragged his coffee table from the center of the downstairs living room, and positioned his door in the floor.

He opened it, closed it, and opened it again. He did this several more times, as if working bellows or fanning his tunnel's fragrant promise to blue guys throughout the city. Finally, he propped the door open, sat on the couch, blindfolded himself, squeezed the last of Dr. Tot's serum into his mouth, and tossed the hollow heart like a smoked cigarette.

Hours as long as calendar pages passed. He lost track of time. How long had he been sitting there? Long enough to be surprised when he heard soft footsteps and excited whispers. Whatever was in the room remembered the alarm system, so it stepped cautiously.

"Bubbles of Earth . . . Bubbles of Earth . . ." it warbled.

Ludwig didn't lower his blindfold to check because he didn't need to. Nothing else used that phrase, and nothing else could sneak into his apartment so gracefully: Lonesome Johnny knocked; people rang; Mr. Blueberry whined; and blue guys appeared from nowhere, a place they returned to just as effortlessly.

The blue guy assessed the blindfolded doorbearer, who, despite their previous battle, might as well have been a broom. Ludwig didn't matter; the door did. And the door was all the way open. The blue guy's years-long search was over. Returning to its sane, green form was just a few ladders, some worms, and a little rest away.

"I'm not going to hurt you," Ludwig said. "You want to go home, don't you? Away from the bad noises and dark basements? I know how you feel; I hid underground too. Give that big green bitch my regards."

The blue guy had not been home in as much as two decades and likely didn't know or couldn't remember that the way to Broken Throat was fortified explicitly with it in mind. But it wanted to go home—to be a regular fairy again. What An Exalted Northwind did to create the blue guys was punishment, she once told Ludwig, not murder. She said a death sentence against fairies took as long to create as a powerful enchantment because of their nebulous and bureaucratic internal politics. When her client-housemates defied her, she took their time and sanity. He would make the blue guy a martyr, her a murderer, and tarnish her reputation forever. His plan might even oust her from Broken Throat and transform her into a blue guy. The irony! He hoped that Gilda Fiorella and her crystal ball were watching.

The gun trembled in his hand as the blue guy inspected him. If necessary, all he had to do was pull the trigger. Would it work?

It didn't matter.

The blue guy jumped through the door and floated down, scaffold to scaffold, as if attached to a magic umbrella.

"Bubbles of Earth! Bubbles of Earth!"

It ran into Ludwig's tunnel, and Desolate Phil gave chase.

"You should not be here, o punished one!" Desolate Phil roared. He caught up to the blue guy, filled his fist with its green hair, and thrust Bluebane the Onionscourge's Sword-Spear of Puncturing through its back.

The blue guy simply popped, releasing blue fluid that painted the tunnel, but not a drop touched Desolate Phil, who dodged them all.

The plan had worked. Desolate Phil did what he existed to do, and the blue guy bled blue fluid that made every worm it touched bark madly at a sky it had never seen.

Ludwig kicked the door shut.

14

Polyampulation [pol-ee-am-pyuh-ley-shuhn]. Noun. The euphoria that a person experiences upon waking up with more limbs than they're supposed to have.

—*Chloe Knopf's Encyclopedia of Mystical Maladies*

THE PERPETUAL RAIN that flooded basements and subway platforms across the city waned, but the obsidian summer clouds that incubated the tempest as it traveled east from the American plains went nowhere as if waiting for another, greater storm to begin. Meteorologists struggled to describe the phenomenon, which, for lack of a scientific label, they called cloudscape paralysis. And yet, there was nothing scientific about what New Yorkers were seeing. A Manhattan fairy, a living manifestation of nature's endless grace and absolute beauty, had passed on. As the Earth mourned, the sky gathered around New York to pay its respects.

The spectral torches that lined Broken Throat's corridors, common areas, and apartments no longer revealed prisms of rare, shape-shifting light. Instead, they burned bright, radiant black, alerting the fairies who lived there that one of their own was dead.

None of this was part of their deal with An Exalted Northwind, who knew better than to attend the blue guy's funeral since her client-housemates, without a nearby human to blame for its fate, would blame her. So until responsibility could be convincingly reassigned to Ludwig, her power and esteem stood jeopardized.

Lonesome Johnny reported that her client-housemates were gathering in the receiving room beside her list of rules, several of which they broke just by being there. Rather than voice their disgust with her to Lonesome Johnny, An Exalted Northwind's most faithful servant, they hissed and gave him death stares because Lonesome Johnny could not teleport them into the calamitous, noisy metropolis above with a flick of his wrist, so he absorbed their scorn—to do so was one of the myriad reasons for his existence.

Instead of mourning, An Exalted Northwind raced to control the damage that Ludwig had caused by drafting a letter for Lonesome Johnny to deliver.

"Do you know what this letter is?"

"I do."

"Do you know who it is for?"

Lonesome Johnny had delivered another letter like it once and remembered well its aftermath. He understood that the colossal parchment, which likely contained only a few paragraphs, boded ill for Ludwig.

"Yes. My lady-lord and benefactor, please, even though it is not my place to question your wisdom, I fear this is not only a bridge too far but one in the wrong direction. Mr. Ludwig may still be necessary."

"That is why the letter bears no orders for the beast to kill Ludwig."

"I urge you to reconsider this course of action. This path is the path of pain," Lonesome Johnny said. "I—we, you, Mr. Ludwig, all of us—are better than this. We are better than *him*."

"Is that not heresy? He is the first bucketbearer."

"And a servant to no one. He is an insult to my order, a disloyal, vulgar, crude, obnoxious monstrosity."

"Yes, and who does that remind you of?" she asked.

"Surely not Mr. Ludwig! He is so tenderhearted and hard-working. I do not mean to question or doubt you. I am simply loath to see someone so graceless acting on behalf of your infinite grace," Lonesome Johnny said, tap-dancing nervously in place.

"He has already been useful once. Or did you forget that it was he who informed us that a human had heard, rather than said, *muumbazza*? In a sense, he brought Ludwig to us. So it's only fitting that he should relieve us of him."

"He did this not out of service or altruism! He was paid handsomely for that information."

"Yes, he was. And he will be paid handsomely for this. Who knows what priceless baubles Ludwig's rubies have afforded him? Wet Henry can have his pick; I only want the pig and the hollow heart. I'm afraid that my client-housemates are days from openly rebelling or, worse, firing me. And where would I go? I can't leave this place without being summoned again, and after so many blunders, who would summon me? No, the fae of Broken Throat need to see that we are taking Thornfell Littlefog's death seriously before we ourselves are exiled. This measure shows that we are. If Ludwig is to reenter my employ someday, he must do so of his own accord. Until then, we are beyond the realm of a PIP. We must close this forsaken chapter. Now, take this letter and deliver it to Wet Henry."

Desolate Phil sifted through tools in Lonesome Johnny's basement until he found what he needed: a push broom, a box filled with matches, and an unopened oil canister. The canister's wax label depicted burning Europeans tied to stakes, all in varying degrees of immolation from just ignited and still screaming to limbless, withered charcoal husks.

The march back to his outpost felt different this time, even as the bucketbearer who, by design, felt the least. The worms that lined the muddy corridor followed him, leading to the formation of shifting, putrid dunes. He wasn't alone and could feel the scrutiny of fifty-six individual fairy eyes.

More from protocol than necessity, Desolate Phil dodged the fluid that leaked from where Bluebane the Onionscourge's Sword-Spear of Puncturing had struck down Ludwig's blue guy, whose common name was Thornfell Littlefog. If the fluid had been handled by the bucketbearer, it wouldn't have affected him like humans and fairies. However, Phil was a perfectionist and valued that reputation like his creator. Besides his fabled sword, his reputation was all he valued.

He dragged the blue guy's deflated body into the worms.

"Eat now. Play your part in a bloody proper fairy funeral," Desolate Phil said. "You are alive and well, Thornfell Littlefog. Your exile is ended. Where you go now, you go in silence."

As the worms feasted, he recited the blue guy's true name. Both took hours. When he was satisfied that they had consumed all of the insanity-inducing blue fluid, all that remained was a tuft of green hair, a tongue, and some inedible teeth and eyeballs.

Desolate Phil corralled the moonstruck worms with the push broom into rowboat-sized piles. He doused each in oil and then dropped match after match, while all around him, the fairies' kin chanted quiet goodbyes to the first fairy from Broken Throat ever to defy An Exalted Northwind.

DESPITE SOME ANXIETY about impending retaliation, "New York, New York," regained some of its appeal, and Ludwig's spirit lifted. Hassan had been avenged, and An Exalted Northwind thwarted. She would fire him, he knew; he didn't need a crystal ball or tarot cards to see that. It was just a matter of when and how. So he turned up the volume and took stock of his future.

If selling even one of his six briolette rubies was possible, it would easily carry him through the rest of his life, even if Mr. Blueberry never produced another. He owned a lavish apartment, which, in an emergency, could easily be flipped by Kenneth Branagh. He had profitable Vermin Milk, though he had no salary, but as the number of decisions that affected others' livelihoods and well-being increased, which Lulu would say wasn't many, his interest in being the boss of a fashion company faltered. What he had once told his coworkers about only being in it for clothes that made him look and feel like an urban druid was true. Now that he had the clothes, he wondered if he was just incompatible with leadership, even when he was the leader. Because of his connection to the fairies, he was dangerous to those around him, and he knew it. More importantly, so did Lulu.

Lost in half-formed plans for his post-fairy future, Ludwig never noticed the frozen halo of dark, observant clouds circling New York. No, what concerned him was what to tell Lulu about Hassan. If it came from him, the truth was out of the question—she was clear about never wanting to see lightning, polka-dotted or otherwise, ever again. If Hassan could speak, they might have already spoken. But Hassan wasn't the sort to gather around the office refrigerator and tell competitive, pity-seeking tales of personal woe. So whether their hypothetical conversation had lifted the burden of disclosure from Ludwig remained unknown.

As part of his nightly ritual, Mr. Blueberry inspected Zeal for anything enchanted or out of the ordinary. When satisfied that the apartment was of one reality, he fell into a deep sleep full of meadows rich with copper flowers and soft pennies falling from nostalgically blue skies.

Having just warded off one invader, Ludwig didn't think An Exalted Northwind would send another—it was too predictable.

So when the lid of his margarita machine, which was running and filled to the top, hit the kitchen floor, he didn't expect it, nor did he expect the gloved hand and wet, dripping chain mail–robed arm that emerged from its reservoir seconds later. Nor did he expect the arm that followed the first, nor the arm that followed the previous two. As the number of armored limbs emerging from the margarita machine increased, so did the malleability of its rigid, plastic reservoir. Once four arms had appeared, the hands attached to them searched the kitchen for things to grasp, finding the microwave, the handle of a cabinet, the refrigerator door, and the silverware drawer. Next, a bucket followed by three more arms emerged, and the margarita machine's reservoir stretched until its circumference exceeded that of a manhole cover. Finally, a chain mail–encased torso and three legs materialized, knocking the margarita machine to the floor, shattering all but its plastic reservoir.

Ludwig didn't need the testimony from his eyes to know that the base of the margarita machine had been broken. He just did; he knew it in his heart, like how a mother knows when something has befallen one of her children. Was this An Exalted Northwind's revenge? To destroy what was one of his closest, only, and most dependable friends? As he slowly sprinted into the kitchen (he had only sprinted twice since childhood), his soul tore at the sight of the broken machine and all of its wasted, slushy, 14.5% ABV glory.

He sniffled. Then he beheld the bucketbearer.

Ludwig counted seven arms: two that started at its shoulders, where arms belonged; three rose from its back like featherless wings; one reached forth from its belly, and one emerged from beneath its bucket like an egregious tumor. Besides its many appendages, it was distinct from the other bucketbearers in another way: It had no face, painted or otherwise. There was only the bucket, which stood two buckets above Lonesome Johnny's and Desolate Phil's.

As he was, at this point, at least a journeyman at challenging the supernatural, Ludwig ran for the closet and the sword Kenneth Branagh had requisitioned. The creature gave no chase.

No bucketbearer had ever injured or threatened him, but this one's unexpected arrival, seven arms, and armored body foreshadowed menace.

Ludwig drew the sword from its scabbard, charged back into the kitchen, and without hesitation, swung. The bucketbearer seemed to place itself directly in the blade's path, causing the arm that started beneath its bucket to drop from its body.

"O-M-G! O-M-G!" the six-armed bucketbearer wailed in a voice that brought to mind someone who was unjustifiably proud to be from Long Island. "Why you do that, bro? It hurts! Please don't hurt me, bro!"

Ludwig raised the sword until it was parallel to his shoulders, mimicking an offensive stance he knew only from movies and didn't really understand the purpose of, before limping in to separate the bucket from the creature's shoulders.

The six-armed bucketbearer sidestepped the sword and dealt Ludwig's neck two fists at once, causing him and the blade to clatter across the floor.

"I was just kidding, bro! J-K! J-K! I ain't hurt. Gonna take a lot more than that."

The ungodly avatar retrieved its severed arm and reattached it as if corking a bottle; then, it used that arm to confiscate Ludwig's sword.

"Where you get this? This ain't human-made, bro. This rare shit. Dingle get this for you? You know Dingle, right?"

"Hoo eth Jingle?" Ludwig wheezed.

"Oh, thass right! He Lonesome Jackoff to you. He juss Dingle to us. 'My lady-lord and benefucktor' this, 'my benevolent whatever-da-fuck' that. Real dingle, that guy. I known the treehouse bitch a long time, but I ain't never care for her myself. I ain't even really want to do this job, you know? Fuck the bosses. But sometimes they pay, right? Thass why I gotta go through all your stuff. Big treehouse bitch says I can keep whatever I find. My name's Wet Henry, by the way. Nice to meet you. Anyways, le's see what you got in here! Real nice place you got. Hey, whass this song?" Wet Henry asked about "New York, New York." "I know this song! Ol' Frankie Blue Eyes! Eyyy, my guy!"

Wet Henry wrapped a cold, sticky, margarita-soaked hand around Ludwig's throat and dragged him from room to room.

"Bro, you like memes? I love memes. I got four phones for maximum memeage. You ever see the one with the karate sunglasses guy that's like, bro, 'What if I told you . . . ?' Or the one with the bearded guy who's like, 'One does not simply . . . ?' You see those? Sooo funny."

Wet Henry's grip prevented Ludwig from voicing his disagreement.

"You got safes, bro? Seems like you got safes. Big place, rich guy—therefore safes!" Wet Henry quickly discovered the safe in Ludwig's bedroom and instructed him to open it. As the door clicked open, Ludwig reached in and retrieved his revolver, aimed, and shot Wet Henry twice in the bucket, giving him deep black eyes. Then he fired twice more, piercing his left leg and belly. Wet Henry's grip remained firm.

"Shit! Why you shoot me, bro? Ow, my face! Ow, ow, ow!" Ludwig pressed the gun against Wet Henry's chest and fired again. "O-M-G! I'm bleeding out! I'm gonna die!"

But like Lonesome Johnny, Wet Henry had no blood. "L-O-L, just kidding! I'm OK. Bullets ain't really do shit to me, y'know? I'm Wet Henry, bro! I lived through the Ice Age, the Inquisition, the Fairy Wars, the 1970s, Earth God Island, the McRib. L-O-L, the McRib! Where you get a gun, bro? Guns hard to get in the city." Wet Henry removed the weapon from Ludwig's grip by bending his fingers until they broke. Ludwig howled. Wet Henry ejected the last bullet with another hand, then slid the revolver under Ludwig's bed. "I'd take it, but I ain't got a license. Gun license tough to get in this town, you know?"

From the safe, Wet Henry extracted mementos, cash, sharpened bullets, a hard drive, company-formation documents, the clairvoyance-blocking blue fairy glass that Ludwig had been instructed to crush underfoot, Mr. Blueberry's vaccination records, and a folded Trader Joe's bag containing $300,000,000 worth of rubies.

"What you got in here? You like Trader Joe's, bro? I love Trader Joe's." He turned the bag upside down and caught each falling ruby with a different hand. "Bro! Bro! How you get these? Oh, thass right! You got a fairy pig. Sorry, bro. The big treehouse bitch wants pig back. Ain't it fucked up, like, how bosses can just take your stuff cause you signed some papers? Really sorry for your loss, bro."

Ludwig tried to force words out as the bucketbearer moved on to inspecting the closet, but Wet Henry's grip prevented them from being spoken.

"Thass right! You the naked fashion guy. I *gotta* upgrade my wardrobe, bro. My shit's Middle Ages. How come you ain't make swag for seven-arm people? You got a problem with seven-arm people? Thass not cool, bro. I thought we was bros. Hey, wassup with all these buttons everywhere?" Wet Henry stomped on one, and the five-story building swayed with paralyzing sound. "Guess somebody's got a blue guy problem!

That's why the treehouse bitch called me. You kill one? Pretty impressive, bro. Bet you didn't do it with this sword, though. It's dope, except only one sword kills blue guys."

Mr. Blueberry entered the closet to investigate the alarm, then turned on his hoofs to run. Wet Henry was faster and fell over him with arms flailing like a trapdoor spider. The three protruding from his back lifted Mr. Blueberry into the air and trapped him there.

"Welp, that was easy! Thought I'd have to chase his fat ass around. Sorry to do this to your bro, bro," Wet Henry said to Ludwig, "but a job's a job! Big treehouse bitch says you got something else she wants back. Can't remember what it was." Ludwig heard the chirps of incoming text messages, but his phone wasn't with him, and Mr. Blueberry didn't have one. "Oh, hold up—iss my bitches!"

Wet Henry flipped Ludwig onto his bed like dirty laundry, then sat on him and farted. Ludwig watched in horror as Wet Henry's free arms produced two phones and typed the same passcode into both: 6-9-6-9.

"Ain't that funny, bro? My passcode's sixty-nine, sixty-nine! All my bros are like, bro, you should have been a comedian. Only thing funnier would be four twenty, four twenty. I'd probably forget it, though. L-O-L."

Ludwig couldn't see the text messages' contents, but he saw the names of their senders: Crestfallen Kate and Malignant Lindsay.

"Oh, bro! They're sending me memes. You gotta see these."

Wet Henry held the phones inches from Ludwig's face.

The first meme portrayed a pensive dinosaur making a profound observation about fast food drive-through lanes. The other portrayed Willy Wonka leaning on his hand and delivering an obnoxious insult.

There were undeniably worse ways to die; the blue guy had shown Ludwig that, but this wasn't so much better than them:

memed to death by an enchanted, flatulent, easily amused bucket bro. The images were somehow less funny than watching his guts be pulled apart in an operating room to the sounds of an accordion played by septuagenarian acquaintances.

Wet Henry resumed his grip on Ludwig's throat and stood up. His bucket began to rotate like a beacon searching for something that could have been anywhere—until he stepped on it.

"Oh, oh! Thass it!"

He stepped back and retrieved the object.

"These things expensive! Gargoyles' hearts rare as hell, bro. The big treehouse bitch told me she want it back. I don't think I'm gonna give it, though. She been really shit to you, I figure, so why help her? You and me bros now. And it feels good to defy the boss, right? I got one more thing I need, though. I need you to open your door in the floor. Don't worry! Don't worry! We ain't going down there, though. I ain't really want to see Lonesome Dingle and Desolate Dingus either, y'know? Just need you to open it real quick for me." Wet Henry's grip on Ludwig's throat tightened until his head swelled and air couldn't enter, so he did as he was told.

Wet Henry lowered Mr. Blueberry into the tunnel, depositing him into Desolate Phil's open arms.

"Peace, pig bro!"

Desolate Phil held out his hand for the hollow heart.

"Nah!"

Wet Henry kicked the door closed, then loosened his grip on Ludwig's throat. With the hollow heart and bag of rubies in hand, Wet Henry returned to the kitchen, filled the margarita machine's unbroken plastic reservoir with water, and disappeared into it.

"Later, person bro!"

It had all once been so exciting for Lulu: the rubies, the pig, the lightning that nearly cleaved her into separate Lus; knowing, or at least thinking she knew, that magic was real and that she might be made a part of it.

But she hadn't been. Not really.

Ludwig never permitted her entry to that world—apparently, with good reason. She bore him no malice for that; in fact, just knowing of that world's existence had value since it alleviated some of her fears about death, even if it paved the way for other, more existential concerns about what happened after it. Did the lights just go out? And if not, was there a Hell or something worse? If magic existed, what did souls do without bodies? Did they become fuel for magic-making, pawns in the games of wizards and archmages?

Ludwig's reasons for missing work, like Hassan's injuries and the Muumbazza line's canceled launch, were not what they seemed. Ludwig didn't have to say so; she just knew and was envious. Even being hospitalized by magic had some morbid appeal. At least then, she'd have a receipt.

Lulu had entered the world of auction houses not for prestige or money but because magic seemed like an inseparable fixture of its hundred-million-year-old gemstones, one-of-a-kind artworks, and antiquated timepieces that thread the needle of the unknown through reality's dull, damp fabric. Like New York, auction houses had their own kind of magic, except it wasn't *magic* magic. Only Ludwig's magic was that, and it infringed on the lives of his employees who, in truth, seemed more like hers than his. He had become dangerous, despite not deserving to be. To protect Vermin Milk's employees, Ludwig needed to be pushed out. Once again, she was stuck playing the grown-up when she only wanted to play the Ludwig.

With his penthouse utterly defiled and without serum to withstand another blue guy attack, Ludwig ventured to the only place that still felt like home, though it admittedly felt less like one lately. It was a place where his door in the floor had never been. An office, home? It was hard to fathom.

Ludwig looked like a nuclear silo as he entered his and Lulu's shared office with his hand in a cast and his neck in a brace, which he tried to conceal by wearing Vermin Milk's signature Druidic Traveler hoodie pulled over both.

"Muumbazza you battle an ogre?" Lulu asked.

"Haven't seen an ogre, to be honest. Hoping I get to skip that one. So what's the plan?" he said casually, as if he didn't care to know the answer. "What did I miss?"

"The plan?"

"Yeah, the plan. What are we working on? I thought we had samples to review or something."

"Ludwig, muumbazza anyone see you come in?"

"What, you're worried about this?" he said, indicating his cast and brace. "No one saw me. I came up the fire escape."

"Do you not see how needing to sneak your injuries and misadventures around employees is a problem? Are you trying to add fuel to the rumors? Half the company already thinks you're in bad with a loan shark, and Savannah convinced the others that you owe a favor to a Lapland witch," she said.

"What is a Lapland witch?"

"I presume it's a kind of muumbazza, Ludwig. You would know."

"If only my problems were with loan sharks," he said. "So two things. First, we have to talk about money."

"What happened to Mr. Blueberry?" she asked, displaying more concern for the pig than she ever had for him.

"He's fine, I think. But let's put a pin in that. Second, the team doesn't care about my misadventures. They are paid too well."

"They will care once they muumbazza that your presence puts them in danger. Money isn't everything, Ludwig. You have become dangerous in ways I don't think you understand: all those people on the subway, the lightning, Hassan's injuries, your injuries, the muumbazza, whatever's in your backpack, whatever almost killed that reporter in our *Kingdom of New York* profile. Oh, you thought I didn't notice? This stuff isn't just a distraction—it's a liability." Lulu had only ever fired one person and didn't want to again, though whether she even could depended on her securing votes. She wanted to push him to the company's icy fringes, where he posed less harm to everyone, including himself. "Until you are free from muumbazza, I am asking—no, I am telling you—that you muumbazza step down as CEO. You can transfer into a nonexecutive muumbazza role and oversee products from afar. You can no longer be this brand's day-in, day-out face. Until you are muumbazza from this, you cannot continue putting us at risk. We cannot have another Hassan."

"Where is he, anyway?" Ludwig asked.

"You don't know? How do you not know? He quit. He moved back to Michigan to be with his family." He was, frankly, unsurprised by the news. Without Dr. Tot's serum, no one would have stayed within whatever geography had facilitated a confrontation with a blue guy.

"I think I might be free now," Ludwig said. He didn't know if, after surviving Wet Henry, his association and conflict with An Exalted Northwind had reached its end. If so, he was free. If not—well, he took her point.

"Can muumbazza prove it?" she asked.

"Do you see a mysterious throbbing backpack?"

She didn't.

"I don't think that's the right question. Can you tell me in detail where your rubies come from?"

Could he? He hadn't tested whether he was still under

the deed's surveillance since Wet Henry took everything enchanted from his apartment. But if the enchantment's nondisclosure clauses cremated Lulu, it would only further her point.

"I don't think I can."

"Then you aren't free."

She was right. He, as the boss, put everyone in danger. And though he liked the companionship that came with being surrounded by people, which every leader usually did, the mantle of leadership upholding him was a threat to everyone. Perhaps it was once again time to go his own way.

"Look, honestly—yeah, it's OK. You take over. You're right," he said as if sliding an anchor from his shoulders. "I don't know when or if this will be over, or if it's already over, but I don't need another person getting hurt because of what I'm going through."

"Really?" she said, feeling as if she might hug him for the first time, though the neck brace curbed her from doing so. Being in charge wasn't what she wanted most, but it was something.

"You have always been the essential one. Consider yourself CEO," Ludwig said. "But—but!—I am not signing off on my own execution. I retain the right to veto product decisions from a distance. I also want to make a goodbye speech."

"I don't think you should say anything. I will," she said.

"It's my company. I'm the founder."

"You are muumbazza giving any speeches."

"It will only take a minute."

"On *day fucking one*, you dodged a question from Hassan by triggering an earthquake." Was it an earthquake? He still didn't know. "I want what's best for this company. And, right now, that isn't you."

Later that night, during a sniffling fit, Ludwig called Lulu to talk through the details. The call went to voicemail.

"Hello, you've reached Lulu Vaillancourt, the Chief Executive Officer of Vermin Milk. Unfortunately, I can't come to the phone right now, but please leave a brief message after the beep if you would like me to return your call. Thank you."

Already?

An Exalted Northwind sought to inform the anxious, breathlessly waiting universe that her search for the next doorbearer had begun, so she whispered an enchantment that should have reached the stars. Her call into the beyond rose only as high as the streets of Times Square, where sweaty, disoriented tourists unwittingly trampled it to death.

The deed couldn't be burned since its clauses about privacy were still needed. She couldn't let him use his door in the floor, perhaps ever again, so she sealed the deed in moss and candle wax, then ordered Lonesome Johnny to store it in his basement. Ludwig had the door, but she had the deed. Without both, it wouldn't open. It was once again just a door.

The dark summer storm clouds that had circled the city drifted away, back to Oklahoma or Nebraska or other places that had once been quiet but had become noisy, which fairies had abandoned long ago, perhaps even once upon a time.

15

Everyone wants a time machine, but everyone already has one. Focus on any clock, and time slows down. Forget the clock, and time speeds up. And if your clock breaks, at least you won't be pulled apart by a pious inquisition, devoured by living proof of the fossil record, turned inside out by some extinct malady, or stranded in an impossible-to-identify epoch, wondering how much longer you can survive on small handful after smaller handful of primordial goo.

—Dr. Tot's journal, 860,390,199 BC

GIUSTINA DIED AND, with her, so did the best mozzarella in the city, perhaps the world. She was ninety-six. To Ludwig, she didn't look a day over eighty-seven.

Her funeral took place only a few blocks from the shop whose window she'd sat behind for over seventy years. Those in attendance were aging New Yorkers whose community, with every new death, became less like the New York they knew, which they could do little to preserve. Like the neighborhood itself, everyone from the Old Neighborhood was on their way out of this world. Some of those mourning Giustina found themselves at two wakes per week. Despite this, they had never seen the weeping fashion icon dressed in formfitting black tapered sweats. Who was he?

The blue guys' interest in Ludwig had waned, reducing his finely tailored alarm system to an outdated relic of a life few would ever believe possible. Ludwig closed the circuit that connected them to his building's grid. Without the deed, he was just a regular person, and the blue guys had little interest in regular people. They wanted the doorbearer and its door, not a plank of wood and a plank of man. Because An Exalted Northwind's search for the next doorbearer had gone nowhere, so had the blue guys, and they retreated into cellars and access tunnels that New Yorkers had long forgotten.

That no replacement existed for such an incompetent, noncommittal employee in an eight-million-person city seemed inconceivable even to An Exalted Northwind, someone used to being sought out by strange truths.

Ludwig's dismissal and punishment had quelled Broken Throat's fairy rebellion. Like the blue guys to whom they were either acquainted or related, the fairies retreated into less downtrodden, though still gloomy, underground accommodations—by punishing the person responsible for Thornfell Littlefog's plight, An Exalted Northwind had deflected the blame that was rightly hers onto Ludwig. And the fairies, who knew better, went along with it—she was still their best chance at stopping the spotted-blue scourge from turning their slender green bodies into big blue onions.

Ludwig's limp disappeared step by step, then all at once, and his badly broken fingers healed faster than bones ever had. Doctors said it was impossible, but he had nowhere to go even after the limp was gone. So he stayed home and played nostalgia-rich retro video games, researched a replacement for his margarita machine, read fantasy paperbacks from no-longer-middling, still-canonical piles that teetered everywhere like Roman ruins, and searched for the next industry to conquer. Did he even want that? Did he want another job? He already enjoyed comfort supreme without a manager or responsibility in sight. That's what he'd wanted, wasn't it?

Wasn't it?

He was free from the time-constraining shackles of employment, even those imposed on him by the company he had founded. He had time to do whatever he wanted, unless what he wanted was prohibitively expensive, since Wet Henry's fairy-commissioned kleptomania had forced him to begin rationing his once-endless wealth. Had he needed to tip all those delivery people, couriers, and cab drivers $2,000 wads? Ludwig sympathized with anyone who worked for a living; that's who he was. But he might need to work for a living once again, and his sympathies quickly shifted from them to himself, especially now that fashion industry magazines and trade publications often featured Lulu, Ayonia, and Uchu. They still mentioned Ludwig, though, usually somewhere in the piece's lede. But as the months passed and more articles arrived, his tenure at Vermin Milk faded further into the background until no one mentioned him except to remind readers about his naked escapades. A grown-up was in charge now, the blogs said.

But, as ever, there was another problem, the most persistent in Ludwig's life: Everyone was saying *muumbazza*, and they said it all the time.

During some conversations, the entire English language became *muumbazza*, a word that wasn't even English. So whenever an interaction with Lulu or the company was required, he took it in writing because *muumbazza* never appeared on the page. This evasive strategy worked until he started seeing *muumbazza* in text messages. And then in emails. And then in the subtitles of movies and TV shows. Books were the only place he had never encountered it until he encountered it there too, continuing the case, unbeknownst to his ex-employer, for him to be her ideal troubleshooter, someone who was irreplaceable only by dumb luck. Even online encyclopedia entries about him were a fog of *m*'s, *u*'s, *b*'s, *z*'s, and *a*'s.

Ludwig had had enough of fairy magic, but with it no longer in his life, his attention turned to New York's other spell chaser. *He* had invented athleisure. The company only made sense with him in charge. What had he been thinking?

On a bright and muggy morning in early September, when the rising sun's eastern light turned every glass tower into a beaming lighthouse, Ludwig fired up his company laptop and made his move. To communicate, he had to read between the *muumbazza*s.

LUDWIG: Hey, what do you think of the company's direction?

NAVEENA: You're alive?

LUDWIG: You thought I was dead?

NAVEENA: Muumbazza.

LUDWIG: Why would you think I was dead?

NAVEENA: Lulu said you were taking a muumbazza back, which I took to muumbazza that she finally killed you.

LUDWIG: OK, but what do you think of where the company is?

NAVEENA: Should I be muumbazza to you?

LUDWIG: Why wouldn't you be talking to me?

NAVEENA: You were muumbazza to be stepping back. Now you're muumbazza about the muumbazza direction.

LUDWIG: It's in my agreement that I still have veto power over product decisions.

NAVEENA: Is there something wrong with muumbazza and muumbazza?

LUDWIG: That's what I'm asking you.

NAVEENA: I am not muumbazza part in a coup. Muumbazza muumbazza.

LUDWIG: Hey, what do you think of the company's direction?

IGOR:

LUDWIG: Hey, what do you think of the company's direction?

AYONIA: What do you muumbazza?

LUDWIG: I feel like I'm too old for all the druid shit, and our fan base is heading in the same direction. I have this thesis that there could be a future in cardigans and moccasins.

AYONIA: Can muumbazza hold on one muumbazza.

LUDWIG: Sure.

AYONIA:

LUDWIG:

AYONIA:

LUDWIG:

AYONIA:

LUDWIG:

AYONIA: I'm back.

LUDWIG: Great. What do you think?
AYONIA: (Ayonia is typing . . .)
LUDWIG:
AYONIA: Respectfully, I don't muumbazza we're Tommy Muumbazza. Our style is ATHleisure, not leisure. Urban, not log cabin. That feels like selling out the muumbazza and doing what all brands eventually do, which is forget what made them muumbazza to begin with. Our fans would muumbazza on us. People would burn our muumbazza in the streets. I am finally a respected fashion muumbazza, and I don't want to muumbazza that. Yes, you gave me this muumbazza. But that does not give you the right to muumbazza it back. Lulu is my CEO.
LUDWIG: Selling out the movement? I invented the movement! I put extra-large hoods on sleeveless windbreakers. Not Lulu. Me! I'm the entrepreneur! This is a margaritas and cozy Swiss alpine fireplaces culture now.
AYONIA: That's not a real culture.
LUDWIG: Athleisure wasn't a real culture until I invented it, just like I invented all of you!
AYONIA:
LUDWIG: Hello?
AYONIA:
LUDWIG: Ayonia?

LULU: Stop it.

LUDWIG: Stop what?

LULU: Don't you dare muumbazza what I am making. We had a muumbazza that I was CEO. I cannot be a muumbazza if you are sowing muumbazza and second-muumbazza me in every channel. Do this again, and I will make sure we vote you out.

LUDWIG: There's no way they would vote me out. I made them. You all owe me. Especially you.

LULU: Muumbazza muumbazza, you muumbazza. Muumbazza! Muumbazza muumbazza muumbazza muumbazza muumbazza muumbazza muumbazza. Muumbazza MUUMBAZZA muumbazza MUUMBAZZA muumbazza muumbazza. Muumbazza muumbazza! If you muumbazza want to help muumbazza, find your pig.

LUDWIG: This is no way for a family to behave. You never understood that this business is a family.

A week later, they voted him out. He had his shares; they had the power.

Then Ludwig put on jeans.

Years passed.

THE CITY THAT NEVER SLEEPS

Fall 2021

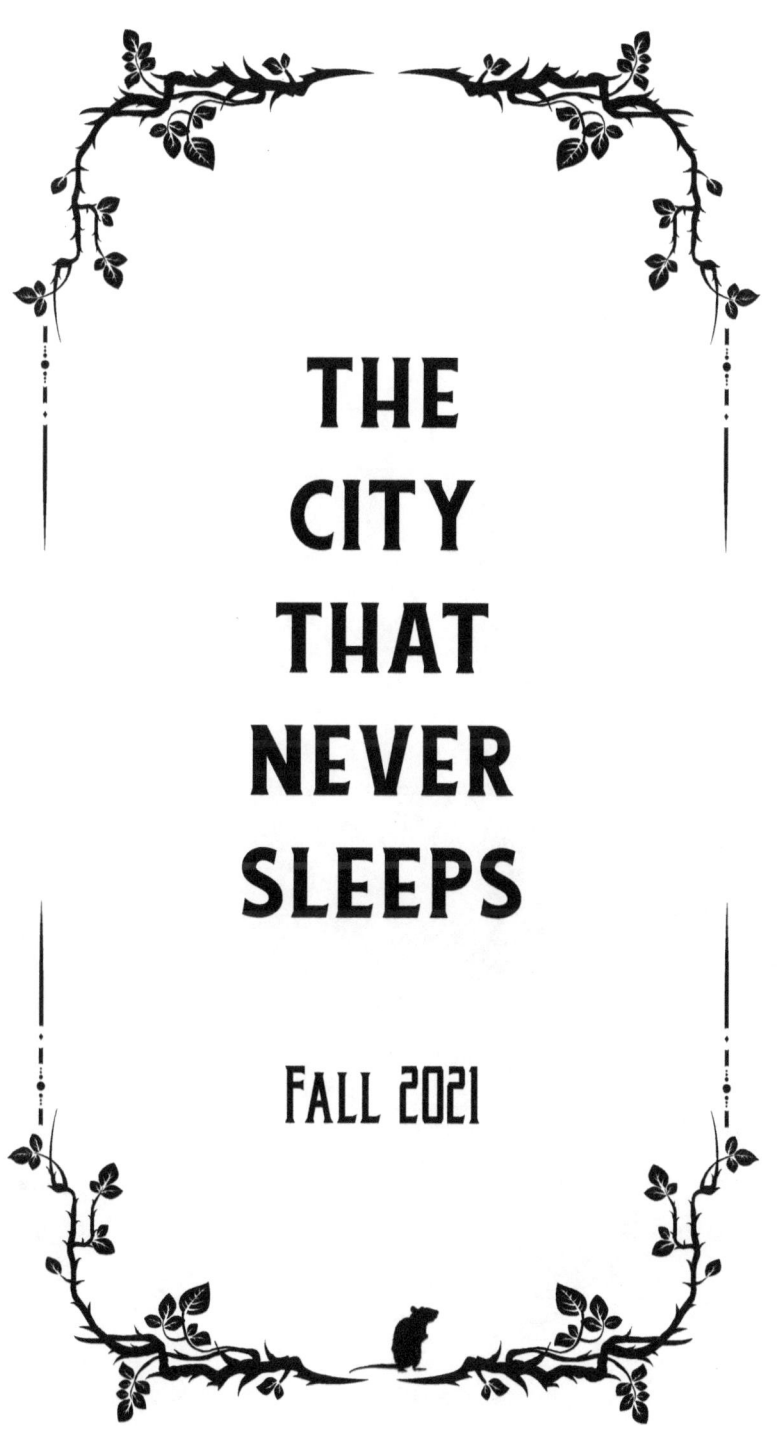

16

Muumbazza.

—Every New Yorker, Nearly All the Time

When Ludwig listened to music, he listened only to the instrumentals. Otherwise, every song, even the ones he knew best, became the word.

No longer able to comprehend written and spoken communication, he avoided them and, if spoken to, feigned deafness while gesturing to the uncharged hearing aids he wore everywhere. "Too many Q-tips," he'd say. What else could he do? What they said, he could not say.

On rare occasions when someone fluent in sign language acknowledged Ludwig's inability to communicate verbally, they brandished hand gestures that undoubtedly represented something to them and many others, but, to Ludwig, appeared only in the shapes of the five letters that controlled his every interaction with other sentient life.

Ludwig no longer saw himself as the exception to an enchantment but as the singular sufferer of a curse. So the concept of joining some new community evaded him, just as it had when he lived belowground. Only fairies and their servants didn't say *muumbazza*. Seven years after his PIP, there were no longer any of them in his life, and when Ludwig made conversation, he made it with himself, the only person who didn't say *muumbazza*.

Without employment to encumber the daylight hours, unlimited free time took him to every major New York museum and art gallery, where it was taboo to start conversations with strangers, so no one ever approached with a question or trite third- or fourth-hand observation that he couldn't understand. In crowds, instead of hearing aids, earplugs thwarted the legions of second- and third-hand *muumbazza*s fighting for a way into his mind's inner keep.

Ludwig gorged on natural history, ancient artifacts, and modern art, the last of which inspired a transformation of Zeal's second living room into an abstract expressionist painting studio. Its open floor plan easily accommodated the flinging and dripping of car and house paints at parking spot–sized canvases with mixing sticks, spoons, and improperly cleaned, stiff, otherwise unusable brushes. Controlling the descent and splatter of those orchid white, iris blue, monarch orange, proofreader red, and arachnid black strands felt like casting spells.

Cooking also felt like magic or some adulterated form of alchemy. If potion making as a vocation couldn't happen, perhaps village cheese maker could; that guild, like him and Giustina, his guru, belonged to another time.

To replicate her mozzarella, he contemplated asking her family for the recipe. Had she written it down? If so, what would *muumbazza* let him learn from it? Less and less every day. So he attempted her mozzarella, via many trials and just as many errors. All he had was unwanted time.

Unpasteurized milk was the most challenging component

to find, more so than even rennet (a complex set of enzymes produced in the stomach lining of some mammals), especially for someone whose ability to communicate was comparable to a stop sign—he could talk, but nothing could talk back.

Visually, the two milks were identical: white in a jug. Where had Giustina found hers? A secret of the old Italian community, perhaps, and he was neither Italian nor a part of any community, though against his will, he kept many secrets. So when bottles of unpasteurized milk were found—which he identified by mandated, colorful warning labels about dangerous microorganisms that he could not read—he bought them in bulk, and his refrigerator and freezer bulged with heavy glass bottles dated using variously colored electrical tape.

Despite online tutorials promising thirty-muumbazza mozzarella, early attempts to replicate Giustina's consumed many multiples of that. Written recipes required immeasurable R & D since *muumbazza* substituted everything from ingredients and portions to instructions. Video tutorials circumvented some of these problems by offering visual cues.

His version went like this:

1. *Mix 1.5 teaspoons of citric acid into one cup of water. Meanwhile, add 1.5 teaspoons of liquid rennet to a quarter cup of room-temperature water.*
2. *Mix one gallon of unpasteurized milk with the citric acid in a cold pot and stir until the mixture clings to a whisk.*
3. *Heat the combination over medium heat and stir until 90 degrees.*
4. *Remove the mixture from the heat, add the rennet, and work it while counting "one muumbazza, two muumbazza" until thirty muumbazzas.*
5. *Place the lid on and let the mixture sit for five minutes until soft, ghostly curds float to the top.*

Then, use a knife to cut a crosshatch pattern into the curd.

6. *Place the pot on medium-low heat and gently stir the curd. When it reaches 105 degrees, remove it from the heat and let it sit for five minutes.*
7. *Move the curds to a strainer and squeeze out the whey. Season the left-behind liquids, raise the heat to 180 degrees, and pour them over the curds. Let sit for fifteen seconds.*
8. *Once the cheese is soft and malleable, pull the curds in two directions and let gravity do the rest. Repeat roughly five times until there is one even mass.*
9. *Press the curd through a closed fist to shape and fold it into individual units.*
10. *Finally, let each ball of mozzarella cool for fifteen minutes.*

By 2021, Ludwig could make mozzarella blindfolded, but never like she could. His version looked right and smelled perfect.

But it tasted like shit.

In a five-story walk-up beneath Times Square, in an archival laboratory that only a lonely, comfort-obsessed New York fashion icon and a few dozen fantasy creatures knew about, a fourteen-foot-tall member of the latter group had chased her own elusive recipe for almost thirty years.

Unlike An Exalted Northwind's attempts to forge a powerful and unprecedented enchantment, Ludwig's recipe for Vermin Milk had been simple: two cups of transcendent comfort here, a dash of New York City street savoir faire there, fold in 100 percent cotton or other flexible fabric, stir in some free publicity, and top with a handful of talented, ambitious people who trusted him; bring to a boil and simmer until glowing magazine profiles.

Ludwig had an advantage that An Exalted Northwind did not: New York's endless pool of resourceful, talented, and driven Upstairs Neighbors, from which he had drawn Lulu, Uchu, Ayonia, Naveena, Igor, Hassan, and many others. From the same pool, An Exalted Northwind had only drawn Ludwig. If not for what seemed like dumb luck, Lulu could have been An Exalted Northwind's troubleshooter—she was broadly micro and precisely macro, could follow orders and take the initiative when there was none, she was ambitious but rarely to anyone's detriment, and above all else, she was willing to do anything that would bring a trace of magic into her life. Not even Ayonia or Uchu, who had been equally long shots taken on a hunch, possessed all that. Despite this, Lulu had never heard *muumbazza*, the only qualification her dream job required.

What Ludwig and An Exalted Northwind had in common was a sense that ungrateful charity cases had betrayed them, so he pitied and even related to her. Before their betrayal, his sympathies had always been with fellow workers, despite having never been much of one. He no longer knew whom they were with.

Becoming a boss necessitated a certain sense of ownership and, over time, sympathizing with his once master—in a way, he owed her. She helped him elevate many lives (not including those who lost theirs). Regardless, her client-housemates had turned on her just as his employees had turned on him, forcing him to see the wisdom in her draconian stances on insubordinate employees, clients, housemates, client-housemates, blue guys, Upstairs Neighbors, higher beings—everyone except the bucketbearers, it seemed. However, whereas the lives of his employees improved because of her, her fairies' lives did not improve at all because of him. They stewed in basement apartments like he once had. She'd helped him, but he had not helped her. Instead, he'd made things worse.

"I believe it is possible to create an enchantment that lets my client-housemates occupy the city as you do, without hurting humans or vice versa," she had said. This mission would secure her "legacy as the greatest enchantress of any age." She also said, "The fae of this house won't see it that way; they would prefer I drown you all in an inferno of gargantuan, flaming mosquitoes." Without Ludwig alleviating how long her enchantment might take, would the harmless enchantment for which he had originally been recruited still be possible? Would she still be motivated to complete her work without cutting corners? And if not, what did that mean for New York?

To save time, an enchantment that would drown the city in flaming, flying bloodsuckers might not only be in the works but nearing completion. If he was right, he had to act.

THE TSA AGENT examining Ludwig's nearly expired passport bulged from his uniform like popped corn from its kernel. The document approached its ninth birthday, yet the face looking up at the agent from it was identical to the one before him, as if the photo had been taken only hours earlier.

"You muumbazza aged a muumbazza. Muumbazza's muumbazza muumbazza?"

"Not wearing a suit." Occasionally, he got one.

"Muumbazza, muumbazza muumbazza. Muumbazza?"

He shrugged.

An Exalted Northwind's enchantment had always seemed specific to New York; her mandate was, after all, to liberate the first New Yorkers from the latter kind. It had nothing to say about other cities, states, or nations. Yet in ten years, its range remained untested; *muumbazza* made doing anything into work, especially travel. So when he boarded the direct flight to Rome with a first-class ticket in hand—one that required days' worth of guesswork to acquire, followed by hours spent searching for its corresponding gate—he did so enthusiastically. Though people would speak Italian when the plane landed, they wouldn't say *muumbazza*.

"Muumbazza or muumbazza?" a flight attendant, who in a fairer society would have been retired, asked as she offered a tray supporting a dozen glasses of champagne and orange juice.

"A little bit of both," Ludwig said, certain he'd interpreted *business or pleasure*, correctly. Her confused look suggested that he hadn't. She mixed one glass with another and handed him a mimosa.

As the flight broke cruising altitude, Ludwig searched his backpack for a pill in the shape of a big blue oval that he had bought from a dead woman's kin during his basement days. He chased it with the mimosa and blacked out so suddenly that he never got the chance to recline his seat into a bed, defeating the first-class ticket's purpose.

A different flight attendant shook him awake on the tarmac in Rome.

"Muumbazziano?" He could always tell when it was a question.

"Are we there?"

"Muumbazzidolce."

Perhaps he had to shake out the enchantment's residuals, like waiting out a stiff neck or the delirium and congestion that follow the flu. As life often reminded him, it was not the world that *muumbazza* had conquered; it was him.

Customs was another concern. With *muumbazza* still in effect, would they ask him unanswerable questions that jeopardized his entry and mission? He followed the crowd down an arduously long hallway that ended in front of uniformed Italians behind bulletproof glass.

"Muumbazzafino?" was all they asked, from which he correctly inferred "passport?" They stamped it without looking, and he went right through. He already loved this country.

Without reading comprehension, Rome's Fiumicino Airport, like New York's JFK, could only be navigated using universal, language-neutral iconography; everything else was an Italian-sounding riff on *muumbazza*. Bathrooms were easy enough, but telling signs for the cab stand from the rental car department proved challenging, which forced Ludwig, who didn't travel and therefore didn't own a rolling suitcase, to carry and then eventually drag a loaded, conceptual Vermin Milk duffel bag from wrong location to wrong location until he discovered the shared office space of twelve rental car companies.

Their diverse, brightly colored logos circled the room, as though he had stepped back into his past and arrived at the pitch for one of their rebrandings. Color and typography once again proved his compasses.

Ludwig slid a liberally tanned and perfumed front desk attendant his passport and driver's license, and she slid back five pages of forms. Thrice, he filled them out incorrectly, causing the already overworked and under-appreciated employee to become the most Italian that he had seen a person become, Italian or not. His hearing aids garnered him little sympathy. To her, he appeared not only deaf but blind. Fatigued and finally with keys in hand, he dragged himself into the six-floor car garage's only SUV with automatic transmission. The vehicle's speedometer looked back not in MPH or KPH but MBSPH.

Because money only became tighter without income, he settled for the four-bedroom villa (the one with olive trees and the cement lap pool) overlooking the hills of Calenzano north of Florence instead of the seven-bedroom villa-farmhouse (the one with the famous, photogenic vineyards and the slate infinity pool) overlooking Tuscany's famed and iconic SR 222. Mozzarella originated there, or so mindlessly clicking through search engine results suggested, making the trip more like espionage than a sabbatical.

Photos of the BnB featured a winding, arduous dirt road that led from the foot of a soaring hill to a driveway overlooking summits populated with natural, evergreen wonders fertilized by dead Romans.

Unable to manually enter the BnB's address into his phone since its keyboard lacked twenty-one crucial letters (Italian without *e* and *i* and *o* could hardly be called Italian at all), he frustratedly stabbed and swiped at the screen until it surrendered and let him copy and paste the unfettered address. Was the drive possible without the power to recognize names or understand voice directions? Could *muumbazza* corrupt the application's little blue dot and navigational arrow? Neither glyph appeared in any alphabet. There was, as there had often been with his handicap, only one way to know. Things were not going as planned. Despite this, he continued, expecting that *muumbazza* just needed time to recognize that Italy, despite many similarities, was not New York.

From Rome's western outskirts, he passed carefully preserved ruins, fragments of his former employer's age, past landmarks with names he would never be able to divine. Eventually, he'd be deposited in lumpy, picturesque Tuscany, a place where he imagined settling down until it became evident that *muumbazza* might settle there too.

Along the autostrada, ads looked and read little differently from those loitering among New York's crowded streets and highways ("Muumbazzafini muumbazzadonna? Muumbazzatripa!"), except for Italians' much higher tolerance for the nearly naked human form. Even license plates read as variations of *muumbazza*'s two vowels and three consonants: MBMBZA, MUBBA, MZZBAM, MMMBZA. In a country whose language Ludwig didn't speak, *muumbazza*'s ubiquity disoriented him less than when he had the rightful expectation of understanding speech. But Italians had other ways of communicating.

Their assertiveness at the wheel startled him as someone who rarely drove. Each time he neared the passing lane, a fuel-efficient two-door manual sedan swooped in with high beams flashing and horn honking like a territorial goose beating its wings. Were these ancestral relatives of the immigrants who gave New York its reputation so different from those he knew, with their fondness for temperamental, automotive outbursts, street harassment, and unchallenged self-confidence? Is that what confused the enchantment?

Derelict offices, factories, and parking lots interrupted Umbria's green hills and bucolic pastures, confirming a lingering suspicion that this once nine-to-five economy had surrendered to the siren song of capital and become a rental market for the seeds of Western civilization. Like Williamsburg, its connection to history weakened before Ludwig. People couldn't be faulted for making money the easy way, at least not by him, even if it meant becoming a nation of property managers.

Crisscrossing, geometric fields of orderly grape vines multiplied before farmhouses and villas painted summer colors. Haunted-looking trees that resembled people tightly wrapped in winter cloaks grew everywhere in dotted lines along old roads like marching soldiers. The landscape soared as the long drive approached its end.

As Tuscan hills aspired to become mountains, small pastel villages with their own tourism boards rode the earth into the clouds until they resembled floating islands—the labor it must have required to lift stone and timber into the clouds all those centuries earlier! But the thought stopped there, and so did the clouds, as the road disappeared through tunnel after tunnel, nearly the length of New York subway lines. Exiting the last of these placed him within ten minutes of Brunelleschi's Duomo, once the highest structure in Europe, which appeared as boldly and suddenly as lightning on the horizon.

His phone came to life.

"Muumbazzabubliano muumbazzainace muumbazziazi muumbazzifatto muumbazzabibi muumbazzodonno," the voice navigation said. Or had it asked? Did voice navigation ask? Without the capacity for language, technology's relentless advance had been, if not lost on him, then placed just out of reach.

Ludwig veered off the autostrada and down a Florentine side street so narrow that even swarms of death-tempting mopeds driven by helmetless operators could only access it single file. He rode their wake, assuming they knew the way. The way to where? Up and down cobbled walkways that rumbled the unseasoned vehicle. *Wubba-wubba-wubba-wub. Wubba-wubba-wubba-wub.*

Though not quite an international city—Florence's tiny airport made such a designation unlikely—it was nevertheless a cosmopolitan city, meaning that a small percentage of its downtown undoubtedly possessed a fashion district where tourists shopped for the kind of designer apparel that Ludwig had once warred against.

New York had SoHo, London had Carnaby Street, Paris had the Faubourg Saint-Honoré District, Seoul had Gangnam, Tokyo had Harajuku, Los Angeles had the preposterously named Los Angeles Fashion District, and Florence had whatever this was called, all of them homes to brands that prioritized aesthetics over comfort, unaware that the two things stood forever together, like crises and opportunities. A comfortable person looked good; a comfortable person did not need high fashion to lift their low self-worth.

Or so he had, in another life, believed.

The river of two-wheeled traffic passed the illegible but—using by now familiar tricks—decipherable brand names of sworn enemies from a previous life: the Fendis, the Pradas, the Guccis, the Manolo Blahniks, the Jimmy Choos, the Balenciagas, the Valentinos, and the Vermin Milks.

He raised his foot from the gas until the car crawled over the cobblestones. *Wubba . . . wubba . . . wubba . . . wub.*

What was this treacherous shit? he wondered, sitting in an itchy cardigan, support-free boat shoes, a time-consuming button-up, and stiff jeans supported by a belt that wasn't even 1 percent elastic. Did it matter whether Vermin Milk now belonged to the whole world instead of just New York? To him, it did because he was its founder and visionary—it was his legacy to betray, not Lulu's. Vermin Milk belonged to New York, not these preening, cured lard–licking prima donnas.

He belonged to the fellowship of entrepreneurs, despite not having been one for seven years. Hypocrisy was his right, not Lulu's. As Vermin Milk's founder, he would always outrank her. So nothing was his fault, especially this, and nothing could be. That's what employees were for.

Perhaps Ludwig's lady-lord and benefactor had been right.

WITHOUT ANY MEANS to communicate, the question of whether his hosts would greet him at the villa remained open. Had they offered to give him a tour? Had he agreed? What had that one long paragraph been about? Would antiquated skeleton keys from another time dangle like wind chimes from the lock?

Though he was visibly seething from the revelation downtown, he still wanted his hosts' company—these days, he always wanted company, but the ordinary kind, where parties exchanged words they could understand until both emerged slightly more knowledgeable than before. Perhaps the Italian penchant for speaking with one's hands would trigger a breakthrough. He popped in his hearing aids and hoped this place, on an isolated hill thousands of miles from New York, would prove *muumbazza*'s last stand.

There they were, waiting for him as though he were family—the embodiment of hospitaliano.

The test would be the tour his hosts gave him after depositing his bags into the largest of four approximately medieval bedrooms.

"Muumbazza muumbazza muumbazza, muumbazza muumbazza," his hosts said and said, and on they continued with the tour, and politely, so did Ludwig. Italian guy number one and two were at least bilingual since that many *muumbazza*s without vowel-intensive suffixes signaled English; whether it was good English would forever remain another mystery.

As he had thought, even the villa's newest wing appeared older than his country. No one had to say so, or perhaps they had, and he couldn't understand them. It wore its age nobly. Everything was stone, and everything else was petrified wood. The only plastics in the vicinity were on his backpack and coating the electrical wires. The numbers suggested that someone had died in at least one of these rooms, where he hoped to meet a ghost whose corporeal form expired years before the enchantment went into effect.

Since the villa (Muumbazza, it was called, like the town and his hosts and the model of his rental car) had been carved into a steep, rocky hillside, the villa's ground-floor living room dipped twenty degrees Fahrenheit lower than the second. Both spaces boasted cavernous fireplaces that swallowed what little light the dim electric lamps and sconces produced.

Farther down, in the cellar, walls of old farm tools that

originated before industrial manufacturing hung coated in sheaths of rust. They were not weapons, although Ludwig's imagination could make anything look like one.

In the villa's three-story tower, which had rightfully received the most attention from the BnB's photographer, his hosts flashed seven fingers followed by two closed fists: *seven hundred years old*. Once again, occasionally, one got through. Perhaps even the enchantment lacked the force of will to stop Italians from signaling with their hands. Someone had died up there, where it was all view for miles upon green, hilly miles; the steepness and elevation made it difficult to imagine anyone venturing so high without a car, except perhaps by donkey, which is what hanging, ghostly photos showed hitched to posts surrounding the villa.

The tour revealed additional *muumbazza*s, printed on old brittle tomes lining shelves and cabinets and on an easel bearing a disintegrating sheet-music book. Perhaps, out in the wilderness that engulfed the villa, *muumbazza* would not follow him unless a passing crow cawed the word or the singing wind pronounced it.

He had come to recreate Giustina's mozzarella, a task that, without being able to shake out the word, he recognized was impossible. Many Italians spoke English, but they only spoke *muumbazza* to him. He had traveled four thousand miles, and so had the enchantment. Perhaps it had already been here.

The tour ended, and he was alone again.

Again.

"Muumbazz-*caw*. Muumbazz-*caw*," a crow declared, mocking his pain.

ALTHOUGH HE SELDOM drank drinks that weren't frozen and green, things quickly changed. He possessed no power to improve his situation, but he could perhaps make himself too stupid to care.

Ludwig drank the complimentary bottles left behind by his hosts in a single evening, then imbibed seven more the following day. Quality wine was sold everywhere, even at gas stations and convenience stores. He bought it by the case. How could *muumbazza* have followed him so far? He was supposed to be the exception to the enchantment, not its epicenter. Had An Exalted Northwind meant to drape the whole world in the word?

Again and again, all *muumbazza* gave him was time and frustration, and finally, a question: Had this always been An Exalted Northwind's plan, to split New York and the world into nonoverlapping realities? What would that require? What would that look like? What would be the point? And had she already done it?

Several bottles later, Ludwig extracted an ancient scythe from the cellar and used it like a golf club to tee fresh olives into the distance. Then he blacked out on a white couch and wet it and himself. To hide the embarrassing truth from his hosts, he carried both couch cushions to the fire pit adjacent to the swimming pool, soaked them in kerosene, and burned them.

With ten days left in Tuscany, Ludwig did his best to be a tourist. He drove some of the scenic SR 222, but sitting alone in a car whose GPS felt like it was taunting him only increased his loneliness. Things worsened when he learned that his vehicle, which he thought was gasoline-powered, was, in fact, electric-powered and that charging it, which should have been a simple affair (wall, plug), was not.

The villa's million-year-old electrical sockets, which seemed to predate the harnessing of electricity, weren't compatible with the car's complimentary charging cable. He needed a third-party kiosk, all of which required apps to work, which Ludwig could not read, stranding him at the villa. He could have written to his hosts, had he not already destroyed thousands of Euros' worth of their furniture. The food he had would have to last.

He threw farm tools at trees, knocking loose olives, which he feasted on. Then, after breaking all of the cellar's farm tools and weapons, he threw empty wine bottles at trees, lizards, an old olive-crushing millstone, the villa's roof, his dead vehicle, and that fucking bird. "Muumbazz-*caw*, muumbazz-*caw*."

He spent his time drinking and crying, usually in that order, though not always. Sometimes the drinking resolved the crying, and sometimes vice versa. He hadn't touched water in days. He ate very little; he should have been dead.

On two occasions, less from darkness and depression than frustration and powerlessness, he chased wild boars into the wilderness with a bottle of white in one hand and a bottle of red in the other, like a very specific kind of phantasm that could exist nowhere except Tuscany. If he could have, he would have returned home, but his handicap made finding an early flight back to New York, where he could at least lose touch with reality on his terms and in his own home, impossible.

Ludwig the Prisoner.

As his remaining days in Italy ticked by at the speed of a closely watched clock, he felt the presence of the blue guys, despite being thousands of miles from any. He wondered whether their real power had been to show someone not their worst fears but fears that could make them morbidly lonely, which Ludwig, after seven years of *muumbazza*, recognized was, or should have been, among his worst fears—and the blue guys had known it, if they knew anything besides the location of doors in people's floors.

When he had watched his family and acquaintances die by the frostbitten blade of some unseen executioner, it was not only the violent spectacle of their deaths; it was imagining life without them, even though his mother and father were already, at that point, long dead. When the women in his life had conspired to process him into food, it was not only the gruesomeness of being ground into cans—though that undeniably played a part—but the horror of them doing so without recognizing his existence. In that call center in Maryland, it wasn't knowing that he could never leave, but the thought of having no one to talk to about it except other versions of himself, which proved the same thing as talking to oneself. Then, finally, there was the funeral home, utterly bereft of even a single memento from those he knew, except for the ones who hated him most. Other people, he was learning, were life—and loneliness was death.

In addition to drinking, Ludwig burned books, paper grocery bags, tree branches, cardboard boxes, blankets, and furniture that was older than him and probably more valuable even than the designer kind that populated Zeal.

Ludwig found more to burn each night, and the flames rose, and their explicit, embedded messages grew unmistakable in their projections.

In the fire, he saw images of what *muumbazza* portended. Unable to communicate, short on money without Mr. Blueberry or the ability to hold a job, he saw what remained of his sanity and wealth blown away like ash until he was destitute and sedated in one of Bellevue's hallways.

Then, one night, dressed only in underwear and a T-shirt stained by sweat, ash, jarred puttanesca sauce, wine, and olive oil, he looked into the flames and saw *muumbazza*, not carried aloft by the cawing of some bird or the singing of the wind, but written in the fire by flames that resembled smoldering ghosts.

Muumbazzaaa! Muumbazzaaa! the bonfire howled.

Until An Exalted Northwind succeeded at her enchantment, which might be centuries, *muumbazza* was the way—a way he could no longer abide.

He took the pills he remembered to bring and gathered those left behind by the hosts and previous tourists. These were not, he imagined, the fun kind, since who would leave those behind? Their labels gave nothing away about them except for the countries they came from.

"Muumbazzagugenschfart." German.

"Muumbazzquestatorfilla." Spanish.

"Muumbazzhindaio." Japanese.

On the thirteenth night, hours before Ludwig should have returned to New York, he asked himself what the point was, cupped all the discovered pills into his open palm, shoveled them into his mouth, and chased them with a bottle of wine.

A life with *muumbazza* was not a life worth living.

A life with *muumbazza* was a life alone.

His eyes closed, and he dreamed of nothing, not even the word.

As Tuscany's broiling late summer sun rose, Ludwig felt someone cradling him in their bony arms, tenderly consoling him in a way he wasn't sure he needed or wanted. The man's scratchy red beard tickled his unshaven face.

Ludwig's hands searched his stained T-shirt for vomit, blood, and insects scouring for food. He found none. Perhaps he was in Heaven, a place that he suspected, having made contact with the sublime, might exist (the thought that he belonged in Hell never occurred to him).

Several things struck him as curious all at once: He was not dead, despite having taken over sixty pills of mixed origins; he was not in pain of any kind, and in fine enough health to ask the person cradling him who he was.

"Non abbiate paura, amici. Lavoravo in un ospedale," a familiar voice said to two men, the villa's owners, as they stormed around the house, shouting about this or that broken, burnt, and missing thing. They displayed no concern for Ludwig's health, while the red-haired man with the impeccable smile, holding him upright, showed no concern for that of the villa, despite being a committed and prolific real estate man.

"Muumbazza like us, Mr. Ludwig," Kenneth Branagh said. Only two beings, fairies and their servants, could speak English without *muumbazza*. But only one human could talk without it, sometimes. "Real estate and partying. Our curses, wouldn't you muumbazza? What a muumbazza to see you here, so far from our muumbazza home after so much muumbazza."

For unknown reasons, Kenneth Branagh pierced *muumbazza*'s nearly impenetrable veil so frequently that Ludwig had sometimes wondered whether he was faking it, as if the enchantment couldn't keep up with the frenetic real estate agent. So the frenetic real estate agent filled in the gaps on his own. To ask Branagh why this was the case would be to threaten his life, whether in the form of a swamp ghoul drowning him in the swimming pool, a Komodo dragon leaping from the refrigerator to inject him with a paralyzing neurotoxin, or something as simple as a mounted knight cleaving him in half with a glaive.

Ludwig's hosts rightfully wanted him dead or at the very least in court, but after a quick wrist flick from Kenneth Branagh, like the one that An Exalted Northwind had used to teleport Ludwig from her presence, they snapped to attention like two soldiers and marched shoulder to shoulder down the impossible hill, kicking dust past their bald heads the whole way.

"Why are you here?" Ludwig asked as he freed himself from Kenneth Branagh's coddling, unsettling embrace.

"Muumbazza here helps me muumbazza." Always just enough for Ludwig to understand. Even with Kenneth Branagh's *muumbazza* exceptionalism, comprehending his meaning was still like seeing down a long road during fierce snow. One could make out shapes if they tried, but never perfectly.

"I appreciate you cradling me like this; it's adorable. But I think I can support myself. I feel fine," Ludwig said, and he did. "Where did my hosts go? Probably better I get out of here before they get back. What brings you here? Getting into the Tuscany real estate market? It seems like it's booming."

"Oh, muumbazza a coincidence. What brings me here has nothing to do with any of muumbazza. I am a real estate muumbazza, and though I muumbazza my work, even I need the odd break or two each muumbazza. It is no muumbazza to me, as it is no surprise to you that we would meet muumbazza, having such similar taste in real estate. Plus, I have an old friend I come to see muumbazza I can."

"What do they do? It's mostly BnBs and tacky gift shops out here."

"She's muumbazza of a florist and a collector of things," Kenneth Branagh said. "She loves quiet, which I frankly muumbazza unsettling if absorbed for too muumbazza. So I try not to stay longer than a week or muumbazza. The real question, Mr. Ludwig: What brings you out here?"

"A broken dream. I thought I could help preserve someone's important legacy, but I couldn't. Though it has crossed my mind that I am here because I am running from more important unfinished business in New York, the kind I should have done for someone who did right by me despite our many disagreements, who I did not do right by in return." He did not mention that he needed *muumbazza* to stop, that he still held out hopes of learning magic, and that not even suicide had failed to slow *muumbazza* down. How was he still alive?

He sniffled.

"Oh, Mr. Muumbazza. There's nothing worse than unfinished muumbazza. How unfinished is it?"

"Very. I skipped out long before the job was done, and in

doing so, I also made it difficult for her to finish the work. I fucked up pretty bad, KB. This could have far-reaching consequences."

"Are you still in touch with muumbazza?"

"No. Dead cold," Ludwig said.

"Is this related to your fashion muumbazza?"

"No. Well, yes. Sort of. It's hard to explain. She made that possible; then I used what she gave me to pursue that instead of the job I was given."

"Well, it sounds like this person is a woman. You muumbazza how women are—muumbazza love gifts! They're like fairies," he said, eliciting a stare from Ludwig, but Kenneth Branagh betrayed nothing behind his smile. "Fairies love gifts," he said, then paused as if waiting for the hook to set. "Gifts will get muumbazza back in her good graces. On a muumbazza of 1 to 10, how unfinished did you muumbazza the business?"

"Thirty-eight," Ludwig said.

"In that muumbazza, you might need more than one gift," Kenneth Branagh said. "My strong muumbazza is that you offer three. One gift for her, which is something she muumbazza; one for her people, which is muumbazza they need; and one for all of them, which muumbazza won't see coming."

"Maybe you can help me. You're good at finding things. How insane would it sound if I asked you to find something completely insane? I worded that badly. It's been a long time since I talked to anyone."

"What do you seek?" Kenneth Branagh asked.

"A crystal ball."

"Any muumbazza shop should have one of those muumbazza."

"The real kind."

"That's tough. Mr. Ludwig, just this muumbazza, I don't think I can muumbazza you. But there muumbazza be something else I can do. My ear is still to the muumbazza since you asked me to help you learn magic. Perhaps a crystal muumbazza will be easier. Who knows what a man in my position might find? Now, it muumbazza like you need help charging that muumbazza car so that you don't miss your flight? I will handle the owners."

"KB?" Ludwig asked.

"Yes?"

"What are you?" It was a question he had entertained since their first meeting in Kenneth Branagh's office nine years before.

"Why, I'm your friend, Mr. Ludwig! But muumbazza is also my client. And I'd erase New York from the map muumbazza either. Not literally, of course. It's just an expression. Muumbazza."

Ludwig hadn't heard that expression. Whatever Kenneth Branagh was, he didn't seem like a threat. He was an ally. Perhaps one of only two he'd ever had, and certainly the only ally he still had.

For the entire ride to the airport, Ludwig played the instrumental version of "New York, New York," singing along with the words as he went, the taste of death's failure to claim him still in his mouth.

The trip hadn't been a complete failure. He had realized something about himself: He needed companionship, whether human or fairy didn't matter. But to regain either, he needed his job again.

He needed Her.

17

God was watching, and in His wisdom, God was mum.

—Old Chiseltooth

NOTES OF WINTER were in the air, sailing all around, looking for places to convene like listless youth who had arrived too early to a party. Some New Yorkers chose to say—like they always chose to say around that time every year—what everyone already knew: Winter was still two calendar pages away, and yet, there it was, invisibly slipping through brown leaves for all to see.

That evening, renewed by possibility, Ludwig filled a coffee mug with premium gin and a mackerel he carefully situated as if planting some rare, exotic flower. The combination rested on the windowsill until the fish began deteriorating, making it more like tinned sardine than wild mackerel.

When one of his few remaining bipedal friends hadn't appeared after two days, Ludwig dropped the fish into his garbage disposal instead of letting it pointlessly waft from the trash, as if he could smell anything over his sniffling. As he reached for the switch, he thought better of it. *If it smelled too bad for the trash . . .* So with two cautious fingers like forceps, Ludwig lifted the decomposing mackerel by its tail, walked to the balcony, scanned the street for activity, and threw it over the railing. *Thwop.*

The next day, disappointed by the result that a small amount of premium gin and freshwater fish produced, Ludwig purchased three additional gallons of the dandy Englishman gin and an entire adult grouper, a gross-looking but sumptuous, slow-moving ocean fish with huge, puffy lips, from the chatty fishmonger who resembled the deep sea animal in disquieting ways.

Ludwig relocated his old margarita machine's remains (he had been unable to part with them via the trash, a burial, or cremation) to the balcony and filled its three-gallon reservoir first with the fish and then with so much gin that it splashed over the rim; the big fish's upright tail gave it the impression of having crash-landed there. He took three steps back from the bizarre confluence of expensive things, placed his hands on his hips, and tilted his head like a painter examining their work. Was it done? Only time would tell.

A day passed, during which the mixture summoned summer's final surviving flies and a lingering smell worse than the one commemorating his previous attempt. As the grouper hit Ludlow Street, the vast fish exploded, and rats descended.

An Exalted Northwind might have deactivated the lure or changed its formula to prevent precisely what he was doing, having once said that Lonesome Johnny was more loyal to him than her, and Ludwig was counting on it.

Though it required the kind of manual labor he seldom failed to avoid, it was worth trying the formula again if it broke the curse and reunited him with an old friend not bound by *muumbazza.*

The following day, Ludwig purchased every drop of premium gin (including the airplane bottles) from three liquor stores, netting him thirty-six gallons, a far cry from what his eight-person hot tub required. For three additional days, he marched from liquor store to liquor store and cab to cab, collecting as much of it as his sagging muscles allowed. He attached a hose and drained the heavily chlorinated hot tub into the building's gutters.

He returned to the fishmonger with his uncharged hearing aids in, carrying a labeled drawing that bore a specific request: an adult blue marlin, which Ludwig drew from memory because he could perfectly picture any shape involving a sword. He left a stack of cash, his apartment's address, and a time on the counter: *10/24, 1:00 PM*. To Ludwig, it read: *MM/BS, A:SA MM*. But like the fishmonger's look of disbelief as the man who had just overpaid by $2,000 strode out the door, it didn't matter. Soon, he might again be employed by An Exalted Northwind, meaning that money would be a concern only for other people. What shape would that money take? Perhaps golden eggs laid by a blue goose who, like Mr. Blueberry, would be a great hang. The goose would be cleaner if nothing else.

On the drop-off day, he emptied the gin into his hot tub. Although he possessed only enough to fill it two-thirds, his math told him that the marlin would displace enough to make the hot tub appear full.

After three hours of pouring gin, the buzzer rang.

Through his building's front door camera, he watched three men lift a wheelbarrow shrouded in rope and canvas, giving them the appearance of museum employees moving Michelangelo's *David*. To avoid the ensuing, indecipherable small talk, Ludwig squeezed in his hearing aids. He braced for the kind of question-and-answer session one expects whenever eight hundred pounds of marlin are delivered to a penthouse's gin-filled hot tub.

"It's for a photo shoot," he told them. "Brands. Models and stuff. You know—fashion. Thanks for your time."

"Muumbazza muumbazza, muumbazza muumbazza muumbazza, muumbazza," one said.

"Muumbazza muumbazza," another confirmed.

Ludwig placed $2,000 in each of their hands.

By nightfall, the lure produced nothing with a bucket for a head or a Civil War uniform and straw for a body. If this didn't work, nothing would, including a swimming pool filled with gin and an inebriated, soon-to-expire whale shark, making the lure's formula another relic of his once enviable, legendary life.

To amplify the emanating signal, he stirred the ingredients by wrapping his gloved hands around the marlin's bill and pushing as though he worked a Middle Ages millstone or wound the gears of a clock tower. The odor collected in his nostrils like hot ammonia or burning hair, giving him one last idea. He plugged in the hot tub, walked to the control panel, and turned all the knobs.

The hot tub bubbled like a cauldron and emitted colors that matched those emanating from the Empire State Building in the distance. Then, having forgotten that he once paired the tub to his phone, he was surprised when the instrumental version of "New York, New York" burst from the machine's Bluetooth-enabled speakers.

The noxious vapors became more toxic as the tub's temperature rose, causing a nuclear plume of gaseous gin and billfish fog to form over the Lower East Side. This fusion served no other purpose than to alert the senses of a subcategory of fairy servants who did not even possess the organs required to be nauseated by it.

Ludwig returned to the sixth-floor kitchen, shut the door, and rinsed his face and mouth with cold water before searching his bathroom for eye drops that might suppress the burning.

Finally, he flipped his replacement margarita machine on, collapsed into a chair, and fell asleep.

There came a knock on the balcony door, a pause, a second knock, and a second pause. Desiring months of sleep after almost an entire week of manual labor, Ludwig ignored them.

Knock-knock-knock-knock-knock-knock!

His snores were heard and felt through the glass.

Klang-klang-klang-klang-klang-klang-klang-klang!

What was that?

He rose, startled, searching for the sound's source. Behind the glass, a once crisp and proudly kept Civil War uniform stained years earlier by something wet and brown that had clung to it in globs like French onion soup bounced a dented bucket off the sliding glass door. Tears and rips in the uniform revealed bits of frayed straw and black feathers. Two climbing spikes and a pick-axe appeared in its white-gloved grip. Muffled by the glass, the strange shape cried: "Oh, Mr. Ludwig! Please don't leave me out here with this awful song!"

Ludwig tripped on things that weren't even in his way as he sped toward the door, threw it open, and embraced Lonesome Johnny.

"How are you, buddy?" Ludwig asked, unwilling to let go, an affectionate gesture that Lonesome Johnny happily indulged.

"That's right! We *are* buddies! I have to say that this jubilant combination of fish and gin is the most triumphant of the many that have summoned me," he said, inspecting the hot tub as Ludwig paused "New York, New York." "So of course it was your design. What an artist you are! What an inventor! You are Leonardo da Ludwig or Ludwig da Vinci, whatever you prefer. I prefer whatever makes you happiest."

"I was worried you wouldn't come. I tried fancy gin with fresh mackerel and even a grouper. You couldn't detect them?"

"I'm afraid not. My lady-lord and benefactor has forbidden me from those olfactory frequencies. She adjusted my senses exactly so that you couldn't contact me. But with enough fish and gin"—he spun in place like a figure skater—"well, here I am. Believing that there might have been some emergency—I am so glad to see that there isn't!—I implored her to make an exception and allow this sojourn, which she did, of course, because it is my belief, what with all your talent, diligence, and moxie, that you remain the key to her success."

"There kind of is an emergency," Ludwig said.

"Oh no! Has some villain run a rapier through your pudgy belly? Such a thing is amongst my worst fears, which I will now recite in alphabetical order: abyss ants, aerosol, aneurysms, archons (of the gnostic variety), athlete's foot, Australian jellyfish, avalanches—"

"No, no," Ludwig said, despite curiosity about his remaining fears. "It's worse than that."

"Worse than avalanches?" Lonesome Johnny exclaimed. "We must act now!"

"The whole world is saying *muumbazza*. You're the first living thing I have spoken to in seven years who could speak without saying it."

Lonesome Johnny's bucket percolated. "Where have you been that the word was so ubiquitous?"

"Italy."

"Italia?"

"Yes."

"The ancestral homeland of fairies?"

"Yes. Wait, it is?"

"Some believe it is England or Ireland," Lonesome Johnny said, "but not so. The fae were first driven from their wilds and back into Fairie by the emperor Tiberius Caesar Augustus—a worthy opponent indeed! The same happened to those who found new wilds in England and Ireland. The New York fairies are among the last free fairies. Only an odd straggler or all-powerful matriarch, such as that notorious interloper Gilda Fiorella, remains worldwide. As such, no one more than twenty miles from Times Square should be saying *muumbazza*. My lady-lord and benefactor would not make the mistake of blanketing the whole world with an enchantment meant only for an island. Tell me, could you hear the word on your flight? If you have chartered a yacht, steamship, or sailboat, the question is the same."

"I, uh, *slept* on the flight out." He didn't want to worry Lonesome Johnny with his recent drug use or what he had tried to do in Italy, though someone showing concern for him had an appeal equal to having a conversation. "But on the flight back, people were saying it all the time, over Europe, Canada, and even the ocean."

"I must report this to my lady-lord and benefactor at once," he said as he reequipped the climbing spikes.

"Would you like to stay and have a conversation? To talk? Just for a little while?" Ludwig pleaded.

"Nothing would delight me more, except I must relay this information at once. Now that you are back on the grid, expect my imminent return!"

"You can use the elevator, you know. There is an elevator."

"No time, Mr. Ludwig!"

"Wait, wait!" Ludwig said, blocking Lonesome Johnny's path to the balcony and the side of the building. "I've always wondered, How do you get into and out of Broken Throat? I know that she can portal people out, I've experienced that, but I didn't think she could portal people in. I thought only I could go in."

"Ah, Mr. Ludwig! So clever, your mind. A natural detective of the supernatural, you are. I'm afraid that this trade secret must remain one. Tell me, What will you do with all that fish?"

"Trade secret," he said and headed for the closet, where a Swiffer, a broom, and a custom-forged longsword rested against one another like a quiver of strange arrows.

THOUGH FAINT AND minor compared to her client-housemates', the spots on An Exalted Northwind's neck continued to spread, overtaking her bony, green shoulders. She expected the scourge to finish her last since she was the most powerful among the New York fae and had been underground for the fewest years. But by the time it consumed her client-housemates, Broken Throat would no longer be safe, and there would be nowhere for her to run.

"My lady-lord and benefactor, I bring disturbing news from my rendezvous with Mr. Ludwig."

"That I believe," she said. "Go on."

"Mr. Ludwig has, I believe, brought us information that might help you troubleshoot your enchantment or perhaps expose a glaring mistake."

Lonesome Johnny recited Ludwig's story to her without missing a syllable. He even performed an applause-worthy impression of Ludwig.

This was strange news indeed. *What can this mean?* An Exalted Northwind wondered. Though unhappy to admit it, by reporting this defect, Ludwig had done his job—seven years after being released from it.

"Puppet," she said, "retrieve Ludwig's deed."

"Right-oh-ho, Joe!"

LUDWIG PACED BETWEEN his front door and Zeal's second floor. Which one Lonesome Johnny might appear at was as unknowable as the bucketbearer himself. So, without the hollow heart to calm his nerves, he fired up the replacement margarita machine.

Bzzz.

Ludwig quickstepped to the door, expecting Lonesome Johnny to have remembered the elevator's existence, then slowed to a mosey at the thought of a neighbor inquiring about all the fish.

On the little screen that displayed his building's entrance in grainy black and white, he saw no stained, mid-nineteenth-century uniform with a bucket head nor any unhappy, bearded, leather jacket–wearing creative director from a neighboring apartment. Instead, someone average-looking and instantly forgettable who blended into a crowd of one returned his gaze. Could such a man possess a name? Even John Doe felt too specific, too personal. John Doe had at least been a person; this was no one.

Curious about what a no one might wear, Ludwig interrogated its wardrobe. As his eyes settled on vanilla garment after vanilla garment, boredom quickly set in, followed by distraction and a short-circuiting of his attention span that caused his focus to roll away like rain from the windshield of a speeding car. Whoever he was or wasn't, he reminded Ludwig of Kenneth Branagh's receptionist. Had there been a receptionist? He wouldn't bet on it. Perhaps that was the point.

The plain man flashed a package just smaller than a fantasy paperback. The parcel bore no address, markings, or labels except for "Muumbazza" inked across its surface in silver. Beneath the obfuscated letters, it could have been a name—perhaps Ludwig's.

"Are you with the post office? Just leave whatever that is in the lobby." Who would send him, one of the city's foremost pariahs, a package? Even junk mail and taxes had stopped coming years earlier.

The plain man spoke what were certainly words. They varied from one to the next, adhered to a version of grammar, and appeared more than once in what might have been sentences. But they weren't words that the deed's enchantment bothered to translate, as if the enchantment found the courier too dull to interpret. This caused Ludwig to wonder if this, the most boilerplate man in a city full of unforgettable characters, the default setting from innumerable video game character customization screens, was human at all.

Watching the manlike figure's lips form the shapes that disseminated sounds felt unnatural and uncomfortable, as if Ludwig had spoken to a doll and the doll had spoken back. His words were just sounds, plain as unshaped clay, without disposition or identity, geographical origins or meaning; they were all just noise, signifying nothing.

"I can't understand you. I think it's this fucking video shit," Ludwig said.

Words.

"Just leave it in the lobby."

Words.

Could this be another enchanted courier? It was hard to say since enchantments made the ordinary extraordinary in some way, and nothing about this man was extraordinary except for his evident lack of extraordinariness. If he were an enchanted courier, who sent him? And to what purpose?

"Fine. I'm buzzing you in."

Bzzz.

It occurred to him that moments like this were why people owned guns and other weapons, things that his apartment had, but he was already at the door, and those were over, well, maybe there or there. In the safe? Perhaps. Yet weapons were only ever appropriate as responses to danger, which the plain man did not elicit.

The elevator, which had already arrived in the lobby,

proved unneeded. The plain man climbed all five floors like a windup toy, taking one step every 2.4 seconds—neither fast nor slow, as if a median speed for climbing stairs existed and should be observed.

Standing face-to-plain-face with the courier, even with a featureless white wall behind him like something encountered at the DMV, Ludwig couldn't focus on the man's face, clothes, or movements, as if he were not a person but a portrait of a blurry portrait of one. He was 5′9″ exactly, the absolute average height for an American male, which, as a former fashion mogul, Ludwig could eyeball blindfolded.

Words.

No longer able to comprehend words, Ludwig increasingly excelled at guessing them; thanks to *muumbazza,* not even card players and psychiatrists could read physical queues and unspoken context like he could. The plain man wanted him to sign for the package, so he did.

The man shape left without saying *thank you, goodbye, muumbazza,* or anything as it descended the steps at the same pace it ascended. Ludwig watched him depart through the video screen, confident they would never meet again. What the man looked like would remain a mystery, like the origins of life, the nature of time, or why humanity believed world peace was possible on a planet where people still talked in movie theaters.

Inside the plastic package, he discovered first a bag made from green burlap stained by something purple, a wax sheet like a raincoat protecting something else, and a treated pinewood box guarding seventy-eight moldy, yellow-and-brown, deteriorating tarot cards.

Where had they come from? How were they on his dining table?

"Hello?" he asked, searching his apartment. "Hello?"

He had already forgotten the plain man.

THE POWER TO wield magic wasn't necessary to understand that these were the cards that An Exalted Northwind once claimed warranted a high price—a price she claimed she would pay. How had they come into his possession? Was their presence serendipity, fate, or something else?

If he surrendered them to An Exalted Northwind without charge, they would surely qualify as a gift that might warrant his return to full-time employment, her tutelage, and a community where no one said *muumbazza.* Twenty-nine non-bucket-bearing, verbal beings lived in Broken Throat, and he believed he could talk to all of them, despite only having spoken to two. He quickly found the failure in his logic: They all wanted, at the very least, to see him picked apart by starving crows while swinging from an oak tree.

He could imagine An Exalted Northwind putting aside her ill will in exchange for the cards. She was a pragmatist, but the twenty-eight fairies (minus Galilea) whose friend and family member Ludwig had led Desolate Phil to slaughter, might not be so forgiving.

Kenneth Branagh was right again. At least two gifts were necessary, perhaps even a third. One for An Exalted Northwind (the cards), one for her client-housemates, and another for . . . ? Possibly two gifts for her client-housemates were called for. Inventing one gift would be challenging enough. Perhaps the cards had an opinion.

Ludwig carefully shuffled the fragile deck to avoid inflicting more damage than had already been dealt to them by years spent beneath a leaky pipe, in a toilet, buried under wet ground, or whatever was responsible for their present state.

He could not read tarot cards, at least not how fortune tellers who plied their trade on credulous, middle-aged women could. Yet cards bought from bookstores and trinket shops weren't actual tarot cards, were they? If they were, those curbside clairvoyants would all be rich and powerful beyond imagining.

Despite knowing that magic existed, he still considered tarot more like astrology or alchemy than anything scientific. It was subjective, a figment of the reader's imagination, and imagination remained among his few virtues. His interest in high and low fantasy and their genre-specific tropes familiarized him with the gold standard of tarot, the Rider-Waite deck. These were not them, and the first card confirmed it.

The Reborn. At least they had been printed in English.

The card depicted a green child being extracted from its mother, not headfirst, but by its feet. Was this supposed to be Ludwig, reborn backward from exile to serve An Exalted Northwind?

He expected that he might learn more from the cards by not scanning the deck and biasing himself. If there were a dragon somewhere in there, he would invent whatever justifications were needed to see himself in it, reducing the remaining cards to pictures on moldy paper. Ludwig slid the card away and drew another.

The Ten of Wings. Did coffee shop mystics and other charlatans even include the Minor Arcana when reading people's cards? He placed the card beside the Reborn and turned over the next.

The Oven. Did the cards want him to put newborn, winged creatures into an oven? Perhaps an angel? Did the cards want him to broil an angel? Did angels exist? Demons did. An Exalted Northwind had told him, though he hadn't met any.

The Mob. These were An Exalted Northwind's client-housemates; they could also have been his former employees. He paused, considering all the people who hated him and the revelations thus far. He was tempted to turn over another, but paused at the possibility that adding more cards to his hand might confuse his reading.

All he sought from the cards was a second gift that could allay the fairies' contempt for him.

The Reborn. The Ten of Wings. The Oven. The Mob. What were they trying to tell him? He sensed the cards growing impatient, as if they could not have been clearer or he dumber.

He drew another card. Then he sniffled some more.

The Gathering. Gathering a mob made sense. Amassing a mob into an oven didn't. The deck continued rumbling. What else was a gathering? A conference? A congregation? A party? A convention? A banquet?

Lonesome Johnny and An Exalted Northwind once told Ludwig that there was no sustenance the fae coveted more than the roasted birds from their fairy banquets. The paintings on Broken Throat's walls testified to this fact. A gathering was a banquet and vice versa. The birds' wings wouldn't be raised again in a conventional sense but placed in an oven and reborn as food. The second gift was suddenly obvious: He would host a banquet for An Exalted Northwind's client-housemates, one that, even if they never forgave him, might at least let him back in their good graces long enough to help An Exalted Northwind finish her enchantment. But he'd need a farm to feed that many eight-foot fairies. He'd also need his door.

He had two gifts. What about the third?

Kenneth Branagh had recommended something unexpected and from the heart for all of them. What form would such a gift take? And could it take that form in the time he had before Lonesome Johnny returned?

Ludwig shuffled the deck and attempted to draw a card. As if the deck had told him "Enough already," it wouldn't budge. Besides, the gift had to come from the heart, according to Kenneth Branagh—no more clues.

He searched his apartment for something that constituted a gift or a clue to one. An Exalted Northwind had already taken back Mr. Blueberry, a gift that any person would have welcomed, but perhaps not any fairy, who might already have had an unlimited supply of enchanted pigs with gemstone-pumping bowels.

He could bring them a flight of La-Z-Boys, which spoke to his heart. Would it speak to theirs? What about a margarita machine? Did fairies drink alcohol? Introducing a culture to tequila could be either a gift or a curse, like blankets that later turned out to be infected with smallpox.

Despite having little knowledge of post-1920s technology, perhaps the fairies of Broken Throat wanted smartphones. Could they get a signal down there? He never could. Did he want them to have those? No, he did not want to make himself constantly available to over two dozen additional fairies who might want to know about his mission or what had become of their island.

Ludwig explored Mr. Blueberry's room and shed a long, salty tear at the imagined lingering smell of thousand-dollar farts. Finally, he entered his closet and ran his fingers across rows of hanging, comfortable hoodies with overly large hoods and folded sweatpants that tapered to the ankle.

Ludwig fired up his ancient laptop. For this to happen, he needed to work around the device's incorrectly labeled keys.

> To: lululu@verminmilk.com
> From: urbandruid@verminmilk.com
> Subject line: A trade.
>
> Lulu,
> This is Ludwig. I hope you've been well and that my legend lives on at Vermin Milk, even though you ruined the brand, and you know it.
>
> I am writing to offer, if not a truce, then a trade.

I am in dire need of twenty-nine signature series Druidic Traveler garments—the pants and the hoodies—which I am glad to see from our website have not been abandoned in favor of a lot of the dumb shit I see on there now.

Since I know how hard it is to shut down production to create specialty, limited-edition apparel, I am willing to return a quarter of my outstanding shares to the company in exchange for the garments above. Given Vermin Milk's growth, I am sure you need my shares. I can only guess at the correct sizes. Twenty-eight pairs for slender people at least eight feet tall sounds right. The twenty-ninth pair should fit a purely hypothetical fourteen-foot-tall person. You know how much more I can say about this without consequences, so I hope you will believe me when I say this is urgent. City Park Green would be best. All the newer colors suck.

I cannot understand anything you say in response to this email because of my "thing," so send me one word if you're willing to do this or two if it's something you are not. You know my address.

Ludwig

PS: If this goes well (don't count on it), perhaps I can help you get that thing you wanted.

Vermin Milk had, at this point, conquered the building where it originated. All forty-five units, from the first to the ninth floors, were leased by their LLC. And the artists who had once worked there moved on—they had no choice. Lulu had to choose between them and her people. She was intensely principled, just not in the wildly impractical way that Ludwig was.

Lulu received the email while in a meeting planning for the company's upcoming IPO. It had been seven years since his departure and nine since he founded Vermin Milk. But when she received the unexpected email with the difficult-to-ignore subject line, she opened it immediately, knowing who it was from but not what it was about.

A trade.

The idea was simple enough. By then, a quarter of Ludwig's shares were worth millions—an outrageous trade for her not to take, netting Vermin Milk a profit margin of 1:1,000. Illiquid, they were worth nothing. At an IPO price, well, she had to consider this.

Lulu relocated herself and her laptop to a less crowded conference room and scrutinized the unexpected email.

The request was bizarre, but all of Ludwig's communications were. As with everything related to his *thing*, it left her curious and a little afraid since it had nearly killed her on two occasions. No one, not even the tallest athletes, could wear garments that size. She needed to know more.

"Muumbazza," she wrote.

Ten days later, Lonesome Johnny and twenty-nine pairs of elongated, hunter-green athleisurewear arrived. It wasn't what he asked for; Lulu had never had "the eye," but the eye she did have was enough.

18

What do you think of when you think of infinity: a graceful loop that repeats forever or a straight line that charges forward without ever finding an end?

—Sweet Tooth the Trapdoor Spider

LONESOME JOHNNY WAS giddy as a bridesmaid. He gestured for Ludwig to open his door in the floor as if a prize awaited him.

"Won't that summon blue guys?"

"Well thought, Mr. Ludwig."

Nevertheless, Lonesome Johnny insisted that the door worked. What would prove the greater challenge, the hundreds of gallons of gin he had brought up five floors or lowering hundreds of pounds of plucked birds down fifteen flights of ladders? Whatever the answer, the door needed to move after the banquet if the death of Thornfell Littlefog hadn't scared the six remaining blue guys from the Lower East Side forever.

"A friend told me that to get back in our lady-lord and

benefactor's good graces, I should bring gifts. I could use your help bringing them all down. It's a lot," Ludwig said.

"What smart, well-intentioned friends you have! Unfortunately, I am forbidden from entering your door. I will meet you on the other side and help you. I am oh so eager to see these gifts!"

"Johnny?" Ludwig asked. "You are a gentleman, bar none. How would you say you are as a party planner and interior decorator?"

"The finest there is, Mr. Ludwig! Shall I ply my mastery, starting now? Shall I prepare a banquet the likes of which human and fairy eyes have never seen?"

Ludwig had emptied his refrigerator and refilled it with birds from local butcher shops and high-priced grocery stores. Instead of flimsy paper bags, he had stuffed the blue IKEA bags that all New Yorkers owned, even if they had never shopped there. The athleisure suits required no more than four bags, except for An Exalted Northwind's, which nearly needed its own. As for the food, his math told him that he needed one hundred and fifty pounds of birds, plus rosemary, thyme, parsley, salt, pepper, cayenne, and lemon.

Were there enough ovens in Broken Throat, whose first floor never ended if more first floor was needed, to roast that many birds? It was a gamble, but he had to take it.

Ludwig tossed the athleisure suits from scaffold to scaffold. He hooked long ropes to each of the ten bird bags and lowered them as though he were resupplying a fortress under siege. Lastly, in what he considered an act of genius comparable to the creation of athleisure, he lowered the wheelbarrow that had transported the swordfish to the hot tub.

Desolate Phil watched from his throne, and Ludwig watched back.

"Pig stealer," Ludwig called him.

"Faithless degenerate," Desolate Phil replied.

"Name-calling aside, I could use your help. It will benefit the fairies you guard. Lonesome Johnny and I are hosting a banquet for your lady-lord and benefactor's client-housemates. Please call off the worms."

"I will not. This throne is my post, and it is sacred, for reasons that you of all Upstairs Neighbors should understand. My guard is now more essential than ever; that you are even allowed here dismays me. Yet I do not question my lady-lord and benefactor. Is this something she wants?"

"It was her idea." Ludwig bluffed.

"Are you lying?"

"You'd know if I was," Ludwig said, playing into Desolate Phil's pride.

"Then I will briefly offer my aid." Desolate Phil rose from his throne, perhaps for the first time since the funeral of Thornfell Littlefog. He approached the half-mile tunnel to Broken Throat, raised his arms, and a half mile of worms, some still moonstruck, disappeared into the ground, walls, and ceiling. "They won't be gone long."

Ludwig raced (he walked a little faster than usual) the mountain of carcasses from the foot of his tunnel to the door of Broken Throat. Then he chased the wheelbarrow back to Desolate Phil, loaded the athleisure suits, and jogged them back. If the birds and athleisure suits didn't work, it was the cards or *muumbazza* forever.

Before Ludwig could press the illuminating doorbell, which wasn't a bell at all, eleven latches unlocked, and standing before him again, for reasons that still eluded him, was Lonesome Johnny in a neatly pressed and well-maintained uniform. It was as if he owned two—one for staying in, one for going out—a problem that athleisure once successfully set out to solve. It never occurred to him that the bucketbearers might want suits of their own.

"Mr. Ludwig, I think you will be delighted with the large

big great room," Lonesome Johnny said. "I quite 'decked the halls,' as you say, though we are forbidden to do anything that celebrates or references Christendom. So I have decorated not with boughs and tinsel but with fairy lights, gemstones, and human bones. As always, here is the twin to your dear departed hollow heart. It is filled with fresh serum since you will soon be in the presence of twenty-nine fairies—perhaps the most a human has ever accompanied. Drink deeply. Finally, since you know our protocols by now, we request that you step on and crush this blue glass in case dire eyes are watching."

Ludwig added the blue trinket to his collection because he might need the glass following the delivery of the tarot cards to An Exalted Northwind. If stepped on, it would obscure anyone trying to watch him through a crystal ball, tarot cards, or some other surveillance medium he had yet to encounter. Then, unprepared for the flavor after so many years, he spat out his first attempt at ingesting the serum. Although the second and third swigs went down with less resistance, the flavor would follow him throughout the evening, regardless of how much spice he sampled.

"Can you help me with these bags?" Ludwig asked. "Bringing in a muddy wheelbarrow doesn't seem appropriate."

"Of course, Mr. Ludwig! It is not like me to deny guests simple courtesies."

"These ten should go into the kitchen, and we can leave these four in the doorway for now." He kept the tarot cards a secret, even from Lonesome Johnny, who might have been too excited by their presence to withhold telling his lady-lord and benefactor that they were in the building.

"I could use your help prepping the birds," Ludwig said.

"I am so glad to give it, Mr. Ludwig. First, let me show you something."

He led Ludwig through decorated hallways until they reached the large big great room, where silver trays, dishes, and goblets were placed, candelabras lit, and silverware immaculately polished. Lonesome Johnny did, it seemed, have the decorator's touch. How had he done so much so quickly? If Ludwig had known about his flair for Mach-speed, high-fidelity decorating, he would have asked Lonesome Johnny to give Zeal the comfortable-old-theater, dusty-library, cellar-speakeasy, or Florentine-astronomer's-tower aesthetic he aspired to.

Ludwig and Lonesome Johnny seasoned skin, chucked organs, stuffed cavities, and tied twine for six hours. He expected fairies to catch the scent and ransack the room. Did they know Ludwig had come for this purpose, or had they interpreted Lonesome Johnny's decorating binge as just another eccentricity? One fairy, however, had seldom isolated to her apartment as An Exalted Northwind's reign dictated, and she stalked Ludwig with her nose low and nostrils flaring.

"I know that smell," Galilea said, examining Ludwig. "The birds can't hide it from me."

"Do you know what she's talking about?" Ludwig insincerely asked Lonesome Johnny.

"A fairy's sense of smell vastly exceeds that of even a seasoned hound. Lady Galilea, please! Mr. Ludwig needs to focus!"

Galilea hopped onto a counter at the far end of the kitchen, which let her keep her eyes and nose on Ludwig.

When the first three ovens reached their capacity of squab, chicken, and pheasant, the kitchen expanded like an accordion until two more ovens appeared on both sides of the first three, followed by two more, and then again until there were nine. The cards proved surprisingly literal—wings, an oven, a gathering—which was not their reputation. The Mob had yet to appear.

As the birds' aroma wafted through the building, doorknobs turned, and soft footsteps filled the grand halls and stairwells with green creatures no less than two heads taller than Ludwig, who took another swig of serum. Then, to be safe, he took three more. There was no controlling his sniffling, so he plugged his nose with bits of rags.

At first, Ludwig saw the descending fairies over his shoulders as nebulous green shapes, but curiosity overcame him as he turned to exchange one tray of birds for another. His relationship with this building spanned ten years, yet he had encountered only three of its residents in that time.

As expected, they were tall and green but varied more from one to the next than he could have foreseen; they were as much like animals as people.

One possessed a cat's face and tiny shoulders like a waif. Its tattered robes showed too much green skin, as if a cold, determined draft could leave it frozen in some gusty upstairs hallway for centuries. The blue dots along her arms and neck were unmistakable even at a glance. The face of the fairy beside her resembled a wolf whose mane consisted of dry leaves and gemstones.

As Ludwig turned to say hello, the wolf fairy growled, and the cat fairy hissed. Despite how dangerous they appeared, they were undeniably beautiful, like sudden summer storms. They knew what he had done and might never forgive him for it. Still, he thought their willingness to stand so close without attacking suggested that some progress might at least be possible. He had done what he did, not to hurt them, but to seek revenge against An Exalted Northwind, a sentiment they undoubtedly understood.

Where was An Exalted Northwind? Surely, the greatest of the fairies shared their ravenous yearning for that highest of fairy delicacies. Perhaps she, like he, still wasn't welcome in Broken Throat's corridors and communal spaces. This wouldn't help his petition for her to take him back into her employ.

Lonesome Johnny rang a noiseless bell that caused candles and sconces throughout the building to burn burgundy.

"Everyone, please head to the large big great room. Mr. Ludwig and I will begin serving tonight's banquet of chickens, pheasants, ducks, geese, squab, and turkeys," he whispered into a flame.

Hot and dripping birds left the oven in batches, their perfume verifying what Lonesome Johnny claimed through the fire to the other tenants. What filled their apartments besides more tattered green clothes, spell books, and pastimes banned by An Exalted Northwind? Did those rooms expand endlessly as the first floor did? If so, what shape might the house take if excavated?

Graceful green creatures that resembled archetypal woodland animals like deer, boars, owls, and lemurs filed in and filled twenty-eight of the large big great room's thirty-six seats. As they ate, their faces became human faces again, though Ludwig wondered whether they regarded their faces as "human." Ludwig expected such graceful creatures, the ultimate specimens of nature's unfettered beauty, he was told, to eat as they walked, quietly, full of dignity, eloquent, and patient. Instead, the fairies lunged for the food. Chaos consumed the table as green bodies tore through the birds. Bones hit the ceiling, the floor, faraway cabinets, and hanging pictures—so much for conversation. The silverware remained untouched. Lonesome Johnny joyously and quietly clapped his hands as if his child had just performed strongly at a recital.

Only a few short minutes later, the roasted birds were naught but scattered, gnawed bones. A fairy with the face of an eagle raided the trash for the internal organs that Lonesome Johnny and Ludwig had tossed aside. Content, they bulged through their loose green robes, no longer hissing or giving death stares. An Exalted Northwind had yet to appear, except in the surrounding paintings that told ominous stories about life at Broken Throat since she arrived.

"What a wonderful meal," the formerly wolf-faced fairy

declared quietly. English! "I've had better roasted birds, though not in so long. Thank you, Upstairs Neighbor. This gift will not be forgotten. I will petition for your clemency when the time is right to rise from here and drive your kind into the sea." Some fairies nodded in agreement; others indicated nothing, except for Galilea Dazzledark, who grinned seductively toward Ludwig.

"If you would like," Ludwig whispered to the table, "I brought a second gift that might appeal to all of you, especially after that meal. They're a little unusual, I'd imagine, for fairies, so I think I should explain. You all look overdue for a wardrobe upgrade. I used to manage a business called Vermin Milk." The fairies politely applauded the name by tapping their palms with unused spoons. "We made clothes that strongly emphasized comfort, which I am sure you value highly here. You see"—Ludwig continued—"I had this thesis that aesthetically centered social conventions were due for a reckoning. There's a fortune to be made in high-end athletic leisurewear. When you think about it, in New York, it's too hot when it's hot and too cold when it's cold. Apartments are microscopic, claustrophobic, or glorified closets, and the subways are always crowded." At the mention of subways, the fairies hissed individually until they formed a chorus. He hadn't given his pitch in so long that he had forgotten whole swaths. "So shouldn't you guys be the most comfortable you can be? Comfort has always been Vermin Milk's aim, not just once you get home or go to bed but everywhere and all the time. And since you cannot leave here, I suspect they might be perfect for you."

Ludwig and Lonesome Johnny carried the bags into the large big great room and set them at the foot of the table. It was perhaps the fairies' first time seeing plastic, and they were apprehensive about touching it. Ludwig showed them that it was harmless, and then in fits of wonder, they tore into the material, held up the green cotton suits, and traded between themselves for appropriate sizes. Then, they shamelessly stripped naked and changed into druidic hoodies and tapered sweatpants. Galilea stayed naked longer than she needed to, ensuring that Ludwig saw.

She walked over to Ludwig, with her Druidic Traveler hood pulled over her seaweed-and-dark-gemstone-imbued hair, and whispered, "I can smell them, Ludwig. You can't lie to me. I see what you're doing. I won't ruin the surprise."

He was satisfied that they were satisfied with the birds and the clothes, so Ludwig asked Lonesome Johnny for an escort to An Exalted Northwind's archives. He finished half of what remained in the hollow heart as he entered.

"YOU THINK SOME pants and chickens are enough after what you did?"

He realized, facing her, the most practical of the fae, that she was right. This meant that his last gift had to seal the deal, or else it was "muumbazza, muumbazza, muumbazza" until he someday bid farewell to an unfamiliar world.

"Just see what you think of them," he whispered, handing her the bundled outfit. If any fairy needed them, it was the one in the corset, thigh-high boots, three collars (leather, lace, velvet), and robes that were secured by belts and fell to her feet.

"They're cute, Ludwig, though why you would bring me proof of the very thing you prioritized over the job I gave you is beyond even my great powers of perception to comprehend. Let me ask you again," she said, "why should I trust you? Why should I welcome you back or pay you a pinch of ruby dust for work you never accomplished?"

"I . . ."

"Go on. Let me hear it," she said.

"It will be different this time."

"Tell me how it will be different this time. Tell me how I can trust you."

"Because you wouldn't have to trust me."

The instant the cards left his pocket, Galilea scurried into the room on hands and feet like an iguana, first from somewhere on the top floor, perhaps the ceiling, then onto the table that separated them.

"These are them," she cooed. "I knew I could smell them."

"These are what?" An Exalted Northwind asked.

"These are the cards—the actual cards! My cards! Oh, glory, they are here. My beautiful, dear, sweet, idiot, shithead Ludwig, has brought us a gift ten thousand times any human's value." Galilea unwrapped the burlap sack and the wax wrapping, then slid the top from the pine box and dropped them into her hand. Despite their being only cards, Ludwig heard them beat for her like a heart.

An Exalted Northwind retrieved the cards from Galilea's hand and lowered them onto the table. "Why are they warm?"

"Because they are alive."

"And how, Ludwig, did you come into possession of these?"

"I'm not sure. One minute, I was in my dining room. The next, they were in my hand. I used them, and they led me to the banquet idea."

"They let you use them?" Galilea scoffed. "Novice's luck. They were using you to get back to me. They get lonely, as fae and people do, especially for their mothers. I hope they have not suffered all these years."

"You're getting ahead of yourself, Niece. This revelation has the makings of a trap."

"No, Auntie. Look. The Major Arcana are as they should be, and the Minor Arcana too. They are only moldy because they date from the late Roman Empire."

"Galilea, put the cards on the table and stand back." She apprehensively obeyed her aunt, who wriggled her fingers above the deck as if to see whether something unknown might lunge forth and bite her.

"I know you could teleport me from here," Ludwig said. "Or burn my deed and keep the cards for yourself. You also said, years ago, that you would pay a high price for them. Well, here they are, and here is my price. I only want three things, one easy, one advantageous to us both, and one difficult. One: I get my pig back. I don't care if he shits rubies; you can turn that setting off."

"There is no setting, Ludwig. He is a ruby-shitting pig. Why would you even want this? The pig has grown beyond the point that its rubies have value to anyone except dragons. Do you still want the pig?"

"Yes, he's my friend," Ludwig whispered. "Hold on—there *are* dragons?"

An Exalted Northwind shook her head. "Of course there are—or were. Have you ever noticed that every human culture has stories about giant winged lizards? You thought this was a coincidence? Regardless, I consider your first offer a deal. That is simple enough."

"My second request," he said, "is that you do everything in your power, with all the help I can give you, to free your client-housemates from this place and me from *muumbazza*. It is my understanding that our wants are one and the same."

"You are correct. They are. That seems simple and even desirable to me. I gladly agree."

"Now for the big one. This is a direct trade for the cards. You must agree to teach me the art of enchantment. You don't have to teach me much, just enough to know a few spells and learn more on my own. I want to be a tinkerer of enchantments like you are, surrounded by arcane instruments and books. That is my dream job, not searching for shapeless 'distortions in reality' in a city where everything looks like a distortion in reality. And I would like the power to teach what I learn to one—just one!—other person, even if all I can teach her is how to make fire with her fingertips or the history of your people."

"I thought you wanted to be a druid, not a wizard," she said, aware that Galilea was dressed like an urban druid.

"I would still settle for being an urban druid if teaching me enchanting fails or if, as you put it, that ends up a contradiction in terms. So let's keep that in the mix."

She groaned. "Fine, since I am growing desperate, I will teach you *some* enchanting and keep the druid chip 'in the mix.' The cards are a difficult gift to turn down, although I have only a faint idea of how to use them. Do you understand that your life span might not be long enough to learn what you want?"

"We just agreed to a deal! Stop trying to talk me out of it!" he whispered, perhaps too loudly.

"In that case, I must modify your deed." Using the same trick that could have summoned dark spirits from the deck of tarot cards, An Exalted Northwind held her trembling fingers over the letters and lines that constituted the deed until they rose from the page, then placed them back down in new positions. After scrutinizing their wording, she presented the deed to Ludwig. "It is functionally the same deed. However, I made a few small adjustments to ensure you complete your mission and to show that I agreed to your terms in exchange for the cards. It also stipulates that I will make the very basics of enchanting available to you. After that, you are on your own. Finally, it allows you to reveal elements of our existence to one person—but not until I see progress."

Without reading it himself, Ludwig signed the deed.

"I think you have done enough tonight, Ludwig. Go home and rest. And whatever else you do, don't forget to move your door." It felt good even to be spoken down to in English.

She flicked her wrist, and Ludwig found himself standing in Zeal's first-floor living room, clutching his hollow heart and the leash of a happy golden pig the size of a stagecoach.

GALILEA GENTLY CUPPED the cards as if she were nursing a baby bird.

"I would have liked to keep him, just for one night," Galilea said.

"What is with your hunger for human men?"

"I like to be in charge."

"Niece, as hungry as you are for the cards, give me some time to consult with them. They demand due diligence."

"They are them, Auntie. All my senses confirm it. They smell like the woods of Manhattan once smelled. Through them, I hear rain for the first time in one hundred years."

"Things may be at work that your passion is causing you to overlook," An Exalted Northwind said. "Ludwig's story about them suddenly appearing on his dining room table might be true to him, but it can't possibly be true to you. Someone wants him to have them, which means someone wants us to have them. Did you not think it strange that he has no memory of acquiring them, one of the most powerful artifacts known to the mystic arts?"

"He is very stupid," she purred.

"Leave them with me for a day. I cannot read them as you can. Still, perhaps I can read what their sender intends."

"You have twenty-four hours. Then the readings begin."

Alone, An Exalted Northwind inspected the cards, not for prophecies or hints at a universe yet to be, but for eyes looking back at her. It did not surprise her that Ludwig brought the cards because Ludwig seemed to be the exception to so much. Was it simply luck that earned him this prize or something else? Was someone out there working to undermine her plans? Gilda Fiorella was the obvious suspect. Why would she give something so valuable to someone so unreliable, only to see them in the hands of her rival?

Deep in her archives, from a place she barely remembered, she retrieved a jar of incandescent moth-wing powder and, one by one, dusted the cards with a soft brush. The point was not to sanitize the cards, but to make something sneeze if it were alive in there.

Then she drew the first card: the Seven of Guillotines, which featured a basket filled with seven rotting blue heads. The seven fae she banished from Broken Throat. Simple. Perhaps too simple. She drew another.

Contemplation. Again, not difficult. She was contemplating the cards, and so the cards reinforced this fact. It occurred to her that some cards might be meant to trick readers into incorrect interpretations.

The Grand Archives. A joke?

Frustrated, she drew another: the Sun. She knew what that meant, despite having told no one.

She found their simplicity frustrating. Things that should have been subjective and deep with meaning were all objective and shallow. This should not have been so easy; she, the owner of a laboratory and archive and perhaps history's most accomplished enchantress, derived value from observation and experiment, not freewheeling interpretation.

"Puppet, bring my niece. I am satisfied that the deck is not cursed, though my actual ability to read the deck is subpar."

"Impossible!" Lonesome Johnny countered. "That your power and grace could ever be anything—"

Before Lonesome Johnny could retrieve her, Galilea was at her aunt's side, breathing the cards in like a bouquet.

"Be glad you are of my blood," An Exalted Northwind said.

"Every day, Auntie."

"I have drawn these cards, but do not know what to do with them."

"Because you do not understand them. I imagine this is hard for you. With the cards, like in life, things happen more or less randomly, which is why reading the future is so difficult—there are too many possible outcomes. By too many outcomes, I mean that the cards can produce outcomes equal to a number with forty zeroes. This many combinations can show you everything, which is as good as nothing. So when we draw the cards, we have to limit the number of outcomes. Otherwise, the amount of entropy, or randomness, will overwhelm the card bearer." Galilea returned the cards her aunt had overturned to the deck and gently mixed them as though they might crumble like cookies at the slightest application of force. "The correct way to draw is not one at a time from the top. The cards must be tricked. Since there are no duplicates, each draw is special—"

"Please get on with it," An Exalted Northwind said impatiently.

"I'll remember this the next time you lecture me about the utility of ant lion glands," Galilea said, then continued. "This complexity is why we only draw six cards per shuffle, then two guidance cards, and disregard the rest. We reveal the guidance cards only if the first six cards fail to provide meaning. We do this at our peril since the guidance cards may tell us too much or even mislead us."

She carefully fanned the cards across the table and directed An Exalted Northwind to pick six.

"Don't be shy," she said, "the cards reward boldness."

"No one has ever accused me of lacking boldness."

She selected six cards from the arrangement. Following Galilea's instructions, they remained face down. Galilea reshuffled the deck and took one off the top and another off the bottom. She placed those cards at the edge of the table.

"These two are the guidance cards. Because they increase randomness, turning them over is dangerous and can lead us to conclusions that imperil many, including us. On the other hand, they can also reveal absolute truths and precise instructions, depending on the card bearer's skill." Galilea resheathed the remainder of the deck. "Since nearly all shuffles are unique, the odds of you drawing meaning from these six plus the two guidance cards become 1 in 16,777,216—a far more workable number than using the whole deck. In other words, it is doubtful that anyone will ever draw this combination again. It is unique to you—I might even say, to us in this house since you draw on everyone's behalf. In these eight cards, we might learn the truth of many things: our enemies' movements, our friends' mistakes, and the secret schemes of those who plot against us. You must let meaning come to you. The more you force a conclusion, the less accurate it will be. The cards are like a dance. You move together even if neither can say exactly why or how."

"In a dance, one always leads," An Exalted Northwind said.

"That is correct. So let the cards lead. Now pick a card from the six; their order doesn't matter since that is for us to decipher," Galilea instructed.

The Hermit.

"A staple of the Major Arcana," Galilea said. "The next card will add context to why you've drawn the Hermit or obfuscate it, which is itself context. That the first card you drew is such a staple of the deck is no small thing. It means the cards indeed have something to say."

"I should think that the Hermit might be us, here, trapped in the ground."

"Or it might be Ludwig, trapped by *muumbazza*. Try not to project your impressions onto the cards. Now draw the next card."

The Two of Snowflakes.

"Interesting," Galilea murmured as she bounced on her heels. "A very low member of the Minor Arcana. It seems like nothing now, but like a singular spice that brings a dish to life, it could make or break your reading. Draw the next card."

The Sun.

"The greatest of the Major Arcana. Do not think that the Sun refers to the actual sun or immortality. Many card readers have made exactly this mistake, and it has led them to their doom. When the Sun appears, it often does so to tell us that we are overlooking something."

An Exalted Northwind silently laughed. "I begin to think I understand these cards better than you do."

"You don't. Draw."

"Remind me in ten minutes, and we'll see."

The Basement drawn upside down.

"Well, come on!" An Exalted Northwind slapped her palm on the table, causing them both to cover their ears and cringe. "We know what that means and whom it refers to."

"We do not," Galilea said. "For all we know, looking over our cards, it could refer to a sun trapped underground or light snow in a mine shaft. Importantly, this card faces the wrong direction. It might not be a way into a basement. It might be the way out of one. Now draw."

The Fool on the Moon.

"What do you make of this?"

"It is a very rare card that gravitates to the bottoms of decks for unknown reasons. This is noteworthy. Now draw the final card."

The Wheel of Misfortune.

An Exalted Northwind considered the card. "Us?"

"In this case, possibly. However, it could be the city above us. The Wheel of Misfortune is really two cards. One represents chance, the game we now play with the cards. Everyone knows that one, whereas the other is irony. Now let us take stock," Galilea said. "We have the Hermit, the Two of Snowflakes, the Sun, the Basement, the Fool on the Moon, the Wheel of Misfortune, and two guidance cards."

"These appear no more useful than the ramblings of some

curbside clairvoyant. Why did I agree to teach Ludwig for this? I prefer the science of enchantment to this middling superstition. And yet, I, in my wisdom and knowledge," An Exalted Northwind said as if she harbored a secret she could not wait to disclose, "have already discovered the identity of the Sun."

"I strongly doubt that, Auntie. You believe what you want to be true rather than what the cards know is true."

"Is that so? Tell me, my all-knowing niece, did you not find it odd that Ludwig survived in a room with twenty-eight fae without so much as a dizzy spell? Dr. Tot's serum is a miracle, but even its powers have limits."

"Is something wrong with his health? He seemed in good spirits and fair of mind. I am aching with curiosity," Galilea said. "*And* desire."

"Indeed, he did. First, he survived a confrontation with a blue guy and healed within days. And now, his limp from that injury is gone. Then, with his bare hands, he fought the same blue guy again, and triumphed without any psychic impairment. Next, Wet Henry mauled him, leaving him with no lasting injuries. Then, finally, there is his incessant sniffling. When he arrived for tonight's banquet, I tested a thesis I have harbored since we fired him and filled the hollow heart my puppet gave him with a placebo. Even in the company of twenty-eight fae, he lost not a shard of sanity. His frequent and unnecessary consumption of Dr. Tot's Miraculous Sanity Serum has made him—well, you know the side effects."

"The sniffles."

"Yes, the sniffles, but the far rarer side effect is—"

"It can't be."

"And yet it is."

"Our Ludwig? The idiot? My big, stupid boy?"

"Is immortal. It is pure serendipity," An Exalted Northwind said. "We are drowning in the stuff. The perfect troubleshooter, he might still make. Or he might make something else entirely.

Perhaps the cards will tell us. He cannot die or even be injured. He is immortal. He is the Sun. I didn't need your soggy old cards for that."

Galilea examined the card. In the picture, the sun was not floating in the sky, as stars did, but radiating from the head of a comfortable, badly dressed, and out-of-shape man.

19

Humans have no shortage of knowledge. They are utterly bereft of wisdom.

—Gilda Fiorella

Mr. Blueberry had become more elephant than pig, outgrowing the elevator and becoming too strong even to be prevented from barreling through the front doors of banks in search of copper coins. Lifting even one of his legs required Ludwig's entire body and a short breather. Mr. Blueberry's ruby-producing days were over without a machine to shake him. With such a machine, Ludwig's only prize would be gems the size of grapefruits that couldn't be cut down without releasing poisonous green gas and howling, snakelike shadows. So when Mr. Blueberry shit in the apartment, which Ludwig encouraged, he waited until after dark and shoveled his excrement over the railing.

Plop.

No longer able to print wealth by transforming copper

into corundum, Ludwig retired Mr. Blueberry and converted Zeal's first living room into a shared cabana. He was as excited to be home as Ludwig was to have him. But it couldn't be all frozen margaritas and big-pig bonding sessions; Ludwig had a job and meant to do it. He would end *muumbazza* faster than An Exalted Northwind believed possible.

The bugs in her enchantment that had once been challenging to separate from the city's tumultuous essence began to reveal themselves. However, he might have been deciphering how many were bugs instead of the ever-fluctuating byproducts of the city's unstable soul until the enchantment took wing. Nevertheless, An Exalted Northwind was right. The errors were noticeable as long as he made an effort, which he did for fourteen hours a day, seven days a week. The sooner he completed his mission, the sooner he would wield magic. All the job required was fourteen hours a day times seven days a week times fifty-two weeks a year times somewhere between two and ten years, which totaled 10,192 to 50,960 hours. That wasn't so much, was it? Time, that most invaluable of resources, as Ludwig had often said, was worth sacrificing for some enchantments that would let him . . .

Come to think of it, she hadn't said, and he hadn't asked.

Perhaps it didn't matter. Maybe Lulu was right. Sacrificing your time in service to another could provide you with a sense of purpose, income that let you pursue your passions, and a proud family. Said aloud to himself, he found this argument tough to swallow, like a live octopus.

Ludwig purchased a rainbow trout and premium gin.

He waited by the balcony's edge for Lonesome Johnny but heard no familiar, scraping click-clack of climbing spikes or penetrating strikes from the swing of his pickax.

Bzzz. There he was.

"I believe I have discovered bugs in our lady-lord and benefactor's enchantment. They're serendipitous as fucking shit!"

Ludwig said, as if his goal had been to convince himself, not Lonesome Johnny, that they had been worth his limited time on Earth.

Although the news that his "good buddy" was immortal should have been welcome, having once said it was a gift, Lonesome Johnny said nothing of it. Perhaps this was why he chose the elevator over scaling a five-story building. The secret weighed on him and could jeopardize his ascent. Lonesome Johnny knew the stories about life without death. No matter how beloved or well-known someone had been before joining the ranks of the undying, the affliction always ended in loneliness.

"That is so good to hear, Mr. Ludwig. Well, what have you learned?"

"The Strand has been on fire for several days," Ludwig said.

"What is that?"

"It's a bookstore."

"Of size?"

"Yes."

"How strange that a bookstore should be on fire for days. Has anyone noticed?" Lonesome Johnny asked.

"No. People just keep walking in there, and then, half an hour later, they walk out. No burns or anything. Not even a paper cut."

"A distortion in reality indeed. Is that unusual for your kind?"

"Is what unusual?"

"Walking into a burning building for books."

"The buildings don't even have to be burning," Ludwig said. "Oh, I almost forgot; the Brooklyn Bridge is missing."

"You didn't notice that before?"

"I don't really go to Brooklyn."

"You found all this in two weeks?"

"No, I found all this in four days."

Exactly twenty-four hours later, Lonesome Johnny returned with a scroll. It said little for its size:

> *Well done. You have slashed months from our timeline.*

Only months? Not years or decades?

Nevertheless, Ludwig's success as a fairy employee made him feel less alone and isolated. An Exalted Northwind's communications, Mr. Blueberry's roommate status, and Lonesome Johnny's appearances were enough to simulate belonging, at least in the short term. It wasn't much, but options weren't something he had, since not doing this job would mean more time lost to *muumbazza*. Whatever he did, he lost time. But soon, perhaps in only a couple of years, or 10,192 hours on his feet, he'd be having conversations again, and with any people he wanted; then, once their agreement was in place and their overlapping realities pulled apart, he would learn magic, maybe even before he turned forty. The metrics of success were unbalanced. Two to ten years was an insignificant fraction of An Exalted Northwind's life. It could be all that remained of his.

Ludwig turned on the instrumental of "New York, New York" and felt its effusive magic move through him.

AN EXALTED NORTHWIND, still unsure about what the cards portended, interpreted them with Galilea's help, and though it wasn't clear through which card they heard the song, they heard enough to be appalled.

"What is that awful—*eugh*?" An Exalted Northwind asked, searching for a word equal to her disgust.

"It is Mr. Ludwig's favorite song by a musician named Ol'

Blue Eyes," Lonesome Johnny said. "It is called 'New York, New York.' Many consider it the city's official anthem."

"Is that right?" An Exalted Northwind asked. "I guess it would be with that name."

Galilea floated to the six upright tarot cards.

"The Two of Snowflakes," she said, pushing the card to the table's edge. "Ol' Blue Eyes. Two of Snowflakes. It makes sense."

"I admit that it sounds consequential," An Exalted Northwind said. "Let me know when the others produce results."

With Ludwig working, An Exalted Northwind's enchantment progressed faster than anticipated. The eventual fork of their overlapping realities felt inevitable. She had already begun to bargain with herself about what enchantments she would teach him, which were mainly "pocketknife" enchantments—those that were helpful, possessed little power, and could be learned quickly so that she wasn't forced to spend more time than necessary in his presence. Then again, if his work helped show Fairie who was the greater enchantress, her or Gilda Fiorella, she might endure a little more Ludwig.

The only open question was who had sent the cards. If it was Gilda, or someone working for Gilda, An Exalted Northwind still needed to decode the why, having already deciphered the what, the when, and perhaps the who. For now, she waited on the cards.

As Ludwig's reports to Lonesome Johnny continued, *muumbazza* slowly receded, proving that Ludwig's work accelerated An Exalted Northwind's. First, as he was about town tending to his assignment, a noun slipped past *muumbazza*'s gates; then, an adjective and a verb; finally, even chunky, graceless, bottom-heavy adverbs somersaulted out of people's mouths and into his ears—but not quickly enough.

That day's march through the city revealed two additional distortions: Central Park, which had made a 180-degree turn overnight, putting the Harlem Meer near 59th Street and the Pond at Central Park within feet of 110th Street. The second distortion replaced New York's mayor with a fascist, seven-foot-tall tube of toothpaste. But Ludwig didn't call Lonesome Johnny since he first needed to decompress after fourteen hours on his feet, the soreness from which healed quickly, but only once he was off his feet—the thought of spending the next day doing the same lacked appeal.

So when Ludwig arrived home, he reached for the margarita machine, but it was already on—and so was his hot tub.

"Not again with this shit," Ludwig said. Without any attempt at stealth, he marched to his closet and the sword Kenneth Branagh had forged for him.

"Mr. Ludwig!" someone called from the tub. "I hope you don't mind that I let myself in. I made us margaritas as penance for my crime."

Ludwig had wondered when he would see Kenneth Branagh again after their unexpected and inexplicable rendezvous in Tuscany. This wasn't how he had imagined their next meeting.

"No problem," Ludwig said, dragging a chair to the tub. He was too tired from work to care why Kenneth Branagh was in there, so he didn't ask. Why would he? Company and conversations weren't things he could afford to turn down. Though when he tried to turn their duo into a trio by summoning Mr. Blueberry, the pig kept its distance, which he never had before around people.

"I wish my apartment had one of these babies, but I am only a humble real estate man, living off commissions. While I would never presume to tell someone what to do with their own beloved hot tub, you should really get in here. The water is fine and smells like a gin martini!"

Ludwig changed, poured two frozen margaritas, and joined Kenneth Branagh in the tub.

They toasted.

Ludwig had still not heard a *muumbazza.* Kenneth Branagh had seemed, if not immune to it, then at least resistant. Since Kenneth Branagh had broken all kinds of rules by entering Zeal without permission, Ludwig broke one too.

"How come you aren't saying it?" Ludwig asked.

"What is *it*?"

"Come on, KB."

Kenneth Branagh unveiled that glowing crescent-moon smile. In the light, it was welcoming, but in the dark, it wasn't something anyone wanted to see around an unfamiliar corner.

"Oh, you mean *muumbazza*," Kenneth Branagh said. His hope that Ludwig would be surprised by this revelation died on the spot.

"I always suspected you were faking it."

"So sorry, Mr. Ludwig. I have never been good at faking anything. We can dispense with the whole *muumbazza* charade, especially since I want what I came here to say to be clearer than a crystal ball. Do you recall a day nine years ago when we scoured the city for a place your start-up could call home? And you asked me to help you learn the mystic arts? I may have found a way to help in this regard. And I can do it without forcing you to march through the city for fourteen hours a day."

How did he know?

"What are you?" Ludwig asked. "A fairy? A fairy servant?" The deed's privacy-protecting enchantment issued not even a determined mosquito.

"A demon, Mr. Ludwig!" he growled and made claws with his fingers. "And a servant, but only to my clients. My true name is Kenneth 'the Furnace of Face-Eating Death' Branagh, though, in my dealings with lesser beings, I go by Kenneth 'New York Pinnacle of Prestige Boutique Realtor of the Year'

Branagh, or Kenneth Branagh, or just . . . KB! Please don't confuse what I am with stories about my species. We aren't the monsters we are made out to be."

A name like the "Furnace of Face-Eating Death" made not confusing Kenneth Branagh with historical tales of demons a challenge, though no more than the paintings throughout Broken Throat made hosting a fairy banquet challenging.

"And, yes, you could call me a fairy servant of sorts."

"Who do you serve?" Ludwig asked.

"My clients! Now and always."

"You know what I mean."

"I work for . . . my lady-lord and benefactor!"

"You know An Exalted Northwind?"

"No, Mr. Ludwig. An Exalted Northwind is a hack. I have my own lady-lord and benefactor. She is an enchantress too," he said. "But she is also proficient in other schools of magic, ones that don't require decades to learn a few simple spells. Or didn't An Exalted Northwind tell you that those exist?"

She had not told him, unsurprisingly, given everything else she had concealed.

"I'm listening," Ludwig said.

"Under her tutelage, you could learn how to shape fire, summon magic arrows, walk through walls, or stop time by clapping your hands. We will turn your Zeal into the real Zeal, the one you told me about all those years ago! A floating palace in the clouds where you could study the mystic arts!"

"Could I show this magic to anyone I want?" Ludwig asked.

"My lady-lord and benefactor is not the sort to make you sign away your freedom in exchange for entry to a worm-infested hole in the ground."

"Is she the one you were visiting in Italy?"

"Correct!"

"Is her name Gilda Fiorella?"

Kenneth Branagh said nothing, but his smile said everything.

"Did you give me the tarot cards to give to An Exalted Northwind?"

"Of course!"

"So what are you and Gilda offering me?" Ludwig said. "Spells, yes?"

"Yes. Visit Italy, and she will teach you to your heart's content."

"That's fine. I enjoyed Italy," he said, though if anyone knew that was a lie, it was Kenneth Branagh. "Wealth?"

"Gemstones and beyond. A golden egg–laying goose to go with your pig if you want."

"What about *muumbazza*?"

"My lady-lord and benefactor can dispel that enchantment."

"And in exchange?"

"I'm glad you asked! We know you weren't crushing the fairy glass An Exalted Northwind's puppet gave you. Starting tonight, stomp one. Then, in ten days, stomp another. Do this until you are out. As you must have surmised by now, my lady-lord and benefactor has been watching you through her crystal ball. Once you do this, she will lose sight of you, but so will the cards. We aim to frustrate An Exalted Northwind into doing something reckless, which will cause her to be laughed out of Fairie forever."

"What will happen to the fairies of Broken Throat?"

"They will be looked after. My lady-lord and benefactor's rivalry isn't with them."

"So my job is to do nothing?" Ludwig said.

"Yes, Mr. Ludwig. Is this something you are capable of?"

FOR THIRTY DAYS, the cards augured nothing. This stagnancy was a sign to Galilea but not to An Exalted Northwind, who chided her for their perceived sloth.

Hovering over the cards, Galilea scrutinized everything that might contain something covert. The Basement drew her attention as if something had been happening down there. No, too simple; that's what her aunt would think. The Basement faced up. So perhaps the thing that hid from her wasn't in the ground but above it. After a week of meditating that led her to make several false or outright implausible conclusions, she discovered that Ludwig had been keeping another secret. At some point in time, he had broken blue fairy glass, obfuscating the cards' view of him. But best not to reveal that to her aunt just yet. First, she wanted to know why.

"So that's the Two of Snowflakes and the Basement," she said to no one. "Four to go."

With the fairy glass broken and the cards' extrasensory compass temporarily askew, Galilea asked more questions than the cards usually called for. How long ago had Ludwig shattered the glass? Did he have more of it? What would the cards besides the Basement have to say if Ludwig had not prevented them from saying anything?

Her aunt might have even been right that the fae were the Hermit, but that revelation felt too literal, varnished, and apparent. More than likely, like the Basement, the Hermit portended another mystery. Ludwig's isolation via the muumbazza enchantment certainly made him a hermit, although perhaps not *the* Hermit.

But what if . . .

What if, what if, what if . . .

Her mind reached for every thought worth contemplating, no matter how fleeting or thin its veneer.

What if something in Ludwig's actual basement had been the Hermit? What if the Basement had to be read both ways, facing up and down, to clarify whatever the Hermit portended?

Her aunt was no fool; Ludwig may have been the Sun, though not because of his newfound immortality. On the contrary, the enchantment her aunt tested so long ago might have radiated from him like an antenna. He said the word had followed him to Italy and back, which should have been impossible. He should never have heard *muumbazza* farther than twenty miles from Times Square.

But he did.

What if the Hermit was An Exalted Northwind's enchantment, isolated from the world inside of Ludwig? Was it sealed away inside of him like a secret illness? But why would it want to haunt him, Ludwig, of all people?

Now she had the Hermit, the Sun, the Basement, and the Two of Snowflakes. The fairy glass's magic, it seemed, had faded.

That left two cards, the Wheel of Misfortune and the Fool on the Moon. Mercifully, the guidance cards had not yet been drawn.

She summoned her aunt.

"FOURTEEN THOUSAND YEARS of this, and I am still not past surprise. Do you see, Galilea?" An Exalted Northwind asked as she celebrated by drinking directly from another tall, thin decanter of black fluid. "He is not immune to my enchantment, as I believed, but so receptive that it pours from him. If he is the Sun, those New Yorkers and Italians saying *muumbazza* were simply caught in his light. You're clever," she said to the bubbling orange cauldron as she ran a finger along its scalding rim like someone rewarding an obedient pet. "This is serendipity squared. I might only need to make a few adjustments; our Upstairs Neighbors are already saying a word only Ludwig can hear. Changing the enchantment to make him transmit split realities—theirs loud and ours quiet—should be simple. The only catch is that Ludwig cannot leave the island. We're stuck with him."

"How do we make sure that he stays?" Galilea asked.

"We already have." An Exalted Northwind disappeared and returned carrying Ludwig's rolled-up deed across her shoulder as though it were a tree trunk and she a lumberjack. She unfurled it across interconnected tables. "While he was roasting birds and sipping on a placebo, I already knew he was immortal. So when he made his list of amendments to the deed, I made a few of my own. Ludwig will never leave Manhattan or us unless we return to Fairie."

"Even with four cards accounted for, I don't understand why the enchantment chose him of all people."

"What?" An Exalted Northwind said, strutting like a dunghill rooster. "Do the Wheel of Misfortune and the Fool on the Moon not know? Upon releasing my enchantment's first test into the city, it sought out a fae burrow because fae burrows were all it knew. One such burrow, Ludwig's basement apartment, already concealed a fae—the blue guy Thornfell Littlefog. My enchantment mistook Ludwig for him since Ludwig is like a fantasy creature himself. All alone and wanting comfort in such an uncomfortable city, it chose the so-called Most Comfortable Man Alive. Since then, my enchantment has signaled its growth with each *muumbazza*. Now that the word is Ludwig's entire reality, my enchantment is strong enough to do anything we want to New York."

"We should wait on the other cards," Galilea said as softly as a monk. "I have a strong theory about the Wheel of Misfortune. There is tremendous irony in searching for the bugs in something that has walked into our home a dozen times. That brings us to the Fool on the Moon. I believe that Ludwig's decisions, which slowed you down and trapped us here while the scourge spread, were not entirely his own. He had help. Whoever this person is, they or someone they work for wanted us to have the cards, as you said. It's the why that confounds me."

"Who do you have in mind?" An Exalted Northwind asked.

"You know who I have in mind. Ludwig recently stomped on blue fae glass to obfuscate the cards. I don't believe this was a decision he made on his own. I believe he struck some deal with Gilda, but through some intermediary that we have overlooked without the cards or a crystal ball. Perhaps she has a puppet who has been interacting with Ludwig this whole time. This person is the Fool on the Moon. For the last month, the cards have augured very little, while at the same time, Ludwig's reports have stopped. This is not a coincidence. I believe he stomped on blue fae glass to obscure the cards' view of him while he pursued some mission on Gilda's behalf."

An Exalted Northwind looked like a dark cloud ready to release its pent-up storm. Spiders fell from the ceiling and crawled from bookshelves. Cyclones of hot, vile breath wandered the grand archives' aisles. The flames of torches that lit the room softly cried out and moaned Ludwig's name.

"I kept this secret to prevent you from doing something reckless like turning over the guidance cards," Galilea said as she brushed a spider from her hair.

"Reckless? You think that's reckless? He made a deal with Gilda!"

"Volume, Auntie," Galilea said.

"I will do worse than reckless. I will . . . so help me . . ." Wisps of manic fire danced in An Exalted Northwind's cold, windy wake. "My planned enchantment was elegant and effective. My client-housemates have little time left. If he'd focused, he'd have what he wanted, they'd be safe, and so would my reputation. But this! This is the ultimate insult! Now I will settle. I will develop an enchantment that is crude and effective. No more of these nonoverlapping reality commitments. I wanted to take the happily ever after route, the once-upon-a-time route. Regretfully, they no longer seem possible. My reputation will suffer, but I don't believe it is my fault. An immortal from whom the enchantment emanates is a perfect antenna, especially if he can't leave the island. Even if Fairie loses respect for me, it will fear me. It is time."

"Time for what?"

"To pivot."

"At least you finally sound like one of us," Galilea said.

For a fairy, a being well-versed in cruelty, an appropriate manner of revenge was the kind of thing that just came to you, like a memory. That wasn't enough—she wanted something ironic. Because of Ludwig, the city deserved a hundred times worse than it gave. So when her niece left the room, she peeked at the guidance cards.

The Giant Apple and Quietude.

A WEEK LATER, Lonesome Johnny appeared without being summoned for the first time since he watched over Ludwig from his basement window. He had never seemed livelier. He somersaulted and back-flipped beside another massive scroll that could have only come from one being.

Ludwig opened the sliding glass door. "You OK, buddy?"

"Yes, Mr. Ludwig! Very OK indeed! I come with wonderful news. I would tell you myself, but I am sure that my lady-lord and benefactor would want you to hear it directly from her."

He carried the scroll to the threshold of Ludwig's apartment and waited. Why was he standing there?

"Oh," Ludwig said. "You can go in."

Lonesome Johnny spread the scroll across the kitchen table, which Ludwig had never used as anything except a storage shelf since he ate his dinners on the couch or sunk deep into a recliner.

Ludwig,
The aid you provided and the tarot cards you brought to us enabled me to finish my enchantment long before I expected to. You have lived up to your promise, so I will live up to mine.

Please join the fae of this building for a celebration (there is no need for chickens this time) starting tomorrow at noon that will finally split our overlapping realities into separate planes where we can live without harming one another.

While I cannot promise to begin your "magic" lessons tomorrow since adjusting to these new realities may take time, I grant you full access to my archives once we have vacated this building, which was once a home but is now a prison. That should, if nothing else, give you a start.

An Exalted Northwind

PS: Please bring a copy of the song my puppet says you love. Vinyl would be best. I cannot promise that we will play it loud (in fact, I can only promise that we won't). We thought it only fair to play it at least once, given all you have done for New York and us, the first New Yorkers.

So much for Kenneth Branagh and Gilda's plans to frustrate her; perhaps Gilda wasn't the savant everyone, including An Exalted Northwind, made her out to be. Ludwig consented to the invitation since Kenneth Branagh never said what to do once the blue glass ran its course.

Would *muumbazza* really be over tomorrow?

THE NEXT MORNING, with eyes still red from sleeplessness and pig farts, Ludwig sprang from the couch. He visited one of the Lower East Side's inexplicably bountiful vinyl record stores and bought a copy of Sinatra's "New York, New York."

Ludwig returned to his apartment and propped open the door to his tunnel for the last time as *muumbazza*'s only victim. Would he even have to move the door once their meeting had adjourned? He climbed down and waved as he passed Desolate Phil, who happily waved back.

"Brother Johnny has been sent away to tend to other matters, I am afraid," Desolate Phil said. Then, without objection, he extended Ludwig the courtesy of sending the worms into the walls, floor, and ceiling.

The lobby was empty of all life, including peanut butter and jelly sandwich trays. Whatever indisposed Lonesome Johnny, it did so with remarkable force. The door to An Exalted Northwind's grand archives was open, which it had never been before. If this was a surprise party, then why the letter?

An Exalted Northwind sat beside her orange, purple, and green cauldrons in the druidic athleisure suit he had gifted her.

"Welcome to the celebration," she said, letting down her oversized hood. "I'm not one to avoid giving credit where it's due. These garments are wonderful. It feels like wearing the sky on a slightly cloudy spring day."

"This doesn't look like a party. You could have at least gotten Lonesome Johnny to decorate. He's incredible."

"Ludwig, why do you think you're here?"

"To celebrate?"

"To celebrate what?"

"A new reality. No, wait—two new realities."

"Correct."

She held out her hand, and the vinyl record flew from Ludwig's. She examined the photo of Frank Sinatra on the cover.

The Two of Snowflakes indeed.

"If you came here expecting to hear *muumbazza* no longer, you won't. Well, perhaps just once or twice more."

An Exalted Northwind walked to the trio of bubbling green, purple, and orange cauldrons and said some words, stirred in some powders, poured in some liquids, and made a few motions with her hands before removing the vinyl record from its sleeve and breaking it into three pieces.

An Exalted Northwind dropped one piece of the record into each of the three cauldrons, first the orange, then the green, and then the purple. As though they were connected through some unseen portal or plumbing system, their contents turned black.

"You did this to your city, Ludwig. Now you have the privilege of hearing the single-page enchantment I worked toward for thirty years, during which time you peddled pants and fraternized with our enemy."

She began:

Oh, child who has waited for words from me,
Haunting a man whose comfort thee
Chose for a home that you found underground,
Come alive and make years ten thousand of sound.
To this concrete jungle, add a painful addition,
And with these words, prepare a simple transition.
Turn this metropolis into a city of constant song
That will loop and play ten millenniums long.
Let nothing stop you till the fae hear no more
And even then continue to roar.
Then for the rest of those ten thousand years
Give not a moment's peace to a human ear,
Except for the one in whom you took shelter.
From him, you must issue this helter and skelter.

Ludwig felt a welcome change inside as if something dark

had lifted from him, like a cancer, parasite, or curse, until something more nebulous took their place.

"That's the feeling of freedom," she said. "*Muumbazza* is no more."

Whatever else the point of this meeting or that ominously worded enchantment, he was elated, which spoke to how much damage *muumbazza* had done over the last decade.

"The tarot cards taught us much. I had my doubts about them, but I've come to accept my niece's readings. From the six cards we drew, we learned from the Basement that you were avoiding us again. From the Two of Snowflakes, we learned about Ol' Blue Eyes, who wrote your city's anthem. We learned that you are the Sun, not because you radiate light, but because, for a decade, you have radiated the test of my enchantment. Does it surprise you that it has been alive and inside you this whole time? That makes it the Hermit, which is how you could hear *muumbazza* without falling under my enchantment's magic. After all, a star cannot bask in its own light. It discovered you quickly, thinking that you lived in a fae burrow, which, in a sense, you did. My enchantment mistook you for your blue guy. All it wanted was comfort, so it possessed you, the so-called Most Comfortable Man Alive."

"So your enchantment is, what, up my ass?"

"In a sense. All this time," An Exalted Northwind said, stirring the three cauldrons with three iron spoons, "we looked for its signs to improve and evolve it, and it was right in front of us, improving and evolving. That is irony; that is the Wheel of Misfortune. Then there is the Fool on the Moon. It's a deceptive card. Its name implies only a single person, but if you deduce what we now know, it refers to two people: Gilda Fiorella, the moon, and her demon puppet, the fool. Why she wanted us to have the cards eluded me until last night. She wanted to frustrate me into doing something reckless that would damage my reputation without hurting the fae on whose behalf I act."

"That *does* sort of sound exactly like what you're doing," Ludwig countered. She ignored the obvious, insightful slight.

"I struggled with how to punish you for allying with my enemy. We are past public humiliation, and my client-housemates are sicker every day." She beckoned him with her finger, and he marched toward her against his will. "There are two other cards, Ludwig, which my niece, who believes deeply in the cards' rules, says are never to be turned over unless the other cards fail to provide a narrative. These are the guidance cards. The first six did their jobs just fine, but I turned the guidance cards anyway. They pointed me toward appropriate punishment for you and for your city. You should have bothered to read your deed—I added some things. You still get your pig, freedom from *muumbazza*, the right to learn magic and share it with one other person, but I added something for me: You may never leave Manhattan. Just now, at these cauldrons, I reversed the enchantment inside of you; it will no longer be you who hears *muumbazza*, but New Yorkers who will be hearing—well, if you haven't figured it out by now, you will. Your kind has kept my client-housemates underground for one hundred years. We want one hundred times that in return."

"Joke's on you," Ludwig said, finally realizing what kind of conversation this was and that there would be no celebration. "I'll be dead long before then."

"So you think. Your excessive use of Dr. Tot's Miraculous Sanity Serum has made you, well, I wish I were there to see you realize."

"Listen, I get why you hate me. I don't do my job; I'm easily distracted; I prioritized sweatpants, cheese, and the well-being of my pig over your species—and, yes, I allied with your enemy. But can you *finally* tell me what *muumbazza* means?"

"That's your question? After all I just told you?"

"I've learned to live with the unexpected."

"We'll see about that."

"Answer my question."

"It is an old fae word."

"And it means?"

"Are you sure you want to know?"

"That is why I asked."

"Well, how would I put it? You, Upstairs Neighbors, have an identical expression," An Exalted Northwind said.

"Which is?"

"Let me think. I'm sure I know it."

"You're stalling for dramatic effect."

"Is that what I'm doing? Stalling? Well, you're the expert. Ah, I just remembered."

"Sure you did."

"While preparing to test my enchantment at these cauldrons ten years ago, I burned my finger and spat out the word, which is how you came to hear it."

"Oh my god, just tell me."

"I think, in English, it's pronounced *go fuck yourself.*"

"You guys really are the first New Yorkers."

"Goodbye, Ludwig. I'm not firing you. I'm freeing you."

She flicked her wrist.

20

> And that's how our story ends: with the first New Yorkers creating the last.
>
> —Unknown

An Exalted Northwind didn't send Ludwig to his old apartment, his penthouse, naked to the top of an iconic skyscraper, or the Gowanus Canal. Instead, she teleported him to the busy and bright corner of Eighth Street and Broadway, next to the Cozy Soup 'n' Burger, a seemingly arbitrary decision for a fairy who never did anything arbitrarily and presumably had never eaten a burger.

She wanted Ludwig to see something there, though it could be seen everywhere—one spot was as good as any other. But what Ludwig saw was not what she intended at first: New Yorkers speaking glorious, clear, and unmistakable English, full of nouns and verbs and slurred New Yorker adjectives. Although there was magic in every language, and the city's people spoke most of them, that kind of magic was not what New Yorkers heard. Instead, they heard something intangible in the air, like a mood. There were no sound waves; there was just sound.

New York, New York,
I want to wake up in a city that never sleeps
And find I'm a number one, top of the list,
King of the hill, a number one.

Where was it coming from? Noise, especially the ambient, difficult-to-locate kind, was nothing foreign to New Yorkers: construction crews, car alarms, sirens, tires peeling, jackhammers, engines revving, dogs barking, shouting matches, things dropping. The city's soundscape was made of what drove Broken Throat underground one hundred years earlier.

New Yorkers stepped out of taxis, pharmacies, subway tunnels, and doorways to search windows and walls for the music's source. It was everywhere, blanketing everything, missing not an inch of even the darkest cellar or highest tower. But Ludwig heard nothing.

The song didn't stop each time it concluded; it simply started over, like music from an ice cream truck. It even seemed to become louder with each loop, though it was difficult to say if this happened because each replay made it more grating.

New York, New York,
I want to wake up in a city that never sleeps
And find I'm a number one, top of the list,
King of the hill, a number one.

Ludwig approached a bewildered halal-cart operator. "What is everybody looking at?"

"You can't hear that?" the man said. Ludwig could not. "Where is it coming from?"

"What is *it*?"

"It's music."

"I don't hear any music."

"Are you deaf?"

"I kind of was," he said. Consumed by the sound, the man thought nothing of the miraculous stranger who had recovered from an incurable condition.

Ludwig had watched An Exalted Northwind split the Sinatra record into three pieces and deposit them into the colored cauldrons he figured were connected to the enchantment inside him. He didn't have to hear the song to guess what she had done. The timing of her enchantment might have caught him unexpectedly, just as it catches everyone unexpectedly when someone starts reading poetry aloud, but it caught him, nonetheless.

As Charlie, his former boss at Electric Guacamole, had told him about the company's implosion: A bad thing had happened, quite frankly, and it wasn't good.

New York, New York,
I want to wake up in a city that never sleeps
And find I'm a number one, top of the list,
King of the hill, a number one.

Was that what New Yorkers were hearing? Ol' Blue Eyes? The Two of Snowflakes?

"Hey, dude. Can you hear that?" a woman asked, catching him off guard after years of not having been spoken to in English.

"I don't hear anything. What is it?"

"It's the song."

"Which song?"

"The song. The Frank Sinatra one. You know, 'If I can make it there, I'll make it anywhere.' That one. Where's it coming from?"

Ludwig knew the answer. Could he give it to her without a coral reef–wielding merman bashing her into salt-watery soup? Was the deed even still active?

The song was an unusual revenge, like something An Exalted Northwind might have considered before deciding on something befitting a fairy tale. She had been clear. Crude was quick, and this was crude; separating overlapping realities was not. In the many works of fiction that Ludwig had grown up with, this was not how New York ended. It ended with meteors, otherworldly storms, tidal waves, earthquakes, monsters, supervillains, diseases, climate disasters, zombies, war, or aliens. No one had ever tried Frank Sinatra.

No one had ever thought of Frank Sinatra.

New York, New York,
I want to wake up in a city that never sleeps
And find I'm a number one, top of the list,
King of the hill, a number one.

Confusion was understandable, even for Ludwig—he was the only unaffected New Yorker, yet the only New Yorker who knew the cause. Music played, but he couldn't hear it, even if he knew what vinyl record she had dropped into those cauldrons, which had, in turn, dropped into him, into his soul, where it would broadcast for the next 10,000 years, she seemed to say, or about the next 9,999 years, 364 days, 23 hours, 33 minutes, and some change. Over 10,000 years, it would play 1,539,393,170 times.

How would it do this if he died in only a few years? She had mentioned something about Dr. Tot's serum. Might this be the answer? What were the side effects again? He sniffled.

Oh.

Fruitlessly, New Yorkers continued searching for the source. As time passed, searching wasn't enough. People wanted answers. The novelty quickly waned, and curiosity turned to frustration with the song. Some suspected terrorism, as they always did.

Whether Ludwig stood right next to someone, eight miles away in the Bronx, on the outskirts of Queens, or in one of Staten Island's nameless neighborhoods, the song hit everyone simultaneously and at the same volume. Even Hoboken, Fort Lee, Jersey City, and their suburbs, to which the song didn't belong, caught echoes of Ol' Blue Eyes. If someone found themselves within twenty miles of Ludwig, they heard it.

By the two hundredth loop, chaos and bewilderment reigned, and people rightfully doubted that it would stop. Songs stopped, didn't they? It had to stop. Record players burned out. Speakers died. Even phones with streaming music attached to them ran out of batteries or short-circuited. Someone must have stood before a switch, ready to flip it off once the joke was over.

City newspapers somehow published through the noise. None of their newsrooms full of bewildered investigative journalists delivered an explanation or positive diagnosis.

FRANKLY, WE'RE FUCKED

—*New York Post*

IT ISN'T GOING TO STOP

—*Daily News*

GOP STRUGGLES TO SURVIVE VOTE-RIGGING SCANDAL

—*The New York Times*

They were right, except for the *Times*, which could have been right, but Ludwig never paid attention to politics.

Tourists who had just arrived, and some who had been

there for days, thought that perhaps the city was just like this, that the song's lyrics about coming from a small town to tackle a very big town were as essential to its day-to-day character as the hot dogs they believed New Yorkers relied upon for sustenance.

Once New Yorkers realized that life might be like this forever, they got into cars and taxis, loaded into trains and buses, walked across bridges, and fled until they discovered the line twenty miles from Ludwig, where the music finally stopped. But as Ludwig moved, so did the line, making an exact border never more than approximate.

New York, New York,
I want to wake up in a city that never sleeps
And find I'm a number one, top of the list,
King of the hill, a number one.

Searching for the source was pointless. No one, from news teams to social media addicts to even NASA, had found it. Many claimed otherwise; misinformation and bold lying were common in those early days.

Radio antennas and lightning rods were the sources of endless suspicion and conspiracy theories. For a while, people blamed hackers. But even shutting off the city's electrical grid did nothing to stop the music. No one was looking for a New York fashion icon cursed by crude but effective fairy magic.

New York, New York,
I want to wake up in a city that never sleeps
And find I'm a number one, top of the list,
King of the hill, a number one.

What would the city look like in weeks, months, or years? Would any New Yorkers be left? Empty was his guess and her intent. Could there be a New York without New Yorkers? It only took a moment to discover her ulterior motive; that he would live every day with the knowledge that he caused his city's downfall and would continue causing it.

Of course, Lulu, Uchu, Ayonia, Igor, Naveena, and the rest had already escaped, perhaps to set up new Vermin Milk offices elsewhere. He suspected only Lulu would persist in trying to discover the song's origins. Even if she hadn't stayed (how could she?), her thoughts were on Ludwig. She might already be looking for him, but his cell phone was . . . Where was it?

He never knew.

New York, New York,
I want to wake up in a city that never sleeps
And find I'm a number one, top of the list,
King of the hill, a number one.

The grim truth settled in at a national level. The song didn't play several miles into New Jersey, Pennsylvania, Delaware, Connecticut, or even upstate New York—only the city. People who had families or second homes elsewhere left and never returned.

Those who had never known homes beyond the boroughs held on to the belief that the song was something passing, like days of rain or heartbreak, though the longer it played, the more the truth resembled the guidance cards: Quietude over the Giant Apple. Galilea still had not touched the guidance cards for fear of what they might reveal, not realizing that she would soon be looking at their aftermath. Instead, she shuffled them back into the deck, never to know.

Soon, the fae would come out, and the city would be theirs again.

The greatest migration in American history had begun.

And if I can make it there, I'm gonna make it anywhere.
It's up to you, New York, New York.

His door in the floor still worked, of course; An Exalted Northwind wouldn't compromise the deed. To do so would jeopardize the trap that made Ludwig her antenna, forever caught in limbo between Manhattan's Inwood and Battery Park. Once the fairies abandoned Broken Throat, An Exalted Northwind's archive might be his.

He thought of Lulu.

Ludwig patted Mr. Blueberry's cheek and told him he might not return for a while. Mr. Blueberry never heard him; instead, he snored through dreams of copper funnel cakes and fire hydrants that spewed his weight in pennies. "If I am not back in a day, the door to the stairwell requires only a push. Humans won't be outside much longer. Sooner or later, you can leave here."

Mr. Blueberry grunted an imprecise acknowledgment.

Ludwig descended the ladders to Broken Throat rung by rung and already noticed changes. It was windy and cold, like a blizzard without snow. And then there was Desolate Phil.

He did not occupy his golden throne, leaning against Bluebane the Onionscourge's Sword-Spear of Puncturing; instead, he lay collapsed, a pile of straw, cotton, and fine clothes. He was all lumps and fabric. Ludwig thought about what this might mean and, without regard for Phil, searched the room for signs of Lonesome Johnny. None were visible. He kicked Desolate Phil's body, but nothing chastised or insulted him, meaning he was dead for certain.

"Johnny! Johnny!"

Ludwig removed Desolate Phil's bucket, placed it on his head, faced the tunnel, and copied the motions that Phil had once used to disband the worms. None worked. Unsure of what he might find ahead, he unsheathed Bluebane's sword.

Ludwig ran, slipping and falling over piles of slick worms, muddying his cotton clothes with muck and worm guts.

At the foot of Broken Throat, Ludwig discovered a pile of navy-blue laundry that still possessed some of its human shape. Whereas Desolate Phil had simply checked out when An Exalted Northwind released him from his duties, Lonesome Johnny clung to life.

"Johnny! Johnny! Can you hear me? Buddy, can you hear me? It's me, Mr. Ludwig." Ludwig attempted to cradle Lonesome Johnny. Without life to give him shape, he yielded to every touch.

"Oh, Mr. Ludwig, my good buddy, I knew you would look for me."

"You look like shit," he said. "Tell me what spell she used to enchant you. Give me the words."

"I'm afraid I am past the point of help, Mr. Ludwig. Once my lady-lord and benefactor completed her enchantment, she no longer required us. When the Upstairs Neighbors vacate the city, she won't require this building. No fairy will. Manhattan will be theirs once again. I know not where she will go next. Perhaps to Fairie."

"So that's it? You do all that for her, give her all that time and loyalty, and this is how she leaves you?"

"I am afraid that is the purpose of my order, Mr. Ludwig. We exist to serve."

"No one should 'exist to serve.' Service is not the point of existence. I bet Wet Henry isn't dying. He's probably up there laughing at his own farts."

"Too true, Mr. Ludwig. Although he has not been a member of my order for so long."

Ludwig stormed up to Broken Throat's mercurially carved living door and pounded his fists. Carelessly, he impaled his hand on one of the blue guy–deterring spikes. The wound healed instantly.

He stabbed the door several times, causing clean punctures but none that would undo the lock. The carvings dodged and cartwheeled away from each strike, but the door wouldn't open.

"Please don't die, Johnny."

"My fate is notarized and sealed, my good buddy. You were right about bosses, about what they are. It was not in my power to disobey them, but I am no longer under their influence. So, muumbazza, I say to them."

"Muumbazza to them," Ludwig said, his eyes welling up. "Muumbazza, muumbazza, muumbazza." He added: "Right-oh-ho, Joe."

Ludwig curled beside Lonesome Johnny and cradled his bucket until it was clear that whatever gave him life had passed.

Somewhere above, the remaining New Yorkers were still deciding what to do about the song. It would be months before Ludwig became the last.

IT WAS SNOWING again.

Ludwig could once again speak to anyone, but there was no one to speak to. The city was empty, except for military patrols and NYPD barricades that forced stragglers, mostly those who had already been questioning what was real, to leave the city since the number of suicides following the creation of what had been dubbed the Sinatra Zone grew every day. The people who stayed had nowhere else to go; their homes and things were there, and they made peace with the song until they hanged, drowned, or poisoned themselves or leaped out of windows.

Ludwig carried the door through the city, more the door-bearer than ever, escaping into the ground like a rat when the men with guns detected him. These armed units worked in short shifts and rapidly switched posts to protect their sanity.

Months later, as military and police presences vanished, only looters visited New York, and then only briefly. No one could withstand the song.

LUDWIG DROPPED HIS door onto a deserted pizza shop's floor and descended. The torches and sconces from the tunnel and the building it connected to had become the city's last lights. He reached the final rung and wondered where the worms had gone. Without the fairies of Broken Throat, they were out of a job. Where else would they find employment? It was a fun thought, if not a pointless one.

His walk to Broken Throat had never been easier, and the directory had never been simpler. They were finally, really, truly gone.

5G
5F
5E
5D
5C
5B
5A
4G
4F
4E
4D
4C
4B
4A
3L
3G
3F

3E
3D
3C
3B
3A
2L
2G
2F
2E
2D
2C
2B
2A
1L
1G
1F
1E
1D
1C
1B
1A
B1 Lonesome Johnny

Once they were green again, the six remaining blue guys departed basements, cellars, and tunnels and reunited with An Exalted Northwind's client-housemates. Both groups of fairies quickly lost interest in Ludwig. However, one fairy who had not been in attendance at the banquet Ludwig had hosted, which meant that it had once been a blue guy, tipped its hat to Ludwig and disappeared into the city for ten thousand years, never again to be seen by him.

He tried again to enter Broken Throat once the fairies were gone, but there was still no key. He brandished Bluebane the Onionscourge's Sword-Spear of Puncturing and threatened the wooden motifs with impalement if they didn't open the door, but they scattered and ran, perhaps to some other door. Frustrated by wanting to begin his magical education but being unable to do so, he banged Desolate Phil's bucket against the door until a key like a small tree branch with eleven bits slid from it.

The door opened.

It was the last place in the city with working lights or dependable food supplies. And, free from fairies, he could finally explore it.

The house's remaining floors were both less and more strange than he had imagined. Of course, he knew about the archives, the common areas, and the large big great room, but he was surprised to learn that the fairies of Broken Throat were keen decorators and artisans. In their apartments, no inch of wood went uncarved (quietly, he imagined), and no rafter went unadorned. Broken Throat's rooms looked exactly how he had imagined Zeal should: like old theaters, dusty libraries, cellar speakeasies, and Florentine astronomers' towers. If not for their disagreements, he could have happily lived there; as their disagreements no longer mattered, he might.

In the basement, he found the answer to the question that had dogged him since he became the doorbearer.

A dozen Lonesome Johnnys on clothes hangers hung from pipes in an isolated basement apartment full of mounted swords, disintegrating books, and antiquated art mounted in bulging gold-painted frames. None lived, but it explained why the Lonesome Johnny he knew best, the one aboveground, was permanently soiled and covered in brown stains. The Lonesome Johnnys belowground were spotless, immaculate, and freshly laundered. Where had An Exalted Northwind found so many Civil War uniforms without bullet holes?

To combat loneliness, Ludwig distributed lifeless Lonesome Johnnys throughout the house and spoke to them. Some he slung over stalagmites to give their uniforms the impression of sitting upright, while others hung over couches or lamps or from clothes hangers in doorways. Ludwig quickly developed a passable impression of him, one that he would need over the coming millennia.

Would his first goal as a magic user be to return one of these Lonesome Johnnys to life? Perhaps.

Then vengeance.

Who knew what he could learn in ten thousand years if only he had help, whether Lonesome Johnny's or Lulu's—or both, if only.

WHILE SEARCHING THE quiet, empty city for a margarita machine, a car battery, and some clamps to connect the former and latter, he recognized that he was a short walk from where Branagh & Bloom had once been headquartered. He visited, but there was nothing to see. The business was gone, and the building it called home had vanished if it had ever really been there.

There was a tap on his shoulder. Turning wasn't required to ascertain its author.

"Mr. Ludwig! I owe you an apology. Certain things my lady-lord and benefactor promised you may no longer be in scope. It seems that she has deceived us both!" he laughed. "Those 'other schools of magic' that I mentioned are only available to fairies, and since you cannot leave Manhattan to visit her in Italy, she can't teach you those that you would be able to learn. Also, she made clear that she doesn't want to teach an immortal the art of enchanting since that would be like creating another rival. Perhaps you should have gotten your agreement in writing. As a real estate man, I can tell you that deals are always better in writing."

"Are you staying in the city? Does the song affect you?" Ludwig asked.

"Not at all, Mr. Ludwig. But I am afraid I won't be staying. Why would I? There won't be a real estate market here for another ten thousand years. Perhaps once this is all over, we can work together. Branagh & Ludwig has a nice ring to it. See you then, Mr. Ludwig! Thousands of years go by faster than you think!"

He hugged Ludwig, stepped back several paces, then disappeared in a swirling plume of brilliant hellfire.

THERE WAS STILL only one New Yorker whom Ludwig wanted to see, the one who must have stuck around longer than any other, the one whose curiosity about Ludwig's "thing" would prove even more irresistible than it had before. She wanted to hear his story, not to learn magic or gain power, but to know the truth behind polka-dotted lightning, ruby-shitting pigs, Frank Sinatra, and everything else.

It had been months since Ludwig surrendered a quarter of his shares in Vermin Milk to secure twenty-nine oversized, signature-series athleisure suits. The timing of that request and what had happened to New York—neither could be a coincidence.

And yet, she couldn't find him. No one could. He was the last doorbearer, and without a deed of her own or his invitation, such a person could not be found, at least not by humans. The song made a single day as long as a year at the dentist's.

But that night, someone knocked on Broken Throat's front door, an act that its previous tenants would have strongly prohibited. With Bluebane the Onionscourge's Sword-Spear of Puncturing in hand, he opened the door to find Lulu, who had pointlessly donned several pairs of earmuffs.

Not a moment separated their embrace.

"How—"

"Mr. Blueberry," she said, "he took me right to you. I found him at Tompkins Square Park chewing through copper wiring. Is this it? Is this the place? Who am I kidding? Of course, this is the place!"

"Lulu, come in! Come in! Can you still hear the song?"

"Yes, and it's deafening. I don't think I can stay long. You're going to have to talk louder." Had those words ever been used before in Broken Throat?

Ludwig sped her around the house. He pointed at the sizes of things, explained what purpose each room served, and showed her the common rooms, which had the most to say about what the fairies were like. Then they visited the room that Ludwig knew would interest her above all others, the grand archives, although she would never be able to use it while Ludwig, the enchantment's mantle, remained in New York, which he would until long after her death. Sitting on a table, whose legs Ludwig had sawed to make it lower to the floor, was a document releasing all except one of his Vermin Milk shares back to the company.

He told her everything he could remember, which took hours, but she listened despite Sinatra's constant crooning. Then Ludwig revealed his immortality.

"I cannot leave the city, not for ten thousand years. As long as I exist, so does the song. I tried to save the city by jumping off the Queensboro Bridge, but I landed in a pond filled with marshmallows."

"Why the Queensboro?"

"Because it's not in Brooklyn. I tried shooting myself in the head—"

"Jesus, Ludwig."

"And the bullet turned to slow-moving Jell-O."

"The life you've lived."

"Maybe you can return and bring me the new lines whenever they drop."

"Ludwig, I can't keep coming back here. You don't know what this is like. But maybe. Maybe someday. There's so much I want to know about what happened. Not just about the *you* parts—about all of it."

"That is something I can give you without magic."

He invited her to follow him up three flights of impossibly tall stairs, which she enthusiastically did, despite tripping several times. He took her into what he told her was the apartment of the strangest fairy and handed Lulu a nearly two-thousand-page book called *The Decline and Fall of the Fae Kingdom of Manhattan* by Galilea Dazzledark.

"It doesn't look like she'll finish it now. There are fifteen pages about peanut butter that you'll probably have to edit out."

Lulu returned to the surface and saddled Mr. Blueberry, leaving Ludwig to a quiet, certain fate. She never returned.

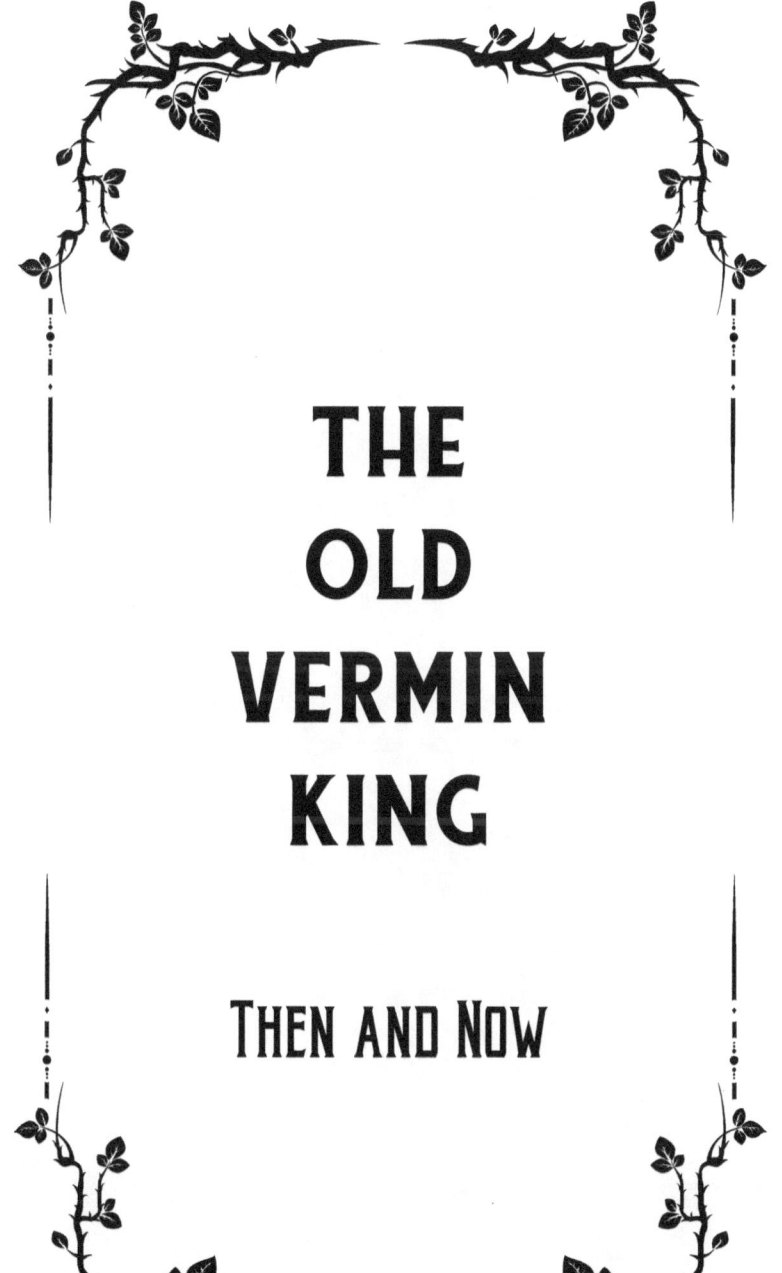

THE OLD VERMIN KING

Then and Now

21

It is well known that the metropolitan population center known as New York City ended in the years that followed the appearance of the Sinatra Zone. What is less known is how the Sinatra Zone came into existence. The already strange truth is far stranger than is usually acknowledged and starts millennia before Ol' Blue Eyes or Henry Hudson ever set foot there. This book aims not only to tell our readers how the city really ended, but how it really began.

—Excerpt from *The Decline and Fall of the Fae Kingdom of Manhattan*, by Galilea Dazzledark and Lulu Vaillancourt

THE FAIRIES WHO remained each claimed neighborhoods of Manhattan for themselves, creating fairy fiefdoms within a fairy kingdom. Some districts, like Times Square and Turtle Bay, went unclaimed forever.

The free fairies of Manhattan avoided the immortal door-bearer, who studied enchanting underground in a five-story apartment building they could hardly remember. There were rumors that mushrooms grew from the walls, and birds lived in the rafters. Other animals found their way in and quickly made homes in the attic. It was like that all over the city, greener and wilder, with nature retaking what it wanted without resistance. Plants grew where plants never had. Animals came back, but none more so than the kind that preyed on rats. A satellite photographed a bear crossing the Queensboro Bridge. Was that a pig over there? No, too big.

One of the last reasons to go into the city and brave the song was to loot (jewelry stores, department stores, electronics stores). That stopped being profitable after a year. People had even robbed Vermin Milk stores. To further the compliment, judging by what was missing, the looters had been women.

No one stole books, so Ludwig smashed bookstore windows and filled shopping carts with formidable piles of not-always-canonical-or-genre-specific paperbacks. He had so much time. As an immortal, he was done reading fantasies. As an immortal, he was living a fantasy.

Teenagers and young adults went into the city to dance all night or for as long as possible. There was even a name for it: Franking. In the winter, Ludwig could tell how long they endured the music from their snowy boot prints.

In later years, people born deaf were brought to the edge of the Sinatra Zone to hear both sound and music for the first time. As they returned to Connecticut, New Jersey, or Pennsylvania, the music faded until it stopped, as it had before fairy magic.

In the end, Ludwig had his own New York, just as he had in his childhood bedroom.

They used to say that if you came to New York and lasted a certain amount of time, you were a New Yorker, usually years, more than five but no less than seven. There were no New Yorkers anymore, just the one. And he could last longer than any New Yorker before him. He had to. He was, against his will, An Exalted Northwind's most committed employee.

Her great work was complete, and she had her single-page enchantment, but not the one she wanted or imagined. What would become of her reputation, especially since Gilda Fiorella both knew of her failure and had orchestrated it? Nothing good, it seemed. An Exalted Northwind, too, had fallen for fairy tricks.

Ludwig could be alone in An Exalted Northwind's archives for the remainder of his sentence if he chose. What would he learn down there? Could he sever his immortality? Resurrecting Lonesome Johnny seemed important. So did issuing Lulu a deed, even if it took decades.

If An Exalted Northwind returned, he'd be there, the ultimate boss versus the ultimate bad employee.

LUDWIG USED LONESOME Johnny's bucket and the building's unlimited milk to make mozzarella. He made citric acid from the fruits of a fourteen-foot-tall lime tree and stole rennet from abandoned grocery stores because what looter wanted the enzymes produced by the fourth stomach of an infant cow?

Something about cheese making down there gave his mozzarella a taste and a texture like Giustina's. Perhaps that's what his version had always missed: love and sacrifice.

In the early days, he kept his enchanted door closed, but as people quit the city and the risk of someone discovering the apartment building in the ground became zero, he let in fresh air that filled the tunnel. Rats followed it.

They filled the tunnel as worms once had. Broken Throat was the last source of the human food they had once thrived on and a haven from the predators who eventually populated the island.

Ludwig fed them cheese and peanut butter sandwiches and named them one by one. He even bathed them; he was that lonely. In a way, he owed them—one of their own had saved his life. By tending to the rats and newly grown wildlife throughout the city, Ludwig became an urban druid.

The free fairies of New York told stories to the land about an immortal man who commanded a river of rats. They called him the Old Vermin King, a king who never wished to be king, ruling over the quietest place on earth.

ABOUT THE AUTHOR

HOMESICK FOR PLACES he can imagine but never visit, Ken Ziegler is a lifelong writer and world builder whose stories marry the mundane and the make-believe in unpredictable ways. Besides filling notebooks and sketch pads with ideas for worlds he hopes to someday share with others, his favorite activity is illustrating abstract monsters at kenandpencil.com. In his downtime, he is the creative director of a tech company within a tech company. His seldom-shared thoughts and opinions can be found on X @NYPD (no affiliation). *The Loudest Place on Earth* is his debut novel.

www.ingramcontent.com/pod-product-compliance
Lightning Source LLC
LaVergne TN
LVHW040038080526
838202LV00045B/3384